THE
SATURDAY
MORNING
MURDER

THE SATURDAY MORNING MURDER

A Psychoanalytic Case

BATYA GUR

Translated from the
Hebrew by Dalya Bilu

Aaron Asher Books
HarperCollins*Publishers*

37586
MYS
GUR

HarperCollins books may be purchased for educational, business, or sales promotional use. For information, please call or write: Special Markets Department, Harper-Collins Publishers, Inc., 10 East 53rd Street, New York, NY 10022. Telephone: (212) 207-7528; Fax: (212) 207-7222.

FIRST EDITION

Designed by Claudyne Bianco

Library of Congress Cataloging-in-Publication Data

Gur, Batya.
   [Retsah be-Shabat ba-boker. English]
   The Saturday morning murder: a psychoanalytic case/Batya Gur: translated from the Hebrew by Dalya Bilu.—1st U.S. ed.
     p. cm
   Translation of: Retsah be-Shabat ba-boker.
   ISBN 0-06-019024-8
   I. Title.
PJ5054.G637r413   1992   91-58346
892.4'36—dc20

92 93 94 95 96 ❖/HC 10 9 8 7 6 5 4 3 2 1

THE
SATURDAY
MORNING
MURDER

It would take years, Shlomo Gold knew, before he would be able to park his car in front of the Institute on Disraeli Street without feeling a cold hand gripping his heart. Sometimes he even thought that the analytic society should change its premises from Talbieh, just so he would not have to feel this recurrent anxiety. He had also considered requesting special permission to treat his patients elsewhere, but his supervisors thought that he should confront the situation with his own inner resources and not by means of external changes.

He could still hear old Hildesheimer's words reverberating in his mind. The building was not the issue, the old man had said: it was not the building that was causing his anxiety; it was his own feelings in relation to the event. Ever since the day it had happened, Gold heard the words, in their heavy German accent, whenever he approached the building. Especially the sentence about how it was his own emotions he had to face, not the stone walls.

Naturally, Hildesheimer had said then, the fact that it was his,

Gold's, analyst who was involved had to be taken into account, and perhaps—the old man gave him a shrewd, inquiring look—he should try to "derive the maximum from the difficulties of the situation." But Shlomo Gold, who had once been so proud of being given the keys to the building, could no longer enter his room at the Institute without an anxiety attack.

And to think of what he had gone through before they entrusted him with the keys! It was only at the end of his second year as a student at the Institute that the Training Committee had convened and graciously found him suitable to try and be a real analyst and treat his first patient (under supervision, of course). And now it was all gone: the keys and his pride and the thrill of ownership every time he opened the door—nothing had been the same since that Saturday.

There were some people who sneered at Gold's attitude toward the round Arab-style building that the Institute had taken as its premises. Until that Saturday morning, Gold had shown off the stone house to every visitor to Jerusalem. He never hid the sense of belonging the place evoked in him. He would fling out his arms as if to embrace the squat two-story house with its round porch, its big garden in which roses bloomed throughout the year, its double stairway curving up on either side of the porch and leading to the entrance. Then he would wait expectantly for the words of approbation, for the acknowledgment that the regal building was indeed suited to its purpose.

And now all that naïveté, the unreserved admiration, the feeling of belonging to an esoteric tribe, the pride in his first patient, had vanished, to be replaced by the oppression, the anxiety, that had haunted him since "Black Saturday," as he called it to himself—the Saturday on which he had volunteered to prepare the building for the lecture to be given by Dr. Eva Neidorf, who had just returned from a month's visit with her daughter in Chicago.

On that Saturday, Shlomo Gold had approached the Institute without suspecting that his life was about to be changed completely. A Saturday in March, with the sun shining and the birds chirping, when Gold, excited at the prospect of his meeting with Eva Neidorf, had left his home in Beit Hakerem early in order to tidy the hall, set up the folding chairs from the storeroom, and fill the huge urn with water. Everybody would want coffee on a Saturday morning. The lecture was scheduled to start at half past ten, and a few minutes before nine, his car coasted smoothly down the hill.

There was a Sabbath hush in the air, and the old Jerusalem neighborhood, always quiet, was now absolutely still. When he passed the President's residence near Jabotinsky Street, he noticed the absence of even security guards.

Gold breathed in the pure, clean air and carefully avoided the black cat that was crossing the street with elegant disdain. He smiled to himself at the superstitions of so-called rational people—a smile that was to be his last on the subject, for in this respect, too, his attitude changed from that Saturday on.

The thought of the approaching lecture filled him with a glow of anticipation: he was about to see his analyst after a four-week interval.

During the four years of Gold's analysis with Neidorf, he had heard her give numerous lectures. Each had been thrilling. True, he always felt a certain insignificance, a dull suspicion that he would never become a great therapist; but on the other hand, there was the unique learning experience and the knowledge that he, Gold, was a witness to the rare, God-given gift possessed by Eva Neidorf—the blessed intuition, the absolute knowledge of when to speak, when to remain silent, the precise perception of the required degree of warmth, all of which he had been fortunate to receive as her analysand.

The agenda for that Saturday bore the name of Neidorf's lecture: "Some Aspects of the Ethical and Forensic Problems Involved in Analytic Treatment."

Nobody was taken in by the understatement "Some Aspects."

Shlomo Gold knew that today's lecture, after a modest introduction, would be a world and the fullness thereof. It would be published in the professional journals and give rise to passionate debates, reactions, and counterreactions, and he relished the thought of seeing the slight changes that Neidorf would introduce in the published version. Once more he would be able to enjoy the intoxicating sense that he

■ 3 ■

had "been there," like someone listening to the broadcast of a concert he had heard live.

Gold parked on the still-empty street in front of the building. From the glove compartment he removed the Institute key ring, with its keys to the front door, the telephone lock, and the storeroom. He opened the green iron gate, with its discreet gold plaque identifying the building's function. He walked up one of the curving stairways to the wooden door, which was invisible from the street. As usual, he could not resist the temptation to turn his head and look down from the porch onto the street and the big, blooming garden, exuding its scents of jasmine and honeysuckle, and then, with a faint smile on his lips, he opened the door into the dark foyer.

The windows were closed, and heavy curtains covered them; they definitely fulfilled their role. Every invisible detail of the foyer was as familiar to Gold as his childhood home. The foyer gave onto six rooms with heavy wooden doors, all shut.

Looking back, it all began with the sound of shattering glass. He had just succeeded in pushing the conference table to the wall and was leaning heavily against it. When he heard the glass shatter he didn't even have to raise his eyes. In spite of his momentary paralysis, he knew exactly which photograph had fallen.

After years of sitting in the lecture hall, listening to case presentations and theoretical debates while his eyes roamed over the walls, he knew, just like everyone else, precisely where every photograph was situated.

The portraits of the dead took up all the space on the walls, and after the last photograph was hung, a few months before, someone had joked that everyone else would now have to remain immortal. Gold had spent many an hour gazing into the eyes of the dead, and there was nothing about their expressions that he didn't know. He remembered, for example, the laughing eyes of Fruma Hollander, a supervisor at the Institute, a member of the generation after the founding generation, who had died suddenly of a heart attack at the age of sixty-one. She hung to the right of the entrance, and anyone sitting at the right-hand end of the hall could see her eyes without being dazzled by the glass. To the left of the door hung the portrait of Seymour Levenstein, who had come to the Institute from the New York society and died of cancer at the age of fifty-two. The years of birth and death were engraved beneath the name on the picture frames. A therapist waiting for a dilatory patient could go from portrait to portrait, contemplating the features of all the Institute's dead.

The fallen photograph was that of Mimi Zilberthal. Gold remembered asking one of the senior analysts what she had died of and getting a withering look, together with an inquiry into its importance to him. Someone else might have pursued the matter, but Gold sensed that there was something particularly unpleasant involved, and he preferred not to know.

But that Saturday, after everything had fallen apart, Gold overheard a snatch of conversation between Joe Linder and Nahum Rosenfeld. Joe brandished the glassless picture and said defiantly to Rosenfeld, almost yelling, that just because they had been presented with an opportunity to get rid of the picture didn't mean that they had the right to do so. And the words Gold remembered were these: "You don't take someone's picture off the wall just because they commit suicide." The two of them were in the kitchen, and they didn't notice Gold standing in the doorway. After everything he had been through that morning, he was not particularly shocked.

Gold quickly swept up the broken glass and put the photo in the kitchen, next to the little refrigerator, after which he went to the storeroom to get the chairs. It was only a few minutes past nine, and he still had plenty of time, even though he calculated that he would need about a hundred chairs (people came from all over the country to hear Eva Neidorf lecture). After arranging all the folding chairs in semicircular rows, he regarded his work with satisfaction but nevertheless decided to bring more chairs from the surrounding rooms.

Whenever he went into the Institute's rooms, especially if he happened to be alone in the building, he was struck anew by their amazing suitability to their function. The first room he entered, the one to the right of the entrance, was dim like all the rest, and the high windows and heavy furniture created a solemn, mysterious atmosphere. Whenever he drew the heavy curtains aside, he saw in his imagination the interior of a Gothic cathedral.

Each room contained a couch and, behind the couch, the analyst's heavy armchair, which looked more comfortable than it was. (Everyone who worked at the Institute complained of back pains. Many of the therapists would discreetly slip a small cushion behind their backs during therapy sessions.) In every room there were dim paintings and a few extra chairs used for seminars.

Weekly seminars were held in the evenings, usually on Tuesdays, and all the Institute students would attend. The rooms would be lit up, the gloomy atmosphere slightly dispelled. In every room the chairs were arranged in circles, and the aroma of coffee and cake drifted from the kitchen, waiting for the break, when everyone would descend on the refreshments.

Once a week, to the satisfaction of Hildesheimer, who wanted to "see the building live and breathe," there was a hubbub at the Institute, the street was jammed with cars, and during the coffee break, sounds of talking and even laughter rose into the air, as teachers and students mingled and told each other anecdotes about their experiences since the previous week.

But there was nothing like Saturdays.

On the seminar days, there was always someone popping out of one of the rooms at the last moment and asking the early arrivals to retire to the kitchen for a moment, so that a patient could be seen to the front door without his or her identity being disclosed. But on Saturdays, even the early birds found the doors to the rooms wide open and knew that if they felt like it, they could whistle a silly tune without intruding on the inner worlds of the people on the couches.

True, the rooms were too few to hold the thirty candidates and all the patients too.

True, there were problems in allocating the rooms, in scheduling the hours, but whenever complaints were brought up at the Training Committee meetings, old Hildesheimer insisted upon the candidates' continuing to see their patients at the Institute until they became full-fledged members. The building had to be used, it had to be lived in, he was quoted as saying.

You couldn't say that people actually fought over the rooms, but you could certainly sense the differences in seniority and status among the candidates. It was clear that a beginning candidate would be allocated the little room, just as it was clear that a senior candidate with three patients would be able to choose whichever room he wanted.

The little room was small, indeed, but its main drawback was its location, next to the kitchen: the voices of the coffee drinkers conducting whispered conversations in the short breaks between patients; the telephone ringing; the slow, hesitant voice of the secretary answering—all succeeded in penetrating the room despite continued attempts to insulate it, including the double curtain hanging over the inside of the door.

The patients treated in this room invariably reacted to the phenomenon. Gold spent hours making different interpretations of his second case, a woman who never overcame her suspicions that her words could be heard outside the room.

But on Saturdays, when the members of the Institute met for lectures and voting, everything was permitted. The windows were opened wide, the clean golden light of Jerusalem and the outside world penetrated the rooms. Now Gold entered the little room, whistling to himself, to get the last of the chairs. The little room, the room where he worked, had a friendly, familiar air. Gold's attitude to "his" room was one of affection, even though he couldn't wait for the day when he would be considered senior enough to move to the first room on the right of the entrance, which he referred to privately as "Fruma's room," because Fruma Hollander, a childless spinster, had willed her heavy, cozy furniture to the Institute, and something of her own kindly warmth, her joie de vivre, still clung to the furniture and even to the dim oil paintings in the room.

Gold stopped on the threshold of the little room. The curtains were drawn, and the room was so dark that he could hardly see the outlines of the furniture. He pulled the curtains, thinking that he had not yet arranged the coffee cups or set out the ashtrays. He himself didn't smoke, but others did.

Professor Nahum Rosenfeld, for example, whose slender cigars perpetually stuck in the corner of his mouth gave him an angry, surly look; he left the space around him littered with brown stubs unless someone took care to place an ashtray next to him. Something of Rosenfeld's character was revealed in the way he ground out the old cigar and went on indifferently to the next. Sometimes Gold would shudder in sympathetic identification with the crushed cigar.

He turned away from the window and looked around the room. And he stopped breathing, literally stopped breathing. Later on, when he tried to describe his feelings, he spoke of shock, of his heart skipping a beat.

On the armchair, the analyst's armchair, sat Dr. Eva Neidorf. "She herself was sitting there," Gold kept repeating later. Naturally, he couldn't believe his eyes. Her lecture was supposed to begin at half past ten, and it wasn't even half past nine yet; she had returned from Chicago only the day before; and she never arrived early anyway.

Neidorf sat in the armchair without moving, leaning back, her left hand supporting her cheek, her head inclined slightly to the left.

The sleeping Neidorf seemed to Gold like someone in whose presence he had no right to remain. It was not only the feeling that he was intruding on her privacy; he felt that she was being revealed to him in another, forbidden persona. He remembered the first time he had seen her drinking coffee. How difficult it was for him to see her as an ordinary person. He even remembered the faint tremor in the hand that held her cup. He had known, of course, that this attitude toward the analyst was a significant issue in the field of psychotherapy, one discussed in all the analytic theories.

He stood there and asked himself how he should address her. He whispered several times: "Dr. Neidorf." She did not react. Something inside him, as he later explained, forced him to go on, to persist in his timid attempts to wake her. He did not understand what lay behind this behavior; the only thing he understood was his own embarrassment at the thought of her discomfort when she awoke and saw him there.

He paused and looked into her face. It bore a strange expression, one he had never seen there before. A kind of slackness, he thought, perhaps even a lifelessness, in a face that always radiated an intensity which dominated every other expression. This peculiar slackness probably stemmed from the fact that her eyes were closed. The source of her energy was her eyes, with their unique penetrating gaze. On the few occasions when he had dared to look her straight in the eye, he had felt scalded. For the first time, he now permitted himself to stare at her from close up, like a child looking at his mother getting dressed when she thinks he is asleep.

Everyone agreed that Eva Neidorf was an exceptionally good-looking woman. The most beautiful woman at the Institute, Joe Linder would say, and add that the competition wasn't all that tough. But the truth was that in spite of her fifty-one years, everyone still looked up when she entered a room. Her beauty evoked a response from women as well as men. She knew that she was beautiful, but she wasn't vain; she simply gave something that needed care and attention its due, as if she and her body were two separate entities. Her wardrobe was the subject of lengthy discussions, even among the men. Candidates, supervisees, and analysts—no one could remain indifferent to her appearance. Even old Hildesheimer, as everyone knew, had a soft spot for Eva Neidorf. At lectures he would give her confidential smiles. During the coffee breaks they would converse in corners, looking serious. They would put their heads together, and the sense of a bond of intimate understanding between them would pass through the room like a high-frequency wave.

Now, as she sat sleeping in the analyst's chair, Gold could subject her to a thorough examination. Her hair, gathered in a chignon on top of her head, was streaked with gray, and the heavy layer of makeup was clearly visible, especially on her delicate cheekbones and pointed chin. Her eyelids, too, were heavily made up. At such close quarters Gold was able to see that she had aged greatly recently. He thought about the fact that she was a grandmother now, about her son, about how tired she had begun to look after her husband died. He had often thought about her relations with her husband, but every time he tried to imagine her at home, he would see her dressed up in one of her elegant outfits, like the one she wore now, a seemingly simple white dress that even to his inexperienced eyes looked expensive and special.

He and Neidorf had devoted many hours to his inability to relate to her as an ordinary person or imagine her existing outside the therapy sessions. He claimed that he couldn't "get her out of her dress," that he could on no account picture her, say, in the kitchen. And he wasn't the only one. No one could imagine her in a dressing gown. Some people even argued passionately that they were sure she never ate.

There was no question about her powers as a therapist. And as for her skills as a supervisor—no one could touch her. All her supervisees paid the most scrupulous attention to her comments. They never tired of praising her "insight," her "rare intuition," her "endless reservoirs of energy." Everyone she supervised tried to adopt her style of therapy. But no one could copy her instincts, which always told her what the right moment was to say what.

When Neidorf lectured on Saturday mornings at the Institute, people came from Haifa and Tel Aviv, and even the two kibbutz members would travel up from their homes outside Beersheba. Her lectures invariably gave rise to stormy debates and controversies; she always had something new and original to say. Sometimes phrases he had heard in her lectures would reverberate in Gold's mind for days, getting mixed up with things she said in his therapy sessions.

Now he held his breath and gently touched her arm. The fabric of her dress was soft. He was glad that it was winter now; the long white sleeve prevented his hand from coming in contact with her bare skin. As it was, he had to suppress an impulse to continue stroking the sleeve. He was shocked by the contradictory impulses and fears assailing him, and he thought that he would never have imagined her capable of abandoning herself to such deep sleep. If he had ever stopped to think about it, he would have been sure that she was a light sleeper.

At that moment he asked himself again, almost aloud, what she was doing at the Institute so early in the morning. She still had not wakened, and he touched her again, this time with anxiety.

It was instinctive, he explained afterward, touching her wrist—which was cold. But since the gas heater wasn't on, and she was so thin, he didn't attach too much importance to it at first. He felt the delicate wrist again, unconsciously seeking the pulse, and abruptly he felt as if he were back at the hospital on the long night shifts at the beginning of his psychiatric residency. There was no pulse. The word "dead" had not yet shaped itself in his mind; he thought only about her pulse. Suddenly he remembered all the stories about similar cases, stories he had always considered apocryphal. The story about the therapist sitting in his chair without reacting, while the patient gave vent to all his pent-up feelings of anger against him, and when the hour was over and he still said nothing, the patient sat up on the couch and looked at him and realized that he was dead. And the story about the first patient of the morning opening the door of the clinic when nobody answered his ring and finding the analyst sitting dead in his chair, having given up the ghost, it transpired, after his regular morning run.

But these were only stories—folklore, one could almost call them—whereas now there was this terrible void in his own stomach. He stood in the middle of the room and felt that he should do something. He repeated the facts to himself: Neidorf, armchair, Institute, Saturday morning, dead.

Gold, who had completed his residency in psychiatry at Hadassah Ein Kerem not long before, had already encountered death. As a doctor he had succeeded in adopting defense mechanisms that enabled him to live with it. He had more or less succeeded, as he once explained to Neidorf, in creating a healthy emotional distance between himself and the dead person: whenever he was summoned into the presence of the dead, a veil would descend on what he called his "feeling glands."

But this time the familiar veil did not descend. Instead, a veil of a different kind came floating down. Everything was wrapped in the mists of a dream, not necessarily a bad one: the floor lost its usual solidity, the door opened as if of its own accord, and although he felt that his limbs did not belong to him, it was nevertheless his hand that gently closed the door and his feet that carried him out of the room.

He collapsed into a chair outside the room and gazed at the picture of the late Erich Levin, who smiled at him genially from behind the glass. Then he told himself composedly—or with what seemed at the time to be composure, although he was dimly aware of the fact that his reactions displayed the classic textbook symptoms of shock—that he had to do something.

He was conscious and at the same time unconscious of standing up, bowing his head, taking a deep breath, and somehow making his way to the telephone in the kitchen.

Not only was the telephone unlocked; the lock lay right next to it, with a key still inside. At the time, Gold did not ask himself who could have left the telephone unlocked or been in such a hurry that he had left his key ring on the kitchen table. Afterward he remembered the key ring clearly, and the fine leather case with the lacy pattern embossed on it.

He remembered lots of details afterward: the almost full cup of coffee in the sink (under the printed notice saying: "Please wash your cups well after use and don't forget to remove the plug from the wall. The last urn had to be replaced only last month because of a burned-out element," and signed by the secretary, Pnina, in her vague scrawl); the dripping tap. But at the time, all his attention was concentrated on the telephone, and as he dialed the number, he sat down heavily in the secretary's chair.

After what seemed like years, someone lifted the phone on the other end and an elderly female voice said in a ponderous German accent: "Yes."

Gold was well acquainted with the stories about Frau Doktor Hildesheimer, and the one word he heard now over the phone verified all the legends. The lady in question, it was said, related to the telephone, the doorbell, and the mailbox as if they were representatives of a hostile foreign power coming to rob her of her husband, to kill him by their endless demands.

Some said that it was thanks to her and her only that Hildesheimer had succeeded in reaching his present age (eighty the following month) without—and here the speaker would usually knock on wood—a single serious illness.

Not only had the old man's daily routine remained unchanged for the past fifty years (eight hours work a day for the first thirty years: from eight to one and from four to seven; and six hours in the last twenty years: four in the morning and two in the afternoon—from two o'clock till four he ceased to exist as far as the rest of the world was concerned); she was also extremely strict in matters usually regarded as less energy-consuming than patients—for example, the number of lectures she allowed him to attend, as lecturer or as auditor, and the number of hours she permitted him to teach at the Institute. Legend had it that it was actually impossible to reach Hildesheimer without first obtaining permission from his lady.

Frau Hildesheimer pronounced her "Yes," and Gold found himself announcing, in a clear voice, his name and the fact that he was speaking from the building (she did not, of course, need to ask which building). After a short pause, Gold apologized for disturbing them on a Saturday and explained that it was an emergency. There was no sound from the other end, and Gold was not certain that she was still there. He repeated the words "an emergency," and in the end the miracle occurred.

The old man's voice sounded as if he never slept, alert and prepared for any eventuality. Gold knew that he was expected at the lecture later that morning and assumed that he intended walking. His home was not far from the Institute, and on fine days his wife encouraged physical activity—in moderation.

The moment Gold heard the old man's "Hello," he felt as if he had been relieved of all responsibility. Since he did not know exactly how to say what had to be said, he announced once more that it was Shlomo Gold speaking, that he was at the Institute, and that he had gone there early in order to get everything ready. Hildesheimer uttered a long, expectant "Ye-es," and when Gold was silent—he could not find words—the old man said, in a slightly worried voice: "Dr. Gold?" and Gold reassured him that he was still there. Then he quickly added that something terrible had happened, really terrible—his voice was trembling—and he thought Dr. Hildesheimer should come right away. A few seconds passed before the old man replied. "Good, I'm coming," he said.

Gold replaced the receiver with a feeling of tremendous relief. Then he switched on the urn, an action lacking in all logic since the water would take an hour to boil, but the idea of doing something practical calmed him.

Outside, through the open windows, the birds must have been singing, but Gold's attention was focused on one sound alone, which when it finally came was like the most glorious music to his ears—the noise of the engine of the cab bringing Hildesheimer. Gold dashed to the front door and looked outside.

The curve of the two flights of stairs leading up to the entrance porch made it impossible to see the person ascending them; Dr. Hildesheimer's round bald head appeared suddenly on the top step of the right-hand flight of stairs. It was hard to believe that the time was only half past nine.

Until the moment of Hildesheimer's actual appearance, Gold had avoided thinking about what he was going to say to him. But as soon as he saw the bald head at the top of the stairs, he realized that he would have to tell the old man about the death of Eva Neidorf, his ex-patient, ex-supervisee, and close friend—some claimed she was the great love of his life—the person who was to have succeeded him as head of the Training Committee. As these thoughts came swimming into his consciousness, the relief Gold had felt after the telephone conversation began to give way to anxiety, and a bottomless pit opened up in his stomach again.

Hildesheimer approached Gold, who was standing next to the front door, with an expression of inquiry and concern on his face. Gold discovered that his throat was very dry, his tongue paralyzed, and in the end he stretched out his hand and beckoned the old man to follow him inside.

Hildesheimer walked briskly behind Gold, who led him to the little room and then stepped aside, flinging out his arm to invite the other in.

E rnst Hildesheimer came out of the room and closed the door
behind him. Gold sat on a chair between the little room and
the kitchen and waited anxiously for his verdict. The old man
was very pale, his lips were pursed, and there was a look in his eyes that
Gold only later identified as fear. His face contained an anger whose
source Gold did not understand.

In a very quiet voice, Hildesheimer asked Gold if he had taken any
other steps besides phoning him. Gold looked at him distractedly and
said that he had not yet called for an ambulance. And Hildesheimer,
who did not seem surprised, mumbled that he understood that Gold
would prefer to leave the police to him.

The old man strode to the kitchen, with Gold behind him, the
knot in his stomach tightening, and there in the kitchen, watching the
old man's knuckles turn blue as his hand gripped the table edge, he
heard for the first time about the pistol.

Afterward he could not remember the conversation in full, only
snatches of sentences and unconnected words. He remembered the

word "pistol" being repeated several times, he remembered Hildesheimer's voice pronouncing the word "perhaps" and also the word "accident." The fragments of information that penetrated his consciousness as he sat facing the old man in the Institute kitchen shed such a nightmarish light on the situation that he suddenly rose to his feet, gasping for breath and seeing nothing but black circles. He could not focus his eyes, he felt the blood draining from his face, felt the rhythmic pounding in his temples, and he knew that for the next hour he would be incapable of doing anything because he was about to succumb to what he later called "the worst migraine of my life."

Gold had suffered from frequent migraines in his youth. Until his training analysis with Neidorf, he had not succeeded in identifying the recurrent syndrome that led up to them. With Neidorf, the hypothesis had emerged that they were the result of unexpressed anger. (As if she was there, very close to him, he heard her soft voice saying "anger that you did not express" and remembered asking her if she meant repressed anger, and how after a brief pause she had gently reminded him that they had agreed not to use professional terminology in relation to his own case and then said no, that was not what she meant, but actual anger for which he had not succeeded in finding an outlet.) He knew that now, in addition to the horror, he felt anger, perhaps similar to the anger registered on old Hildesheimer's pale face. But it was only afterward that he thought about the childish anger he had felt at this stage. The morning was spoiled, the Institute was spoiled. At the time, the fact that Neidorf was dead was so unreal to him that she was completely irrelevant. He closed his eyes, opened them again, and went over to the medicine cabinet on the wall above the kitchen table (Band-Aids, aspirin, iodine, Panadol—"like the first-aid cupboard in a kindergarten; all that's missing is the suppositories," Joe Linder would remark dryly whenever he needed a pill). The idea of swallowing water nauseated him, and he swallowed the aspirins without it.

Hildesheimer stood next to the window and said nothing. It was almost ten now, and Gold thought in a panic—but also with a kind of malicious enjoyment—that the place would soon be full of shocked and frightened people. He did not fully understand the matter of the pistol and the police, and Hildesheimer seemed so aloof and remote that he could not imagine approaching him in any way at all, let alone demanding explanations from him. Gold therefore decided to wait stoically until things became clear of their own accord, and just then he heard the old man's voice saying that it must have been a terrible experience for him, finding her like that. He was truly sorry, said the old man, and Gold, grateful for every word, marveled at the strength he was showing. But you're always marveling at something or other about the old man, he thought. If it's not his courage, then it's his intelligence, or the way he copes with his age, his attention to detail, his modesty, his unpretentiousness.

Until he'd met Hildesheimer, Gold could not have imagined a myth becoming flesh and blood. Now his very presence held a kind of reassurance that everything had not collapsed completely: if Hildesheimer was still capable of saying the words that needed to be said, something was still standing. Although, he admitted to himself, the statement had lacked the warmth and emotional support that invariably accompanied his reactions; these had been replaced by a self-control that awed Gold and prevented him from giving free rein to his bewilderment; it was impossible, for example, to wonder aloud about the pistol. He decided to go on waiting.

And just as he decided to go on waiting in silence, the commotion broke out, a commotion whose echoes went on ringing in his head from that day forward whenever he approached the Institute.

The doctor, who arrived with a Red Magen David ambulance and two paramedics, knocked on the door, which was locked, and Hildesheimer, with an agility incredible for a man of his age, leapt to open it; from then on, nobody knocked or rang the bell. The door, which had always been closed against the world, the door that protected what Gold privately thought of as the most protected place in the world, remained open the whole morning, and through it broke things that did not belong, things that up to now had been, at most, part of the fears and fantasies of patients. Now they had come true, and nothing belonged to anything anymore.

Gold found it difficult to keep up with what was happening. He went from group to group of the people clustering in various corners in order to collect fragments of information—but he didn't understand who was who, or what were the roles of the various figures rushing to and fro and taking over the place so successfully that within a few minutes they seemed to have made it their own. Nothing belonged to the Institute members anymore; the telephone, the tables, the chairs, even the coffee cups had been commandeered.

When that night Gold tried to reconstruct the events of the morning in their correct sequence, he remembered that right after the doctor, a policeman, whose rank he had not noticed, arrived. He remembered the policeman going into the little room after the doctor and Hildesheimer, and also the speed with which he came out again and ran, not to the telephone, but outside. Gold, who followed him out to the front porch, heard voices coming from the patrol car, where the policeman was crouching with a two-way radio in his hand. And in the street, which was still completely deserted, strange, unfamiliar expressions floated in the air: "U.D. event," "Criminal ID Div," "arena of event," and other expressions, no less outlandish.

The policeman remained next to the car; the street was still quiet, and Gold could hear the voices coming out of the radio. The blue light on the car roof seemed silly and incongruous. He did not want to go back inside, where the doctor and the two medics and Hildesheimer, who he suddenly remembered was also a doctor, were still busy and where he felt threatened and superfluous. And anyway, he said to himself, people were going to start arriving in a few minutes, and in the meantime he might as well stand here on the porch, looking at the garden and pretending that nothing had happened, noticing the empty tennis court adjacent to the Immigrants Club, soaking up the March sunshine, and smelling the honeysuckle, whose sweetness did not belong to the morning's events but reminded him of the German Colony, which reminded him of Neidorf, and with the last memory the pleasant warmth of the sunshine vanished and was transformed into something irritatingly bright and harsh. And then another car drew up, a Renault with a police license plate, and a tall man got out of it with slow, deliberate movements, followed by a shorter man, with curly reddish hair. The uniformed policeman moved away from the patrol car, and Gold heard him call: "I didn't know you were the duty officer today," and he saw the tall man reply, but he couldn't catch what he said. Then the redhead said aloud: "That's what you get for hanging around Control waiting for trouble," and he patted the tall man, whose shoulder he did not quite reach, on the arm. The three of them moved toward the gate, and Gold, without knowing why, escaped into the building, leaving the door wide open behind him. He sat down on one of the chairs that were still arranged in rows, and he watched the policemen. He noticed that the tall one, who came in on the heels of the officer in uniform, was wearing jeans and a shirt checked in various shades of blue. Without thinking about what he was doing, Gold took in everything, down to the smallest details. He noticed that despite the youthful impression the tall policeman had given from a distance, up close he looked like a man who had passed forty.

Even before he had exchanged a single word with him, Gold was annoyed by the light, relaxed way in which he bore his boyish body, and above all he felt hostile toward the dark, piercing eyes that regarded him from between high cheekbones and long, thick eyebrows. Gold first noticed his eyes when he asked if he was the one who had notified the police.

Gold, suddenly feeling small and chubby and superfluous, shook his head and pointed to the little room, which the trio entered after the man in uniform had whispered something to the tall one, who turned back and asked Gold to wait. Then he disappeared inside, with the redhead close on his heels.

Shortly afterward troops of people began streaming into the building, and Gold felt lost in the melee. A strapping girl, holding a number of equipment cases and accompanied by two men, strode confidently past him, and the tall detective, hearing the noise, emerged from the little room and announced through the open door that the mobile lab had arrived. And the photographer too, he added.

Then five more people arrived, whom Gold, to his great relief, knew well—they were the people from Haifa, the first to arrive for Eva

Neidorf's lecture. As always, the ones who traveled the greatest distance arrived first, thought Gold as the younger members of the party assailed him with questions about the police cars parked outside and demanded to know if the Institute had been broken into.

With Litzie Sternfeld, who was nearly seventy, standing next to them, a bewildered expression on her face, Gold felt unable to reply, and he knocked on the door of the little room and asked Hildesheimer to come out and speak to the newcomers. Hildesheimer came rushing out and dragged Litzie into the kitchen, and shortly afterward cries of dismay were heard in German, and soft male murmurs, also in German, and harsh, guttural sobs, presumably female. The four other Haifa people turned to Gold with expressions of alarm, and it would not have been possible to put off the explanations any longer but for the fact that at this moment three more people arrived Gold was unable to remember in what order, precisely—who he knew by now were police officers despite their civilian clothes, and who he also guessed were more important than the ones who had arrived up to now, and without being asked, he pointed to the door of the little room and wondered if there would be room enough for them all. The three men were—he heard them being introduced to Hildesheimer later—the Jerusalem Subdistrict commander (the fat, short one), the Southern District commander (the elderly-looking one), and the Jerusalem Subdistrict spokesman (the young, blond one with the mustache).

After them came another man, who introduced himself to Gold as an intelligence officer, asked, "Where is everybody?" and hurried to the little room, from which the redhead now emerged to announce that all those present were requested to go outside to the porch or, at least, to remain seated in the lecture hall, and he proceeded to direct the members of the Institute, now turning up in droves and crowding at the door, to remain on the porch.

Everyone who came in asked what the police cars were doing outside and what all the commotion was about. The redhead, later referred to by the spokesman as the "shift officer," turned to another policeman who had just arrived, whom he addressed as "Sir," and after exchanging a few words with him he stuck his head in at the door and announced that the departmental I.O. had arrived, after which he remained standing outside for a minute. By this time Gold's head was spinning with ranks and titles and initials, and he stopped paying attention to the police personnel turning up in an endless stream.

Joe Linder, who had arrived in the meantime, remarked that perhaps some burglars had broken in at last and stolen all the armchairs, and that now a new generation of analysts would grow up at the Institute without knowing the meaning of backaches. For a moment Gold wished that it had been Linder who had found Neidorf. What wouldn't he have given to see the man speechless for once!

But no one else was in the mood for jokes; anyone who popped into the kitchen popped out again double quick, and they all looked at each other questioningly. No one, thank God, thought of getting an explanation from Gold, who did his best to see without being seen.

The doctor emerged from the little room, with the two medics behind him. They left the building without saying a word, and the tall detective came out after them and whispered something to the shift officer, the redhead, who also left the building, only to return after a few minutes, open the door of the little room, and announce: "The pathologist's on his way, and Forensics too."

Some people stood around and others sat on the chairs that Gold had arranged when everything was still normal. In the large crowd he caught a split-second glimpse of the two kibbutzniks from the south. Standing next to them were two men with leather briefcases, which they opened to extract small instruments that proved on closer inspection to be tape recorders. The din was becoming unbearable, and Gold decided to retire to the kitchen (the idea of deserting the building did not occur to him) and leave the uproar behind him.

Things were no better there. He intruded on the privacy of the two old people, who were sitting very close to each other. Litzie Sternfeld was wiping her eyes with a neatly ironed man's handkerchief, which apparently came from Hildesheimer's pocket, and he was stroking her hand, something Gold had never seen him do before, but which was obviously the right thing to do in the circumstances, when the tall policeman stepped into the kitchen and asked Hildesheimer: "What exactly is this place?" with heavy stress on "exactly." Hildesheimer looked at him wearily at first, and then keenly, and he explained, choosing his words carefully, that it was a place where psychoanalysis was performed. The explanation left the policeman's face with an interrogative expression, and Gold assumed that the term was unfamiliar to him, but then, to his surprise, the latter opened his mouth and asked: "You mean analysis? The couch and all that stuff?" The old man nodded, and a faint smile appeared on the officer's face, which he immediately suppressed, and he said, almost apologetically, that he didn't know such things were still done, or that there was a special institute for the purpose. He obviously realized that the old man didn't encourage jokes on the subject, not even at the best of times. And indeed, as soon as he heard the note of apology in the policeman's voice, Hildesheimer went on to explain in his heavy German accent that at the Institute students learned to treat patients by this method, and he began to enlarge a little on the subject of what, "exactly," they did at "this place."

At first the policeman's face expressed astonishment, but as the old man went on talking, his expression changed to one of close attention, and he seemed to be listening as if he really wanted to know. Gold was aware of the fact that the policeman's reaction surprised him.

He felt a certain embarrassment at his prejudice, but his reflections on the need to improve his attitudes were interrupted by the sound of a loud voice outside. He peeped through the kitchen doorway and saw that the blond fellow with the mustache, who had introduced himself as the Jerusalem Subdistrict spokesman and insisted that everybody wait outside, had come back indoors after spending a few minutes on the porch talking to the Institute people there. He seized the two men with the tape recorders by their arms. "When I said leave the building I meant everyone—reporters too," he said. "Please wait outside."

Gold, appalled to discover that the two men were reporters, decided that Hildesheimer had to be notified at once. But before he could do anything about it, a general exodus from the lecture hall began, with some of those present demanding loudly and aggressively to know what had happened. The rumor that a death had taken place began to spread, and looks of alarm and consternation appeared on many faces. People huddled in twos and threes on the porch, but nobody left the premises.

Out of the corner of his eye Gold saw the two important officers, the District C.O. and the Jerusalem C.O., emerging from the little room and heading for the kitchen, apparently in the wake of the tall policeman, who was still in there with Hildesheimer. Gold approached the kitchen, with nobody stopping him, and stood next to the door, listening to the conversation. The tall policeman presented the Jerusalem police chief with what he called the "problem of publicity." The problem, as Dr. Hildesheimer had just explained to him, was that the reporters had to be prevented from publishing the story at this stage, since the deceased (Gold could not bear the word) had patients in treatment and they had to be notified tactfully. He had a serious expression on his face.

The Jerusalem C.O. said that he doubted if it would be possible to ban reportage of the "event," as he called it, and suggested giving the newsmen "a bit of candy instead." Hildesheimer interrupted him and inquired with restrained rage how the reporters had managed to get there so quickly.

The tall policeman explained patiently that it was a question of radio frequencies: the crime reporters' radios had the same frequency as the police broadcasts. This explanation left Hildesheimer with grimly pursed lips. He turned to Litzie, who had stopped crying, and shrugged his shoulders helplessly. It was then, recalled Gold, that he had overheard the Jerusalem police chief saying to the tall one: "Come along, Ohayon; let's get a few things settled."

The three of them, Ohayon and his superior officers, went into one of the rooms, trailed, in a solemn procession that Gold was later to remember as the sole comic episode of the day, by all the law enforcement officers in the building. Thanks to one of the reporters, who had succeeded in stealing back into the building and stood by the door of the room, talking into his tape recorder, Gold was able to identify all the personages, with their titles and ranks.

The reporter, an energetic little man, informed the tape recorder that Chief Inspector Michael Ohayon, deputy head of the Investigations Division of the Jerusalem Subdistrict, had entered the room, and after him the Commander Southern District and the Commander Jerusalem Subdistrict and the Jerusalem Subdistrict spokesman. The spokesman gave the reporter an annihilating stare, and the latter stopped talking into his tape for a moment, only to resume as soon as the other had gone inside. He informed the little box that the shift officer had now entered the room, together with the people from the mobile lab. He mentioned the name of a woman whose title Gold could not remember, and then the names of the intelligence officer, the departmental investigations officer, the head of the Major Crimes Unit, and the head of the Jerusalem Investigations Division.

When the procession emerged from the room, the last to come out was Michael Ohayon, deep in conversation with his direct superior officer, the head of the Jerusalem Investigations Division. Gold managed to catch only snatches of their conversation—a sentence spoken by Ohayon: "Okay, we'll wait until the lab and the pathologist are through, and then maybe we'll know a bit more"; and three words from his chief's reply: "your personal charm . . ." in a somewhat jocular tone.

And then they were out of Gold's hearing. Ohayon, together with the district and subdistrict commanders, made for the front door, where an uproar broke out. Gold saw the three of them surrounded by a mob of people demanding information in loud, indignant voices. He heard the district commander raising his voice to a near shout: "Gentlemen, gentlemen. Please calm down." And then: "This is Chief Inspector Ohayon. He is the officer in charge of the investigation and will answer all your questions in good time." And so saying, he vanished quickly from the scene, leaving behind him an impatient crowd of anxious people.

A heavy silence fell, which it was clear would not last for more than a few seconds. Apparently sensing this, Ohayon turned to Professor Hildesheimer, who was standing behind him, and asked him to explain to his colleagues what had happened. He asked him not to go into too

much detail and to keep to the essential facts. Gold watched as they all came inside and sat down on the chairs he had arranged earlier that morning. Nobody said a word. Hildesheimer, who was standing next to the little table intended for the lecturer, waited patiently.

Gold was prevented from hearing what Hildesheimer said by the chief inspector, who chose that moment to come up and ask him politely if he could talk to him for a few minutes in one of the rooms; and without waiting for a reply, he opened the door to "Fruma's room."

In addition to the couch and the analyst's chair behind it, there were two armchairs in the room, which usually stood in a corner but were now arranged at a forty-five-degree angle to each other. This particular alignment was always used for the preliminary meeting between patient and analyst, the meeting before the analytic treatment began, and was intended to enable the patient to avoid looking directly at the therapist, if he so wished. The analyst always sat in the chair closer to the door. And this, too, had a certain logic. Now Ohayon seated himself in this chair, indicating that Gold take the other seat. Gold was unable to think of any way of registering his protest. He did not even have an answer to the question of what exactly he wished to protest against; but he was very well aware of the tremendous rage swelling up inside him against this casual, relaxed intruder, who had begun to represent in his eyes the breakdown of all the rules.

At first there was a silence between them, and Gold grew increasingly tense while at the same time feeling sure that the policeman was growing increasingly relaxed. Suddenly Ohayon's face seemed sharp and pantherlike, but at that very moment the chief inspector's quiet, cultured voice broke in on Gold's thoughts, refuting his fears and exposing them for what they were—projection, as his colleagues would have said, the projection of his own anxieties onto the person sitting opposite him. A quiet, pleasant voice asked him to recount the morning's events in detail and as accurately as possible.

Gold's throat was dry and parched, but since it was obviously out of the question for him to leave the room now for something to drink, he cleared his throat and tried to begin talking. He had to start the sentence a number of times before he succeeded in producing an intelligible sound. His temples were still pounding with the remnants of the migraine, which threatened to flare up again at any moment. Ohayon was extremely patient. He sat leaning back in the chair, listening attentively, his long legs stretched out in front of him and his arms folded; he did not open his mouth until he was sure that Gold had nothing more to say. Then he asked: "And when you arrived here this morning, you didn't see anyone in the vicinity?"

Gold conjured up the deserted street, the black cat, and shook his head.

Ohayon asked if he had seen any cars in the street. Gold explained that the downhill slope of the terrain made it possible to take in the whole street at a glance but in the immediate vicinity of the Institute there had been no cars at all. There was no parking problem, he said dryly. And then the chief inspector began a slow, agonizing reconstruction of the morning's events, which was to go on for over an hour.

Afterward Gold told Hildesheimer about the humiliation of being made to feel like a suspect, obliged to prove that he was telling the truth; about the traps his interrogator had set for him in the attempt to catch him in contradictions; about the innumerable times he had been required to explain why he had volunteered to prepare the building for the lecture, to describe his every movement from the moment he got up in the morning, his movements of the night before, to explain where he had got his knowledge of firearms (his army reserve unit)— "And what not?" he complained that night to his wife. "There was nothing he didn't ask me about; he kept on and on until I myself was no longer sure of what was true and what wasn't. By the time he was through with me, there wasn't a second of the morning left unexamined: did I see any clues, did I leave any clues, did I see a revolver, did I shoot one! . . . And after all that I still had the feeling that he didn't believe me!"

Only when Ohayon asked what car Dr. Neidorf drove and Gold described the white Peugeot in detail—the model, the year, everything—only then had he begun to feel that the interrogation was taking a different turn. "Toward the end he got off my back a bit," he mumbled as he lay in bed, listening to the rain. Mina was already fast asleep.

How, in his opinion, asked the policeman, had Neidorf reached the Institute, and where had she parked her car?

He really had no idea. Maybe someone had brought her, said Gold, and immediately regretted it, without knowing why. He quickly added that she might have come by taxi or by foot. It was a fifteen-minute walk from Neidorf's house on Lloyd George Street in the German Colony to the Institute. She loved to take a shortcut that meandered along the old Lepers Hospital and then past the Jerusalem Theater.

Here he began to explain about her visit to Chicago, her return the day before, speculated that she had probably left her car with her son, and finally, suspecting that he was babbling, he fell silent.

Then Ohayon asked if he could tell him something about Neidorf's personality, stressing that he should say anything that came into his head; it was all important. Gold could not believe his ears. The expression "anything that comes into your head" was one of the key phrases used by the therapist in the analytic process. He looked suspiciously at Ohayon's face, searching for a sign of mockery or the consciousness of parody, but he could find no trace of anything of the kind.

Gold suggested that he address his question to Dr. Hildesheimer. At first he made the suggestion aggressively, but when Ohayon failed to react to his aggression, he explained that Hildesheimer knew Dr. Neidorf very well; in fact, he knew her better than anyone else did. Here Ohayon smiled for the first time, a tolerant smile, and said that he would certainly ask Dr. Hildesheimer too.

Gold began to wonder just what the policeman knew about him and where he had obtained his knowledge. He remembered that he had shut himself up in the little room with Hildesheimer; the old man had probably given him his name, informed him of the nature of Gold's professional relationship with Neidorf, and revealed that it was Gold who had discovered the body. Ohayon said nothing, but it was evident that he was going to insist. There was no point in arguing.

Gold began with her professional status. Speaking in the present tense, he said that she was a senior analyst, a member of the Institute's Training Committee, a senior teacher, and also—and here he paused for a moment and then decided not to bother with explanations—most important of all, she was a training analyst.

Ohayon stopped him with a gesture and asked the meaning of the term.

A training analyst was one entitled to treat candidates for membership in a psychoanalytic institute, said Gold, adding with a certain pride that there were only a few of them in the whole world, and in Israel you could count them on the fingers of one hand.

How did someone become a training analyst, Ohayon inquired, and why was training analysis necessary? He would be grateful if Gold explained everything slowly, he added apologetically, since he was unfamiliar with the terms.

Now, for the first time since finding Neidorf's body, Gold felt at ease, to a certain extent at least, and he began a thorough explanation. Every candidate at the Institute had to undergo analysis as an integral, ongoing part of his training. A candidate at the Institute was not permitted to begin treating patients unless he was in analysis himself: Gold had found the formula that seemed to put it all in a nutshell.

Michael Ohayon, who without taking his eyes off Gold played with a matchbox he had taken out of his pocket, asked how long the process lasted, and the question made Gold smile. It depends, he answered. Sometimes four years, sometimes five or six, and sometimes even seven.

"And how long does the training at the Institute take?" the policeman asked, and the question made Gold smile again and say that it was possible, with a great effort, to complete the training in seven years. Here he looked at Ohayon for a moment and asked hesitantly if he didn't think he should take notes, since it was all quite complicated.

The chief inspector replied that at the moment he saw no need for taking notes. Gold, feeling snubbed, fell silent and waited.

The door opened, and the photographer came in and said that in his opinion he had finished and asked if there was any need for him to stay. Ohayon replied: "Only until they take her out of there," and Gold shuddered. Then a woman's voice said from the doorway: "Michael, I'm finished. Is there anything else you want?" Ohayon turned his head, and Gold, too, looked at the broad, rosy-cheeked face, which he could in no way associate with the occupation the owner of the face had chosen. When Ohayon replied in the negative, she added: "As far as we're concerned, the room's at your disposal. I asked Lerner to see that nobody went in. If you need anything else, you know where to find me." Ohayon stood up and went over to the woman, took her by the arm, and led her out of the room. Gold heard her brisk, cheerful voice saying: "The pathologist wants to go too," and then the door shut. After a few moments it opened again, and once more the chief inspector sat down opposite him at an angle of forty-five degrees.

The reaction that Gold usually got to the kind of information he had just given the policeman was almost invariably a mixture of astonishment, incredulity, and mirth. When he explained about the duration and nature of the Institute training to people he called "outsiders," the questions came first, and then the jokes, equally predictable: "You have to be crazy to do it!" "Anyone who does it really needs analysis." Worst of all were his physician friends, especially the ones who had specialized in psychiatry but not chosen the psychoanalytic direction. He was used to hearing remarks such as: "After all the years of medical school and specialization, you must be out of your mind. Look at me—I'm already head of a psychiatric ward." That was the style of response he was used to. His parents, for example, had never understood what exactly he did at work.

But not Ohayon. He did not make a single sarcastic remark or joke, he expressed no astonishment—only pure and simple interest. He tried to come to grips with the subject and understand it, and that was all.

For some mysterious reason, however, the policeman succeeded in making Gold feel insecure. With the expression of a dedicated student on his face, he asked Gold to go on describing the course of the training and reminded him that the question was: How did a person become a training analyst?

Once again Gold overcame his misgivings, and he dared to ask why it was so important for him to know—after all, it had nothing to do with the subject.

Ohayon's only reply was the patient expectation of someone who knew that in the end he would get what he wanted, and again Gold felt that he had been presumptuous—it was the same kind of tension and lack of confidence he sometimes experienced in the presence of Hildesheimer.

"Well," he said hesitantly, "on principle, the Institute accepts as candidates psychiatrists or clinical psychologists with a few years' experience," and he quickly added, "and even then not everybody is accepted."

"How many are accepted?" came the next question, Ohayon never taking his eyes off Gold's face, while playing incessantly with the matchbox, and Gold replied fifteen at the most, in every course.

"Course; is there a new course every year?" asked Ohayon, and he emptied the matchbox on the little table standing between them. He took a squashed pack of cigarettes out of his shirt pocket and lit a cigarette. He used the matchbox as an ashtray.

No, not every year. A new course began every two years, answered Gold, refusing the battered cigarette offered him. He had never smoked, he explained; in all his thirty-five years, he had never touched a cigarette.

The chief inspector motioned with his hand that he continue, and Gold tried to remember where he had left off. Muffled voices came from beyond the door. He was tired, very tired, and wished that he were on the other side of the door now, in the company of those who had arrived at the Institute a couple of hours after him that morning.

How were the applicants selected? the chief inspector persisted, and he received a detailed explanation about letters of recommendation and the three interviews that every candidate had to undergo. Long, grueling interviews, which left the interviewee with a pain in the guts. Afterward the Training Committee met and selected the candidates according to the impression they had made on their interviewers.

The obvious question was then asked. "Who are the interviewers?" asked Ohayon, looking as if he already knew the answer.

"The senior analysts, the training analysts, are the interviewers."

"Which brings us back"—Ohayon smiled—"to the opening question: How does someone become a training analyst?"

Gold remembered a remark once made by another patient of Neidorf's, when they were comparing notes a couple of years before. "She's like a bulldog," said the candidate. "She seizes on something you say and never lets go until she gets right down to the marrow of the bone." There were some people, thought Gold, whose perseverance, or even the thought of whose perseverance, was exhausting. The policeman sitting opposite him was wearing him out. It was clear that he would never forget or overlook a question. The only thing that wasn't clear was why Gold felt such resistance and reluctance to answer.

He said that after an unspecified number of years, the Training Committee of the Institute decided who would be a training analyst.

"Ah." The chief inspector let out a comprehending, perhaps also slightly disappointed, sigh. "It's simply a question of seniority."

Gold explained that this wasn't exactly so. In the eyes of an outside observer, the decision might seem arbitrary, a matter of procedure, but that was not the case. They appointed the people who seemed to them suitable. By a two thirds majority, he added, to make it quite clear that it was a serious matter.

And who were the people on this committee that made so many important decisions? asked Ohayon. He would like to get an idea of the hierarchy.

The Training Committee consisted of ten people chosen in anonymous elections, all of them qualified analysts. No, candidates certainly did not participate in this vote, or in any other vote. Yes, at the moment Hildesheimer was at the head of the Training Committee. For ten years. They kept on reelecting him.

Ohayon asked if they could get back to Neidorf now.

Gold did not want to get back to Neidorf; he wanted to get out of the building, which seemed to be deserted. But he nevertheless replied that she had been his analyst. He noticed that he had begun speaking in the past tense. He stole a look at his watch and saw that it was twelve o'clock.

Ohayon was obliged to repeat his question. "Enemies?" Gold echoed the last word in the question, as if he couldn't believe his ears. "What is this? TV?" No, of course not; everyone had admired her. There may have been some people who were jealous of her, as a person, a woman, a professional, but "Nobody wished her any harm, as they say in detective novels."

He had not even realized that she had been shot. And he had certainly not seen a pistol. He thought it was a sudden death from a stroke, or something of the kind. Yes, of course he was a doctor, but he couldn't bring himself to touch her. No, he wasn't afraid; it had nothing to do with being afraid; it was a question of the relationship between them. She was his analyst! The last words were uttered in something approaching a yell, and then Gold lowered his voice and said, almost whispering, that for him she was not someone who could be touched.

The policeman asked the next question while lighting another cigarette and without taking his eyes off Gold, who sat staring at the matchbox full of ash and cigarette stubs. He nearly jumped out of his skin. No, suicide was out of the question! And in the Institute yet! An angry shake of the head accompanied the word "No," which was repeated: "No, she wasn't that kind of person." "No, not her." "No, quite out of the question." Why—he went on arguing with the outrageous proposition—she had to give a lecture that morning. A person as responsible as she was? No.

And then came the most infuriating moment of all, when Ohayon asked him to accompany the shift officer (Gold knew by now that this meant the redhead) to the police station in the Russian Compound, to sign a statement. At first Gold tried to suggest putting it off to the next day, but Ohayon explained politely but firmly that this was the procedure and opened the door to the foyer, where the redhead was waiting. He smiled at Gold and even opened the front door for him.

"How long will it take?" Gold asked Ohayon, who was standing and looking at them. "Not long," said the redhead, and he led him to the Renault from which he had emerged with Ohayon earlier that morning.

The scene that Gold saw before leaving the building remained engraved in his memory for a long time afterward: in the lecture hall, the members of the Training Committee were seated around the round conference table, which someone had returned to its place in the middle of the room. The folding chairs had disappeared, and Hildesheimer, a steaming cup in his hands, raised his eyes and signaled Ohayon to join the people sitting nervously around the table, preparing themselves to tackle a problem they had never dealt with before. They did not look particularly strong to Gold, no stronger, in fact, than he felt himself.

The sun was still warming the street. After a rainy week, the Institute from outside looked the same as always: the green gate leading into the big garden, with the round porch above it and behind the porch the large Arab-style building. It was impossible to avoid the banal thought that it was all only a bad dream, that perhaps it hadn't really happened at all, perhaps he had only imagined it in some kind of psychotic delusion. But the car that he got into was real enough, and so was the redhead sitting behind the wheel, and the people standing outside the gate and wiping their eyes were real too. There was no room for doubt: he knew with absolute certainty that the world would never be the same again.

3

They're only human, said Michael Ohayon to himself, his face expressionless, when he realized that the nine people at the heavy round table were none other than the Institute Training Committee.

From the other rooms he could hear the muffled voices of the two mobile lab technicians, whom he had asked to go over the whole place "inch by inch."

Hildesheimer, who sat next to him, reported in a whisper that in the open meeting he had told the committee members that Dr. Neidorf had been found dead in the building but had made no mention of the pistol, thinking that the chief inspector might prefer to tell them himself. It was with this in mind that he had asked him to join them in "this forum." The old man's hands gripped his coffee cup as he said that everyone had taken the death very badly. Michael inquired if anyone had reacted in a way that had struck him as surprising or strange, and the old man was silent for a moment and then said that he could not recall anything in particular—at the moment, he added cautiously;

there had been some emotional outbursts, but they were only to be expected.

At normal volume he asked the chief inspector if he wanted anything to drink, and Michael, breathing in the tantalizing smell of the coffee in the old man's cup, said that he would be glad of a cup of coffee, if it wasn't too much trouble. A little man sitting on Hildesheimer's other side asked in an undefinable accent what kind of coffee he would prefer, Turkish or Nescafé without milk, and Michael said, "Turkish," and added immediately, "with three spoons of sugar, please."

The little man, who wore a black turtleneck sweater and had a childish face with a petulant expression, raised a thin eyebrow and repeated inquiringly: "Three?"

Michael smiled and confirmed: "Three spoons, if that's the size of the cup," pointing at Hildesheimer's mug. Now Hildesheimer began to introduce the people sitting around the table; he prefaced the introductions by remarking that it would probably be difficult for Michael to remember all their names.

The chief inspector did not contradict him, but he looked hard at the people as they were introduced to him one by one. Remembering nine names, one of which he already knew, did not pose any difficulties for someone who had majored in medieval history and aroused the envy of his fellow students by his ability to remember the names of all the popes and royal dynasties of Europe. In the present situation, however, he preferred to keep this gift to himself, not out of false modesty but because it was a card he did not want to show at this stage of the game.

The man who brought the coffee was Joe Linder—Doctor, naturally; they were all doctors here—and the two women who were sitting close together, pale but tearless, were Nehama Zold (the younger of the two, solidly and severely dressed, in her middle forties, hard-faced, basically attractive but making what seemed like a deliberate attempt to hide it, Michael noted) and Sarah Shenhar (like a benevolent fairy godmother, a big sweater wrapped around her shoulders, at least sixty, an expression of shock on her kindly face).

Then there was the skinny man called Rosenfeld, Nahum, with the mane of white hair and the small, thin cigar that he never took out of his mouth, who reminded Michael of the sentence he had heard from his mother throughout his childhood: "Eat, Michael, eat, so you won't end up with no flesh on your bones and bad thoughts in your head"; which was no doubt why he always felt uneasy and somewhat suspicious in the company of excessively thin people. And then there was a very handsome man, also apparently in his fifties, named Daniel Voller, and another four men sitting farthest from Michael at the circular table, who all looked in their sixties, three in the early sixties and one pushing seventy, Shalom Kirshner, a very fat, bald man. They did not utter a word throughout the meeting.

Nehama Zold was smoking cigarettes, leaving lipstick marks on the stubs, Joe Linder puffed on a pipe, and Rosenfeld was of course smoking a cigar. Michael took the squashed pack out of his pocket, and someone pushed an ashtray in his direction.

When Hildesheimer had finished introducing his colleagues, he presented Michael to them, mentioning his rank, which did not seem to impress anyone, and saying that he was the police officer "in charge of investigating our tragedy." Then he said: "Chief Inspector Ohayon has kindly consented to join us in order to clarify certain matters, at my request, and help us in any way he can." In the ensuing silence, Michael leaned back in his chair, puffing on his cigarette, without daring to take a sip of the hot coffee in the cup standing in front of him. Everyone stared at him, and the air was so thick with suspicion that he could almost touch it. These people, he thought, are not at all sure of my ability to solve anything and are full of prejudices about policemen and probably about people whose parents didn't come from Europe.

At this point he called himself to order and warned his weaker side not to give way to irrelevant impulses, such as the need to make an impression. It was time to get to work.

With all their eyes on him, he had to make a strenuous effort to begin to talk. The safest thing was to ask, and quickly, the question that had been bothering him ever since Hildesheimer had brought it up when they stood next to the body. There was absolute silence in the room after he had finished asking what Dr. Neidorf had been doing in the building so early in the morning. As he sipped his coffee, he observed the expressions of the people sitting around the table.

Rosenfeld's expression was blank, Linder's puzzled, Nehama Zold's inquiring, and Sarah Shenhar's frightened. Hildesheimer himself was busy observing his colleagues, while the others were shifting about uneasily.

Joe Linder broke the silence and said that perhaps she had come to polish up her lecture notes. From the expression on his face, he didn't seem to believe this hypothesis himself. Nehama Zold dismissed it immediately, inquiring in a nasal drawl who would have prevented her from doing so in her own big empty house. Sarah Shenhar nodded in agreement and mumbled something about Neidorf's children leaving home and the peace and quiet she had gained as a result.

Rosenfeld remarked that her lecture must have been word perfect. Everyone knew how much work she put into preparing for her lectures. They all nodded. "The lecture must have been ready weeks ago," he asserted.

"What about her family," asked Nehama. "Who's going to inform the children?" And she wiped her right eye with the back of her hand. Hildesheimer explained that her son was on a biological field trip in the Galilee, which was why he had not gone to meet her at the airport. The police—here he glanced at Michael, who hastily nodded his head—were trying to locate him at this very minute. "Her daughter's husband, who came back on the same flight as Eva, is in Tel Aviv, at his parents' place. He must have been notified already." He looked at Michael, who nodded again.

Then Michael asked if there was any possibility that Neidorf had made an appointment to see someone in the Institute that morning.

This time a babble of voices greeted his question, with the words "patient" and "supervisee" rising in the air. Once again it was Joe Linder who cut through the babble. Dr. Neidorf received her patients in her consulting room at home, he said, and there was no reason for her to deviate from her usual practice, although perhaps after her trip. . . His voice gradually faltered and died. There were doubtful nods.

Michael, taking one last sip of coffee and lighting another cigarette, asked if he could have a list of Dr. Neidorf's patients.

From the uproar that ensued, anyone would have thought a bomb had been dropped on the room. Except for Dr. Hildesheimer, everyone talked at once, a couple of them yelling. The general tone was one of indignation. Rosenfeld removed the cigar from his mouth and said severely that Chief Inspector Ohayon must surely be aware of the fact that he was requesting the impossible. The information was confidential. And that was that. Everyone acclaimed his stand.

Yes, said Michael, quietly, I understand that the information is confidential, but we're dealing with a case of unnatural death. On the other hand, I also understand that the patients are candidates in the Institute and the analysis is an important part of their training. Perhaps someone would be kind enough to explain to me what's so confidential about all this?

The silence was absolute. Even Hildesheimer stared at Michael, who busied himself with his cigarette, observing them with enjoyment as they confronted his knowledgeability.

"It appears that Eva Neidorf died from a bullet wound in the temple. Under the circumstances, I'm sure you'll agree, we must know who was with her this morning. The possibility also exists that she shot herself. In that case, however, we must ask why the pistol that caused her death was not found next to the body. Either way, someone was obviously with her, before or after she died. We are of course looking for the pistol, and what I expect from you is the fullest possible cooperation and answers to all my questions. For example: Is it conceivable that she shot herself; and if so, who removed the pistol?" He fell silent and scanned their faces, one after the other: they all seemed paralyzed with horror.

He did not tell them that the pathologist had said—with the usual caveat that he would not know for certain until after the postmortem—that the range at which the bullet had been fired ruled out suicide; nor did he tell them that he could get permission from the courts to violate medical confidentiality. He waited patiently.

Hildesheimer silently requested permission to speak, and Michael gave it. With a slight tremor in his voice, the old man confirmed what the policeman had said and went on to describe the events of the morning in detail. Rosenfeld's face, which was drained of blood, began to twitch; Joe Linder leapt to his feet; Nehama Zold trembled violently. Hildesheimer apologized for the manner in which the news had been broken; nobody said anything. Michael was thinking that they were a very restained group of people. For a few long moments, he, too, said nothing. He scrutinized their faces but found nothing untoward: there were expressions of horror and shock, sorrow too, but mainly he saw fear and disbelief. Finally his gaze came to rest on Joe Linder. Linder raised his eyes, and Michael, following their direction, looked with him at the pictures of the dead.

"I ask myself," he continued as if nothing had intervened, "if it was murder, why didn't the murderer leave the weapon—let's assume it was a pistol—in Dr. Neidorf's hand, to make it look like suicide and put us off the scent at least in the initial stages of the investigation? Whichever way you look at it, someone else had to be involved, someone who knows more than we do." He spoke very slowly, uncertain of how much his audience in their present state of shock were capable of taking in.

The members of the Training Committee looked at him and then at one another. Joe Linder said that Eva had not killed herself. Rosenfeld explained that even if she had decided to take her own life, which he did not for a moment believe, the Institute was the last place in the world in which she would have done it. You had to understand, he explained to Michael, that suicide was an act of revenge and hatred against those closest to the person committing it. Eva Neidorf, he said loudly and slowly, in a controlled, deliberate voice, was a person free of hate. She was not selfish enough to do such a thing in the Institute, or anywhere else for that matter, he said, and lit another cigar with a trembling hand. Even if she had found out that she had some terminal disease—he looked around the table—she would have waited. He was sure of it.

Daniel Voller's handsome face took on a critical expression, which deepened the longer Rosenfeld went on talking. Finally he opened his mouth, then closed it without saying anything. He averted his face and looked first in the direction of the window and then at Hildesheimer.

All the others were unanimous in their support for Rosenfeld's statement, nodding their heads and uttering murmurs of agreement.

Joe Linder rose to his feet again and said that there was no point in trying to hide their heads in the sand. Eva Neidorf would not have committed suicide, if at all, without putting her affairs in order—patients, supervisees, the lecture this morning, her daughter, who had given birth a month before. No way. He knew that our knowledge of human beings was limited, he was aware of the fact that the unexpected could happen—and here he raised his eyes to the portrait gallery, and an expression of anger crossed his face. He wasn't saying that analysts were immune to depressions or emotional outbreaks, or even to suicide, but not Eva.

Hildesheimer was the last to speak, and summing up the statements made by previous speakers, he said, in a tone that was apologetic but at the same time firm, that Eva Neidorf had been very close to him, he could not imagine that she would not have confided in him if anything was troubling her, he had spoken to her only the day before, when she came home from Ben-Gurion Airport, and she had sounded cheerful and optimistic; a little tired from the flight, obviously, a little tense, but on the whole happy. Happy about the birth of her grandson, happy to be home, and even happy about the lecture.

Michael sighed and asked if the implications of what they had all been saying were clear to them.

Now everyone looked at Hildesheimer, who suddenly resembled a sad, kindly walrus, and he said very softly, almost in a whisper, that he was very much afraid that it was a question of murder; there was no point in denying it and trying to talk about an accident, for how could such an accident possibly happen in the Institute? After all, he said slowly, how could anyone have met her here if he didn't belong to the Institute? And none of the Institute people were in the habit of wandering around on Saturday morning with weapons in their pockets.

"To my deep regret," he said, his voice nearly breaking, "we will have to cope with this terrible fact as well as mourning for our departed friend and colleague."

Joe Linder asked if it was impossible that someone had broken in from outside.

No, replied Michael, there were no signs of a break-in, and in any case, she must have come here to meet someone. There were no signs that her body had been moved here from somewhere else. And why else would she have come to the Institute so early in the morning?

Rosenfeld said in a shaking voice that Eva could not have met anyone here without making an appointment in advance. "And altogether," he summed up, "on the morning of the lecture"—here he paused reflectively—"only something extremely urgent, something in the nature of an emergency, could have brought her to the Institute at so ungodly an hour."

"Unless the meeting took place yesterday," said Joe Linder, desperately, and they all jumped. "How do we know when she passed away, I mean died," and he made an abrupt gesture as if to banish the word he had just dared to utter.

Hildesheimer said that the doctor who had examined the body was of the opinion that the death had occurred not long before, although of course it had to be confirmed.

And so Michael took up again where he had left off. He must ask them again for the names of all Dr. Neidorf's patients, as well as the names of all the people connected with the Institute: members, candidates, everyone.

And what about the supervisees? Joe Linder wanted to know. Why wasn't he interested in a separate list of supervisees?

Michael quickly went over all the information he had received from Gold. No mention had been made of supervisees. He looked at Linder inquiringly, and the latter responded with a provocative glance, as if to say: I thought you knew everything there was to know about the place; but he quickly recovered his gravity under Hildesheimer's look and explained that every candidate had to have supervision on every analytic case: for every case, a different supervisor; "three cases—

three supervisors," he summed up with a macabre relish. Who were the supervisors? asked Ohayon. Were they restricted to the members of the Training Committee, or did they come from all the members of the Institute?

"Anyone the Training Committee deems fit to supervise," replied Rosenfeld, who had recovered his composure. His hands were no longer shaking.

Michael stood up and said that he would meet each of them separately later; in the meantime he would like their addresses and telephone numbers. If they could give him a short account in writing of their movements over the past twenty-four hours he would be grateful, he added, and lit another cigarette. Someone seemed about to protest, but Hildesheimer said in a tone of authority that he expected the full cooperation of everyone present; they had nothing to hide.

"The guilty person must be found," he said, his voice reverberating in the big entrance hall. "We can't go on living here together as long as this matter remains unresolved. Too many people depend on us for us to be able to afford not to know which of us is capable of murder."

So it had finally been said, thought Michael, as he nodded in the direction of the two policemen who had finished going over the rooms at last and were on their way to wait for him outside the building, as arranged. He looked at the photographs of the dead again, going over them one by one as he listened to the old man saying that it would be up to them, the members of the Training Committee and the three who also served on the Institute Committee, to deal with all the problems arising from Eva Neidorf's death: both from the fact itself, he explained, "and from the terrible manner in which she was taken from us." He went on to say that they would have to deal with all her patients and supervisees, to be capable of helping, to cope with all the mistrust that people were going to feel toward one another, and he concluded by saying that they were all about to experience "an extremely difficult period. We must do everything in our power to help get the police side of the matter, at least, over as quickly as possible. I'm asking you all not to take offense, and to comply with the chief inspector's request."

Joe Linder apologized and asked if Chief Inspector Ohayon would permit him to cancel a luncheon appointment, which he had already missed but had to explain—"unless nobody is allowed to leave the room until their alibis have been confirmed, like in an Agatha Christie novel."

Nobody smiled at this last pleasantry. Michael accompanied Linder to the kitchen, where a uniformed policeman was sitting, and nodded his permission. Then he left the room and waited outside, close to the door, and heard Joe Linder saying in an intimate voice, to someone called Yoav, that he would not be able to meet him as arranged. "No, it's not a committee meeting," said Joe into the phone. "Eva Neidorf has been found dead in the Institute." He said nothing about a pistol. Or about murder.

The papers rustled and the notes were handed in, and the members of the Training Committee left the Institute one after the other. The last to leave was Ernst Hildesheimer, who, although he may not have known it, had acquired a new admirer in the course of the morning.

By the time they succeeded in locating him, it was nearly evening. Chief Inspector Ohayon was on his way back from Tel Aviv, where he had spoken, very briefly, to Neidorf's son-in-law, Hillel, who now had to call his wife in Chicago and tell her the news and then would make funeral arrangements—all from his mother's bedside in Ichilov Hospital, where she was being treated for lung edema induced by heart failure. Confronted in the waiting room outside cardiac intensive care, Hillel had paled and removed his spectacles, but Michael sensed that he had not yet taken it in. As he left the room, Michael could still hear him muttering: "It's not possible. I don't believe it." He had been unable to provide Ohayon with any possible leads.

At the control center, they simply could not understand why Michael's radio had not picked up any messages until he reached Motza, the closest suburb to Jerusalem. The frequency, as Naftali from Control reminded him, was supposed to transmit as far as Tel Aviv. Michael did not supply the explanation: all he had to do was push the right button to be alone at last. As he had tried to gather his thoughts, his inner world took over and made the distance from Tel Aviv to Jerusalem nonexistent. His life was difficult enough without this latest investigation, he thought rebelliously.

A woman he loved had once said that only someone who knew him intimately could tell when he was troubled: he became less and less there, his eyes grew glazed and his reactions mechanical. "You're fading away again; soon you'll disappear completely," she would have said if she were in the car with him now. He drove automatically, oblivious to the other cars on the road, signaling and passing and obeying the speed limit without awareness.

Inside him the seed of longing for this woman swelled and grew, until at the entrance to Abu Ghosh he even found a faint echo of her smell in the car. Finally he brought the radio back to life in order to break out of the longing and the pain. Saturday was never their day, as she had put it years before: "Thieves don't meet on the Sabbath day," she said then, and she didn't laugh.

Control said that the radio would have to be seen to as soon as he got back. Michael agreed.

"To come to the point," said Naftali, "somebody's looking for you, everybody's looking for you—the boys on your team and some guy with a long name who keeps calling and wanting to talk to you."

Michael asked for the man's name, Naftali stumbled over it, then spelled it out, and Michael said that he knew the person in question.

He asked Naftali to tell the men on the special investigating team that he would make contact from town to inform them of his whereabouts, then he asked what Hildesheimer had wanted. "He didn't say. He left a phone number." Michael asked for the number. It was already half past eight, and the town was crowded with people. Saturday night in Jerusalem was not the ideal time for driving downtown, and Michael turned into Narkis, a quiet side street, and looked for a phone booth.

Three tokens went down the tube before he found a phone in working order. Hildesheimer answered as if he had been waiting for the phone to ring, his hand on the receiver. After apologizing for the lateness of the hour and the trouble he was putting him to, the old man wondered if he could meet him. Michael asked what place would be convenient for him, and the old man inquired hesitantly where he was phoning from, and in the end Chief Inspector Ohayon found himself on his way to the Hildesheimer residence on Alfasi Street in the heart of Rehavia, a few minutes away.

As he could have guessed, the apartment was in one of the old houses inhabited by German immigrants who had come to the country in the thirties. It had not been renovated, unlike many of the homes that were bought by wealthy American Orthodox Jews who had made Aliyah after 1967.

On the first floor of a three-story building, a small sign announced: "Professor Ernst Hildesheimer, Psychiatrist, Specialist in Nervous Diseases and Psychoanalyst."

At the first ring of the doorbell, the door was opened by a woman whose head was covered with tight gray curls and whose eyes were blue, sharp, and hostile. It was impossible to guess her age or to imagine whether she had ever been beautiful. She looked as if she had never concerned herself with such things as age or beauty.

In a thick German accent, she said that the professor was waiting in his study. Leading Michael to the study as if someone were twisting her arm, she looked back over her shoulder from time to time, muttering unintelligibly.

Hildesheimer opened the study door, introduced his wife to Michael, and asked her to bring them something hot to drink. The request was answered by a growl, which brought a broad smile to Hildesheimer's face. In Michael, the professor's lady gave rise to something approaching awe.

While he was still on his way to one of the two armchairs his host indicated, Michael began examining his surroundings. There were a number of bookcases, all crammed with books. In one of the corners stood a large old-fashioned desk made of dark, heavy wood. The desktop was covered with thick glass, at the center of which a long, narrow booklet with a green cover lay facedown. Despite his sharp eyesight, Michael was unable to read the title. His eyes shifted to the couch, which appeared very comfortable, and from there to the Scandinavian-design leather armchair behind it. This chair was the only modern item of furniture in the room.

Michael raised his eyes and looked at the pictures hanging between the bookcases: dim pictures among which he made out a portrait of Freud, a pencil sketch, and a number of oil paintings of foreign landscapes. It was only after he had become completely absorbed in trying to discern the gold-lettered titles of the leather volumes in the bookcase behind the Scandinavian armchair, and discovered Arnold Toynbee's name next to that of Goethe that he suddenly sensed Hildesheimer's eyes on him. The old man was sitting opposite him and waiting patiently for him to finish examining his room.

Embarrassed, Michael asked if there was anything in particular that Dr. Hildesheimer had wanted to talk to him about.

Hildesheimer picked up the big bunch of keys that lay on the table between their chairs and held it out to him, saying that the keys—which were attached to a finely patterned leather case—had belonged to Eva Neidorf and had been found next to the telephone in the Institute kitchen. He had slipped them into his pocket when he locked the phone and had intended handing them over this morning, but he had forgotten. The last words were uttered with profound and puzzled sadness. Professor Hildesheimer was evidently not accustomed to forgetting things.

He had been trying to contact Chief Inspector Ohayon since noon—he had remembered as soon as he got home—but it was impossible to get hold of him, he continued apologetically.

Michael seemed more interested in the telephone. How did the keys relate to the telephone: was the telephone in the Institute locked?

It was, replied the old man. Recently the members and also the candidates had been provided with keys, because they simply could not afford to pay the bills, which were "something shocking."

No, he had to admit that the situation had not improved since the advent of the lock. He smiled in response to Michael's inquiry, a smile that illuminated his round face with a childish innocence.

No, nobody could get into the Institute except members and

candidates, who had keys to the front door as well as the telephone.

"And what about the patients?" asked Michael, doing his best to ignore the wave of affection for the old man he felt flooding him. Hildesheimer replied that the patients did not have keys; the therapists let them in and accompanied them to the door when the sessions were over. In any case, only the candidates received patients in the Institute, and in recent years, due to overcrowding, candidates too, in their fifth year, had been permitted to work outside the Institute.

The door opened, and Mrs. Hildesheimer brought in a tray—hot cocoa for her husband, its smell filling the room, and tea with lemon in a delicate glass for Michael. There were biscuits too. They thanked her, and she went out again, muttering to herself, taking the tray with her.

A strong wind was blowing outside, and through the window, whose green iron shutter was open, flashes of lightning were visible. They drank in silence, without remarking on the change in the weather.

Hildesheimer rested his chin on his hand and said, as if to himself, that the matter of the keys had been bothering him all day. "First of all," he said, "it's not at all like Eva to leave her keys in the kitchen. Analysts in general"—he smiled again—"are a compulsive lot, and she"—here his smile vanished—"was particularly compulsive and orderly, so it would be quite out of character for her to leave the telephone unlocked, to forget her keys, unless . . ." and he fell silent.

"Unless," he repeated thoughtfully, "someone rang the doorbell. Not just anyone, but someone she had made an appointment with, someone she didn't want to keep waiting. Otherwise it doesn't make sense."

"Someone who didn't have a key," Michael pointed out. "Or perhaps someone who preferred not to use his key . . ."

"And secondly"—Hildesheimer stubbornly persisted with his own train of thought—"why didn't she make the phone call from her house before she left? Which brings us back to the questions"—here he sat up straight in his chair—"whom did she meet, why at the Institute, and whom did she call?" The questions came out in a rush, without a pause for breath between them.

"The time bothers me too," he said with a sigh. "Whom could she have been calling so early in the morning, and on a Saturday? It wasn't a family call—she would make that from home—and she didn't call me. So who was it?

"Besides the fact that I was very attached to her," he continued, tears in his eyes, "I'm afraid that what has happened will destroy the Institute, its inner life, the sense of belonging our people feel toward it. I want to get it all over with as quickly as possible," he said emotionally. "And I really wanted to ask you: in your experience, Chief Inspector Ohayon, how long can an investigation of this kind take?"

Michael was silent. Finally he waved his hand and said that it would take some time, certainly, although it was impossible to tell. Maybe a month, if someone broke, and if not, maybe a year.

Despite the embarrassment he felt when the old man wiped his eyes with his hand, Michael looked straight at him.

"I must stress," said Hildesheimer, "that I am convinced it was no suicide."

Michael nodded and said that this seemed a reasonable assumption, in the light of everything he had heard, but that in some cases it was easier to accept the thought of murder, or manslaughter, than suicide. "For a senior psychoanalyst to commit suicide," he said, as gently as he could.

"It's happened before," Hildesheimer interjected. "Not a senior psychoanalyst, to be sure; a psychoanalyst at the beginning of her career, but she already had three cases. And it was very hard, very hard indeed. We kept it as quiet as we could, but it was a shock, there's no denying that it was a shock." He sighed. "That was a good few years ago, when I was younger and perhaps less vulnerable. And now I find the fact that Eva is gone very hard to accept. I'm not sure," he went on, almost whispering, "that it isn't even harder, or at least just as hard, to get used to the idea that one of us is a murderer."

"Maybe," Michael amended.

"As things appear to stand at present." The old man repeated the reservation in a different, but apparently no more consoling, formula.

Michael was quiet. A sympathetic, attentive silence. He knew how to exert pressure when necessary. There were some people who claimed that they had seen him in the act and that it was not a spectacle they would easily forget. But here he sensed that he had to proceed with the greatest possible delicacy, the only way to get onto the wavelength of the person sitting opposite him and pick up those ostensibly trivial things, the things people said between the lines and sometimes never said at all, that in the last analysis provided the master key to solving the mystery. And there was also what he privately referred to as "my historical need." In other words, the historian's need to obtain a full picture, to see everything concerning human beings as part of an overall process, like a historical process possessing laws of its own, which—he never tired of explaining—if only we are able to grasp their meaning, provide us with the tools for going right to the heart of the problem.

The main thing in the initial stage of an investigation, Michael Ohayon would repeat to his subordinates—he never could define what he meant exactly but succeeded only in demonstrating it—the main thing, he stubbornly claimed, was to understand the people involved in the case. Even if this understanding might not seem to play any role in the investigation at first. Which was why he always tried to penetrate as deeply as possible into the emotional and intellectual world under investigation. Superficially this was manifested by the fact that investigations of which he was in charge began too slowly, according to his superiors. Now, for example, he made no attempt to contact the members of his team, because he didn't want to miss the meeting with Hildesheimer even for the sake of a new lead. He was unwilling to hear facts that might oblige him to cut short his conversation with the old man. He knew that one talk with Hildesheimer would help him to understand the spirit of the place where the murder had occurred and the forces activating the characters more than would any fact discovered in the field. Naturally, he was in conflict; he was tense, and he suspected that there would be a price to pay for his absence: he would have to explain himself, and he knew in advance that he would not be understood. Shorer, his immediate superior, was always attacking him for his "eccentricities." But he was sure that he was right: you had to start slowly, with a kind of theoretical introduction, and speed things up, as much as possible, only later.

Hildesheimer closed his eyes for a moment and, opening them, gave Michael a long look. Then he said hesitantly that he was afraid he was going to have to break some rules. Even though his wife claimed that he understood nothing at all about people unless they were his patients, he felt that he could trust Chief Inspector Ohayon. Not that it was a secret; it simply wasn't done to talk about internal matters to outsiders, but as he had already said, he was interested in getting the case solved as quickly as possible.

Michael followed his train of thought and asked himself where it was leading.

Generally, said the old man, when people in the psychoanalytic community or outside it asked him questions about the Institute, he was careful to ascertain *why* they were asking: there were all kinds of situations in which thoughtless replies could cause a lot of pain. On the other hand, Chief Inspector Ohayon himself was asking questions whose answers would certainly be painful, but here he felt he had no alternative, since in any case what had happened was irreversible, the damage already done. He begged the chief inspector's pardon for the digression: it was intended to explain his reservations about discussing the Institute on principle and why he was about to depart from custom.

By the time the rain began coming down, in big, quiet drops, Hildesheimer was already in the middle of his story. When he had started to speak of the thirties in Vienna and his decision to emigrate to Palestine, Michael, without asking permission, lit a cigarette from the new pack of Noblesse he took out of his pocket, and by the time the professor reached the house in the old Bukharan Quarter, not far from Mea Shearim, there were already three stubs in the ashtray that the old man had taken from the shelf under the little table. He himself had stood up and taken a dark pipe from a drawer in his desk, stuffing it as he spoke. The smell of the tobacco spread sweetly through the room, and the china ashtray filled with burned matches.

Even before he said it in so many words, Michael knew that he was talking about his life's work.

The most painful things were said in the most matter-of-fact tone.

The need to put Michael as fully as possible in the picture was explained by the fact that "the person in charge of this case has to understand exactly what he's dealing with; he can't afford to make any mistakes. He has to be aware of the gravity of his responsibility." Then he said that the entire future of the Psychoanalytic Institute depended on the question of whether there was a murderer actually in its midst, that the whole basis of the lives of the members would be threatened if it was "really impossible to ever know in advance what the person facing you was capable of." (Michael thought that it was, indeed, impossible, but he said nothing.) The old man spoke of his own personal need to discover the truth, of the fact that what was at stake was the thing to which he had dedicated his life.

It was only after his introduction, and after looking searchingly into Michael's eyes, that he began, in a monotone, to tell his story.

In 1937, when it was already clear what was going to happen, he had concluded his analytic training and was about to begin his professional life. He decided to emigrate to Palestine.

With him was a small group of people at a similar stage in their careers. They had been preceded to Palestine by Stefan Deutsch, whose training and experience were more serious than theirs—"after all, he had undergone analysis with Ferenczi, a personal friend and disciple of Freud's." With some money he had inherited, Deutsch bought a large house in the Bukharan Quarter in Jerusalem.

To this house Hildesheimer came with Ilse, his wife, and with the Levines, a husband and wife who were both analysts at the outset of their careers. In the course of time, said the old man, the house became, without anyone intending it, the first home of the Psychoanalytic Institute. Ilse took charge of the administrative side, and the Levines and he himself practiced analysis, and they all lived together in the house in the Bukharan Quarter. He half smiled as he recalled the high round ceilings and the chipped, painted tile floors of the old Arab house. Winters were traumatic, with the rain seeping through, but the summers were pleasant. They used to spend the evenings summing up their days, sitting in the open courtyard, surrounded by jasmine smells and the drying laundry hanging from the neighbors' clothesline. After many months they found this apartment in Rehavia and came to live here, but they still spent most of their time in the house in the Bukharan Quarter. Later on, others came to join them there, especially in 1938 and '39.

It was raining harder. Hildesheimer puffed on his pipe and then restuffed it, first extracting the burned tobacco from the bowl with a used match. The china ashtray was overflowing, and he emptied it into a wastepaper basket next to the table and then stood up and opened the window, though it was pouring. Michael sank down deeper into the armchair and went on listening to the flow of German-accented words.

It was in these years that Fruma Hollander, for example, who was still very young, had arrived, and Litzie Sternfeld (Michael remembered the figure in the kitchen). They both underwent analysis with Deutsch and stayed in his house for a long period, until they found somewhere to live. Fruma was already dead, and Litzie, like himself, wasn't getting any younger.

The rain grew weaker, the wind stronger, and an odor of good earth spread through the room, overpowering the smell of the tobacco.

Life was very hard, from every point of view: the analytic training was extremely arduous, and they earned hardly any money. Deutsch insisted that they treat the children and adolescents sent out of Germany without their parents, wards of the Youth Aliyah, and they, of course, could not pay. In fact, Deutsch supported them, all the—he searched for the right word—the candidates, that's what they really were, he and the Levines and Fruma and Litzie, candidates for the as yet nonexistent institute. And Deutsch was their supervisor.

It was only after five years of work that he had allowed Hildesheimer to treat patients independently, and then, too, clinical seminars had been held, where all the members of the group had to present their cases and Deutsch would comment. Here Hildesheimer made a few remarks about Deutsch's professional skills, his seriousness, his sense of responsibility, and the indebtedness that he, Hildesheimer, felt toward him to this very day.

It was a pioneering atmosphere. The financial situation and the slowness of their professional advancement did not really bother any of them. Yes, there were tensions; that went without saying. The tensions were related mainly to Deutsch's dominant personality but also to the conditions of the country. The heat was terrible. The dryness of the Jerusalem summers. There were language difficulties too. He glanced at the bookcase and went on talking. All the seminars were held in German, and the therapy itself was conducted in a mixture of languages, including broken Hebrew—and he smiled his childish smile again. Now of course it was hard to imagine that then he had not known a word of Hebrew, but the effort! What an effort! Here he paused to ask Michael if he himself had been born in Israel.

No, but he had come to the country when he was three years old.

For children the language does not present such difficulties.

No, Michael agreed, but there were other difficulties.

Yes, said the old man, and looked at him keenly.

Michael breathed in the scent of the jasmine that apparently grew right underneath the window, and he lit another cigarette. The sixth, he counted.

Afterward Hildesheimer and the Levines became proper, qualified analysts, and they were the supervisors of the group that arrived in the country after the war. Deutsch was then the only training analyst. At first only psychiatrists were accepted; later, psychologists too. And there was someone they accepted from another field entirely, a thing that would be impossible today: Deutsch was so impressed by his personality and intuition that he undertook to train him from beginning to end. Hildesheimer himself had given him supervision, and today he was a highly respected member of the Institute. Michael was not quite sure, but he sensed that he should know who the person was, that the old man was trying, without mentioning names, to tell him something. He knew that the knowledge of who it was would come to him with time. It was clear to him, although nothing had actually been said, that Hildesheimer did not like this "highly respected member."

And then—it was the beginning of the fifties—there were twenty analysts and another five candidates, and the house grew too small to hold them. Deutsch was worn out and wanted a place of his own. The

Levines were in London, taking a course. Deutsch and Hildesheimer between them had found the house in which Michael had been that morning, and Deutsch later bequeathed it to the Institute (which was why it was called after him). When the present building no longer met their needs, the old man continued—there were already a hundred twenty members, including candidates, and when there was a lecture, like today (an expression of anguish clouded his face) it was hard to fit them all in—they would build on the roof. Or if a candidate had to make a presentation— And here he was brought up short by the question on the chief inspector's face.

Michael asked him what this presentation was, and the old man explained that after the candidate had met the conditions—that is, after he had three cases in analysis, on which he received supervision, in addition to the training analysis he himself was undergoing—he applied to the Institute Training Committee for permission to present one of the cases; if the committee had no objections, and if his supervisors approved, he was invited to write up his case and send it to the Training Committee. The committee could approve it immediately or request corrections, and then a date was set and the candidate had his presentation printed and distributed to the members of the committee. After they had all read it, he delivered a lecture on the case to all the Institute people.

Here, the old man continued to explain to Michael, who sat listening attentively to the description of this Via Dolorosa, people could ask questions, express criticism or praise. And then the candidate went out of the room, leaving behind, only members who were not candidates, and if there was a quorum (two thirds of the members had to be present, he said in answer to Michael's silent question), the candidate was accepted as an associate member of the Psychoanalytic Institute.

Michael raised his eyebrows, and the old man explained the meaning of the term "associate member."

"But what does it mean in practical terms to be an associate member?" Michael persisted.

"*Ach!*" Hildesheimer exclaimed in pure German. The candidate became an independent analyst, he did not require supervision, and he received the full fee for treatment. A candidate was entitled to demand only half the usual fee, in addition to which he could not choose his own patients but received them from the Institute.

And how did an associate member become a full member, inquired Michael.

"*Ach so*," replied Hildesheimer. Two years after the initial presentation, an associate member was entitled to present another lecture, which had to include a theoretical innovation, and then, following an additional vote, conducted on the model of the previous one, he might be accepted as a full member.

Michael quickly digested the new information. The silence lasted a few minutes, until he knew what the question was that he had to ask.

"A candidate," said Michael, "undergoes years of therapy; he gives therapy for half the price; he has to get supervision on every case. . . ." The old man added that there were also fortnightly seminars throughout the years of training. "Good," said Michael, "we'll add that to the list." And now, he wanted to know, what was the function of the vote Hildesheimer had mentioned? Why couldn't they make do with the approval of the Training Committee, which, if he had understood correctly, was the representative body?

These were two completely different matters, stressed Hildesheimer. The Training Committee could find that someone was suitable or unsuitable to be an analyst. The membership, on the other hand, voted on the question of whether they were interested in having a certain person as a colleague or not. Two completely different matters! The phrase, repeated with even greater emphasis, was still echoing in the room when the next question was asked.

Had the Training Committee ever failed to approve a candidate's presentation?

"There was one case, or actually two," said Hildesheimer, with a certain air of discomfort. One of them had abandoned the whole business in a huff and become one of the main detractors of the analytic approach; the second had refused to give in. He had gone back into analysis and after a few years had resubmitted his presentation for approval, and in the end he was accepted, and today he was a full member.

"And has it ever happened," Michael persisted, "that the Training Committee approved someone's application and the membership voted against him? I want to understand if the members actually make use of their right not to accept a candidate on the grounds of personal unsuitability?"

Hildesheimer admitted that nothing like that had ever happened. Up to now, he added cautiously. But certainly some people abstained from voting, and occasionally some members had voted against a candidate, although there had never been enough people opposing a candidate to reject his application for membership. "In that case," reflected Michael aloud, "it would be correct to say that the Training Committee has a decisive influence on the candidate's fate? In fact, his fate is determined by the vote of the Training Committee?"

"Yes," Hildesheimer agreed unwillingly, "the Training Committee and the supervisors—the three supervisors that every candidate has to have. That's why every candidate has three supervisors instead of one; and if all three supervisors criticize him severely or cast grave doubts on his suitability, a candidate will not be able to become an analyst. The main role of the Training Committee, however, is to formulate the Institute's policy and structure its curriculum."

Hildesheimer sighed and placed his pipe on the corner of the desk. The room was becoming chilly, and he folded his arms across his chest.

Michael asked what kind of supervisor Neidorf had been.

What kind of a supervisor was Eva, repeated Hildesheimer with a smile. About this, he imagined, opinions were unanimous. She was a wonderful supervisor. While it was true that she was rather imperious, her supervisees accepted her authority, which stemmed from the highest therapeutic and moral—here he raised his index finger and wagged it at Michael—standards. And then there were her tremendous energy and powers of concentration, which together with her skills as a therapist enabled her to make the most of every hour of supervision. But here, he warned, they were already approaching technical aspects of psychotherapy, and he was afraid that it was impossible to cram the whole theory into one short conversation.

But what was it, probed Michael, in the last analysis, that made people subject themselves to this long and arduous apprenticeship? What was the difference, ultimately, between being a psychologist or a psychiatrist and a psychoanalyst? If he might be permitted, he said cautiously, to express a personal opinion, for whatever it was worth—here he paused, and the old man nodded—he got the impression that the Institute had something in common with the guilds of the Middle Ages and the Renaissance. A certain rigidity. Things were made as difficult as possible for the candidate on the grounds of maintaining professional standards, but it was impossible to ignore the fact that there was another factor operating here: competition—economic and class competition. After all, you couldn't have an infinite number of psychoanalysts, especially in a country as small as Israel. In short, said Michael, he had the impression that they were protecting themselves by means of a set of regulations that limited the number of participants. The teacher-pupil/master-apprentice model that had existed in the professional guilds was particularly applicable here.

Hildesheimer did not answer at once. When he did reply, the effort and sincerity evident in his words touched Michael's heart. As he listened, he formulated the main idea behind the long speech, and after dismissing the preamble ("the best clinical training available . . . the highest possible stage of formal training"), he was left with what Hildesheimer referred to as "the loneliness of the therapist."

A member of the profession not working in the public health service—a hospital, a mental health clinic, or some other institution—found himself sitting and listening day after day, for hours on end, to patients; with one ear he listened to the plots of the stories being recounted, with the other to the associations accompanying the stories, and with yet another to the patient's "music," or tone, while simultaneously combining everything he heard into the patterns of thought characteristic of the person in the room with him. The patient, he added, spoke about the therapist, too, but never saw him as he really was. In the patient's mind the therapist took on many different guises. At one and the same time he was all the significant figures in the patient's life: his mother and father, his brothers and sisters, his teachers, friends, wife, children, boss—all in accordance with the projections of his own personality structure. "As anyone with any knowledge of the field knows," said the old man, "we never relate to people emotionally 'as they are.' We are always in thrall to modes of relating that are determined at a very early stage. In other words, when the patient relates to the therapist according to his mode of relating to his wife, for example, we must remember that he doesn't see his wife 'as she is,' either, but 'as she is' in his eyes." Sometimes, the old man went on, in a less didactic manner, the patient's attitude to the people around him was completely divorced from reality. "If the therapy is successful"—Hildesheimer's voice rose—"and only if it is successful, the patient will relate to the therapist as the embodiment of all his own patterns of interrelationship; and then the patient will sometimes hate the therapist, attack him, and so on, and sometimes he will also love him, but none of this will have any connection to reality and to the question of who the therapist actually is."

Michael asked for an example.

"Good," said the old man. "For example, when a patient tells you bitterly that you can't understand his suffering because you are a happily married, rich, handsome, important man, whereas you may well be widowed, divorced, ill, and in trouble with the tax bureau. This is what we call 'transference'; and without transference there is no therapy. Actually, transference always takes place to some degree, negative or positive. But the most important thing is the warm, human contact that makes a relationship of trust between the patient and the therapist possible."

The therapist, the old man continued, had to be able to point out the patterns and repeat the same things over and over again, sometimes even in exactly the same words. That was his role in the therapeutic situation, where the gratification of his own manifest needs could have no place at all. He personally, for example, objected to the therapist's smoking during the therapy session, since then he would be occupied with satisfying his own needs; and he had always made a point of this with the candidates he supervised.

And when a man spends hour upon hour with people in whose company he has to efface his own needs, allowing them to level unrealistic accusations against him, or to love him for qualities he has never possessed, he begins to feel a powerful need to be in the company of his colleagues, to exchange experiences, to learn, to feel secure, to obtain encouragement and support, even to hear objective criticism: to feel a sense of belonging to a framework, a tradition backing his work.

Sometimes (Michael noted the gesture of helplessness: hands outspread in front of him) the therapist could lose his sense of proportion, and then he needed a new perspective, which only his colleagues could provide. Not to mention the fact that he had to keep a constant distance between himself and his patients, never allowing any details of his private life to be exposed, in order to allow the patient's imagination as much freedom as possible in which to bring up all his fantasies around the figure of the therapist.

Michael would remember this whole speech almost by heart. He could quote the conclusion word for word: "I can tell you that these two things—intensive professional training at the highest possible level and the sense of belonging—are the main reasons why young people come to us at the Institute."

And then, as a comic interlude, the old man told him an anecdote. In an interview for admission to the Institute, one of the candidates replied to the standard question: Why do you want to be a psychoanalyst? "Because the work is easy, the pay is high, and you can take a vacation whenever you feel like it," and he grinned impudently.

Michael asked curiously if he had been accepted. Hildesheimer answered with a question. Before he replied, he would be interested to know if Chief Inspector Ohayon would have accepted him.

Michael said that he would. The old man wanted to know why. Michael replied that in spite of its childish impertinence, the answer showed daring and defiance, since he assumed that the candidate knew that this was not the answer expected of him and the reply was an expression of his anger at being asked so banal a question. The old man looked at Michael with an expression that could have been interpreted as affection.

"And what really happened to him?" inquired Michael.

Yes, they accepted him. He had qualities that enabled him to be a good analyst. But the things mentioned by Chief Inspector Ohayon had also been taken into account. And with a broad smile, he added that they had wanted him to find out for himself just how wrong he was.

If they were already discussing banalities, said Michael hesitantly, he would like to ask the professor a question that he had no doubt had been asked many times before: What was the difference between regular psychotherapy (which he happened to know something about, he refrained from saying) and psychoanalysis? As a method of therapy, that is. Did the difference boil down to sitting on a chair versus lying on a couch?

And did the difference in question, said Hildesheimer dryly, seem insignificant to the chief inspector? Was a police interrogation conducted in the suspect's home, over a cup of coffee, the same as one conducted in Ohayon's office, under a blinding light?

Michael apologized. He had not intended to belittle the technical aspect, but he would like to understand the more essential differences.

That was one of the essential differences, said the Professor humorously. First, he should know that not everyone who applied for help was suitable for analysis. (Michael asked himself if he was suitable. As if it was some test of status! He scolded himself.) This was a method of therapy that demanded, among other things, more ego resources than those required by other methods. Second, the patient not only lay on the couch; he also came to therapy sessions four times a week. And this, too, he said, looking searchingly at Michael, was not simply a quantitative difference. These two features—the couch and the four weekly meetings—enabled the patient to reach greater depths, to return to the basic experiences of his past. It was impossible to go into it properly now, but he could also say, in brief, that in psychoanalysis the transference was the crux of the matter.

The transference was facilitated, as he had already mentioned, by the opaqueness of the figure of the therapist, and the opaqueness was obviously greater when the therapist sat behind the couch and the patient could not see him but only sense his supportive presence.

"But you mustn't think that the patient can talk to nobody. All the stories about talking to a computer are nonsense invented by people who don't understand the main thing—the patient has to be supported, held. And all those caricatures about analysts falling asleep behind the couch are nothing but reflections of patients' fears that the therapist is not there with them," he said unsmilingly.

"A good analysis is one in which the analyst succeeds in making the patient feel sufficiently supported to enable him, precisely because of the fact that they meet four times a week, to go further, deeper, into his primary experiences and deal with them anew."

A full minute passed before Michael asked if the patient, because of the transference, could hate the analyst enough to murder him.

Hildesheimer relit his pipe and said: "Even in the closed ward of a mental hospital that would be rare, and analysis is a form of therapy intended for relatively healthy people, what we call neurotics. A patient in analysis might have fantasies about murder, but I have yet to hear of an actual murder attempt. In reality the patient in analysis would harm himself rather than his analyst."

He puffed on his pipe and went on: "And you must remember that most of Eva's patients are people from the Institute, candidates, because there are very few training analysts. She had very few patients who weren't connected to the Institute."

"Isn't a situation possible," Michael wondered aloud, "where the analyst would have incriminating or confidential information about one of his patients, who might be afraid of the consequences? Who might feel threatened, endangered?" Hildesheimer was silent for a while, and then he said that this was exactly the subject of Eva's lecture.

"Just a minute," requested Michael. "There are a few things I have to know about her before we go on to discuss the lecture."

"What do you want to know?" asked Hildesheimer, emptying his pipe into the china ashtray.

"How did she come to the Institute? What did she do before?" Michael felt himself growing tense without knowing why.

Eva had worked for years as a psychologist in the public health service. She had come to the Institute at a relatively late age. Thirty-seven was the maximum age at which candidates were accepted, and she was thirty-six when she joined them. From the beginning it was obvious that she was gifted. Six years ago she had become a training analyst. Before this she had been a member of the Training Committee; he had thought that she would become the head of the committee after his retirement; he was to retire next month, and it was obvious that she would be elected.

When Michael asked about her family life, the old man told him that her husband had been a businessman, who had not appreciated her work or even understood how successful she was in her profession. This had caused her difficulties, which nobody except for him knew about. She had kept the family together while at the same time fighting for her rights: her husband had not wanted her to work at all. In the end, the old man said with a hint of pride, her husband had come to value her as an independent woman. "They were very attached to each other," he said sadly.

She had been his patient, then his colleague, and even more. Her husband had died suddenly, three years ago; he had been several years older than she was and had died of a stroke, in the middle of a business trip, in the airport in New York. She had to fly there to bring the body back. And then there were problems with the property, because she had not taken any interest in the business, and her husband had a lot of business affairs, and the son—well, the son had become a bit of a crank about nature and conservationism, whose main interest in life was the Nature Protection Society. A nice, intelligent boy, but not the least bit interested in business. Finally the son-in-law, her daughter's husband, had agreed to take charge of the estate, which was a great relief to everyone.

Michael asked about her relations with her children. Hildesheimer replied, choosing his words carefully, that she had been very close to her daughter. Too close, he thought sometimes. Nava was very dependent; she had never taken a single step without consulting her mother. Since she and her husband had moved to Chicago, however, he thought that there had been a change for the better. He had always thought that Eva had blind spots about her children. With the son things were more complicated; the points of contact had been weaker, and not only as far as their spheres of interest were concerned. There was also the problem of the son's identification with his father and his objections to his mother's profession, but here, too, there had been an improvement after he found himself this job with the Nature Protection Society.

And the son-in-law, asked Michael, what were her relations with her son-in-law like?

Correct, Hildesheimer thought, perhaps not particularly warm, especially in comparison to her relationship with her daughter, but he admired her very much, and she, for her part, was very grateful to him for relieving her of the responsibility for the business. Michael asked for further clarification, if possible, about the business affairs. He did not mention that he had already met Hillel Zehavi, the son-in-law, in Tel Aviv.

Hildesheimer was not familiar with the details. All he knew was that they had flown back together from Chicago, Eva and Hillel, for a big board meeting that was supposed to take place on Sunday morning. He knew this because Eva had taken an extra day's leave from work to attend the meeting. When they spoke on the phone, Eva had complained that on the flight to Tel Aviv, she had had to learn everything she had refused to learn for years. For four consecutive hours Hillel had explained to her what they were going to vote about at the board meeting and how she was to cast her vote. Both of them, she and Hillel, had the right to sign documents.

Without changing his position or his tone of voice, making a great effort not to reveal his excitement, Michael asked if there had been arguments between them.

The old man laughed out loud, a hoarse guffaw. "Eva and arguments about business! She wanted to hand everything over to him long ago, but Hillel wouldn't hear of it; he insisted on getting her approval on everything. She often complained about it." Hildesheimer gave Michael a sharp look, suddenly understanding the thrust of his thoughts. He shook his head disbelievingly and said he was barking up the wrong tree.

Michael pointed out that it was quite possible that someone had committed the murder in the Institute in order to throw suspicion on its members. Hildesheimer replied that while he would obviously prefer to think it was someone outside the Institute, it could not possibly be Hillel: he had no motive, certainly not a financial one. He shook his head several times and looked at Michael with new eyes, as if he was having second thoughts about his first impression. Michael said that he had to investigate all the possibilities. The old man shifted uneasily in his chair and in the end seemed to recover his composure. Michael felt guilty for not telling him about his meeting with Hillel, who had a watertight alibi: from the moment he landed at Ben-Gurion Airport he had been at his mother's bedside in intensive care. He wondered what devil was stopping him from mentioning the meeting to the old man, even now.

And then it was time to ask about the lecture.

Was it true, he inquired casually, that Dr. Neidorf always prepared her lectures well in advance, as he had been told this morning?

Hildesheimer replied that his informants, whoever they were, didn't have the faintest idea of what they were talking about. Nobody, nobody in the world, knew with what fear and trembling she had approached every single lecture. Dozens of handwritten drafts before typing, and then—

"Who did her typing?" Michael interrupted.

"She did it herself," said the old man. Sometimes he had been obliged to read every version, every word. And she wanted his comments on everything, of course. And when she had a version that satisfied her at last, she would make three copies. One was for herself—she always read her lectures. Eva was not a spontaneous person, and she didn't know how to improvise.

"And the other copies?" asked Michael, feeling the perspiration break out on his back.

The second copy was intended for him, said Hildesheimer, and the third she kept in her study at home, "just to be on the safe side." He used to make jokes about it, and so did she. "She really was an incorrigible perfectionist," he said with a sigh, "in every area of life." But only in relation to herself, he added. Apart from questions of morality, where her attitude might be called rigid. As far as what she called "unethical behavior" was concerned, she was completely unforgiving. But he didn't want to give the wrong impression: Eva was not a self-righteous prig or an interfering busybody. It was mainly a question of professional demands—the good of the patient, discretion, and so on. He had almost always agreed with her.

The lecture, asked Michael, the copy in Hildesheimer's possession—could he see it?

But no, replied the old man, and Michael stopped breathing. This time he didn't have a copy. She had prepared the lecture in America, they had agreed that it was time for her to free herself of her dependence, he had refused to see any but the final version, which she had to decide on herself. She kept claiming that this time there was a special problem involved, but he had insisted on being surprised.

Michael asked if anyone else knew about her habit of showing him her lecture drafts and final versions. Hildesheimer shrugged his shoulders. He had never discussed it with anyone, but there were few secrets in the Institute. She, in her honesty, always made a point of thanking him for his help at the beginning of every lecture.

Michael sensed the blood draining from his face even before the old man asked him if he felt all right.

He asked about Neidorf's own copy. Hildesheimer said that it had presumably been found among her possessions. He looked very sad.

"What, exactly, was the subject of the lecture?"

The answer was brief: questions of morality and forensics. Questions, in other words, that had been perplexing psychotherapists since the birth of their profession. A classic dilemma. Was it right for the therapist to keep his patients' secrets even if they had broken the law? Not when crimes like murder or robbery were involved, but in questions of professional ethics, for example. Information revealed in the course of therapy, or information passed on to the supervisor by the supervisee. But there was no point in speculating any further. In the handbag he had seen next to her chair in the Institute, Inspector Ohayon would find the text of the lecture, and he would be able to read it for himself.

That was precisely the problem, said Michael. Nothing had been found: no lecture, no papers, and no keys either: only the usual feminine paraphernalia, personal documents, and a little money.

For the first time, Hildesheimer looked like a confused old man, like someone who didn't know what was going on around him. But only for a second, after which he recovered and asked Chief Inspector Ohayon to please make himself clear.

All that afternoon—in fact, from the moment they had begun searching the building, while Michael was still sitting in the lecture hall with the Training Committee—a special team had been combing the Institute for anything resembling lecture notes. He himself had searched her handbag thoroughly as soon as the police surgeon had completed his examination. And the people from the lab, the Criminal Identification Division—everyone had had a go at it. He had a detailed list of the contents of the bag, he began to say, but the old man waved his hand impatiently. He understood, he said, but they had to find a copy in her study at home. He knew she had another copy at home; he knew it because she had promised to give it to him later for a keepsake.

Michael Ohayon looked at his watch and saw that it was eleven o'clock. A strong wind was blowing, blotting out the sound of the rain. He rose from his seat, and the old man stood up, too, and asked him if he was going to go to Neidorf's house now. Michael took the hint and asked if he would like to accompany him, adding something about the lateness of the hour and the bad weather. Hildesheimer brushed his reservations aside with a sweep of his hand and said that he had already lived quite long enough, in his opinion, and that in any case he would not be able to sleep tonight. As he spoke, he led Michael to the coatrack in the corner of the long hallway, took down a heavy winter overcoat, and put in on. The house was dark and silent, and the two of them let themselves out. Outside it was very cold. Michael, who had kept his jacket on all the time he was sitting in the study, felt the wind like an icy blow and was glad to get into the police Renault.

He activated the radio, which responded immediately. Control tried to tell him something in a tired female voice; he listened patiently. Everyone was looking for him, everyone said it was urgent. "Okay; tell them I'll be in touch later. And tell my team that I'm in the middle of something." Control sighed and said, "Will do."

Hildesheimer sat next to him, sunk in thought, and Michael was obiged to repeat his question twice before the old man nodded and gave him Dr. Neidorf's address, the same address that Michael had seen on the identification card in her bag in the course of his repeated rummagings through its contents that morning.

It was a little street in the German Colony. Almost every time Michael passed Emek Refaim Street, he thought of the Knights of the German Templars who founded this neighborhood in 1878. How pathetic were their hopes for redemption, symbolized by the remnants of their flour mill, still visible on the corner. Michael maneuvered the Renault through the narrow alleys and parked carefully. He opened the door for Hildesheimer and helped him out of the small car. The two of them went through the little gate and walked up the path leading to the front door, where the old man stepped back to let Michael open the heavy wooden door.

Michael tried all the keys, at first in the light of the streetlamp and then in the light of all the matches left in the box, which Hildesheimer lit one after the other with an admirably steady hand. Finally they both resigned themselves to the fact that the key to the house was not on the ring. Neither said a word about where it might be.

Michael went to his car and came back a few seconds later, a sharp object in his hand. He mumbled something to Hildesheimer about the skills one acquired during the course of one's life, then he set to work on the lock. Hildesheimer went on lighting matches—Michael had brought a new box from the car—and ten minutes later they were standing in Eva Neidorf's house.

Michael shut the door.

In the bright light illuminating the entrance hall, he saw the old man's pale face. His grimly pursed lips expressed what they had both already realized: someone had preceded them.

5

Standing in the doorway to the consulting room, in the other wing of the house, Michael, with his hand on the door handle, thought about the record of the Brahms clarinet quintet, worn and scratched, on the turntable of the record player.

In the large living room, with its pale, heavy furniture, the atmosphere was one of refinement and restraint. The big abstract paintings with their bright colors, the flowers growing in the pots and window boxes as if there were no winter in Jerusalem, the thick, dark carpet, did not succeed in banishing the chill. The clarinet quintet on the open record player in the corner, next to the French window, betrayed a passion that was not expressed anywhere else in the room.

As soon as they were inside the consulting room, Michael asked Hildesheimer, who sank down into the armchair—his big body seemed shrunken, his face pale and exhausted—about the record.

"Yes," the old man replied with a sigh, and drew the heavy winter coat, which he had not taken off upon entering the house, more tightly around him. "I always thought that she had a sentimental side too. She had a preference for Romantic music. We sometimes joked about it."

He smiled sadly and appeared completely absorbed in his own thoughts. Michael, who felt an almost physical urge to protect him, quickly suppressed it and sat at the antique desk. Producing a pair of gloves from his pocket, he pulled them laboriously onto his long hands and started opening the drawers one after the other, handling them with extreme care and explaining to Hildesheimer that they must try not to leave fingerprints. He emptied the contents of the drawers onto the couch that stood next to the wall, opposite the desk.

When he reached the third drawer, Hildesheimer, who was watching with intense concentration, said that he would be able to find a list of Eva's patients and supervisees there. He got up from the armchair and said that underneath the papers in the third drawer was a list of names and telephone numbers. He knew this because whenever she went abroad, she would ask him to inform her patients if anything happened to prevent her from coming home on time. In which case he was supposed to contact the maid, gain entry into the house, take out the list, and inform the patients. The old man buried his face in his hands. A few minutes passed before he recovered and wiped his eyes with the big handkerchief he had removed from his coat pocket.

Michael pointed to the pile of papers on the couch, warned him not to touch, and began showing them to him one after the other, taking care not to change their order. Still standing, the old man examined the papers, and Michael transferred them one by one to the heavy rug at the foot of the couch, which showed signs of dust.

Hildesheimer, his face disturbingly pale, said in a tremulous voice: "No, I don't see it here. There's no list here."

Michael went on rapidly emptying the contents of the desk, the papers accumulating on the couch. They both examined every piece of paper. There were all kinds of bills, lecture notes, tear sheets of articles, checkbooks, bank statements, letters, everything you might expect to find in desk drawers. But there was no rough draft or typed copy of the lecture she was supposed to have given that morning. And there was no list either, except for a roster of the Institute members and candidates, which Michael put down on the side of the desk. Nor was there the address book that Hildesheimer had described in detail; he took from his pocket a little notebook with a blue plastic cover and said: "Here you are—the same as this," and held it out to Michael, adding: "But it would have been in her bag, of course; it was always in her bag."

"We'll have to try and find it here in the house, because as I told you before, there was no address book in her bag," said Michael carefully.

Michael looked at the little notebook, and Hildesheimer said: "You can open it if you like."

He turned the first page of the notebook, and Hildesheimer, looking over his shoulder, explained that it contained the roster of daily meetings with patients and their phone numbers. Michael examined every corner of the desk, including the spring-locking secret compartment that was a feature of most antique writing desks, which he emptied of its contents. The old man said excitedly that this secret drawer was where she kept the notes she made after her preliminary sessions with a new patient.

"The first two meetings," he explained breathlessly, "are what we call 'intake,' and it's usual to concentrate on the more—well—biographical, objective details, such as age and family status, parents, marriage, occupation, as well as discussing the reasons that led the patient to seek therapy. Anyway, some people take notes during these preliminary meetings. I personally am against this. Eva took notes, but only after the hour was over."

They both searched, but the notes were not there. Michael looked around him.

He had made a mental inventory of everything in the room the minute he entered it. As in Hildesheimer's consulting room, there were two easy chairs, a couch with the analyst's chair behind it, a bookcase (only one, containing professional literature), and a few lamps. Yellow parchment lampshades lent the room a warm, cozy air. Prominent in the bookcase was a small compartment with a key in the lock, which turned out to contain a pile of booklets with thin covers in different colors. Hildesheimer explained that these were all the case histories that had been presented at the Institute. Michael leafed through the booklets, glanced at the titles on the covers, all of them at least two lines long; apart from the prepositions and articles, he could not understand a single word. All the booklets bore the words "Confidential, Internal."

Hildesheimer explained that the identity of the patient was disguised for the purposes of the case presentation: the name was a pseudonym, the occupation was not stated, all identifying particulars were changed. As an added precaution, the booklets were handed to members in person, never sent by mail.

From the pile of papers that had accumulated on the couch, Michael picked up a page written in a small, cramped hand. He examined it closely and asked Hildesheimer if it was Eva's handwriting. The old man answered in the affirmative. It was a list of book titles, the bibliography for a course she had been scheduled to give at the Institute in the last trimester of the year. Freud's name was the only one he recognized. There was noplace left in the room to search for documents, lists of names, lecture notes, address books, or any other source of information.

Michael lit a cigarette, his first since entering the house. There was an ashtray on the table between the two easy chairs. There was also a box of tissues there. He noticed that despite the similarity between Hildesheimer's consulting room and Neidorf's, the atmosphere in the two rooms was completely different. This room was feminine. The dominant colors were red and brown, in the curtains, the carpet, and the upholstery of the couch. The easy chairs were lighter, but there was no trace here of the pale tones that prevailed in the living room. Nor were there any large, impressive abstract paintings like the ones on the living room walls, paintings that Michael found incomprehensible but whose colors captivated him. Here the pictures were black and white, woodcuts and pencil sketches.

He asked Hildesheimer where the bedroom was. In a dry, matter-of-fact tone, the old man replied that it was on the second floor. Michael felt somewhat uncomfortable at not being able to stop himself from speculating about the nature of the relationship between them.

On their way upstairs, he asked if they had been in the habit of meeting often. From Hildesheimer's reply he gathered that they had met frequently at her house and that they had not been in the habit of going out together. He also concluded that there had been a father-daughter relationship between them, and more. He didn't dare wonder aloud about the meaning of the "more."

Standing in the bedroom doorway, Hildesheimer showed no signs of embarrassment, only of brokenheartedness. A large window, white curtains, a big bed, neatly made, a dressing table, makeup, a vast closet. Hockney's swimming-pool pictures, a suitcase on the carpet. Michael's glance swept the room like a camera lens and zoomed in on the suitcase.

It wasn't locked. Michael knelt down and emptied its contents carefully onto the carpet at the foot of the bed: clothes, underwear, makeup. He asked himself why this supertidy woman hadn't unpacked as soon as she came home and wondered if she had spent any time in the bedroom at all, in the light of the clarinet quintet on the record player and the ashtray full of cigarette stubs next to one of the easy chairs in the living room.

He searched through all the pockets in the case, and finally he turned to Hildesheimer, who was still standing by the door, and shook his head. No address book, no lecture, no notes, nothing.

It was two o'clock in the morning when Chief Inspector Michael Ohayon phoned the control center from Dr. Eva Neidorf's bedroom, gave them her address, and asked them to send his team around to search the house. "And send a fingerprint man from Forensics too," he added in a tired voice. He glanced skeptically around the room, which looked lifeless, as if it had not been occupied for a long time, yet contained a number of dust-free surfaces. He understood the meaning of this only too well, and when he replaced the receiver he said to Hildesheimer that someone had definitely been there before them, someone who had done his work carefully and not left any fingerprints behind him.

They went down to the living room and waited for the police.

Hildesheimer sat huddled in one of the big easy chairs. Michael prowled nervously about and asked himself what it was that made the room so elegant. He looked at the high ceiling, at the arched alcoves, the record collection, the ornaments, and thought about the time, money, and energy that had been invested in this house. He asked himself about the motives, and thought about people who found an outlet for artistic drives in the decoration of their homes. For reasons that he preferred to ignore, the thought aroused his hostility, but in spite of his hostility he could not help feeling admiration.

For the hundredth time he asked himself and in the end he asked Hildesheimer, too, if he could think of anyone who might be able to tell them what there was in the lecture to have made it disappear from the face of the earth. The old man shook his head and said that he had no idea, nor any idea of where the notes could possibly be. He couldn't stop thinking about it, he said in a cracked voice.

The room was very cold, and both of them sat huddled in their coats until the doorbell rang. Michael jumped up to open it. Outside in the pouring rain stood Eli and Tzilla, his regular team, and, behind them, Shaul, from Forensics.

Tzilla's mouth was wide open, ready to say things that Michael could guess in advance, mainly where on earth had he been all night, but he got in first with a detailed description of the latest developments. Michael watched their faces and saw them register the significance of the missing address book and lecture notes. He concluded with the words "Outside too: tire marks, footprints; inside, every single scrap of paper—sort them out, don't throw anything away, and don't move from here until replacements arrive; answer the phone, but be careful," and the three of them slipped past Hildesheimer and literally ran upstairs to the second floor.

Hildesheimer had stood by silently, studying their faces during Michael's briefing. When they left the room, Michael explained that the team would search all the rooms of the house, for fingerprints too—although he had little hope for those, in view of the paucity of dust both in the downstairs rooms and in the bedroom.

Hildesheimer looked as if he had no hope at all. He said that Eva was such a private, reserved person, and now her world was being rudely invaded. He concluded with a despairing "*Ach!*" Michael offered gently to drive him home, but the old man brushed the offer impatiently aside. He wanted to stay and see if they found anything. Michael nodded, took off his gloves, thrust them into his pocket, and began prowling around the room.

Hildesheimer inquired if he spent many nights like this, and he received a sigh in reply. How could he stand it? the old man asked, and Michael replied that between one case and another he tried to rest. When asked about his family life and how it stood up to the strain of a "job like this," he shrugged and said: "Who says it does?" And with a miserable smile, he added that after his divorce, the greatest difficulty was keeping up the relationship with his son, and after thinking for a minute he said that his was lonely work too.

Hildesheimer nodded and dropped his head, with no further questions, and Michael resumed his inspection of the big room. He stopped in front of a painting, a statuette, and in the end he wandered into the kitchen and stared at the round rustic-style table. Suddenly he felt a chill, which led him to look at the window, and what he saw there filled him with rage against his own dullness.

He stepped out of the kitchen and called loudly: "Shaul! Shaul!" Shaul appeared at a run, with Tzilla close behind him. Eli was in the other wing and didn't hear him call. Michael dragged them to the window. One of the windowpanes was missing, and there were splinters of glass on the floor; the white bars of the grille were bent.

Shaul came closer. "Move out of the way; you're in my light." Tzilla and Michael moved aside and stood at the entrance to the kitchen. Hildesheimer got up and came to stand next to them—there was no door between the living room and kitchen, only a wide opening. Shaul went out of the room and returned a moment later with a big case. After putting on rubber gloves and examining and measuring (powders, magnifying glass, powerful flashlight) and taking photographs, he went out again; they heard the outside door opening, and a few minutes later his head popped up on the other side of the kitchen window, where he repeated the whole procedure.

Effortlessly Shaul detached the grille and called Michael to join him outside. The people in the kitchen heard him explaining: "Look at the grille; someone bent it and ripped it out, broke the glass to open the lock, and got in through the window. And here, you can see where his shoe scraped the wall, where he climbed onto the windowsill. And look how the ground's been dug up under the window; whoever did it took care to cover up his footprints, used gloves, left the same way he came in, and put the grille back in place."

In the kitchen they heard Michael's quiet voice: "What do you think he used to loosen the grille?"

"It looks to me like an iron bar. You may be able to find it somewhere in the vicinity, if he didn't take it with him."

Their voices began to recede, and a few minutes later they were back in the kitchen. Shaul went down on his knees under the window and with a little brush began sweeping splinters of glass into a plastic bag, which he put carefully into his case. "You see, the broken glass fell inside, and whoever broke in swept it up, but he didn't get it all. He tried to straighten the grille from outside, too, and push it back into place. Where's the trash?" He turned to Hildesheimer, who pointed to the usual place under the sink.

Shaul rose to his feet and carefully opened the door of the cupboard under the sink, removed the trash basket, dusted it with powder, remarking that the best they could hope for were prints of gloves. He pointed to the contents: "There's the glass." Then he said that if he had decent lighting, he was sure he could find a footprint, and went outside to the police van. He returned with two big flashlights, one of which he gave to Michael. "Before I ask for help, let's go and see if we can find a print."

Tzilla leaned against the wall and looked outside, where big beams of light soon appeared, shifting back and forth. And then Michael called from the far end of the garden: "Shaul! Shaul!" and a few minutes later Shaul came into the kitchen and went out again with the big black case. When they returned, Shaul was carrying a cast, which he showed proudly to Tzilla, saying: "Anyone who thinks he can cover up his tracks after a week of rain without flying should think again. Just have a look at that sole."

Tzilla looked curiously at the cast and asked whether there was anything special about the print.

"No," said Shaul, the triumph fading sightly from his voice. "It looks like an ordinary sport shoe, but I'm always cleverer in the morning." He put the cast down on the rustic table, said that it had to dry completely, and wiped his big hands on each other.

"Just a minute." Hildesheimer suddenly spoke up. "There's something here I don't understand. Whoever it was took the key to the house from the key ring, didn't he? The key to the house was missing from the ring. So why did he need to break in through the window?"

Everyone was silent. Michael was the first to speak, hesitantly, almost as if he were talking to himself: "First there were no papers or keys in her bag. Then we came here to look for a copy of the lecture, and the key was missing from the ring. We couldn't find a copy of the lecture, or a list of patients, or an appointment diary, and now it turns out that somebody broke in through the kitchen window and attempted to cover up the break-in. The question is, were they looking for anything else, apart from papers? Does anything valuable appear to be missing?" he asked Hildesheimer.

The old doctor shook his head and said: "Not at first sight, no. The paintings are very valuable, and they're all here. But I think you'll have to ask the family. I still don't understand why anyone would have to break in if he had a key."

Michael replied hesitantly that he didn't know. He could only guess: maybe the key didn't fit and the culprit was unable to force the door open by other means. He would have to think about it.

"If there was property missing, if there were any signs of the usual mess after a burglary, it might have been possible to think that we were dealing with two separate events," said Tzilla. "But the way things look at the moment, it really doesn't make any sense unless there was some kind of problem with the key."

Michael asked Hildesheimer to look again, just to make sure, and see if anything valuable was missing, and the two of them went into the living room. The old man cast his eyes over the furniture, the paintings, the carpet—it was hand woven, he explained, Chinese, worth a fortune—over two ivory statuettes, whose value he stressed. Of two oil paintings he said that they were originals, very valuable, and mentioned the names of artists Michael had never heard of. Finally he answered Michael's question about jewelry: "Whenever she went abroad, she left her jewelry in her safe-deposit box in the bank—she only took a few pieces with her—and since she only came back on Friday, I doubt whether she had time to bring them home. Besides which, I think there were some jewels she left in the bank permanently, because she didn't like wearing them. But you'll have to ask the children."

By the time they were finished, it was four in the morning. There was a pile of sacks in the entrance hall. Michael helped Eli to load them onto the van. Tzilla remarked that at this stage it was impossible to find anything; they would go through everything thoroughly later, in the office. Shaul said that he had found different fingerprints; presumably some of them were Michael's and the doctor's—gesturing in Hildesheimer's direction and giving Michael a rebuking look—but they would all have to be checked.

Only after everyone had left the house did the old man agree to let Michael drive him home.

On the way, Michael tried once more to find out if Hildesheimer's habit of helping Neidorf prepare her lectures was known to their colleagues. Again he gained the impression that his companion did not understand the question, and he reformulated it: Was it possible that anyone might think he had a copy of her latest lecture in his possession?

The old man understood. Yes, he thought it very possible that people might think so, although no one had asked him about it.

"Not yet," said Michael, "not yet. But I'm afraid you might still be asked, and not only asked."

The old man only uttered a comprehending "Ah." He did not sound surprised or excited, certainly not frightened. Only as if he had understood some new technical detail. Michael, on the other hand, was quite worried. He thought about the extremes to which Neidorf's murderer had gone in order to get rid of the lecture copies and the patient lists.

Examining the old man's face as he sat next to him, staring into the darkness, he wondered how far he should take him into his confidence, and in the end he asked him not to tell anyone that he did not have a copy of the lecture. Although he would be putting himself in danger, the danger might bear fruit, he said, and felt the sour taste of a guilty conscience.

The old man nodded absentmindedly, still not showing any anxiety, which only made Michael feel worse.

He dropped Hildesheimer off outside his front door and waited until a white car appeared with two plainclothes policemen inside it, in compliance with the request he had made over the radio.

After ensuring that there would be round-the-clock surveillance on the house, he returned to his office. It was after five in the morning, and it was still dark, and the rain had stopped. The air was very cold.

6

Joe Linder could not fall asleep. This was nothing unusual in itself, but tonight it was harder than usual to bear. From his side of the bed, next to the window, whose blind he had left open, he could see the drops of rain falling from the branches of the cypress tree that reached almost to the roof.

He saw the ray of light cast by the streetlamp on Agnon Boulevard, the one that Daniel, his four-year-old son, claimed prevented him, too, from falling asleep. Joe, rather impatiently, had advised him this evening, not for the first time, to count white elephants until the arrival of the Sandman, who strewed sand in children's eyes and made them sleep. The child protested. He was afraid of the story about the Sandman, he was afraid of the sand, he didn't know what white elephants looked like, he could only count to twenty, and most of all, he could sense that his father was somewhere else, far away from him. But Joe was firm and refused to go on sitting next to Daniel's bed. The day's events had made it impossible for him to relax and sit still with his son.

The expression on Hildesheimer's face when he emerged from the little room returned to confront him every time he closed his eyes.

He picked up the clock from the bedside table and saw that it was two o'clock. Sighing, he got out of bed, trying not to make a noise. He glanced at his wife's face and was relieved to see that Dalya had not stirred. The last thing he felt like now was a heart-to-heart conversation about what it was that was keeping him awake this time.

He wasn't sure himself. Eva Neidorf's death caused him neither grief nor pain, because he had never liked her, had even been a little afraid of her. He realized that if she had shown him any warmth he might have regarded her differently. But his overriding feeling now was not one of guilt. No, it wasn't guilt that he felt now, not even now that she was dead. His strongest feeling toward her was still one of resentment, for all the ways in which she had conveyed her mistrust of him and her lack of confidence in his ability as a therapist. She had made him believe that her disapproval of him was basic and that there was nothing he could do to change it.

Joe was sure that Hildesheimer would not have prevented his becoming a training analyst but for Neidorf's firm and consistent opposition—Neidorf, who had started her career at the Institute years after him and gotten so far ahead of him, who made him feel in her presence like a child whose desperate eagerness to please was transparently obvious to everyone.

To be quite frank, he even felt a certain spiteful satisfaction at her death, perhaps even at the way in which she had died. And the thought that there might be a murderer in their midst did not overwhelm him with anxiety: there was a certain apprehension, but chiefly curiosity.

He had always taken it for granted that everyone, with the exception of Hildesheimer, was capable of anything. Even the thought of Hildesheimer, of the old man's heartbreak, gave rise in him to a childish, malicious glee, alloyed by the bitter taste of his own pettiness. Joe Linder, who often congratulated himself on his unflinching honesty, who was second to none in self-criticism, who always argued passionately that he was prepared to face up to the very worst of his thoughts, did not dare admit to himself that he did not really love the old man.

He had never had the guts to say a single word against him. Even to himself he claimed that the old man was the acme of perfection, as an analyst, that is, and as a leading member of the Institute. The truth was that it cost him a great effort to cover up his pain at the old man's failure to clasp him to his breast, to choose him as his successor, or even to show any interest in him anymore.

He was prepared to admit his yearning to be on intimate terms with Hildesheimer, and his fierce jealousy of Eva Neidorf—"Her Ladyship" as he called her, although only to himself and his close friends— and of the special relationship she enjoyed with "old Ernst," as he called him behind his back, despising himself as he did so, because he knew that he was trying to impress the younger people with his familiarity: and this, too, he was prepared to admit to himself.

He got out of bed, wrapped himself in his old woolen dressing gown, ignoring the unpleasant smell of stale sweat that it gave off, and allowed the green-eyed monster to overwhelm him.

No, he was not in the least sorry for the old man. It served him right. If he had taken him, Joe, under his wing instead of Her Ladyship, he would have been spared all this grief. It was Joe's belief that angels existed only in heaven, and now Eva Neidorf had provided the proof. Nobody, for instance, would have bothered to murder Joe Linder. What could she have done, he wondered, to have so violently provoked someone who belonged to a group that stood, more than any other, for social order and control? He had always suspected that people who hid behind coolness and formality, as she did, must have terrible vices to hide. Even now that she was dead, they wouldn't let him be a training analyst. Even if Rosenfeld was able, at long last, to realize his dream and stand at the head of the Training Committee, he wouldn't have the guts, nor perhaps the will, to acknowledge Joe's professional ability.

It was cold. He tightened his dressing-gown belt, pulled up the collar, and padded into the kitchen. As usual, the sink was full of dishes, and a giant cockroach was slowly making its way from the refrigerator to the marble counter. Until the housekeeper came on Monday, the sticky dishes would remain in the sink, unless he washed them himself. He swore when he failed to find a single clean glass, then poured the milk he took from the refrigerator into a glass containing the dregs of Daniel's supper cocoa, after which he went into the living room, which was separated from the kitchen by a low partition, dropped into the TV chair, stretched out his legs, switched on the reading lamp, put the glass on the table next to him, and tried once again to come to grips with Janet Malcolm's controversial book *In the Freud Archives.*

"Only someone who hates himself the way you do would read a book that upset him so much," Dalya had said to him that morning. The sentence rang in his ears as he tried to find the place where he had stopped reading.

She had delivered this salvo in the course of their daily skirmish, to put an end to which he had picked up the book as a declaration of noncooperation and boredom with the subject. He couldn't reconstruct the beginning of the quarrel, but he vividly remembered a couple of her sallies that had succeeded in silencing even him, notorious for his sarcastic repartee.

He lit a cigarette and considered the reasons for his attraction to the book, which had been upsetting his peace of mind for a number of days now. It discussed an episode that had thrown the psychoanalytic world into turmoil. Joe asked himself right out if he thought that he had anything in common with Jeffrey Masson, the brilliant young analyst in the book, and once he had taken the plunge and the question was asked, he had no alternative but to answer it in the affirmative. Like Masson, he had come to the Institute from another field, had made a big impression on everyone—in the first years, at least—with his erudition, his charm, his wit, his sense of humor, his clear, swift insight into his patients' problems. He had never had any trouble in identifying other people's problems. Even today, when he was out of favor, nobody cast doubt on his diagnostic ability. Joe couldn't understand how things had begun to go wrong or pinpoint the moment when he stopped being a promising young analyst, when a tinge of bitterness had begun to color his point of view instead of the compassion he had once felt.

He knew, without quite understanding why, that the problem lay in the monotony of the daily routine, that it was the loneliness of the therapeutic situation, the lack of reinforcement, year in, year out, which had caused his failure. He would often repeat to himself, jokingly but also painfully, a number of the key phrases he had heard from Deutsch right at the beginning, in those early years. One of them Deutsch had been in the habit of repeating like a mantra: "There are no shortcuts in our business. Every shortcut only makes the road longer. The process is agonizingly slow; it involves suffering. Sometimes it's like chiseling marble, sometimes like carving ice, but there are never any shortcuts."

Dimly Joe sensed that he had got his priorities wrong. Not the good of the patient had been foremost in his mind, but his own good, his own needs. He himself had not been taken in by what he called the "new methods" he had begun to employ in his treatments. And Hildesheimer, who had not been convinced of the purity of his motives either, had accused him outright of using them to cover up his own need for new stimuli and his craving for excitement.

Hildesheimer's most vehement outburst against him had actually taken place in another context—in the wake of a lecture on the interpretation of dreams, which Joe had delivered to first-year students at the Institute. "In order to break the ice," as he tried to explain to the old man afterward, "who were so tense and nervous that I felt really sorry for them," his own, private dreams, "for a bit of comic relief—what's so terrible about that? Why must everything always be so solemn?" Needless to say, his dreams were full of incident and packed with highly personal details. The candidates were embarrassed, and they told tales—he never found out whom they told, or how the information reached Hildesheimer, whose reaction was uncompromising and outraged.

Joe tried to calm the fear of God that the old man instilled in him then by telling himself that these outbursts of fury were typically German and that the whole thing had nothing to do with him. It was the first time he had ever seen the old man lose control completely and raise his voice. Harsh things were said. Inter alia, Hildesheimer said:

"You're losing all standards of judgment and acting simply to gratify your own needs. The need to be loved is making you take leave of your senses. Things can't go on like this. How long, how long do you think you can go on deceiving your patients? What you're doing isn't analysis—it's nothing but a circus!"

In his heart he knew that there was some truth in Hildesheimer's accusations. Deep inside himself he *was* tired of listening day after day to his patients, absorbed in their private pain, of demanding associations, of insisting on the truth. The sentence "And what does that remind you of?" had turned into a farce in his mind, and sometimes he was unable to bring it out in the proper intonation. Some of his patients sensed it. He couldn't say exactly when his practice had begun to dwindle. He didn't actually have any free hours yet, but he didn't have a waiting list either, and lately there were no applications from candidates wanting supervision. He had only two supervisees left, and they both dated from way back.

He had begun to notice that the moment he opened his mouth to speak, before he uttered a word, smiles appeared on the faces of his listeners, and he recognized the role of court jester with which he had gradually become identified. His perceptiveness and diagnostic astuteness were still unquestioned. Nobody smiled who came to consult him—unofficially, of course—about a particularly problematic patient, and everyone admitted that he was always right. But lately he had become convinced that a process of decline had set in and he was on his way downhill.

In addition to everything else, or before everything else, there was the knowledge that his marriage was breaking up, and the fact that it was his second marriage intensified the feeling of despair, the cynicism, and the pessimism that enveloped every detail of his daily life.

To be fifty years old, the father of a four-year-old child—how often could a person begin his life over and find himself again and again at the end of his chosen road? This was what he had been asking his face in the mirror every morning when he shaved.

Whenever he thought about his previous career and his first marriage, he was forced to admit that there wasn't even anybody he could blame. He had been given every possible opportunity, and he was responsible for making a mess of things himself.

He could always blame Deutsch for not doing a good job, but the knowledge that the analysis he had undergone had not solved all his problems did not make him feel any better.

And then there were the incessant thoughts, night after night, about his first wife and the question of what would have happened if he had not let her go, if he had not insisted on her having an abortion, if he had not been so opposed to becoming a parent. His first wife—the missed opportunity of his life, as he had discovered a few years before—had made a new, full life for herself. If only he had understood then how much the marriage depended on him, on his ability to accept things (the things he actually longed for more than anything else), to undertake the deep commitment on which she sought to base their lives together, to appreciate her candor, her good sense, her optimism—if only he had understood then, he would have stopped her. He should never have let her go.

He should never have insisted on the abortion. He himself no longer remembered the arguments he had advanced to justify his decision never to bring children into the world. But he did remember, and vividly, the day he brought her home, pale and weak, the tears streaming from her eyes, to the unheated apartment, where she lay shivering for two days, while he brought her cups of tea that failed to warm her up. He could not bring himself to touch her.

Two months later, when he drove her to the airport, her mouth was set in a determined line. She flew to New York. And two years afterward, he put no difficulties in her way when she said that she wanted to "make it official" and came back to Israel for a divorce. Something in her expression then made it impossible for him even to hint at a reconciliation. She had not forgiven him.

The truth was, thought Joe as he stared at the cover of the book, that he had loved her very much, in his limited, childish way, but his way of showing it then had been so twisted that any idea of making a new start was doomed at the outset.

Twenty years had passed since then, and seven since he had married Dalya, who had told him about her pregnancy only when it was too late to do anything about it. Whenever he looked at Daniel he felt joy, love, but also a sea of anxiety, especially at night, when he woke up and went to see if the boy was still alive. Only with his son, thought Joe, looking at the book on his knees, did he feel the warmth and security of being unconditionally loved.

And also—sometimes—with Yoav.

The relationship with Yoav—which he regarded as one of the wonders of his life—was a source of never-ending tension between Dalya and himself. Late at night, usually, with her face to the wall, Dalya would ask rhetorically: "So why is it different with Yoav? Just because he's younger than you are and admires you without any reservations? Accepts you as you are? Or is there a little queer hiding behind the ex–Don Juan? That's what you are, at bottom, isn't it?"

Joe would smile. Like anyone else in his profession, he assumed that there was latent homosexuality in everyone; a feminine element in every man, a masculine element in every woman, and a degree of attraction to members of the same sex.

He had explained this to Dalya himself: "We've all got everything inside us, all God's plenty: homosexuality and self-destruction, spite and malevolence, sadism and masochism—the lot. The question is how much of each thing there is in each person: that's the only difference between the sick and the well—how much of everything there is. And I happen to like women. Men too—correct—but in my personality homosexuality is not the dominant factor. That's not the issue." Dalya preferred to ignore the basic argument behind these words.

The first of the accusations she had hurled at him this morning contained a painful truth, although, as usual, there was nothing new in what she said. Yoav Alon, who was ten years younger than he was, admired him unreservedly, was close to him and dependent on him. Joe was obviously a surrogate father figure for him, a big brother. They had never spoken about this explicitly.

Within the relationship, Yoav maintained his self-respect by taking care of practical matters (Joe didn't know how to change a fuse) and keeping them all up-to-date about what was happening in the world (Joe never read the newspapers, and the statement "We'll ask Yoav" became a token in the game of give-and-take: "I'm the expert on the inner man, and you're responsible for the world outside").

They had met when Joe was having an affair with Yoav's sister, soon after the divorce. It was she who had brought him to the apartment in Arnona, where Joe lived many years before it became so popular, and two months later, when she moved on, Yoav continued to turn up with obstinate regularity, without advance warning, sitting for hours on end, listening silently to the conversations of the people who always filled the house. He began sleeping over too, when Joe was not entertaining some woman, and Joe would stay up until the wee hours, talking to him and drawing him out.

He brought Osnat around to introduce her to Joe even before he presented her to his parents. Dalya regarded him as part of her husband's world and accepted him as such, and it was only in the last year that she had begun to complain about the delicate understanding that existed between her husband and the sunburned officer, the sabra whose thorns disappeared when he was in the older man's company.

During the past year, Joe felt, Yoav had withdrawn from him too. Once only, Joe had asked lightly: "What's been eating you lately?" and Yoav, after pretending that he didn't know what his friend was talking about, finally blushed and said: "It's this bloody job; it's sucking the marrow from my bones." Joe tried to put out additional feelers, but Yoav evaded his questions. Now they spent hours together in silence, on small talk and trivialities. Although Joe knew that Yoav's withdrawal had nothing to do with him, it hurt him so much that he could not bring himself to try to break down the barriers. He treated his friend as gently and tactfully as if he were an adolescent child, and he kept his hurt feelings to himself.

Joe Linder knew no greater sacrifice than this—to love someone and to let him be.

But he could not help seeing this, too, as part of the general process of his decline, of the way in which people were beginning to tire of his company. He no longer had the energy to change anything. He did not have Eva Neidorf's enviable capacity for believing in his ability to change the course of his own or other people's lives.

His train of thought ground to a halt. He looked at the book, at the cigarette that had burned down in the ashtray and turned into a cylinder of ash. The room was intensely cold, and when he stood up and went over to the little cabinet to pour himself a whiskey, thanking whatever powers that be for the fact that the wineglasses were clean, he felt a sharp stab of the chronic pain in his back. He returned to his chair, and as he sat down he encountered a curious bulge, which turned out to be Daniel's rubber duck. He stroked its head with his free hand. On a clear day you could see the Judean mountains from the big bay window. Now, at three o'clock in the morning, there was nothing to see but the black sky. Ever since '67 and the big building boom, the apartment—one of four in a building that till then had stood by itself in an island of stillness—had lost all its charms. Only at night did some of the old magic return, and Joe would spend hours contemplating the great darkness outside. Sometimes he would sit in the armchair facing the window until the sky grew light.

There were other nights too. Not many, but they existed nevertheless.

Sometimes it made him happy to have people around him, lots of people. Two weeks before, he had thrown a party for Tammy Zvielli on the Saturday of her case presentation, after the vote. He had made his special punch, which had its usual liberating effect, and they were all there. Dalya had behaved like a hostess. A temporary truce. He had hugged everyone, loved everyone; even his backache had vanished, despite the cold, though they had sat out on the big balcony. The jokes and the feeling of togetherness had seemed to warm the outside air.

Hildesheimer didn't come (he never took part in social events, because "that was precisely the kind of thing that spoiled the transference," and there were always patients of his present at parties), and Eva wasn't there either, and Joe felt free of all inhibitions.

The best part of the party was late at night, when only the young people were left, the ones who still regarded him as an object worthy of admiration. Then he came into his own: clever and witty and full of humor. Even Yoav, who came because of his connection with Tammy, was in high spirits. His eyes shone with the old sparkle when he smiled at Joe. For days afterward Joe felt happy. Even the moment when everyone went home and he was left with the paper cups and the dregs of the punch did not sadden him. He relived the pleasure of their unreserved admiration and basked in its glow.

Now he sighed and stood up. Mechanically he went over to the bookcase and pulled out, almost without looking, a soft leather-bound book whose faded edges had once been gold. He knew every page in it, every line. Legend said that Deutsch had made Joe Linder learn German as a condition for acceptance by the Institute. And Joe, for his part, was happy to cultivate any myth that made him the center of attention and showed him in an interesting, unusual light. Everyone in the Institute admired his fluency in German. In fact, German was his mother tongue, the language he had spoken with his parents, German Jews who had immigrated to Holland.

In his most difficult hours he would return to German poetry, his secret consolation. The book fell open at Hölderlin's "The Middle of Life"; he knew it by heart, but he liked looking at the letters, the lines, the Gothic print, and feeling the thin, delicate paper.

Joe had two secrets, two bright islands: his love for his first, lost wife and his love of poetry.

But this time Hölderlin brought no comfort, and he felt the constriction holding back the tears, the tears for which he could find no outlet.

At half past three in the morning, his little diary showed him that the first patient of the morning was not due before nine. Thoughts of a sleeping pill turned into a decision. He dialed 174 and his home number and asked to be wakened, then he went into the bedroom, a glass of water in his hand, and opened the drawer of the bedside table where he kept his sleeping pills.

He switched on the reading lamp, stretched out his hand, and felt in the drawer for the pills. Rosenfeld provided him with a regular supply, always making the same speech: "Like all shoemakers, you go barefoot. Perhaps you should see someone instead of living on this rubbish?"

This time Joe Linder felt extremely righteous: it was two weeks since he had taken a pill. It's been a hard day, he thought as he swallowed the barbiturate and put the packet back into the drawer. Then he switched off the light and waited for the miracle.

But the minute he began to wait for the pill to take effect, he realized that something had felt different when his hand was groping in the drawer. Something that usually got in the way wasn't there this time.

Afterward Joe Linder would say that the older he grew, the more he realized how right Freud was when he said that there were no accidents. Only determinism could explain why he had remembered the pistol then and not the night before.

The moment he realized what was missing, he put the light on again, got out of bed, pulled out the drawer, and emptied it of its contents. He did not find what he was looking for. Not in the second drawer either, nor anywhere else in the room.

But then the sleeping pill began to take effect, and his body grew heavy and slack. On his way back to bed, he thought that everything could wait until morning, and he fell asleep with the second verse of "The Middle of Life" echoing in his mind: *Alas for me, where shall I get / the flowers when it is winter and where / the sunshine / and shadow of earth? / The walls stand speechless and cold, in the wind / the weather vanes rattle. . . .* He slept soundly until he was wakened by the ringing of the telephone, which merged in his dream with the alarm going off in his burgled car.

When he lifted the receiver he was informed that the time was seven thirty-one, and he went on sitting in bed, wondering how he was going to cancel his first appointment of the morning so that he could go to the police station and report the fact that his pistol was missing.

7

On the Saturday morning that Eva Neidorf was found dead in the Institute, the inmates of the closed ward of the Margoa Hospital were allowed out into the garden. But in spite of the exhortations of the ward nurse ("Come and see, look what a lovely day outside"), the patients of Men 4 were inclined to stay in bed. Nurse Dvora went from bed to bed, trying to persuade them to get up and go out into the sun. Only two of them were persuaded: Shlomo Cohen and Nissim Tubol. They rose heavily from their beds and crossed the large room one after the other like sleepwalkers, stopping at the door to blink in the sunlight.

At the same time, in the garden surrounding the hospital, Ali, the Arab gardener, from the Dehaisha refugee camp, passed from one rosebush to another, leisurely scooping up rubbish and dead leaves with his spade and throwing them into the barrel he dragged along behind him. From time to time he would raise his head and look through the fence at passing cars. He had been working from early in the morning, and it was already ten o'clock when he reached the high fence separating the hospital from the street. For the past few months, Ali had been working on Saturdays instead of Sundays. After doing his work quietly for a year without asking for anything, he had succeeded in persuading the maintenance supervisor to agree to this special arrangement. No one outside the hospital knew about it. The supervisor was afraid of the Health Ministry's reaction to so flagrant a breach of the sanctity of the Sabbath. In the hospital books and work roster, the gardener was listed as working on Sundays. Not that Ali was a believing Christian, as he presented himself; he simply wanted to be at home and enjoy himself with his friends, who had Sundays off from work.

He loved the profound silence surrounding the hospital garden on Saturdays. The street was a quiet one on weekdays too, but on Saturdays there was hardly a car to be seen.

Today the street was full of traffic. The cars drove past the hospital and parked at the bottom of the road. The patrol cars clustering up above, next to the Institute, were invisible to him from the garden of the hospital, which was situated farther down the one-way street.

Until he reached the rosebush nearest the fence, everything was normal. He worked at a leisurely pace and basked in the sun. The ground was still a little muddy. And then, in the rosebush in the row next to the fence, he saw the gleam. Something was glittering there. He put out his hand and touched cold metal. When he saw the object in his hand, a little pearl-handled pistol, he acted fast. He looked to the right and left, and when he was sure nobody was watching, he dropped the pistol and, with his foot, covered it with earth. Then he squatted down next to the bush and considered his next move.

He did not know how the pistol had landed in the hospital grounds or how long it had been tangled there in the rosebush. But he knew very well the kind of trouble he could get into by finding it.

First he contemplated burying it deeper in the ground and pretending he had never seen it. But the thought that someone from the hospital would find it and he, the only gardener, would be called on to explain how it got there was too frightening to contemplate.

Then he considered the possibility of taking it home with him and getting rid of it there. But because of the fine weather, he imagined that there would be many Jewish tourists and also many police on the roads between Jerusalem and what the Jews called the "territories," and this thought frightened him to death. He thought, too, of the searches and arrests in the wake of the murder of the tourist in the Old City, which were probably still going on. He dug his fingers into the damp ground and wondered what to do. More than anything else he feared contact with the authorities. His younger brother had been arrested a few months before on suspicion of hostile activities. Nobody in the hospital knew about it. He realized that he would have no peace of mind until the pistol disappeared from both his sight and his thoughts. He didn't want any trouble.

Ali stood up and looked around him, and then he saw Tubol. He thanked his lucky stars that it was Tubol of all people who had come along at this critical juncture. Tubol was one of his biggest favorites among the mad people. And his great advantage with regard to the problem in hand was his enduring silence. For years nobody had succeeded in getting a single word out of him. It was the maintenance supervisor who had told Ali this, in his broken Arabic, in one of their rare conversations. Naturally, it was not Ali who had started the conversation but the supervisor, who expressed his amazement at the trust placed by Tubol in Ali. The fact that he was prepared to take a cigarette from the gardener was surprising enough, but seeing him follow Ali and sit down to watch him while he worked was cause for astonishment. Ali expressed the hesitant opinion that the man seemed harmless, and the supervisor concurred but saw fit to warn him nevertheless that you could never tell when one of "them" would take it into his head to run amok. The young gardener was not afraid of the patients, however; in all the time he had been working at the hospital, he had not come across a single patient who frightened him. The staff were something else.

Nissim Tubol noticed Ali and approached the rosebush. Ali did not budge until he was sure that Tubol was coming, and then he sat down innocently and took a pack of cigarettes out of his pocket. Tubol sat down a little distance away, and Ali turned his head delicately toward him and smiled. Tubol stood up and came closer, looked timidly around him, and after much hesitation sat down next to Ali and pointed to the cigarettes. Ali offered the pack, and Tubol took three cigarettes. Two of them he tucked carefully into his shirt pocket, and the third he put into his mouth; then he leaned toward the match, which Ali lit with a trembling hand.

They smoked in silence, their backs to the street behind the fence, at which Ali glanced between puffs. Tubol sighed deeply at regular intervals, and from time to time a tremor passed through his little body, until he gradually calmed down. His hunched shoulders slackened, and he stuck his legs out in front of him. If, thought Ali, he avoided sudden, careless movements, Tubol would stay beside him.

After the second cigarette the suspicion vanished from Tubol's face, which resumed its glassy stare. Ali turned his head and looked again at the street behind the fence, where the activity had died down. Slowly, trying not to alarm the sick man, as if he were tracking a deer, with an almost accidental movement, he dug into the damp soil with his fingers. He did not look at his fingers but kept his eyes on Tubol, who puffed intently on his cigarette and followed the movements of the gardener's hand with his opaque gaze.

The moment the pistol was exposed, Ali withdrew his hand from the soil, keeping his eyes on Tubol, who to his amazement jumped up, pounced on the pistol, and held it in a fierce grip, his eyes shining and unintelligible grunts escaping from his mouth. Then he stuck it into the elastic band at the top of his trousers, which resembled pajama bottoms, and looked at Ali with an expression at once triumphant and frightened, like a child who had laid hands on some precious treasure and was afraid that it would be taken away.

The gardener, who had expected to have to invest a lot of effort in coaxing and enticing, and could not believe his luck, pointed quickly to his watch, which showed half past ten, said one word: "Tea," then stood up and began walking toward the building. Tubol rose to his feet and followed him, suddenly breaking into a clumsy run toward Men 4, and disappeared into the big hall.

Ali retreated into the garden, sat down next to the remotest rosebush, breathed a sigh of relief, and lit a cigarette. Even if Tubol suddenly decided to break his silence, even if he went berserk, they would never be able to connect the pistol with the Arab gardener. It was only when he stood up again and went on with his work that he saw the first police car coming down the street. He held his breath, but the car continued down the hill, with two patrol cars behind it, which turned into the side street opposite the hospital. The patrol cars put him into a real panic, and he worked at convincing himself that there was no connection between the police and the revolver, between them and him. With all his strength he resisted the overpowering impulse to run away and go home to the camp, for he knew that it was essential to keep acting as usual. He went on working, pretending that whatever was happening in the street, on the other side of the fence, had nothing to do with him, and then he gradually withdrew deep into the garden, to the fruit trees that were beginning to blossom.

Nurse Dvora noticed that Tubol was in a highly excitable state. Observing him out of the corner of her eye, she saw him lying curled up on his bed, his hand in his trouser pocket and his eyes shining with a gleam she had never seen in them before. She went up to him and said, in the tone that Dr. Baum referred to, and not only behind her back, as her "kindergarten teacher voice," that it would be nice if he, Tubol, came to the table now. There, next to the entrance to the ward, was tea and cake—"a special cake for Saturday," she added in the same bright, gushing tone.

Tubol did not respond, or even turn his eyes—which were fixed on a point on the opposite wall—toward her. She repeated her invitation, and then he looked at her suspiciously and covered himself with the woolen blanket. Nurse Dvora gave up and left the room.

After the tea break was over, she went to the call doctor's room.

That Saturday the doctor on call was Hedva, but Nurse Dvora, who was fond of Hedva, had no intention of consulting her on a professional matter. She knew very well that the senior doctor on call, Dr. Baum, would be at the hospital all day long, because whenever Hedva was on call on Saturday she would ask Dr. Baum, if he was the senior on call at home, to stay with her in the hospital, which gave rise to powerful feelings of anxiety in her when it was in her exclusive charge. Dvora had never been officially informed of this arrangement, but nothing went on in the hospital without her being aware of it, and although she disapproved of Dr. Baum—she didn't like working with him because he "upset the ward and turned everything upside down" with his peculiar methods, which included ignoring her instructions and joking with the patients—at the moment she preferred his medical experience to any advice she could get from Hedva. Baum was sitting in an armchair, with his feet on the coffee table, and when she came into the room he said: "My, my, look who's here! Dropped in for a little rest, have we? How about a cup of coffee?"

"I ask you!" Dvora appealed silently to an invisible audience. "Dropped in for a little rest! Really!"

"Well," continued Baum, his eyes twinkling, "do you want some or not?"

"What? Want what?" asked Dvora, busy with her own thoughts.

"So we don't even know what we want anymore." Baum laughed, fingering his fair mustache. "A fine state of affairs, I must say. I can think of all kinds of possibilities. What do you say?"

Nurse Dvora did not blush, and pointedly ignoring his smile, she said: "I came to tell you that there's something the matter with Tubol again. I think he's starting. This morning when he got up, he was still all right. I don't know what happened since then, but it looks to me as if he's starting again."

Dr. Baum grew serious. He asked: "Are you sure?" without waiting for a reply. He knew that Dvora was more experienced and also more perceptive than a good few doctors he knew. In the last analysis, and in spite of all his jokes at her expense, he valued her work and rapport with the patients. "That's a pity," he said in the end, tugging at his mustache. "He was doing so well last month I was even thinking of transferring him to One." Men 1 was a half-open ward. Or half-closed, depending on your point of view. The patients in it had more freedom than those in Men 4, which was a completely closed ward. "What exactly is wrong with him? What did you see?"

"That's just it," Dvora replied hesitantly. "It's different from usual. He's staying in bed, and he doesn't want to eat, you know, but this time he seems agitated too, unusually agitated—that's my opinion anyway." There was a certain aggressiveness in her last words, as if she was reluctant to commit herself to anything too definite.

"Is he taking his medication?" asked Baum. Dvora nodded, and then he turned to the gray metal filing cabinet in the corner of the room, dragged the armchair over to it with a loud rasp, sat down and, mumbling, "Tubol, Tubol Nissim, what's he on," pulled out a thick cardboard file folder. Dvora began listing the medications out loud, while Baum consulted the file to make sure.

"We could increase the Mellaril," said Baum thoughtfully to himself, "or maybe it would be better to wait till tomorrow or tonight. What do you think?" He didn't wait for a reply but went on: "Good; let's wait till evening. In the meantime I'm here, and you'll call me if there's anything new, right?"

Dvora did not reply. If anyone had asked her opinion, she would have acted right away, increased the Mellaril, increased something. But nobody asked her opinion. She had done what she could. Nurse Dvora shook the floorboards when she left the room. Baum resisted the impulse to pinch her vast backside, smiled to himself, and went back to his book.

He read until he felt hungry. He saw it was one o'clock; if he didn't hurry, there would be nothing left to eat. Since the budget cuts, the standard of the food had dropped to an all-time low, which roused even the depressive patients to indignation. Once he put the book down and went out into the sun, he decided that on his way over to the staff dining room he would drop in to see Tubol. He entered the ward, groping in his pocket to make sure that he had his door handle with him. He was always afraid that he would have to ask Dvora for hers, and then she would have her moment of triumph. She would leave him locked up inside. In the Margoa Hospital, the conventional bunch of keys had been replaced by the door handle. There were no handles on the inside of the doors in the wards, a fact that gave rise to an inexhaustible fund of jokes, some in better taste than others.

The handle was in his pocket, and he entered, nodded to Dvora, and turned in the direction of Tubol's room. It was the first room in the ward and held another eight patients, none of whom was there. He went up to the bed, sat down, and said: "What's up, Nissim? Have we decided to be sick again?"

Tubol lay curled up in bed, covered by the blanket, and did not react. Baum touched his exposed hand, which was hot and dry, and said: "I think you've got a fever; let's have a look." He began pulling off the blanket, but Tubol clung to it with all his might, biting his lips, his body tightly curled in a fetal position. Baum was unable to remove the blanket. He looked at his watch and said he would come back in a little while and then perhaps Tubol would be prepared to behave rationally. On his way out of the ward, he said to Dvora: "Do me a favor: have a look at Tubol; I think he's got a fever. I'm just going to have something to eat. Keep an eye on him, okay?" And without waiting for her to reply, he went outside.

Next to the fence, he paused to look into the street. He saw the cars parked on both sides of the road, made a face, and went into the dining room. Hedva Tamari, the duty doctor, for whom he felt profound affection, was standing in the corner of the room, eating a slice of bread smeared with a red substance that made him feel sick to the stomach. "That tinned jam again?" he asked, and, without waiting for a reply: "Tell me, did you see all those cars outside? Are those lunatics having another one of their Saturday jamborees?"

Hedva pointed to her mouth, which was full, finished chewing, and replied while applying jam to another slice of bread: "You tell me. I'm on call here, remember. I haven't stuck my nose outside since I arrived. What do I know?" Baum knew that it was the second consecutive Saturday that Hedva was on call at the hospital, and accordingly he was not put out by her hostility but smiled and said: "There's no need to bite my head off. I only asked. I thought you knew. They're friends of yours, aren't they?"

"You know very well that I haven't been accepted yet, and I didn't tell you so that you could start making jokes at the top of your voice either." Hedva was hissing, an offended expression on her face.

"Okay, okay, I apologize; stop taking offense at everything," said Baum placatingly, then quickly added: "But there really are a lot of cars; go and see." As he spoke, he helped himself to a large portion of gluey macaroni mixed with what appeared to be ketchup, and some kind of fish rissole. These he bolted down, doing his best to ignore their taste. Unable to face a second helping, he left the dining room, passed the hospital guard's lodge, and went hesitantly outside, into the sun.

He stood looking up the street, which from outside the hospital grounds was visible all the way to the top of the rise, and retraced his steps, almost at a run, to the guardhouse next to the gate, where he asked in alarm: "Hey, did you see all those police cars? Has anything happened?"

The security guard, an old-age pensioner who had not ventured out of the little stone hut all morning, except for making one round of the hospital grounds, stood in his doorway and said: "Search me, Dr. Baum. It's a few hours already I've been seeing them, from the window, like, but I never asked anything."

Baum went outside the gate again, walked up as far as the Institute, crossed the narrow street, and said to the policeman standing outside a patrol car: "Excuse me, please; has anything happened?"

The policeman asked Baum to move along. It was only after he had introduced himself and explained that he was the call doctor at the hospital down the road, inviting the policeman to come and ask the guard if he didn't believe him, that the latter relented and said that there had been an accident. Baum wanted to ask for more details, but the policeman's face was sealed, as if he was determined not to say another word. Baum went back down the road to the hospital. Next to the lodge he stopped, asked for the telephone directory, found the Institute's number, and dialed it eagerly. When he heard a busy signal, he ran back up the hill and stopped outside the green gate, next to which a group of people were gathered. He knew them all; some had studied at medical school with him, and others had worked with him in psychiatric clinics.

He saw Gold, who had studied for the board examinations with him and was now working in the psychiatric department at Hadassah Hospital, emerge from a patrol car and lean against the stone wall, his face ashen. He saw the beautiful Dina Silver, whom he had come to know when she was taking her first steps as a psychologist at the Margoa. He vividly recalled his attempts to seduce her, all of which had come to nothing. She was still beautiful. In her fluffy blue coat, she was something to behold.

He also recognized Joe Linder, about whom he had heard from various people. He remembered some woman saying about him: "The only attractive male at the Institute, and brilliant too."

Next to them were three people he didn't know, standing and asking questions in loud voices. A fat, sweating man holding a microphone was shouting at Dina Silver: "Just the name, that's all I'm asking for—what's so terrible about that?" Dina ignored him, and he kept repeating his question until Linder grabbed hold of his sleeve and dragged him aside, saying something that Baum couldn't catch. The man moved a little way off and took up his stand near the patrol car. Baum approached Gold and asked: "What's going on here?"

Gold, who was even paler than before his last board exam, took Baum by the arm and drew him down the hill in the direction of the Margoa, recounting the events of the morning and completely ignoring the responses of his companion, who kept repeating, with variations, the usual exclamations made by people who know that what they are hearing is the gospel truth but cannot reconcile themselves to it. Gold concluded his story with a reference to the reporters who were hanging around, waiting for information. "They're just like dung beetles; they live on every shitty thing that happens," he said with loathing. Then he expressed concern for Neidorf's patients, at which point he remembered that he was one of them himself and fell silent. Baum exclaimed again: "Who would have believed it! In the Institute! Good God! And Neidorf of all people!" Gold did not respond. Then he said in a stunned voice that he had just come back from police headquarters in the Russian Compound, where he had made a statement; the police officer had interrogated him for ages, he complained.

Baum had heard a number of lectures by Neidorf, who had

worked at the hospital for years, before his time, and still served as a consultant at the outpatients clinic. In both the hospital and the clinic she was admired to the point of veneration. He himself always said about her that she was tops, but in private he allowed himself to scoff a little at her lack of humor.

He said something to Gold about the greenish tinge of his complexion, clucked sympathetically at the trauma he had experienced, and invited him to come and have a cup of coffee in his office. Gold accepted the invitation for reasons that were unclear to him. He had never felt comfortable in Baum's company, and he didn't understand his jokes. Ever since they had completed their studies, he had avoided meeting him. He trailed after him, mumbling that he really should go home.

The coffee that Baum poured him from the thermos in the call doctor's room was lukewarm and muddy, but he drank it without complaint. The muscles in his calves were trembling with weakness, as if in the wake of some tremendous physical effort, and he sat in the armchair with his legs quivering uncontrollably. He attributed the weakness to his migraine.

Baum didn't stop talking for a moment. He talked all the way to the room, he talked while he was pouring the coffee, and he talked now that they were sitting and drinking it. He asked all the questions demanded by the situation: "Who, in your opinion, could have shot her?" "Why should anyone have wanted to shoot her?" And: "What was she doing there anyway? What could have brought her to the Institute at such an unheard-of hour?"

These were precisely the questions that had been nagging at Gold ever since the murder was discovered, but to Baum he said that he had no idea, how should he know, let the police break their heads, that's what they were there for, and the patients would be taken care of by the Institute's big shots, and what's-his-name, the good-looking policeman, the one who had driven him crazy with his questions, would find the murderer, and everything would turn out all right in the end. He didn't mean a word of it; he had no control over what he was saying.

"Or the murderess," said Baum dreamily.

"Why murderess?" asked Gold in confusion.

"Why not?" replied Baum, and smiled broadly. Again Gold didn't understand the joke.

Baum put the empty coffee cup down on the table next to him and said: "From what I've heard up to now, the following questions arise: One"—he raised one finger—"what was she doing there at that ungodly hour? as I said before. Two"—he raised a second finger—"who came there to meet her? Three"—he raised the third—"which of the Institute people possess a pistol, since it was obviously one of your people who did it"—here he expressed a certain satisfaction by twirling his mustache—"because whoever it was had to have a key, although of course she may have opened the door herself. In short," he said with a grin, "the main question is who did it and why. Who profited by her death, or who hated her so much, or even"—and here a gleam appeared in his eye as his voice rose—"who loved her so much?"

Gold looked at Baum in silence. He felt a wave of nausea, his response, he assumed, to the smugness radiating from the person sitting opposite him. Gold now regretted from the bottom of his heart having agreed to accompany him.

After a moment he stood up and said that he had to get home. Mina wouldn't know where he was; it was three o'clock already; she'd made lunch; they were expecting her parents. Baum then delivered himself of a parting blow that drove Gold right up the wall. "Tell me," asked Baum, "didn't anyone tell you that you were a suspect?" Gold was generally slow on the uptake; he was especially so now. At first he felt only surprise, and then, as Baum went on and on with his nonsense, he sensed the anger flushing his face. "Come on, seriously, you know, like in all those detective stories, when the murderer pretends to be a solid citizen and informs the police and it all comes out in the end."

Gold felt his nausea intensifying, and he finally succeeded in saying: "Stop it—it isn't funny," words that came out weakly but demanded vast amounts of energy to pronounce.

But Baum didn't stop. "Look, I didn't say you actually did it, shot her, murdered her; perish the thought. I only asked if anyone else thought so; I'd just like to know." Gold hadn't said a word about his first hour with Ohayon, dismissing his conversation with the detective in a couple of sentences. Now he suppressed the desire to deliver a final, crushing retort and was about to leave the room, when Baum rose from the depths of his chair and said: "Hang on a minute; I'll come with you. In any case, there's nothing to do here, and it's such a nice day outside."

Gold did not protest. He was so exhausted that he didn't know how he was going to drive home. Together they left the call doctor's room and went outside, where they met Hedva Tamari, whom Gold knew from the days of her internship at Hadassah. A few weeks previously, she had come to ask his advice about applying for candidacy at the Institute. The conversation had left him with a faint residue of guilt and uneasiness.

He had held forth at length about the difficulties but had not succeeded in deterring her, since her mind was already made up. He should have known, he thought, that someone who came to ask whether to apply or not wasn't looking for reasons not to do it; what was wanted was reinforcement of a decision already made. He had done the same thing himself. He should never have tried to make Hedva change her mind. During that same conversation it had transpired that she, too, was a patient of Neidorf's.

He was not quick enough to warn Baum, who immediately embarked on a dramatic recital of the morning's events, paying no attention to the way the color was draining from Hedva's face until she suddenly collapsed without a word and fell to the ground, limp as a rag doll.

For a moment the two doctors stood rooted to the spot, and then Baum knelt down next to her, took her pulse, and tried to revive her. Gold abandoned all thoughts of going home. Hedva quickly regained consciousness, but it then became evident that she had injured her ankle in the fall. The ensuing debate about whether to take her to some hospital or other for an X-ray was cut short by Hedva's vigorous protests. A rapid examination of the injured ankle indicated that no bones were broken, and the three of them slowly made their way, the two men supporting Hedva on either side, to the call doctor's room, where Baum bandaged the injured ankle with a gentleness and an expertise that took Gold by surprise. Baum put the bandaged foot up on a chair, sighed, and said it was a good thing the senior on call was already there; then he smiled, winked at her, and asked if she wanted anything for the pain. When she refused, he suggested, with a warmth and tenderness that Gold had never heard in his voice before, that she take a Valium; she actually agreed, and he held out the little yellow pill and proclaimed total rest, doctor's orders.

She shook her curly head and burst into tears, begging them not to leave her alone. At this stage the penny dropped, and he said with a hurt expression: "I thought we were friends; how could you not tell me?"

Between sobs, Hedva replied that she knew he would laugh at her, because he didn't believe in analysis, only in drugs, and then she added that he mustn't feel guilty about the way she had found out; in any case, nothing mattered anymore, and her sobs grew louder. Baum rose from his chair to embrace her, and Gold felt very lonely and excluded again. Nevertheless he did not leave the room but stood in the doorway and asked Hedva how long she had been a patient of Neidorf's. "Over a year; a year and a month," she replied, wiping her eyes with the back of her hand, and he nodded, but she gave no sign of acknowledging his share in their common plight. Gold then said goodbye to both of them and left the hospital to go home, where, he thought despairingly, he would have to tell the whole story all over again.

The novice psychiatrist Dr. Hedva Tamari was the chief reason that the patient Nissim Tubol vanished completely from the mind of the senior physician on call. He put her to sleep on the bed in the office and sat next to her, and he held her hand, as he had promised on his honor to do, until late that evening, deaf to the nurse Dvora's attempts to call him on the house phone, for he had taken the precaution of removing the receiver in order not to disturb Hedva's sleep. The nurse tried desperately, over and over, to get him on the phone, since she did not dare leave her post in the ward, where Nissim Tubol had been sitting up in bed since eight o'clock in the evening, aiming a little pistol at the patient in the opposite bed, a pistol that appeared to Dvora's inexperienced eye to be loaded and cocked.

And since the telephone was on the counter of the nurse's station, in full view of the open door of Tubol's room, it was an hour before she dared, without taking her eyes off him for a second, feeling for the right holes with her finger, to dial the call doctor's number, which gave off a continuous busy signal. But after Tubol fired one shot at the opposite wall and the patients, who till then had been paralyzed with fear, began to go berserk, she stood up and with a no-nonsense expression on her face marched up to Tubol and took the gun away from him without any difficulty at all—he didn't even try to resist—and ran to the doctor's room.

Baum awoke from a deep sleep, full of visions of fractured ankles, to the sound of loud knocking on the door, which he had taken care to lock behind Gold. He stood up and opened it, confused by the light that flooded the room as Dvora pressed the switch. He saw the dazed expression on Hedva's face as she began waking up, and was about to ask what the matter was when his eyes fell on the little pistol in the nurse's hand as she stood there trembling all over and weeping. (No one had ever seen Nurse Dvora cry. This, together with the wild disorder of her blond hair, which was always scraped back and neatly pinned up in a "banana" roll, indicated clearly that a catastophe had occurred.) She began haranguing him about how she couldn't cope with the ward by herself, and where had he been all this time, and in the end, glaring at Hedva, she even screamed that she should have guessed what he had been up to, should have known why the telephone in the call physician's room was busy when Tubol was pointing a loaded gun at the patients in the ward.

Baum didn't wait for the end of the speech. He began to run in the direction of the ward, with Dvora still standing and shouting in the doorway.

When he heard the usual noises and saw the light on in the ward, he began to calm down. He went inside, counted the patients, and breathed a sigh of relief when he saw that they were all present. Tubol was sitting on the corner of his bed and staring into space as if nothing had happened. Baum looked around. The patients were behaving as usual, and it occurred to him that an outside observer, who did not know how to read the signs of tension and anxiety, would have suspected Dvora of making the whole thing up. But he wasn't an outside observer. There was a little pistol in his pocket and a ward on the point of breaking out in front of him.

He returned to the office, to see Dvora still standing in the doorway and Hedva once more asleep. Dvora kept declaring that she wasn't going back to the ward and nobody was going to make her, until Baum announced in a tone of authority such as she had never heard from him that she was going back with him right now, because there were patients in need and work that had to be done. Muttering "Look who's talking," she walked down the corridor behind him, interrupting her protests only to answer his demands for a detailed description of the events in the ward.

The patients' tension and anxiety were becoming overt. Only after Baum and Dvora had succeeded in calming the first two to become violent, and they were lying sedated on their beds, did Baum sit down next to Tubol. In a casual, conversational tone, he asked him where he had found the pistol. Tubol, who was lying in a fetal position, did not even turn his head in Baum's direction. Baum took the pistol out of his pocket, waved it in front of the patient's eyes, and repeated the question. There was no reaction. But when Baum sighed and stood up, Tubol began to scream.

He screamed wordlessly, and even Baum, who was used to patients' outbursts, froze when he heard the dreadful animal howls. The other patients went berserk, each of them expressing his symptoms in a way that demanded an immediate response. Dvora managed to prevent Shlomo Cohen from taking off his clothes, but she called Baum to help her, crying that his strength was uncanny. Baum held him down, and Dvora prepared a syringe. Then they gave Tubol a shot too, and while Dvora had the needle in his arm, Itzik Zimmer, who was famous for his uncontrollable fits of rage, jumped on Baum—who was holding Tubol down and couldn't move—from behind. Huge hands throttled his throat, and he felt the breath being choked out of him, but then Dvora, with a superhuman effort, succeeded in jabbing a needle into Zimmer's arm. The mere sight of the syringe was enough to frighten Zimmer, and he let go of Baum, who fell to the floor in a faint.

When he came to, Baum saw the hospital director, Professor Gruner, and two people he didn't know standing next to his bed. He tried to say something aloud, but all he succeeded in producing was a whisper. The director said, paternally: "Don't strain yourself. You're in my room, the ward's under control, everything's all right, you're going to be fine. There are some people from the police here, who're trying to find out what happened. They're here because of the pistol, not because of the trouble in the ward. They'd like to ask you a few questions now. Dvora's already been questioned, and so has Hedva."

A figure loomed up from behind his head and stood opposite him. Hedva, her eyes red and swollen, stroked his hand. According to the big clock on the wall, it was four o'clock. Four o'clock in the morning? he asked himself. How could he have slept so long? Professor Gruner, as if reading his thoughts, explained: When he arrived at the hospital, he found the ward in an uproar. "Dvora was magnificent. How she managed to get hold of me in the middle of that madhouse I don't know. We called an ambulance, but by the time it got here you were awake, and you even made it here from the ward on your own feet, and then the doctor came and took care of your throat and gave you something to sleep." Baum felt his neck, which was wrapped in a stiff bandage, like a collar. His head was spinning, and his throat was dry and burning. ("As if someone had lit a fire inside it," he told Hedva later on, when he could speak.) "The police think," continued Gruner, "that the pistol that Tubol was holding is connected to Dr. Neidorf's death, and they were waiting for you to wake up in case you could tell them how it came into his possession." Baum looked at Professor Gruner, who was standing opposite him. The light hurt his eyes, and he closed them, waving his hand weakly to indicate that he had no idea. When he opened his eyes again, Gruner still stood opposite him, a worried look on his face. The hands on the clock behind him pointed to four-fifteen.

(Afterward Baum told Hedva that the expression of concern on the face of the professor—the terror of the hospital—"made it all worthwhile. Would you believe it? I hadn't even been sure he knew who I was." To Hedva's response: "Don't talk nonsense," he said: "No, really; sometimes he walks past me as if I'm transparent. Once he even asked me my name. He's only fifty-something—" "Five," said Hedva, pursing her lips. "And don't talk about him like that. I think he's a human being, a real human being. You should have seen the recommendation he gave me to the Institute." "Ah, the Institute! Who am I when it comes to the Institute? As far as you're concerned, anyone connected with the Institute is halfway to God almighty. I'm not saying he's an idiot, but you have to admit he's not a genius, or at least that he's not quite all there, not to say senile.")

The two men who had been introduced as "the police" stepped aside and conferred in undertones. Then one of them asked Gruner something in a whisper, and Gruner shook his head and said: "Only with his hand, if you must," and, turning to Baum: "Dr. Baum, do you know how the pistol came into Tubol's possession? Answer with your hand, please. Sideways for no and up and down for yes." Baum waved his hand negatively, then one of the policemen, the redhead, asked him if he had ever seen the pistol before. Baum waved his hand from side to side again. He was very tired, and when he closed his eyes he heard the redhead say: "Okay, let's get the details on the gun and begin searching the grounds," and then he fell asleep.

L ike Gold, Michael Ohayon scoffed at superstition, but when he walked into Jerusalem police headquarters in the Russian Compound and someone congratulated him on finding the murder weapon, he couldn't help remembering his mother's terror of the "evil eye." His instinctive disclaimers and cautious comments about ballistics tests were greeted with the contempt they no doubt deserved. "Come off it," said Chief Inspector Klein, head of a special task force investigating another murder. "How many pistols can there be in Disraeli Street on one Saturday? How big is the whole bloody street, for God's sake?" Michael didn't smile. Stranger things had happened. He would wait for the answer from the lab. Meanwhile he had to talk to the pathologist and pay a visit to the Margoa Hospital.

The news about the pistol had reached him over his radio at five o'clock in the morning, when he was on his way from Rehavia to the Russian Compound. There was no need, they said, for him to come to the hospital, but he made a detour anyway and drove to Disraeli Street again. At the hospital, the red-haired policeman told him that there were traces of mud on the handgun—a Beretta .22, as they had thought. One bullet had been extracted from the wall in ward Men 4, and another, said the redhead hopefully, would probably be found in the murdered woman's body. He added with a sigh that the gun was full of prints: Dr. Baum's; Nurse Dvora's; the patient Tubol's; and others, still to be identified. But some of the prints would be hard to examine, he explained, "because of the circumstances."

Of all the information printed out by the police computer, the red-haired policeman was most impressed by the fact that the pistol belonged to Joe Linder, who had obtained a permit for it in 1967. The mud bothered him, he added, but they couldn't be sure of anything until Ballistics was through.

Michael looked around him. Light was entering the sky, and he took in the size of the hospital garden, measured the distance from the street, the height of the fence, the distance to the Institute building. Lighting a cigarette, he announced his tentative conclusions to the redhead, who agreed, saying: "Yes; someone must have thrown the gun into the garden from outside, maybe even from a moving car. And the nurse says that the patient went outside. But we'll have to check to make sure."

It was impossible to get anything out of Tubol. All the patients were still sedated, and Baum was sleeping too. There was no choice but to come back later, said Michael, and to bring Baum in for questioning when he was up to it.

Sitting in his room in the Russian Compound, at the end of a curving passage on the second floor—a cubbyhole barely big enough for two chairs, a desk, and a filing cabinet—he looked around him and asked himself where to begin.

Tzilla came in without knocking, as usual, and suggested that he begin with the coffee and rolls that she set on his desk; everything else could wait for a minute. But Michael, his lack of sleep making him feel that if he let up for a minute he would collapse at once, began dialing the pathologist's number with his first sip of coffee. They told him to give them a break, they'd just begun; they'd let him know as soon as they knew anything themselves. It seemed that between Friday night and Saturday morning Neidorf had still been among the living, but they would say nothing for sure.

"I should go down there myself. Eli's too soft with them; he doesn't push them hard enough," thought Michael aloud as he hung up on the Institute for Forensic Medicine and dialed the ballistics laboratory. The line was busy, and he bit into the fresh roll, at the same time searching for the electric shaver in his desk drawer.

Tzilla was not surprised to see Chief Inspector Ohayon beginning to shave himself with one hand while the other still clung to the telephone receiver. She knew how frustrated he was by his limitations, among them the fact that he could never find time for "peripheral" things like eating, drinking, and shaving when he was on a case. He hated being unshaved.

She volunteered to phone back the lab for him, and by the time she got through, Michael had finished his first cup of morning coffee, his shave, and half a roll.

The mud on the pistol, they informed him, was identical to the mud in the hospital grounds. Someone must have picked it up there; it may even have been buried in a flower bed before being found. There were masses of fingerprints; they would never be able to get them all. Meanwhile they had identified Baum's and Tubol's. Yes, they were waiting for the bullet from the body; until they got it, they couldn't say anything definite. They had one of the forensic boys from Criminal Identification there too. The Institute for Forensic Medicine had notified them that they would be sending the bullet around within an hour, and in the meantime there was nothing for Michael to do but wait patiently. They had read the morning papers too, they said.

What about the morning papers? asked Michael cautiously. Did he want the headlines or would he like them to read the whole thing over the phone? Michael said never mind and put the phone down, asking Tzilla if she'd seen the papers yet. Tzilla bent down to the large shoulder bag she had dropped on the floor and pulled out a newspaper.

On the first page was a description of the Institute building and of Disraeli Street; a photograph of Michael, who was called a "star investigator, next in line for Chief of the Jerusalem Investigations Division";

and details about the "case." No other names were given. "Thank God for small mercies," said Michael aloud. Senior woman analyst . . . violent death . . . police baffled . . . funeral arrangements to be announced later today, and that was it.

The telephone rang, and Michael heard the voice of Eli Bahar, who had watched the autopsy. He reported that so far there didn't seem to be any signs of struggle, that so far the cause of death appeared to be the shot in the temple, at close range but not close enough to assume suicide. The time of death, said Eli hesitantly, was probably somewhere between seven and nine on Saturday morning. "They're finishing up now, and the minute they're done I'll be taking the bullet over to Ballistics personally," and Michael caught the quaver in Eli's voice.

Michael didn't like watching autopsies either. For hours afterward he would be horrified by the businesslike way in which the pathologist had cut the cross with his scalpel, slicing the torso from top to bottom and side to side and exposing its inner organs as if it were a chicken.

Eli Bahar was an inspector with the Major Crimes Unit. Michael had worked with him and with Tzilla regularly for a number of years, until Michael had been appointed deputy head of the Investigations Division two years before. Since then he had spent more time on paperwork than in the field. When Michael was made head of the special investigating team on the Neidorf case, it was clear that Eli and Tzilla would be working with him. Tzilla had been appointed coordinator of the task force, but the ingrained habits of years militated against clear-cut demarcations, and Michael knew that just as she had turned up at Neidorf's house last night, she would work at his side until the job was over.

He asked her to inform Hildesheimer that the funeral could be scheduled for the next day, Monday. "Let them decide when, and will he please inform the family and whoever else should be told. I promised I'd let him know as soon as I could." He lit a cigarette.

Tzilla leapt for the phone, but before she began to dial, he asked her if she would please go somewhere else. When she asked him where, exactly, he had in mind, he gave her an annihilating look and asked her if she needed any help moving. She was familiar with Michael's moods after a sleepless night without a shower or a proper shave, before a hard day's work, and she was about to get out while the getting was good, when Joe Linder appeared in the doorway and asked to speak with "Mr. Ohayon."

"Chief Inspector Ohayon." Tzilla corrected him and moved out of his way. Linder entered the room, and she exited, slamming the door behind her.

Joe Linder threw his little body into the chair, unbuttoned his coat with a sigh, and, glancing at his watch, said that he had exactly one hour until his next patient. To come straight to the point, he was here to report the loss of a pistol.

Michael went on smoking calmly, and Joe, with the dark pouches under his eyes giving him a look of simultaneous suffering and debauchery, cast a sidelong glance at the squashed pack lying on the corner of the desk. Michael offered him a cigarette, and after lighting up, Linder began to explain, without being asked, that he was sure that if not for the death (he chose the word after beginning to pronounce the word "murder" and then changing his mind), it would have taken months for him to notice it was missing. He had never used it and had never intended using it. But last night, when he couldn't fall asleep, Providence had guided his hand (here there was a hint of a forced smile) to the drawer of his bedside table, and then he had discovered that the pistol was gone.

Michael, who had managed the day before to read Joe's account of his movements on Friday night and Saturday morning, remembered that on Friday he had entertained friends until the wee hours and on Saturday he had been with his son from six in the morning until he left for the Institute.

He asked what kind of pistol it was and received a reply that included historical and cultural details. (It had been purchased for him by a friend, an army man, in '67, after Joe's house had been broken into—he never locked the door—by a young Arab who claimed that he was being pursued. The break-in had terrified his then girlfriend, and it was for her that he had acquired the gun. That was why it was so feminine-looking, and in general it was an objet d'art, pearl-handled and hand-engraved. Actually it had been bought from a certain art dealer, who was responsible for both the plating and the engraving.)

Assuming an official manner, Michael pulled a form out of the desk drawer and requested particulars regarding the "firearm." Joe took from his wallet a license to carry a .22 caliber Beretta pistol, serial number so-and-so.

Michael then asked what had led Dr. Linder to think there was a connection between the death at the Institute and his pistol. Joe shrugged his shoulders, opened his mouth to say something, changed his mind, and finally said that he didn't know. He just thought so.

Michael looked at the license and asked carefully, scribbling something on the form in front of him, exactly when Dr. Linder had last seen the pistol.

The reply began with a backache and insomnia. Apologetically Joe said: "This may seem irrelevant to you, but actually it's strictly relevant, because the only reason I saw the gun was missing was that I was looking for my sleeping pills, and the way to discover when it was still there is directly related, in my opinion, to the last time I used the pills, and as a matter of fact I remember precisely when it was." And then Linder told him about the night two weeks before when there was a big party at his house. He didn't need the sleeping pills then, and after that he had resolved to stop using them because, as Dr. Rosenfeld had rightly said, he was becoming dependent on them. "Maybe, as an analyst, I shouldn't say this, but in the last resort man is a weak-willed creature, and in any case, perhaps as a result of the tragedy yesterday, I didn't keep my resolution."

Michael completely ignored the frank, intimate tone that Linder had adopted when he talked about the pistol, which increased when he got onto the subject of his insomnia. If he understood correctly, he said, the pistol was last seen on the night before the big party that Dr. Linder mentioned.

Linder nodded and said that there was no need to preface his name with the title "Doctor" every time he was addressed. "Altogether I'm an impostor: not a real doctor and not originally a psychologist or a psychiatrist at all."

It was easy to understand the resistance a man of this type would arouse in Hildesheimer, thought Michael, remembering the old man's words about the single exception to the rule. There was something offputting in the man's demonstrative, exaggerated frankness, as if he was saying: "Look, here are all my shortcomings laid out for you. I've nothing worse to confess, so please accept me as I am."

Women were probably attracted to a man like him, who aroused all Michael's own hunting instincts. Underneath the pathetic facade he sensed the existence of snares and dangers. His expression did not change as he inquired: Where, exactly, had Linder spent Friday night and the early hours of Saturday morning?

Linder glanced at his watch and said that he would have to leave if he wanted to get home in time for his next patient.

In the most formal tone in his repertoire and with all the civility of a British civil servant, Michael explained that he could not allow him to leave and suggested that he cancel all his appointments for the rest of the morning. The reaction was virulent. Things were said about "this country," where you got screwed for behaving like a good citizen and the only way to survive was to "shut up and mind your own business," and how in God's name did he expect him to inform his patients of last-minute cancellations; after this morning's headlines they were probably all hysterical anyway, and why the hell couldn't it wait?

At this point Michael informed him that the description of his missing pistol coincided with that of the pistol that had been found in the vicinity of the Institute, and the serial number was identical too. His tone was unchanged: calm and formal. He maintained a poker face as he added that Dr. Linder must surely realize the extent to which this implicated him in the investigation and understand that it was impossible to do without his presence at the moment. The telephone rang.

The ballistics laboratory was on the line, with the news (unofficial, of course) that the pistol was, in all probability, the one that had been used to shoot Neidorf. The probability would increase, they said, when the bullet arrived, and the official reply would be forthcoming in one week's time. Michael did not utter a word during the conversation, except for "Thank you" at the end. He did not take his eyes off Linder, who appeared excessively tense. His hands were shaking and his face was pale, paler than it had been when he came into the room.

In a cracked voice, he asked if he could at least use the phone. The question sounded familiar, the tone too, and Michael reminded himself to inquire into the telephone call that had been made from the Institute the day before.

Linder dialed a number and spoke at length to someone called Dina. He dictated names and telephone numbers and asked her to make the cancellations. She was to hang a note on the door for the ten o'clock patient if she couldn't reach him in time, and to answer the doorbell even if it didn't ring at her hours. His patients were to be told that he was alive and well but that an act of God had prevented him from coming to work. Here he sent a look at once mocking and offended toward Michael, who didn't blink an eye but rubbed his cheek with his hand, feeling the bristles that were still there and telling himself that he hated electric shavers.

A question was put to Linder, which he answered dryly and shortly: "The Russian Compound," after which he said "Thanks a lot" and put down the phone.

Michael repeated his previous question, and Linder mumbled: "You want an alibi, like in detective stories?" and lit a cigarette from the pack he took out of his pocket, neglecting to offer one to Michael. As he did so, he protested: "But you've got it all written down there; I said it all yesterday. Don't you remember?"

Michael did not react.

"We had friends over on Friday night for supper. I didn't leave the house at all; in our family I'm the cook. They left around two in the morning, two hours too late as far as I was concerned. It wasn't even interesting: colleagues of my wife's."

Michael asked for names and addresses and wrote everything down carefully. The tape recorders weren't always reliable. Finally he inquired: "What did you eat?"

Linder stared at him incredulously and then indignantly, but when Michael did not retract the question, he said: "First course stuffed tomatoes; main course leg of lamb with rice and pine nuts; lettuce salad . . . shall I go on?"

Michael, who was writing down every word, nodded without taking his eyes off Linder, who continued: "Dessert fruit salad, and coffee and cake, of course. You want the wine too?"

"No need," said Michael without reacting to the sarcasm. "And afterward, when the guests left?"

"Afterward it was late. Daniel couldn't sleep; I don't know why. Maybe he's developing something. Daniel's my son. He's four years old. Dalya, my wife, was sleeping, and it was my turn to go to him. I was with Daniel until nearly ten. Dalya was sleeping; she never has any problems about sleeping."

"Where were you with him?" asked Michael, as if the question were printed down on the report in front of him.

"Where do you think I was from six o'clock in the morning? At first in the house: games, stories, breakfast. Then in the yard. It was cold." Here there was a digression about back pains and the difficulties of playing ball when your back hurt. And a detailed description of how he sat on a tree stump and caught the ball.

The hostile note disappeared. Once again Linder went into unasked-for details in a humorous, friendly way, as if he wanted to be as cooperative and helpful as possible.

The police psychologist had once remarked to Michael, as they sat together in the café on the corner, that some people had a comprehensive sense of guilt. They felt the need to incriminate themselves, and therefore they behaved like Raskolnikov, "even though they haven't committed any crime. They need to ingratiate themselves," the psychologist explained. Now Michael reminded himself that analysts were human beings who had studied a certain subject and that this did not endow them with absolute control or absolute awareness of their motives. Outside working hours and when they themselves were the subject under investigation, they didn't look any better than anybody else.

He interrupted Linder, who had gone on to the issue of parent-children relationships in general, and asked: "And who saw you with the child?" Linder said that there were only four apartments in the building, and he didn't know if anyone had looked out the window and seen them. Michael stood up, saying, "Just a moment, please," and went to look for Tzilla. He found her in the next room, where they usually held their morning meetings, and asked her to phone Linder's wife at the Israel Museum, where she worked, and ask her about Friday night and Saturday morning. "Take this—it's his version. And then talk to the neighbors. Get hold of a car: you'll have to go to the museum and then to Arnona, on the other side of town. I want you to finish with the neighbors before he gets home."

He returned to his room, where he found Linder staring into space, sat down briskly behind the desk, and asked about his relations with Dr. Neidorf.

Here Linder grew more hesitant, weighing his words and choosing them carefully. It was evident that he had often brooded about the subject, without arriving at a formula that satisfied him. In the end he revealed that he had not been one of her admirers. It was clear from what he said that there had been no love lost between them.

Without changing his tone, Michael asked Linder how he felt about the fact that Dr. Neidorf was the obvious person in line to replace Professor Hildesheimer as head of the Training Committee.

Linder burst out laughing. He congratulated Ohayon on his social intuition. But there was no need to go overboard. The Training Committee was certainly a very important body—they formulated policy, they made the rules—but hardly important enough to murder for in order to become its head. Anyway, he added more seriously, he did not think that he was slated for election to the committee—even without Neidorf at its head. Detecting bitterness, Michael asked why.

Linder took a deep breath and sighed. He began to say that there were internal matters related to the profession that were hard to explain, but Michael, who was able by now to predict the other's reactions, kept quiet, and Linder, unable to endure the silence, was drawn into a detailed explanation of what he called "professional differences in outlook and so on" between himself and those he referred to, ironically, as "the pillars of the Institute." The term *enfant terrible* also came up.

Glancing at his watch again, Linder said that patients didn't like sudden cancellations. "It makes them tense and anxious," he explained to Michael, who found himself thawing a little and said he was sorry but sometimes it couldn't be avoided and that perhaps they could get back now to the moment of the pistol's disappearance, upon which Linder hastily corrected him, saying that it was out of the question for him to commit himself to any specific moment. He could only say that the night before the party, the pistol was in the drawer, and that he hadn't opened it since then. At Michael's request, he sketched a plan of the apartment and showed him where the bedroom was.

"Who knew that you had a pistol?" asked Michael, and picked up the pen, only to put it down again at the reply: "Who didn't?" Linder explained apologetically that he had often shown off the pistol as a work of art, and when he hadn't actually displayed it he had spoken about it and told the story of how and why it had been acquired.

Michael asked for a list of the guests at the party. He had assumed that it was an ordinary party, and he felt his muscles tighten when Linder said that it had been a party with a special character. At his request, Linder began to describe it. After a candidate "presented his case" and the vote was taken, it was usual to throw a party in his honor; usually the last member to be accepted held the party for the new member. The new member was the one who drew up the guest list, which actually included everybody, especially the members of his class, or year.

This time it was impossible for the previously accepted candidate to hold the party—there wasn't enough room in his house—and since he, Linder, had developed an especially close relationship with the class in question, and Tammy was almost a member of the family, he had volunteered to have the party. It wasn't a surprise party, and everyone tried to come. The popularity of the candidate was measured by the number of guests. Yes, people from outside the Institute were invited too, although not many, only really close friends. To Tammy's party only Yoav had been invited, a close friend of hers. Actually, it was through Yoav that Tammy had come to him, Linder, for supervision. A funny coincidence, because it was Yoav who had acquired the pistol for him, back in '67. But that—the close friendship with Tammy and himself—was the beginning and end of Yoav's connection with the Institute. Linder was smiling slyly, his face less pale. "He thinks it's all nonsense," he said.

Michael asked Linder whom he had phoned from the Institute.

It was Yoav, Linder admitted. He was a close friend—"and I had invited him to come around for beer and sausages to wash away the taste of the Saturday-morning lecture and Training Committee meeting, but under the circumstances, I had to put him off." Here Linder remarked that Michael was a dangerous man and asked him how he remembered.

In response Michael asked if he, Linder, had difficulties in remembering information connected with a patient's problems.

Linder laughed out loud and said that he had never thought of the two things—police work and analysis—as related fields but there was something to it.

Michael took up his pen and asked again who the people at the party were. Linder said that he could no doubt remember their names if Ohayon insisted but that he had a full and exact list at his clinic, and he added sarcastically that if he was ever allowed to go back there, he would be happy to put it at the chief inspector's disposal.

"Why have you got a list?" asked Michael suspiciously. "Surely it's rather unusual to make a list of the people invited to a party?"

"Ah," said Linder, "but it wasn't an ordinary party, although there was dancing at the end; it was really a professional affair, and Tammy dictated the list of the people she wanted me to invite."

Michael stood up and told Linder that he would now go with him to identify the pistol, which would remain in the possession of the police for the time being—"Trial exhibit?" asked Linder ingenuously, and Michael began to like him—and then they would drive to his clinic and go over the list of party guests.

They traveled in Michael's police car, which induced in Linder a childish glee, deriving, he explained, from the wish to shock the bourgeois inhabitants of Rehavia out of their complacency.

The clinic was in a quiet, tree-lined street, and Michael was anticipating how it would be furnished. Linder kept murmuring about his amazement that the pistol that had been found was indeed his pistol.

On the door they found the note that Linder had dictated over the phone to his partner in the clinic. In reply to Michael's question, he explained that she was in the final stages of her candidacy, just before certification by the Training Committee. Of all the senior analysts, he was the only one who failed to maintain strict class distinctions, for he couldn't see any harm in sharing his clinic with a candidate at the end of her training. Although, he admitted, he had taken her in only after she had stopped getting supervision from him. "Nor can I see any harm in being on close terms with my supervisees," he hurried to add, "especially when they're as pretty as she is."

"And what about with your patients?" asked Michael.

"Ah, patients—that's another story entirely. Although with them too, according to Hildesheimer's standards, I'm way out of line," said Linder in a defiant tone.

They sat in the two armchairs, between them the little table with the box of tissues and the ashtray. In the corner stood the couch, a rubber mat at its foot. Behind it was the analyst's easy chair. The pictures were dim, the desk dark and heavy.

Michael asked himself if the rules for furnishing the room were written down in some book of regulations. The differences in the personalities of the analysts were expressed only in the color schemes. Here the couch was covered with a black fabric. Michael smiled to himself at the thought that there were another hundred and fifty rooms almost like this one, and he addressed his thought in the form of a question to Linder, who came back from the kitchen with two cups of coffee. Linder laughed out loud—he had a warm, rich laugh—closed the door with a light kick, put the cups down on the little table, and replied while rummaging through the desk drawer, coming up in the end with two scruffy sheets of paper covered with a big scrawl. He suggested to Michael "not to say things like that to the others, because they won't be amused. Not that they haven't got a sense of humor. They have. But not about those things."

Then he grew more serious. "Yes, the rooms are quite similar. But the work is quite similar too; the analytic patient always lies on a couch, so you need a couch and a chair behind it. Every analyst does psychotherapy too, so they all have two armchairs. Most patients cry sometimes, so you need a box of tissues. You're right, though. I never thought about it before, but there really is something very funny about it."

Michael asked Linder if he could make a list of all the people who had been in his house over the past two weeks.

Nothing easier, Linder said. Until Saturday, no one at all had come to visit them: Daniel had been ill with mumps. "Even people who'd already had it were afraid of coming."

Michael looked at the list of party guests. About half the names were ticked off, and Linder explained that as the sign that they had accepted the invitation. Next to each ticked-off name something to eat was written in brackets, and Linder went on to explain that all the guests had agreed to bring something. Michael remarked that it seemed that more than half the people on the list weren't at the party.

"Yes," said Linder. "The Tel Aviv people come only if it's someone from their own year; the Haifa people don't come at all; and there are a few really old people who never come to anything: they're invited for the sake of politeness and good form. Hildesheimer is prepared to come only if he hasn't got any patients or supervisees there, which never happens, and Eva was abroad, and so were a few others; there was some congress or other at the end of March that they invented so they could take the expenses off their income tax returns before the first of April. But the forty who did come are considered a very respectable number."

"Did anyone know exactly where you kept the gun?" asked Michael.

There was an unhappy look on Linder's face. "It doesn't mean a thing," he said. "So what if someone knew where the gun was? Some of the people at the party were almost part of the family; everyone knows I haven't got a safe; everyone knows I've got a pistol—where else would I keep it?"

Michael kept quiet and waited.

"Okay. Yoav knew exactly where it was, but he wouldn't have had to wait for the party—he's always dropping in. And quite a few others too, and maybe I said something out loud and someone heard me; I don't always remember what I say when." He lit a cigarette, shivered slightly, and stood up to switch on an electric heater. The room was very cold.

Michael asked if by any chance he remembered who left the living room, who wandered around the house.

"Everybody, absolutely everybody; they were all over the place all the time. The coats were in the bedroom, and people kept on going in and out to take them off or put them on or get something out of their bags or whatever. Tammy went to peep at Daniel, who was sleeping in our bed, and a few other people did too. It wasn't the kind of party where people go off together and shut the bedroom door behind them."

Michael asked cautiously if he knew anything about Neidorf's relations with the people at the party.

Linder began to say something, changed his mind, sipped his coffee, glanced at the list, which Michael had placed in his outstretched hand, raised his eyes, and began to say in a different, quiet, hesitant tone that he knew a lot of facts about the people at the party. He knew who the candidates were being analyzed by, who they were getting supervision from, but none of this meant anything, in his opinion. None of them could have murdered her. What motive could they possibly have had?

"You don't understand." His voice grew stronger, and there was now a note of passionate conviction in it. "In their eyes the woman was a paragon of perfection. You couldn't say a word against her. They wouldn't even let me make a joke at her expense. And it's quite inconceivable that a patient in analysis would physically attack his analyst. We're not talking about psychotics here, people who're mentally ill, where anything is theoretically possible. We're talking about healthy people who've got problems with themselves, and they're all in analysis. Everyone at the Institute has analysis to improve his professional abilities; it's an essential condition of our work."

On the other side of the wall, they heard a muffled sound of voices and footsteps, the noise of a door opening and closing. Linder explained that Dina had accompanied a patient to the door and that the next one would probably be there in a minute. The doorbell rang, footsteps and a creaking door were heard, and then dead silence.

"No, Dr. Linder," said Michael quietly, "however painful it is, I have to tell you that even people regarded as healthy can sometimes surprise us. And precisely the people we look up to as models of perfection, precisely those people—as you should know better than I do—are sometimes the targets of attack. And what we're dealing with here, unfortunately, is murder, and I'm asking you for your help."

Linder smoked in silence. The dark circles under his round eyes emphasized his pallor. He took a tissue out of the box on the shelf under the little table and wiped beads of sweat from his forehead.

"Look," said Michael, "just help me to reconstruct her weekly work schedule, the patients' hours and the candidates' hours. Don't think for the moment about who might be a suspect, about who you might be betraying. Only about her work schedule. What do you say?"

Linder cleared his throat, tried to speak, cleared his throat again, and tried again. His voice was hoarse when he said: "Okay, but I'm sure I don't know them all. Only some of them."

And then his eyes lit up, and he cried: "But you'll be able to find it all in her diary, in her notes. Why waste time on guessing here with me?"

Michael explained that he would need details about the people; her notes were beside the point at the moment. He said nothing about his visit to her house.

With a sigh, Linder took a sheet of paper out of his desk drawer, handed it to Michael, invited him with a gesture to move to the wooden desk chair, and said: "The best thing is to draw up a timetable. I often talked to Eva about her work load. I know, as do a lot of other people, that she worked eight or nine hours a day, except Tuesdays, when she only worked six, because in the afternoon she taught at the Institute. And on Fridays she only worked six hours too."

Like a diligent pupil, Michael drew a timetable with days and hours, then he rested his chin on his hand and waited.

"Okay, let's see. We'll begin with supervisions. Only one hour a week for every supervisee. I don't know what days and what hours, but that's not so important. First of all, Dina is—I mean was—in supervision with her, right at the end. Yesterday, after the lecture, they were supposed to approve her case presentation and also another candidate's, from Dina's year; what's his name . . . ?" Linder took a printed list out of another drawer, and Michael, craning his neck, saw that it was a list of the Institute members and candidates, identical to the one he had found in Neidorf's house the day before. Linder ran rapidly through the list, his finger stopping at a certain point on the page. "Dr. Giora Biham."

From then on, Linder consulted the printed list, and Michael slowly wrote name after name on his table. There were six supervisees. "Which is a hell of a lot," said Linder, a note of bitterness creeping into his voice again. Michael asked for an explanation.

"Look, she's got—had—forty-six hours a week; I know exactly. On Sunday she worked eight hours, on Monday nine, on Tuesday six, on Wednesday nine, on Thursday eight and on Friday six. Add it up. She always took a break between one and four, except on Tuesdays and Fridays, when she worked right through. Six supervisees in forty-six hours doesn't leave a lot of time for analysands. Every analysis means four hours a week. And there were psychotherapies too—not too many, we'll see in a minute—which is two hours a week each."

Linder's finger ran down the list again, he read out names, and the table filled up with Michael's neat handwriting. Eight analyses, eight names fitted in four times a week, all of them Institute candidates. Eight squares were empty.

"Okay," said Linder, "in the eight hours left, there may be one analysis I don't know about, of someone from outside, but I can hardly believe that, because Eva had a waiting list of two years, and there are only five training analysts in Jerusalem altogether, and she always insisted that the Institute people came first, because it was inconceivable for there to be demands on the one hand and conditions that made it impossible for the candidates to fulfill them on the other. Typical, of course. Always so fair and decent!"

Michael said nothing. During the morning he had learned that the best way to get information from Linder was simply to keep quiet. Linder would take care to fill the gap.

"So I imagine that the eight hours left are psychotherapy, which can be done in two sessions a week by conservative analysts and once a week by anyone more flexible. Which group do you think Dr. Neidorf belonged to—I'll give you three guesses."

Michael noticed that the more the squares filled up with names, the grumpier Linder grew. The corners of his mouth drooped, like a resentful child's, and his finger drummed irritatingly on the list of names in front of him. Michael asked, with as must tact as he could muster, how many hours a week Dr. Linder himself worked.

"The same number, maybe even a little more, about forty-eight hours a week. But I have only one analysis from the Institute. I'm not a training analyst," he added as if to forestall the next question, "and a candidate has to get special permission from the Training Committee to come to me for analysis."

The expression on his face prevented Michael from pursuing the subject any further for the moment. He made a mental note to find out what Linder had done to get into the Institute's bad books. He could make a few guesses already. There was something so childish and exposed about the man that it was hard for Michael to imagine him sitting behind the couch and listening in silence.

But he couldn't believe that was the whole story. Not after his meeting with Hildesheimer. Hildesheimer must have other, more substantial reasons.

"In short"—Linder raised his voice—"Eva was a training analyst and a training supervisor and everything else you can think of, and so much in demand that there were candidates who refused patients for analysis until she was free to give them supervision. So I can't believe that she was giving analysis to anyone from outside, and I know all the inside people who were with her in analysis. The eight hours left over must have been psychotherapy hours that she was giving to people from outside, but I myself don't know anyone who was in therapy with her."

Michael folded the sheet of squared paper in half, and then, as if having second thoughts, unfolded it again and spread it out on the desk and asked Linder if he could tell him anything about her relations with the people on the list.

"Yes, of course I can. They all worshiped the ground she walked on. I myself think that there was something nauseating about it. You can think I'm jealous if you like"—he fended off an attack that Michael had no intention of making—"but that doesn't change the fact that there was something nauseating about it. The woman was even more of a paragon than Ernst, and believe me, they don't make people like Ernst anymore."

It took Michael a while to realize that he was talking about Hildesheimer. He looked curiously at Linder, who appeared to be absorbed in a world of his own private thoughts.

"But beyond my jealousy, which I don't deny, I have to say that Ernst has qualities of innocence and pure-heartedness and compassion that Eva Neidorf lacked completely. You understand"—his gaze fixed itself on a point on the wall opposite the desk—"it's not only that she didn't have a sense of humor, and believe me, she didn't; she didn't have compassion for any kind of deviance either, not really."

The chief inspector asked how she could have been so good an analyst and such a sought-after supervisor if she lacked compassion; how did Dr. Linder explain it? He took care to ask the question in a curious, interested tone, as if he had no doubts about the truth of what Linder had said.

"Ah," said Linder, "I see that you understand. Yes, you're right, it's impossible to be good at our work without feeling compassion, without being flexible, okay, but I wasn't talking about patients, or even about supervisees; with them she did have compassion and flexibility: that's what they say, and that's what came out in the clinical examples she gave in her lectures. But that's not what I was talking about. I was talking about something else, something hard to define. You understand"—he looked at Michael again—"in our profession there are all kinds of ways of getting around the difficulties with other people that we have in our daily lives. You're so protected in the analytic situation; you know how helpless the patient is. He comes to you for help, and it's sometimes the same with the supervisees. Eva had a proprietary feeling about her patients and her supervisee. Within the framework she accepted their mistakes, but outside it she was merciless. Look at the subject of the lecture she was going to give on Saturday, for example, and more than that I can't explain."

Michael looked at Linder and thought that he understood. There was a charm in his gratuitous frankness, perhaps not only in the eyes of women. But it didn't work on Neidorf, nor did it, apparently, on Hildesheimer.

"And in addition to the admiration you spoke of, can you tell me anything else about her relations with the people on the list?" Michael pointed to the sheet of paper spread out in front of him.

"Nothing I can think of. She kept her distance."

"And relations with people outside the Institute? Friends—women friends? Men?"

He didn't believe, said Linder, that she had had any men since her husband's death. She was a flower with a notice on it saying "Don't Touch." In spite of her beauty, there was something sexless about her, but perhaps it was a question of taste. About her women friends and social life he knew nothing. He didn't know anyone outside the Institute who had any contact with her. And inside the Institute— Hildesheimer. And perhaps also Nehama Zold, a member of the Training Committee. And years ago, before her marriage, perhaps, Voller had been head over heels in love with her. "He never really got over it completely," said Linder, and smiled.

Michael remembered Voller, who was also a member of the Training Committee. He thought that he would have to talk to the two of them too. His head ached and his body ached. The air was thick with cigarette smoke. Both of them were smoking. The big window was closed, and the electric heater gave off an unpleasant warmth. He thought that his physical malaise was the result of accumulated fatigue.

He wanted to get home, to bed. But he sat up straight in his chair and shook his head, as if he had just come out of a shower, and asked about the lecture.

There were printed copies, probably hundreds, said Linder dismissively. Why speculate if Chief Inspector Ohayon could simply read it, and if there was anything he didn't understand, and presumably there would be—he didn't understand everything (stressing the "every"), after all—he, Linder, would be glad to explain. "Ernst always has a copy, so he can go over it and comment before the lecture. I myself, if you were about to ask, never laid eyes on it. I wasn't in her confidence, as they say."

Michael was about to say something in explanation, but as he was wondering how to put it, there was a sound of footsteps and the creak of the door opening and shutting outside. Linder stood up, and without asking, Michael opened the door of the room. A wave of cold blew in from the passage, and then the beautiful Dina Silver entered the room.

The first thought that came into Michael's head was about shaving. Why hadn't he had a proper shave?

When Linder introduced them, Michael noticed that her face was clouded with anxiety. He was used to seeing anxiety on people's faces when he met them in his professional capacity.

She said, "How do you do," and looked at Linder inquiringly. While Linder was busy explaining that he had been asked to assist Chief Inspector Ohayon, Michael—who noted that he omitted to mention the pistol—examined her. The red dress she was wearing, of some soft, flowing material, was in his opinion too thin for such a cold day, but it certainly suited her pale face, her gray eyes, and the black hair which was cut short in a straight line, in a style that emphasized the whiteness and fragility of her neck. Her cheekbones were high, her mouth was full, perhaps a little too fleshy, and except for the thick ankles and blunt, uncared-for hands (he noted the bitten nails), she was perfect.

He hoped that his admiration was not evident. He always tried to control his facial expressions, and his achievements were impressive. Or so, at any rate, said Tzilla, who claimed that he could make a fortune as a professional poker player.

Linder reminded Michael that Dina was one of Dr. Neidorf's supervisees, "the one I told you about, whose presentation was going to be voted on Saturday—" He broke off. Michael remembered. He also noticed the change in Linder's manner. The spontaneity of the last hour had been replaced by tension, and the look traveling between himself and Dina seemed full of suffering. Again the bags under his eyes stood out dark and swollen.

Linder asked Michael if he had finished with him, and Michael said, "Nearly," and suggested that Dina join them.

"I've only got five minutes before my next patient arrives," she said in a soft, slow voice.

Michael insisted.

She sat on the couch and crossed her legs. Michael thought that boots would have solved the problem of her ankles. He couldn't understand why she should have chosen to wear the shoes she had on, whose high heels improved the situation only marginally.

In reply to his question, she said that she had indeed been in supervision with Dr. Neidorf, for four years. "Our relations were excellent. I learned a good deal from her and admired her greatly." She spoke slowly. Every word was stressed, every syllable. The pauses between words were longer than usual. But her voice expressed no feeling whatsoever.

Linder sat and looked at her. By the expression on his face and the increasing nervousness of his manner, Michael guessed that he, too, had noticed something odd about her way of speaking, although in his case he appeared to be registering a phenomenon with which he was already familiar.

The supervision, continued Dina after a short pause, was about to come to an end, on condition of course that the Training Committee approved her case presentation.

Michael asked if the word "condition" implied that there was any doubt about it.

"There are always doubts," she replied, a reply that incurred Linder's anger.

Her modesty was superfluous, he said sharply. There were no doubts, and there never had been. Everyone admired her work; he should know; he had been her supervisor.

Dina Silver folded her hands and said that whatever the objective situation, people were always tense when they submitted their request to present their case. She glanced at her watch.

Michael asked if she could remain with them a little longer.

"Only until the doorbell rings," she said unwillingly.

He showed her the names on his timetable and asked if she knew anyone else who had been in therapy with Dr. Neidorf.

The hand holding the page shook so much that she had to put it on her lap. She looked at the names intently and then raised her eyes to Linder and asked, ignoring Michael: "Did you know that she worked so many hours?"

Linder nodded and said that on the one hand she never stopped complaining about it, but on the other hand she couldn't resist the pressures. Michael asked what pressures he was referring to.

"When someone's a famous analyst, people are referred to him for treatment all the time. Friends and colleagues put pressure on him to take just this one, just that one, and it's sometimes very hard to refuse."

Dina Silver looked again at the page on her knees, and in the end said that she herself had referred someone to Neidorf for psychotherapy, and she knew that the person was, had been, in therapy with Neidorf twice a week, but she was not prepared to give her name without her consent. When the doorbell rang she leapt up, and saying that the chief inspector could get in touch with her later, she went out of the room and closed the door behind her.

Again there was a sound of footsteps in the passage, the door opening and closing, and a murmur of voices, and then a silence, which remained unbroken, because Linder's mood had changed completely and he hung his head and gazed at a point in the middle of the little rug at the foot of the couch.

Michael was obliged to ask his question twice: Had anything new occurred to him?

"No, no, of course not," exclaimed Linder in alarm, but his face showed a dejection and despair that had not been there before. Michael thought about two people as different as Neidorf and Linder both supervising Dina Silver. He asked Linder how the candidates coped with the differences in style.

"It's not just a question of style; it's a question of a general philosophy of life, of a different personality. Though the situation involves difficulties, it also has advantages. But Dina didn't have any problems. I'm sure she brought Neidorf more exact write-ups than she brought me. But you don't know about the write-ups, do you?"

"No," said Michael.

"Once a week the candidate comes to supervision with write-ups of the four hours of his patient's analysis. But the notes aren't made during the hour itself. Why? Because Ernst thinks that then the therapist pays more attention to his notes than to his patient. When are they made, you ask? After the hour. I think that writing up those sessions at the end of the day is the worst punishment in the world. And naturally I would forgive someone whose notes were occasionally brief or even nonexistent. But no one ever did that to Eva. Dina told me that she once came to her for supervision without write-ups and Eva reacted with an immediate interpretation of her motives. I told her that she should be grateful for getting something for nothing, but I don't think she ever dared go to her for supervision again without all her sessions properly written up."

Michael asked if his relations with Dina were close, and if she had adopted his "style."

Linder was silent for a long time. His reply was bitter. His relations with Dina had changed. Once he had been a source of comfort and support, to whom she came with her difficulties with patients, and also with professional and personal problems. But during the course of the past year she had grown away from him. She told him less about herself. The ghost of a smile crossed his face, and he said that she had apparently become independent, she had simply grown up, and this was hard for him to accept.

That's not it, thought Michael. There's something else. Perhaps he's not sure that she's on his side anymore. Perhaps he thinks that she's gone over to Neidorf's camp, something like that.

Dina Silver's name was on the party list, with the word "salad" written next to it, in pencil and in a small script, not Linder's.

Yes, he replied to Michael's question, she was at the party. And the salad too, of course. No, he didn't know if she had been in the bedroom. But yes, of course she had. Her coat: he remembered helping her to take it off and putting it in the bedroom, but he didn't remember getting it for her afterward. Michael was barking up the wrong tree, though. He had seen her for himself, hadn't he—all that fragility didn't go with handguns and shooting, not to mention the motive. What motive could she have had?

No, he didn't know what she was doing on Friday night or Saturday morning. Probably sitting in her big garden and having her breakfast in the sun. She had married money, serious money; he wouldn't be prepared to swear that she hadn't married with the object of being cared for and pampered for the rest of her life. Her husband was some archconservative, some judge. Maybe Michael had heard of him?

Michael had heard of him; he was even acquainted with him. A small, dry, pedantic man. And yes, an archconservative. One of the strictest judges the district had ever seen. He couldn't imagine that beautiful young woman in the same bed as the man everybody called "The Gavel" because he couldn't stand the slightest noise in court and was always hammering with his gavel. Michael calculated that her husband must be at least ten years older than she was. With unabashed curiosity, he asked Linder how old she was.

"Ah, you're interested too. Well, you're not the only one." Linder grinned and replied that she had turned thirty-seven last month, and apart from the money, he couldn't understand what she was doing with that "stuffed shirt" either. But she hadn't been in analysis with him, and she had never encouraged him to talk about it. She had been in analysis with the great man himself, he volunteered without being asked. Then he looked at his watch and said that he had to go and fetch Daniel from kindergarten. It was almost noon.

He stood up and switched off the heater, cleared the cups away, and ushered Michael out of the room. He looked worn out and defeated.

Linder was so preoccupied with his thoughts that he did not even notice when Michael made a detour, crossing all of Rehavia on the way back to the Russian Compound, and drove past Hildesheimer's house. The Peugeot van was there, its curtains drawn; one of his people was next to the open hood, and the other was at the window that faced Hildesheimer's front door.

9

As Joe Linder got out of the car, the radio started crackling. The chief was looking for him, he wanted him in his office right away, they were waiting for him, where was he anyway, asked the unfamiliar voice at the control center. "I'll be there in half a minute," replied Michael as he parked his car next to the Greek Orthodox church, noticing the hue of its pale green dome. It seemed to him that the gold-green color was fading along with the hopes of the Arab families crouched next to the fence surrounding the church and the old stone court building.

He took the stairs two at a time, making straight for the C.O.'s office, the biggest in the building. In the little anteroom, he took the secretary's hand in a manner that led her to expect it to be kissed. He bent down and kissed her hand, although he had not intended doing so, and said a few words about the daring new color of her nail polish. With part of his mind he observed the little scene, which might have been lifted out of a James Bond movie, mockingly. But for all his irony, he always took care to keep on friendly terms with the secretaries. The women in Control all had a soft spot for him. He didn't have to make any promises or tell any lies, only to be nice and listen to their stories so he could remember them next time. His attitude toward them was rather paternalistic, and sometimes he felt sorry for them, without knowing why. There wasn't anything calculating about it—the displays of attention came quite naturally to him—but there were, of course, secondary benefits. Now Gila, the C.O.'s secretary, gave him a big brown envelope. "Something Eli Bahar left for you." Michael opened the envelope and took out the report from the pathology lab and a note from Eli summing up what he had been told by Forensics.

"You've got a couple of minutes. He's on the phone. Here, you can sit down if you like," said Gila, and she took a bulging file off the chair next to her desk.

In the report he found everything he had expected to find: a photograph of the deceased sitting on the armchair, a sketch of her position, a close-up of the wound, a description of the angle of the shot. He paged rapidly through the pathologist's report, which put her death at somewhere between seven and nine on Saturday morning; there were remains of breakfast in her stomach. Michael loathed these details estimating the hour of death according to stomach contents. In any case, he didn't believe they could ever be absolutely accurate. The temperature in the room had been taken into account, and also the position of the corpse. There were a lot of medical terms, which he had learned to skip, and a lot of stuff about the range of fire.

Additional details, on a separate page, looked as if they had been dictated to Eli by Forensics. No clear fingerprints had been found on the victim's body, but there were glove prints on her cheek and her hand. The victim had apparently already been dead, then placed in the position in which she had been found. There were signs that the body had been dragged from the door to the chair, but no traces of blood had been found. In the room itself, a blue thread had been found near the body, a thread that might have been torn from an article of clothing. The words "estimated," "probable," and "presumed" appeared throughout. There was no way of telling, of course, if the thread was related to the murder. It had to be taken into account that the Institute was cleaned only once a week, on Wednesdays. There were many fingerprints on all the door handles. Anything found in any of the rooms could belong to anyone.

Traces of the victim's lipstick were on the cup containing coffee dregs found in the kitchen.

The firearm had been identified, not yet finally, as belonging to Dr. Joe Linder. The bullet removed from the victim's body appeared, on a superficial examination, to be identical to the one removed from the wall in the Margoa Hospital and to the bullets remaining in the chamber of the firearm.

Michael went into the office, where the Jerusalem Subdistrict commander, Ariyeh Levy, was sitting behind a big desk, studying copies of the report and photographs taken at the scene of the crime. He said nothing to Michael, who sat down in the chair opposite him, but wordlessly passed him the photographs, one after the other. Michael's direct superior, Emanuel Shorer, head of the Jerusalem Investigations Division, came in and sat down. Michael handed him the brown envelope, and he began to study its contents.

Superintendent Emanuel Shorer was about to be promoted, and word had it that the promotion was going to be announced within the next couple of months. Michael Ohayon was the obvious candidate for his job: this, too, was common knowledge in the corridors of the Russian Compound. From the beginning they had enjoyed a relationship of mutual understanding and affection. Michael liked and admired Shorer in spite of his rough manners and harsh tongue. "Under that elephant hide," he once said to Tzilla, who complained, "lies true delicacy of spirit, and one day it will be revealed to you. Just be patient."

He himself had been a witness to that delicacy eight years before. It was during his first investigation. One of the team headed by Shorer, he had fallen into a trap set by a false alibi, with the result that the investigation had taken much longer than necessary. Shorer had given him a long talking-to and concluded by saying that there were moments in life when it was better to put one's trust in the human race than to be insanely suspicious. But you had to be able to distinguish between the demands of the profession and your own personality and to act, on occasion, in contradiction to your natural instincts, "probing most carefully just where your faith is most implicit." He hadn't even reprimanded him. Patiently he had described the slow, sometimes excruciatingly slow, procedures governing the proper conduct of a successful criminal investigation. They had been in tough situations together, spent days and sleepless nights together. They had always found subjects of common interest to talk about. From the beginning Emanuel Shorer had treated him with a fatherly tolerance, which had infuriated their co-workers until they got used to it. Michael was sorry that he was going to lose him, in spite of the professional advancement he himself expected to gain by his superior's promotion.

His relations with Levy, on the other hand, were strained. Without understanding how this pattern had come to dominate their relationship, Michael was always on the defensive with him, every encounter somehow giving rise to anger and embarrassment. He always felt an obscure need to apologize to Ariyeh Levy. And in the future he would have to work with him, under him, in this tense, strained atmosphere. This, too, was a reason to regret Shorer's departure.

Michael extracted a cigarette from the pack he had placed on the desk, lit it, and began to talk, as if to himself.

At first, speaking quietly and slowly, he summed up the events of Saturday morning. He described the structure of the Institute, the formal relationships among the members, and the few nuances of a subtler nature that he had succeeded in grasping. He explained the terms "candidate" and "training analysis" and told them about the supervisions, about the Saturday meetings. He described Hildesheimer and Linder. The Training Committee he defined as "the legislature and executive at once—the people in authority and the real power behind the Institute."

Then he told them about the pistol and its bizarre appearance at the hospital. Levy interrupted to ask him when it would be possible to question the patient, Dr. Baum, "anyone who might be able to tell us something about how it got there? And why didn't you get there sooner yourself?"

Michael told them about his trip to Tel Aviv, the meeting with the son-in-law, the conversation with Hildesheimer, the visit to Neidorf's house. "Our problem will be with the type of population involved," he summed up, after describing the search for the extra copy of the lecture.

"We've heard of their type before," said Levy, and drummed the desktop contemptuously. He recalled the case of the murdered mistress of a lawyer, who had been found guilty, and similar cases that had been solved in recent years. "Although, on second thought we'll be dealing here with all kinds of smart-asses of a kind we haven't encountered before. They're psychologists, after all. You'd better look out, Ohayon. Be careful they don't pull the wool over your eyes with their tricks."

"Actually," said Michael, "that's not what I meant at all. I wasn't talking about social status. I was referring to the fact that they're a very closed group, with very special laws and a special power structure. And the patients too: who knows what goes on in their sessions with their patients and their supervisees; it's all between them and the doorpost. And the disappearance of the lecture on the same day, and the list of all the people in therapy with her. I don't exactly know how we're going to reconstruct what happened. But one thing I'm sure of: the murder is connected to someone involved with her professionally. Probably, although not necessarily, someone from the Institute, but in any case someone in therapy or supervision with her. And now the whole lot's gone and disappeared—the lecture, the list of patients, the notes the old man claimed she kept in the place he showed me, and the diary. In short, everything that could have told us something about her professional connections."

For the first time, Shorer opened his mouth. "There's something I don't understand," he said. "You say the key to the house was missing from the key ring but the house was broken into anyway? How do you make sense of that?"

Michael said he didn't know yet, and he looked straight at Ariyeh Levy.

"A key and a break-in," mused Emanuel Shorer. "Either we're dealing with two different people here or someone's trying to put us off the scent. There may be two people involved. And something else. If someone took the key from the Institute, why didn't they take the whole bunch? Maybe to prevent us from getting to the house earlier. If you hadn't found the keys, you would have had the house put under surveillance, no?"

Michael reminded him that he hadn't found the keys. Hildesheimer had given them to him in the evening, when he went to see him at his house.

Levy showed less mercy than Shorer. He looked at Michael sharply and said: "I really can't understand why you didn't get onto the house right away. Apparently someone, the same person who shot her and took the key, went straight from there to the house and found the papers he was looking for. That's elementary, surely. What could you have been thinking of? Leaving the house like that, when the victim's keys were missing! Really! And afterward, as far as I can understand, someone broke in, someone else, who was looking for something and who wouldn't have broken in if there'd been a guard on the house."

Michael tried to defend himself by saying that he was concentrating on the scene of the crime and he wasn't thinking about keys or lecture copies or notes, and the situation at the Institute was chaotic, with all kinds of people and press milling around.

"Yes, but someone from Forensics should have got onto it and suggested putting a guard on the house or something," said Shorer, in an attempt to distract the C.O. from Michael's exclusive responsibility as head of the special investigating team. "And then"—he changed the subject—"I ask myself why at the Institute—why not shoot her at home?"

"That's it exactly!" explained Michael eagerly. "That's what I was getting at with all that background stuff about the Institute—that it had to be someone she wouldn't have been prepared to see at home. They've got all kinds of professional rules that would explain why not at home."

"Yes," said Shorer doubtfully, "but from what you said, I understood that she had a consulting room at home. Why not there?"

"Look, it was obviously Neidorf who decided on the place,"

said Michael, not understanding what his superior was getting at.

"No. What I meant was that the Institute is a risky place to plan a murder. Take that Gold, for instance, who came to arrange the chairs: he could easily have come a bit earlier. And the murder was definitely planned in advance; the pistol was stolen weeks ago. Once you've stolen a pistol, you could be expected to plan things more carefully."

"Yes," said Michael, "but you're forgetting that she only got back to the country the day before yesterday. There probably wasn't any alternative."

"No, I wasn't forgetting. I remember." Shorer put his hands palms down on the desk. "And that's precisely the point: whoever shot her must have had some very urgent reason for doing it where and when he did—there must have been something he had to prevent her from doing. And when we're looking for motive, we should keep that in mind."

Michael nodded in agreement. The C.O. looked from one to the other of them, and Michael could see the moment when the light dawned. "In other words, you think we should concentrate on the lecture?" Levy asked doubtfully, and each of them nodded in turn. Michael sighed and complained that not only did nobody know what was in the lecture; there were even difficulties about locating the list of people in treatment with her.

Shorer chewed a burned match and, gazing at the big window, through which he could see the ivy climbing up to the third floor, remarked that if the deceased was as honest as everybody had insisted she was, she must have had an accountant, who would have copies of all her receipts and whatever else was necessary to discover who her patients were.

Michael looked at him and smiled. It was clear that this was an idea that had not yet occurred to him. After a pause, he said that he would go and see her accountant as soon as he had spoken to her daughter, who was arriving in the country today.

"So you think there was something in the lecture that might have threatened somebody?" asked Levy, picking up the phone and asking Gila for coffee.

"Yes," Michael confirmed, "that's what I think. But there's another possibility: that she had information dangerous to someone who wanted to prevent its discovery."

"The two things aren't mutually exclusive. She may have been about to disclose dangerous information in her lecture," said Shorer and began breaking matchsticks in half.

"Tell me, my learned friend, are you saying that we should discount all the usual motives—money, love—right from the start, just like that?" asked the C.O., as Gila entered the room and deposited a plastic tray with three mugs on the desk. Michael smiled and gave her an invisible wink. The others picked up their mugs without acknowledging her.

"I'm not sure yet, but that's what it looks like to me," replied Michael hesitantly, gazing at the rain that had begun to fall, big drops splashing against the windowpane.

"Because it wouldn't be the first time, you know: setting everything up to point in one direction, when all the time—"

"Which is exactly why I went into all that stuff about the Institute. She wouldn't have met anyone from outside there. Not on Saturday morning, not before her lecture. We looked; there weren't any signs of breaking and entering. Either she opened the door to someone, or that someone had a key. Not to mention the pistol, the party, et cetera."

For once, the C.O. didn't take offense at being interrupted. The atmosphere in the room was peaceful, each of them pursuing his own thoughts. Michael was exhausted; Shorer looked depressed; and Levy fell in with the general mood. Maybe it's the rain, thought Michael, aware of the fact that the atmosphere was more relaxed than usual.

"What about this character Linder? Who's checking his alibi?" inquired Levy, and he raised his eyes as the Jerusalem Police spokesman came into the room with the intelligence officer who had been co-opted onto the team. They both looked tired. Gila came in behind them with two more mugs of coffee, and the spokesman, Gil Kaplan, a fair-haired young man who had just been appointed to the post, fingered his mustache and said he was being pestered by the press all the time with demands for the "latest developments." "I can't get them off my back, and they've already gotten hold of the details and begun to pester people—who for once, I must say, are not letting them have anything for publication."

Ariyeh Levy remarked coldly that if they had arrived at the conference on time, perhaps they would have been able to understand why. In a few sentences, Michael sketched in the background: patients, procedures, and the need to maintain strict confidentiality.

The intelligence officer, Danny Balilty, wanted to know what had happened about Linder and the pistol, and was told that he had an alibi. "Gil"—Balilty defended the spokesman—"came late because the reporters wouldn't let him go; we're dependent on their goodwill not to publish the name of the murder victim, so we can't afford to upset them, and I want to tell you"—he paused for a minute to take a sip of coffee, pulled a face, and went on talking—"that I've never seen anything like it before. All the people involved, but *all* of them—everyone involved in the case, all those psychologists—we've got nothing on them. Absolutely nothing! No information, no charges, no traffic reports; a few handgun licenses, and that's it. I only found one civil suit about a property purchase: someone bought a house and sued the person who sold it to him. Apart from that, there's nothing on any of them. If anyone had told me there were so many law-abiding citizens in the country, I would have asked him why we had to work so hard!"

Balilty finished his coffee and wiped his thick lips with the back of his hand. Then he stood up and straightened his trousers, tucked his shirt into his belt, over which a little paunch swelled, and sat down again, carefully smoothing a tress of hair over his balding head. He folded his arms, sighed, and said: "What a job—I'm telling you!"

An expression of mild disgust passed over the C.O.'s face as he asked what he could tell them about Linder. Balilty explained that the minute it came out that the handgun belonged to Linder, he had run a full inquiry on him. Date of birth and date of immigration from Holland, address of his clinic, residential address, name of his first wife—"the lot, but apart from that I've got nothing on him. His best friend—you want to know who his best friend is? What's-his-name,

Yoav Alon, Colonel Alon, military governor of Edom! What can you say against a guy like that? None of them are even involved in politics. Neither left nor right."

"Well, the way things stand at the moment, you're going to have to examine the alibi of everyone who was at that party at Linder's place, and Linder too, with a magnifying glass, and the people who weren't at the party too: everybody connected with the case. I don't know, it may take years," said Shorer, and he threw a few matches into the wastebasket under the desk.

"We haven't got years!" Levy controlled himself with an effort and turned angrily to Michael. "And don't start giving me that song and dance about getting inside their heads. You know very well that I have to make out a report to my superiors now, and I don't have to tell you what Avital's like. Not to mention the press. Have you got any idea what a meal they're going to make of it? So don't start playing the professor here—this isn't a university, you know."

It was almost with a feeling of relief that Michael listened to the familiar words. The last sentence, which Levy utilized at every possible opportunity, signaled the approaching end of the conference.

After a short silence, Chief Inspector Ohayon explained that as he saw things at the moment, he would have to meet the victim's accountant, go around to the Margoa Hospital again, and begin the spadework of questioning everyone involved. He would put in a request for surveillance and telephone taps the minute he knew who the suspects were; meanwhile all he wanted was a round-the-clock guard on the old man.

Ariyeh Levy stood up, pushed back his chair, and asked on the inside line for the departmental investigations officer to be located and sent to his office pronto. The conference would continue, he announced, until they came up with a few more ideas. "What could Linder's motive be?" asked the intelligence officer. "What could any of their motives be?"

Michael told them about Linder's sense of professional bitterness. The spokesman said he doubted if that kind of grievance could provide a motive for murder. Michael agreed but explained that so far these were the only kinds of tensions that had surfaced.

"And what can you tell us about her, Eva Neidorf?" the C.O. asked Danny Balilty, who rummaged in his papers and began describing her life history: place of birth, high school in Tel Aviv, military service, marriage, children, life style, work, conversations with her neighbors, economic situation, and romantic liaisons: none. Nobody asked where he had obtained all this information.

Michael congratulated himself on having on his team the best intelligence officer in the history of the police force. Balilty had been a legend from the beginning. Suddenly Michael realized how tired he was, remembered that it was twenty-four hours since he had been home, eaten a proper meal, or changed his clothes. He had a long day ahead of him, he said. He simply had to go home first.

Emanuel Shorer went out of the room with him, patted his shoulder encouragingly, and said: "You remember the murder of the lady Communist? You remember how bogged down we got? Did you believe we'd ever solve it?" And then he patted him on the shoulder again. "And there was something else I wanted to say. Happy birthday, Chief Inspector Ohayon. What is it today?"

"Thirty-eight," replied Michael in embarrassment. He had forgotten all about it. He didn't even remember that it was Sunday today.

"So smile," commanded Shorer. "You're a babe in arms. You've got your whole life in front of you. What do you know about it? Ask an old man like me, who can't even remember when he hit forty, it was so long ago."

Michael was still smiling when he opened the door of his office. On the table he found a red rose in a plastic glass and a note: "You can reach me at home. I went to catch up on some sleep. Happy birthday. Details about what I got out of his wife and the neighbors later, in person. Everything confirmed. He's in the clear." The handwriting was Tzilla's.

All the parking places next to his apartment building were taken, and although he ran from the car to the front door, he was wet through. His flat was on the basement level, but it wasn't really a basement. The building was on a hillside of Givat Mordechai, and the basement floor was open to the air and the view of green hills and distant houses.

The moment he opened the door, he sensed someone's presence. Closing the door quietly and stepping inside, he cast his eyes over the little living room, the big blue easy chair, the sofa, the telephone, the bookcase, the striped rug. Nobody was there. Then he went into the bedroom and looked at Yuval, who was lying on the big bed, his shoes sticking out over the edge. The boy appeared to be sleeping, but Michael, who knew how lightly he slept, didn't believe it. He sat down beside him and stroked his curly head, observing the isolated hairs growing on his chin. No doubt about it, the child's grown, he thought. Further proof came in the form of the voice that emerged from the depths of the pillow, the breaking voice of an adolescent boy. Yuval, with his eyes still shut, said: "It's not enough to give somebody a key; you have to be home sometimes too. What kind of a father have I got?"

"Well, what kind?" asked Michael with a sigh. He could guess where it was going to end. He began getting undressed, and the boy lifted his head and looked at him without answering. "Come on, Yuval, give me a break; it's been a rough day, and yesterday too. Have a heart."

"I only wanted to give you a surprise, I even brought you a birthday present. It's your birthday today, isn't it?" said the boy, and sat up. "I thought we had date for last night. Didn't we agree that you'd get in touch?"

"And I'm delighted to see you, I really am. Thanks for the present, sorry about last night, but something came up and I couldn't make it, I couldn't even phone." As he spoke, he regretted every word that came out of his mouth. He knew he wasn't saying what Yuval wanted to hear, but the cold, fatigue, and hunger put him into an irritable mood, which he couldn't control.

"At least tell the truth, that you completely forgot, and don't say you couldn't," said Yuval, a hurt expression on his face. "There's no such thing as 'I couldn't'—if it was important to you, you could have." The ritual was familiar, the source well known to both of them, and Michael burst out laughing. The boy smiled too.

"You see that what your mother says can come in handy sometimes?" asked Michael on his way to the shower.

Yuval stood in the hall while his father showered. "You can come in if you like," Michael called when he turned off the water, and the boy sat on the edge of the bathtub and watched his father as he shaved, bending down to see his face in the mirror. He was wrapped in a big bath towel, and from time to time he used a corner of it to wipe away the steam that kept clouding the mirror.

"And how is she?" asked Michael, who usually avoided speaking to his son about his ex-wife and didn't know why he was breaking his usual silence on the subject now.

"She's okay," said Yuval, keeping any surprise he may have felt to himself. "She wants to go for a holiday abroad. For five weeks. Do you think I can stay here?"

"And what do you think?" replied Michael, scooping a blob of lather from his face and sticking it on the tip of the nose of his son, who grinned shyly and wiped it off.

"When exactly is this supposed to happen?" asked Michael, wiping the rest of the lather from his face.

"In April," said Yuval.

"What do you mean, April? Won't she be at the seder?"

The boy said no.

"And your grandfather, what does he say?" asked the father, regretting the words before they were out of his mouth.

"He's paying; you know how it is," said the boy with a sigh, and Michael, who knew exactly how it was, said nothing and went on wiping his face.

The Passover seder at his ex-father-in-law's house in the nouveau riche suburb of Neve Avivim was an unforgettable experience. Crystal dishes were taken out of glass-fronted cupboards; the diamond merchant and his wife, Fela, invited everyone they could think of. Nira had had to be there every year, with her son and her husband. Michael hadn't been at his mother's for the seder once after his marriage; he was simply unable to stand up to the pressure. Nira would send him to her father, and Youzek would put on his "after all these years and everything I've done for you" expression. There was the painful business of the marriage itself, which had taken place primarily because of "what people would say." "If you were so worried about her having an abortion," Michael had once challenged, "you could have helped her to have the baby; and if you didn't want anyone to know, you could have helped her to have an abortion. But no, you kept repeating that you haven't got anyone in the world but Nira, and at the same time you kept crying about what people would say. You had to have your cake and eat it too; she wasn't allowed to have an abortion, and I had to marry her."

Even today, eight years after the divorce, he felt waves of almost uncontrollable anger when he recalled the miserable scenes of his surrender to a blackmail unlike any other he had encountered.

Youzek, with his round little body and beady little eyes, was too shrewd to try and buy him with money or promises of partnership in the business. They met in a café across from the diamond exchange in Ramat Gan. The whole street smelled of chocolate from the Elite Candy Factory. Youzek kept repeating that he knew Michael was "a decent, responsible boy," who felt something "for our Nira, who is all we've got," etc., etc. After this meeting the marriage was a foregone conclusion. Michael couldn't stand up to them, especially not to Youzek. He tried to argue that they didn't love each other and was answered with contempt. "Love, shmove: married life is habit and compromise; all that talk about love doesn't last five minutes. I know what I'm talking about, believe me." Even though he didn't believe him, even though at the age of twenty-four he already knew that Youzek's married life was not the only model available and other possibilities existed as well, the marriage took place very soon afterward. They stood side by side in the Tel Aviv Hilton, overlooking the Mediterranean Sea, the bride in her white gown the only daughter of a diamond merchant, and the groom a second year university student from Morocco.

They tried to persuade him to change his name, but when he

referred to "my late father" they were shamed into silence. To their business acquaintances and distant relatives they introduced him as a gifted man of letters, a brilliant scholar. When the list of B.A. graduates appeared in the newspaper, including Ohayon, Michael, History (with distinction), they clipped it out. But when his name appeared on the list of M.A. graduates, they failed to save the article, even though now he was one of three students to graduate with distinction. By then there was already talk of divorce.

Michael looked again at Yuval, whose conception had been the cause of all that misery, and asked, stroking his hair: "So you remembered my birthday, did you? And you even bought me a present? And now you're punishing me, and I'm not going to get it? What did you buy me?"

With a pride he couldn't conceal, the boy held out a parcel, and Michael opened it curiously. It held John le Carré's *The Little Drummer Girl*, and on the flyleaf, in childish handwriting: "To Daddy, the big drummer, from your son Yuval, the little drummer boy."

The child's too sentimental, said Michael to himself for the thousandth time.

"You said you liked him," said Yuval, signs of anxiety appearing on his face.

Michael put the book down on the living room sofa and rumpled his son's hair, stroked his cheek, hugged him tightly. Yuval's effort to please him touched Michael deeply. He remembered the pictures Yuval drew for him when he was a small child, and all those obscure collages the boy would spend days cutting out of magazines and pasting onto pages.

Tactfully he asked about the inscription. "You'll understand after you've read it," said Yuval firmly, and Michael asked if he hadn't found the book difficult. "Yes, it wasn't easy, until I got into it. If you're referring to my age, then it wasn't difficult at all." His voice broke at the end of the sentence, and he blushed, shrugged his shoulders, and fell silent. Michael began reading the first page of the book, pretending not to notice Yuval, whose clumsy movements and breaking voice gave rise in him to a powerful desire to hug his son and tell him that it would pass, that he had been through the same thing, clumsy and acne-scarred, imprisoned in vague physical yearnings. But Michael had too much respect for his dignity to do any such thing, and the only protection he could offer him now was to ignore their common awareness of his growing body, his changing voice.

A woman with whom he had had a short affair in the last year of his marriage had once accused him of never being spontaneous, of calculating every move. She didn't know exactly how to answer his question: "Calculated to what end?" and could only say that he did things to please other people.

He was hurt, but later he often remembered what she had said, especially when people looked at him in surprise and asked, "How did you know?" sometimes in words and sometimes with their eyes. There was nothing that gave him greater happiness than a grateful and admiring look in another person's eyes.

When Yuval was small he would sometimes look at him with just that expression. Lately, however, Michael had begun to notice a skeptical gleam in his eye. But whenever he caught his father looking at him, he would quickly lower his eyes. And there were scenes too, typical adolescent scenes. Recently he had taken to accusing his father of hypocrisy. Afterward he would apologize, but Michael knew that he was referring to the same thing that the woman whose name he couldn't even remember had accused him of so many years before.

The telephone rang, and Yuval looked at it with loathing, sighed, picked up the receiver, listened for a minute, and passed it wordlessly to his father, who held it in one hand while trying with the other to touch his son, who evaded him and threw himself onto the sofa, where he lay on his back, staring despairingly at the ceiling.

"Yes," said Michael. "I'm glad you managed to get hold of me; I'm only here by chance."

"I'm at a public phone in Rehavia. I only wanted to report before the next shift takes over that nothing suspicious occurred. I've already reported to Control that everything's okay."

"Nothing at all?" Michael asked one of the two man guarding Hildesheimer's house.

"There was a lot of movement; there've been people here all morning, at one-hour intervals, but I understand that that's normal. And I've just seen the subject himself, fit as a fiddle, talking to some glamour girl in the street."

"Glamour girl?" Michael Ohayon repeated the word, which refused to fit in with the image of Dr. Hildesheimer.

"Yes, some dame who was hanging around in the street, strolling up and down, standing outside his house. He went out to the grocery and came back with a loaf of bread, not more than a minute ago, and met her in the street. A real piece: she's wearing a red dress and she's got black hair."

The noise of a bus came over the line, and Michael formulated his question while he waited for it to pass: Did she go into the house with him? When the reply came in the negative, he went on to ask if he had noticed anything.

"Who? The old man? Not a chance. He was walking with his eyes on the ground; he nearly bumped into a tree. He only saw her when she accosted him. We didn't hear what they said; we were too far away. But he's very much alive, and nobody's tried to attack him."

Michael said nothing. In the end the policeman said: "We'll be pushing off, then. I'll be seeing you tomorrow, right?" Michael agreed, and put the phone down.

It was four o'clock. If the plane from New York had been on schedule, Neidorf's daughter, Nava, should have landed an hour before.

"Look, Yuval." He turned to his son, who was sprawled on the sofa, his eyes half-closed, "I've got a few things to get out of the way first, and then I'll come back for you. We'll go see a movie. What do you say?"

The boy shrugged his shoulders, but Michael was not taken in by his show of indifference and said: "That's settled, then. It's four now. I've got one more call to make, then I have to go out, and I'll be back at about eight. When does school start tomorrow?"

"Twenty past seven, zero hour." Yuval groaned. He went to the same school that Michael had attended. Almost the entire teaching staff had changed, but Michael still felt warmly affectionate toward the institution in Bayit V'gan where he had spent six years as a boarder and to which he attributed almost all his achievements in life. "Zero-hour math, in this weather," said Yuval. "Even the boarders don't make it in time!"

A third of the pupils at the school were boarders. They were carefully selected from all over the country. To the American donors they were presented as "gifted children from disadvantaged families."

"Have you got any homework?" asked Michael, and began dialing the number of the Margoa. He was prevented from listening to Yuval's reply by the hospital's operator, whom he asked to connect him with Dr. Baum. The doctor promised to wait for Chief Inspector Ohayon in his office.

Yuval stood up and asked if he could come with him. There was a childishly imploring note in his voice, and Michael felt the same sorrow he had experienced when he left him alone on his first day at nursery school. He explained that it was impossible but promised faithfully to be back at eight. "And by then you'll be able to finish your homework. I know from experience that they give you a ton of it, right? You've got homework for tomorrow, haven't you?" Yuval nodded disconsolately. His long-lashed gray eyes regarded Michael suspiciously. "Are you sure you'll be able to make it by eight?" He smiled unwillingly when his father replied: "Scout's honor," and raised his hand in the scout's salute.

Michael did not make it by eight, and Yuval greeted him by pointing at his watch and saying: "We can forget about the movies."

"Don't worry, we'll make it," said Michael, and rushed him to the car. Although he stopped to buy a huge sack of popcorn on the way, they arrived just in time for the science fiction film, *Alien Passenger*, that Yuval had been dying to see.

Once Yuval had settled down to watch, Michael was free to relax and think about his tired mind and aching body. There was no hope of sleeping, the visit to the hospital had left him tense. Baum had consented to let him meet Tubol, but as the doctor had predicted, they had not succeeded in getting a single word out of him. Michael had never seen the inside of a mental hospital before, but he maintained his usual deadpan expression and perfect composure, even when he was sitting by the bed of a mute, curled-up psychotic. Haunted by images from the hospital, he missed the first fifteen minutes of the movie.

At first the nurse, Dvora, insisted that she had no idea where Tubol could have got hold of the pistol. But after repeated requests that she try to imagine where he might have gone, Baum, who was sitting and tugging at his mustache, hit on the idea that Tubol must have met the gardener.

Michael pricked up his ears and asked about the gardener's relations with the patients, and Baum sang Ali's praises at length. When asked where Ali could be found, he said he couldn't say; he only knew that Ali lived in Dehaisha. Ohayon shivered when he thought of the wretched conditions of the refugee camp, only a half hour away from Jerusalem. The maintenance supervisor, they said, would know how to find Ali. But the supervisor finished work at three. Yes, they could call him at home. They called, and Michael spoke to him, and the man said that he couldn't remember any details offhand. "Not even his surname?" Michael asked impatiently. No. It was all in the files, but he couldn't come and look now; he was home alone with the baby. No, there was nobody else who could look up the information at this time of day. No, he couldn't take the baby out of the house and come there now, not in this weather. Yes, Ali worked on Saturday, and here the maintenance supervisor became aggressive: it was an internal matter and nobody's bloody business. Ali didn't work on Sunday, but he would be at work the next day. "Can't it wait?"

Michael controlled his frustration and maintained a polite tone and a patient expression for the benefit of Dr. Baum and the nurse. Yes, said the supervisor, he supposed he could come later on, when his wife got home, in about two hours.

Michael returned to the subject of Dr. Neidorf. No, neither Dr. Baum nor Nurse Dvora had any contact with the Institute. Dr. Neidorf had been a special consultant to the hospital and to its outpatients clinic, but they knew her only very superficially.

Baum, it transpired, did know someone in the hospital who had a professional relationship with Neidorf. After Michael had explained how important every little detail was to the investigation, the nurse gave Baum a meaningful look and he began to describe that Saturday's events in detail, mentioning the young doctor Hedva Tamari and describing how she had fainted and how he had found out that she had been one of Dr. Neidorf's patients. He wrote down her telephone number on a prescription slip, which Michael put in his pocket.

In the end the maintenance supervisor arrived, a thin, nervous, bespectacled man. He announced that he had to be back home in half an hour, having left the baby with a neighbor because he didn't want to hold up the police in their work, especially since he felt personally responsible for the gardener, who worked there on Saturday with his permission; he hoped that Ali hadn't done anything wrong.

From the files they learned that Ali's surname was Abu Mustafa, and that was all. The matter of his working on the Sabbath was explained again. He would come to work the next day, Monday, in the morning. Yes, they would inform Chief Inspector Ohayon the moment he arrived. They would also inform him of any developments that came to their attention. If any of the patients talked, said Nurse Dvora, she would immediately phone the number he had given her. Baum was skeptical about the possibility of this happening. They both stressed how important it was for Michael not to come to the hospital in uniform, "so as not to upset people unnecessarily, and that goes for tomorrow morning too," said Baum as he accompanied Michael outside, touching the bandage that wrapped his neck, its top just visible above the black turtleneck sweater. The rain was coming down hard, and it was dark.

Nava Neidorf-Zehavi had arrived, but the baby had cried nonstop all the way from Chicago to New York and from New York to Israel, and she herself was dazed and exhausted. Her husband begged Michael to let her sleep and to wait until after the funeral to talk to her.

He wrote the name of Neidorf's accountants, Zeligman and Zeligman, on a slip of paper. There was no answer from the office and Michael tried a home number. The Zeligman who answered was on his way out, but he promised to have the file ready first thing in the morning.

After going over all the above in his mind, Michael stretched his legs and stole a look at Yuval. The boy was transfixed by what was happening on the screen. The expression on his face wasn't visible, but his body was tense, and the popcorn lay untouched on his lap. Michael began to watch the movie, and within a few minutes he was absorbed in the plot: Seven people from earth discover on a space flight that they have been joined by an eighth traveler, a creature from another planet. Not a creature, really, but an evil presence, impossible to identify because it can change its form at will. One by one it destroys the humans, who can't fight it because they can't tell in advance which of their own forms it will decide to assume.

Any hope of spending the next hour sleeping vanished. Science fiction movies usually bored him. He was interested in the past, not the future, he once jokingly explained to Yuval. But this film filled him with a dread such as he had felt only rarely before, which he attributed to his exhaustion; he kept being reminded of the events of the last two days. As he watched the suspicion and fear of the seven travelers in the spaceship, he could not help remembering what Hildesheimer had said at the end of the Training Committee meeting: "We can't go on living here together as long as this matter remains unresolved. Too many people depend on us for us to be able to afford not to know which of us is capable of murder."

Outside after the movie, Yuval asked his father if he had enjoyed it.

"It was the most frightening film I've ever seen," replied Michael without thinking. Before he could take the words back, he saw the gratified expression spreading over his son's face.

"Some of them are even worse," said Yuval.

10

I read about you in the paper yesterday—how important you are and what you're working on now," said Yuval. He finished his coffee standing up, put the cheese sandwich his father gave him into his backpack, and announced that he was ready. Michael put his coffee cup and the breakfast dishes in the sink. It was seven o'clock, and the boy had to be at school at twenty past. "There's not much traffic now; if we leave right away, you'll get there with time to spare."

"I know you won't talk about it," the boy said seriously, "but I only wanted to ask you what a psychoanalyst does." He pronounced the word laboriously, syllable by syllable. Michael collected his keys, cigarettes, and wallet, put them in his parka pocket, and smiled at his son. "It's like a psychologist. When your mother and I separated and you were small, you went to a woman in a big corner house in Katamon, where there's a child therapy center, and you played with all kinds of toys and talked to her? Remember?"

"I remember," said Yuval, and pulled a face. "I went because of my teacher Zippora, that's what you said then. Anyway, it was a pain in the neck."

"It's quite similar, only you go more often and of course grownups don't play with toys. Some people need it."

The boy said with a sneer: "I think it's all garbage."

Michael smiled and opened the front door. It wasn't raining, but it was very cold, and they both shrank into their parkas. A blustering wind, blowing between the tall apartment buildings, grew stronger on the way to the suburb where Yuval's school was located. "A gray day," said Michael dispiritedly, as if to himself, and even before letting the boy off outside the school he began to think about what was waiting for him. When Yuval got out of the car, Michael insisted on kissing him and stroking his cheek. He always ignored the protests of his son, who by the age of three was already saying: "Ugh! I'm not a baby." But today Yuval did not protest. He hurried to join a girl who was sauntering slowly toward the gate. Michael looked at them. The girl had long legs, and her hair was tied back in a ponytail, and Yuval smiled at her. Michael could see the smile only in profile, but the little scene gave him a feeling of simultaneous happiness and loss, a feeling that did not leave him until he reached the Margoa.

In front of the hospital, Baum was waiting for him next to the guardhouse. It was a quarter to eight. The gardener, Baum explained, should be arriving at any moment. The maintenance supervisor arrived, glanced at his watch, and said that Ali was never late. "He always comes by eight, whatever the weather," he said, but Michael had the feeling that this time the gardener would break his record.

Huddled in their coats, they stood inside the guardhouse, close to the little stove, and waited. At half past eight, Chief Inspector Ohayon said that he had to be somewhere else, he couldn't wait any longer. When the gardener arrived, would they please call him at his office in the Russian Compound. If he wasn't there, they could leave a message at the control center. If the gardener arrived, he added, he would be grateful if they just behaved as if nothing had happened.

Tzilla and Eli Bahar were waiting in his office. Tzilla was sitting at the corner of the desk and bending paper clips, which she took out of a clean ashtray, and Eli looked preoccupied. Michael felt like an intruder. He glanced from one to the other, said "Good morning," obtained a faint response, and asked the switchboard operator to put him in touch with Bethlehem.

The Arab policeman who answered the phone connected him with the officer on duty, who sounded overjoyed to hear his voice.

"Ohayon, my dear fellow, how are you this morning? When are we going to see you? You haven't visited us in ages. Is there something I can do for you? Anything—just say the word!"

Michael performed the social rites, inquired after the health of his wife and children, hoped the little one was over his pneumonia. In his mind's eye he saw the round face and vast paunch of Itzik Gidoni, renowned among his cohorts for his geniality.

"You can put the water on to boil," Michael joked. "I'm coming around for some real coffee."

Cries of joy burst from the receiver.

"But first of all"—Michael grew serious—"you'll have to locate one Ali Abu Mustafa from the Dehaisha camp."

Gidoni, too, changed his tone. "Have you got anything else on him? With them, Abu Mustafa's like Cohen or Levy."

"I know it won't be easy. He works in the Margoa Hospital as a gardener. A young guy, about twenty-five, curly hair, not too tall."

There was a silence, and in the end Gidoni said with a sigh: "We'll do our best; the coffee will keep. I don't know how long it will take. Believe me, the last thing I feel like this morning is going into Dehaisha. But what wouldn't I do for you. And when we find him, should we bring him in and let you know?"

"Yes; right away. If I'm not here, try to get me through Control; they'll know where I am. In any case, I'm counting on a cup of real coffee this morning." And Michael replaced the receiver gently and looked at Tzilla and Eli. Tzilla's slender body was wrapped in a man's parka; her short hair and unmade-up face gave her a boyish air. Eli was unshaven.

"What's the matter with you two this morning?" asked Michael, and when he was answered by mutters about tiredness, he said impatiently: "Stop it; we haven't got the time for moods. There's a lot of work to get through this morning. Let's get the conference over first." He stood up, and they preceded him to the room at the corner of the corridor, where Balilty was waiting with Inspector Raffi Cohen, who announced wearily that he had been attached to the team but it was too early for him to function properly. "There's no need to put me in the picture now," he said. "I spoke to Shorer yesterday, and I know more or less what's going on."

The meeting took an hour, and at half past nine, Michael summed up the plan of action. Most of the time was devoted to Tzilla's report on her conversations with Dalya Linder and the Linder neighbors—one of them had been wakened by the noises Linder and his son made in the yard.

They were all holding cups of coffee, which from time to time they went out to refill. They all looked worn out. Michael mentioned *Alien Passenger,* but no one else had seen it and it gave rise to no associations. It was agreed that Balilty would try to find out more about Ali Abu Mustafa from the military government of the administered territories. Tzilla, who had been in touch with the men watching Hildesheimer's house, reported that nothing noteworthy had happened there, apart from the meeting with Dina Silver.

In the end it was decided that Eli would go to the accountants, Balilty would continue to gather intelligence material, Raffi would pay a visit to Forensics, and Tzilla would contact all the guests at Linder's party and ask them to come in for questioning. Michael summed up. "We've got less than three hours to the funeral, so let's get cracking. Eli, you go over to Zeligman and Zeligman right now"—he pushed the note with the address across to him—"and bring Neidorf's file back here. Maybe we'll have enough time before the funeral to draw up a list of patients and supervisees from the receipts. He's expecting you. And you'd better shave. You look like a jailbird on leave. Here." He held out the keys to the Renault. "It's parked next to the Jaffa Road entrance." Eli took the keys and departed without a word.

Tzilla followed Michael back to his room and sat down, bending paper clips again. Michael looked at her curiously. "Well, what's up?

And don't tell me you're tired. I've seen you and Eli tired before, you know. Or don't you want to talk about it?" Tzilla, with tears in her eyes, shook her head. Michael sighed and said: "Well, maybe a little work will improve your mood," and passed her a list of names. He wondered again about the nature of her relationship with Eli. There were no signs of affection between them, but every now and then there was tension in the air, and sometimes he sensed that he was interrupting them in the middle of a heart-to-heart discussion. He assumed that they met outside working hours, but nothing had ever been said.

Tzilla blew her nose, wiped her eyes, and asked: "What are all these names? What am I supposed to do with them?" An aggrieved note in her voice led Michael to reply impatiently "It's the list of guests at Linder's party, the one where the pistol might have been stolen. Forty people who have to be brought in for questioning. You and me and Eli, and we'll need two more; maybe we can stop watching the old man, and then there won't be such a problem with manpower. We have to find out where they were and what they were doing. Get on the phone and tell them we want to talk to them. And when you've finished with them, we'll begin with patients and supervisees who weren't at the party. But first we'll have to wait for Eli to come back with the file," he said, and tried to ignore her sniffs. "Believe me," he added gently, "there's no cure like work. I don't know what happened, but whatever it is, work will make you forget it. And by the time you get back to me, in about an hour or so, even if you haven't finished—because we have to talk about the funeral too—you'll look like a different person." And in the tone of voice he used with Yuval when he was grumpy and contrary, he added in a whisper: "And then you'll be the best team coordinator in Jerusalem again."

Tzilla folded the paper in four, shook his hand off her shoulder, picked up her big bag, and left the room. Michael stood thinking for a minute, and then he fell on the phone and dialed Dina Silver's number. The phone was answered by someone who said that she was the maid and she didn't know anything. There was nobody at home. Madam had a phone at work, but you were only allowed to call there ten minutes before every hour, she said in a warning tone. As one who had already been burned. Michael wrote down the number. It was nine forty-five: in five minutes he would be able to phone. He left his office and went into Emanuel Shorer's, which was next to his own and not much bigger. Shorer's desk was covered with papers; a large mug of coffee was in his hand. His face lit up.

"What's new?" he asked, indicating the chair opposite him.

Michael remained standing. "Nothing. Bahar's gone to the accountant's, Tzilla's on the phone with a list of people we want to question, and the funeral's today at one. I need photographers and another two for potential surveillance, I can't manage with only three and Intelligence, and I can't take the men off Hildesheimer. Someone could try to get him at the funeral."

"Okay; we'll organize something. At one, you say? How many? Two photographers? And two others? enough. If you need more men ad hoc, let me know and you'll get them. Why do you keep looking at your watch?"

"Because I have to make a call at ten to . . ." And Michael smiled, reminded of Winnie-the-Pooh and the stories he used to read to Yuval. For some reason, he felt like Eeyore.

"Oh, I haven't told you about the gardener." And he told him, concluding with the words: "I've got a funny feeling, as if there's something I haven't thought of, as if something's going to happen. I don't know. . . . Do you understand what I'm talking about?" Shorer looked at him and shook his head. "Never mind. You'll organize two people and another car for Raffi for the funeral?" Shorer nodded, and Michael returned to his office, getting himself a cup of coffee on the way in the "coffee corner," an alcove near his office.

It was five to ten when he put out his hand to dial Dina Silver's number, but instead the phone rang, and he heard Eli Bahar's excited voice on the line. Before he could tell him to call back later, Eli shouted without any preliminaries: "Michael, there's no file! Someone's taken it! You didn't send anyone else, right?"

"What do you mean, someone else? What the hell are you talking about?" said Michael, lighting a match with hands that immediately grew clammy. He wiped the sweat off on his trousers, first one hand and then the other.

"About the fact that there's nothing here! The man says that the police were here and asked for the file. The guy who took it signed a receipt and everything!"

"Just a minute. Take it from the beginning and slowly." Michael drew deeply on his first cigarette of the day. "Are you speaking from Zeligman and Zeligman in Shamai Street?"

"Yes, Zeligman and Zeligman, Accountants, Seventeen Shamai Street. Mr. Zeligman's right here next to me. You'd better come around and see for yourself. Her file's gone. Someone claiming he was a policeman arrived here at half past eight this morning, signed a bit of paper, and went off with the file."

"I'll be there right away. You stay put," said Michael, and charged into Shorer's room. The latter looked at him in astonishment, said no, he certainly hadn't sent anyone to Zeligman and Zeligman, and what the hell was going on anyway? Michael explained and rushed out of the building. Quickly he covered the distance between the Russian Compound and the accountants' office, zigzagging through the crowds on Jaffa Road, nearly stumbling over the blind beggar off Zion Square, running up Ben Yehuda and crossing through the alley of the Atara Coffee Shop. He arrived puffing and panting, his muscles trembling. The Institute people would doubtless have summed up his condition in one word: anxiety.

Zeligman senior was pale and nervous. He hung his head and stammered in a heavy Polish accent: "But you said you would come for it. It never occurred to me that he might not be a policeman. Here's Zmira; ask her. She gave him the receipt, and he signed it."

The flow of words was impossible to stop. The old accountant began with apologies and went over to an attack aimed at proving his absolute guiltlessness. The comparison with Youzek, Michael's father-in-law, was unavoidable. Even the accent was the same, with its guttural *ch* instead of *h*.

In a minute he's going to ask me to apologize, thought Michael wrathfully. All I need is an excuse to hit him. God almighty, what idiots they all are! Eli Bahar, looking as if he had swallowed a bottle of vinegar, stood in a corner stubbornly paging through the tax files from four years back, despite Zeligman junior's repeated attempts to explain that he would only find copies of her income tax returns there and no receipt books. Zmira, a young girl in tight jeans and an even tighter sweater, clasped her hands and cracked the knuckles of her fingers with their bright-red nails. She chewed steadily, and from time to time the lump of pink gum poked between her teeth. With a trembling hand she held out the note to Michael. Below the words: "I have received from Zeligman and Zeligman, Accountants, the income tax files of Eva Neidorf, which I hereby undertake to return in full to the same. Signed," was an illegible scribble.

Michael pushed the piece of paper into his coat pocket. Zeligman senior said for the umpteenth time that if he had been there himself, it would never have happened. He—an honest, upright citizen who had "never had any trouble with the police in his life"—had prepared the file and phoned Zmira first thing in the morning and instructed her to go straight to the office and wait for the police and give it to them when they came.

Eli Bahar raised his eyes from the old files and asked why he himself had not been present in the office. The elder Zeligman explained that he had been obliged to pay an urgent visit to the income tax authorities to prevent one of his clients from getting into serious difficulties. And his son, he explained, always came later. "But he works late. It isn't so easy to get to the center of the city from where he lives," said the old man, looking at his son, who came over to him and put his hand on his shoulder and said: "Calm down, Dad, calm down; it's not your fault." No, thought Michael, it's not his fault, but how does that help me? He could hear Ariyeh Levy saying: "This isn't a university, you know," and more of the same. He could already sense the covert stares and see the suppressed smiles of his ill-wishers, all those who had coveted the plum he was about to pluck: Chief of Investigations, Jerusalem. And on top of everything else there were the members of the Institute's Training Committee, with their suspicious eyes and mistrustful looks.

The facts were simple: At eight o'clock in the morning the file was ready, and at eight-thirty (when I left the hospital; I could have dropped in here myself, thought Michael furiously) a man had presented himself in the accountants' office, a tallish man in his thirties, with a mustache, wearing army uniform. She could see the khaki trousers, said Zmira, under the big parka that came down to his knees. "An army-issue parka," she added. He wore black gloves, and he said he had come for the file. These were the only facts that Michael succeeded in getting out of the girl. "But I already told him," she said, and pointed at Eli, who tightened his lips and said in a menacing tone: "And now you'll please tell us again." She couldn't remember anything else. She couldn't see his rank. "He had this big coat on, like I said. And dark glasses, the kind that hide your eyes. All I could see was his mustache and a mouth full of teeth." She removed the pink lump from her mouth and burst into tears.

Nobody made a move to comfort her. Michael was sitting in a big wicker chair opposite the desk behind which Zeligman senior sat, fingering his tie knot and wiping his forehead. Every now and then he looked at the wall where magnificently framed diplomas testified to the fact that he was a certified accountant and chartered auditor.

On the desk stood a vase made of exquisite Venetian glass, and Michael felt an overpowering urge to pick it up and dash it to the floor and hear the glass shatter. He distracted himself with an effort. There was no one on whom he could wreak his rage. Eli Bahar put the old files down and said they were of no use. "There's nothing here," he said, "nothing but bank accounts." Michael pricked up his ears. "Bank accounts," he repeated, and asked Zeligman senior if he had the numbers of the deceased's bank accounts. Yes, said Zeligman, and straightened his tie. He was able to inform him, he said, that she had one active account and other, inactive accounts. "Are you interested in stocks and shares and business accounts too?" he asked. Everything, said Michael, all her bank accounts. Especially the accounts in which she deposited her patients' payments. "No problem," said the accountant. He even had one of her check right there, postdated to the next month, to deposit for her. She had made the advance payments on her income tax at the end of every month, he explained.

"She didn't want to be bothered with such matters herself. Dr. Neidorf had complete trust in us," he said in a tone of rebuke. "Here. The chief inspector can see for himself," and he opened one of his desk drawers. He bent down and rummaged through the papers in the drawer, and finally he pulled out a thin cardboard file, from which he extracted a checkbook and handed it to Michael. It was from the Discount Bank, German Colony branch, and contained two signed checks, one made out to the income tax bureau and the other to V.A.T. The date on both checks was April 15, and Zeligman quickly explained that she had not yet received her advance payment forms for the next financial year. Every April she would give him a year's supply of signed checks. "This checkbook was full of signed checks; you can look at the stubs—here, see for yourself. Everything was paid on the dot." So we've gone over to the second person, have we, thought Michael; in other words we've stopped being afraid. He remembered his ex-father-in-law, and the point at which he had stopped speaking to people in the third person and begun to address them in more familiar terms.

Eli Bahar said that perhaps they should take the old files too. "Take everything," said Michael dryly. "It's safer with us."

Zeligman junior opened his mouth, but he changed his mind and closed it again. And Zeligman senior nodded his head at Zmira and said: "Give the gentleman an envelope for those papers." As he put the papers in the envelope, Michael delivered his parting shot: "Mr. Zeligman, I want you to think before you answer, and to answer with absolute honesty: we're not from the tax bureau." Zeligman began fingering his tie again, and his son opened his mouth to protest, but Chief Inspector Ohayon raised his hand as a sign that he wanted to finish what he had to say: "My question is about receipts. Was everything entered? Are you sure that she gave all her patients receipts?" Zeligman reacted like a man about to have a heart attack. The defensive tone had disappeared: a lady's honor was at stake, and the Polish gentleman rose to the occasion. His face flushed, he said: "I don't know what kind of people you are accustomed to dealing with, sir. Here we are speaking of Dr. Eva Neidorf, whose acquaintance you obviously never had the honor of making. I don't mind telling you, in confidence, that I even advised her on more than one occasion to work fewer hours, because she was so scrupulous in her reports to the income tax authorities that it simply didn't make sense economically for her to work so much. She always said that she would think about it, but that it was out of the question for her not to give a patient a receipt. 'Mr. Zeligman,' she would say—she had a lot of respect for me—'Mr. Zeligman, in work like mine you have to be moral; you can't behave like a shopkeeper and not give people receipts.' With my hand on my heart I can assure you that she always gave receipts and kept copies of the receipts and that she reported everything. And believe me, I have other clients; I know what I'm talking about."

If Michael was convinced by this speech, he didn't show it, and as they descended in the creaking old elevator, he summed up his attitude to Zeligman in two words: "Pompous ass." Zmira stared from him to Eli with frightened, bulging eyes. A lot of time had been devoted to reassuring her that she had done nothing for which she would be punished. "It's routine; that's the way we work," Eli explained again on their way to the Russian Compound. First he took her to the Identi-Kit artist, after which he obtained a signed statement from her about the events of the morning. On the way, he asked her about the man's voice and manner of speech. She thought he was an Ashkenazi, she said; he didn't have a Sephardi accent anyway. She said she would be able to identify the voice and maybe the man, too, if she ever saw him again, Eli reported to Michael an hour later.

There were some positive developments with which Michael tried to console himself. For example, the minute he walked into his room, at half past eleven, he heard Tzilla saying briskly into the phone: "Here he is, he's just arrived." She was sitting on his chair and scribbling something with a pencil. Michael took the phone from her. They had found Ali Abu Mustafa, announced Gidoni. "You have to admit we did a fast job. You see the benefits of being on friendly terms with the Mukhtar?" Michael said that he would be there around four. To Gidoni's protests about the coffee getting cold, he responded with a feeble joke and an impatience he hoped was not too obvious.

At ten to twelve he succeeded in dialing the number of Dina Silver's clinic. There was no answer. He tried again, a few minutes later and a soft, breathless voice said, "Hello." "Yes, speaking," she replied when he asked if she was Dina Silver. No, she would not be able to talk to him today; she had to go to the funeral at one, and after that she was working until late.

"What's wrong with late?" asked Michael, looking at Tzilla, who appeared tense.

"This evening," said Dina Silver hesitantly. "You mean at home, or something like that?" No, he didn't mean at home, he meant here, at the Russian Compound, after the funeral. "But I have patients from three," said Dina Silver nervously, stressing every word. He could imagine her beautiful, clouded face. "Do you work after nine?"

Michael smiled to himself and replied that they worked twenty-four hours a day, "if necessary."

There was a silence and then, in a more animated tone: "But I can give you the name and number of the girl I referred to Eva Neidorf for treatment over the phone. Perhaps you could skip the meeting tonight?"

He could, said Michael, if she wasn't willing to come after her patients. Something prevented him from asking her to cancel. There was no gun involved here, as in the case of Linder, and he himself wasn't sure that he would be finished with the murdered woman's family by nine. In the end he told her to come to his office the next morning. What time? she asked, her voice strained again. He worked out how long the morning conference would take and then said: "Nine o'clock. But please keep the whole morning free, if it's not too difficult." It would be very difficult, he knew, and he was surprised when she did not protest but listened in silence to his instructions about how to find his office, which he delivered at dictation speed before hanging up the phone.

Tzilla spoke, "I looked for you, but you weren't here, you all disappeared. What happened?"

Michael told her briefly about the morning's events, trying to sound unperturbed.

"What are we going to do now?" said Tzilla anxiously. "How are we going to locate them all? We can hardly put an advertisement in the paper asking everybody who was in treatment with Dr. Neidorf to report to the nearest police station."

"It's not only that. There's someone here who's determined to keep us from finding out. The risk he took this morning was a serious one," said Michael thoughtfully. "But life's not so simple, and it isn't so easy to keep that kind of information hidden. Thank God for banks: imagine if everything were still based on barter and payment in kind—what the hell would we have done then?"

Eli came into the room, to say that they would have to leave for the funeral soon, but when he heard Michael's last sentence, a spark of interest and comprehension appeared in his eyes. "Look," Michael was saying slowly. "There were eight hours we didn't know what she did with, eight hours a week. Of those, six have been accounted for. Four hours a week she analyzed that doctor from the Margoa, Hedva Tamari, who applied to the Institute recently and hasn't yet received an answer; and another two were given to another female patient, whose name I'm going to get tomorrow from the woman I just spoke to on the phone, Dina Silver. Which leaves only two hours unaccounted for. After we've spoken to everyone on our list and found out their days and hours, we'll know where to fit them in on Neidorf's timetable. And after we've gone through all the bank accounts, I hope and pray that we'll know the mystery patient's name too. From this morning's events, we assume it's a man."

Eli opened the brown envelope and said: "Or maybe there were more than one of them, who knows, what with all these break-ins and everything."

"So what are we sitting here for? We have to get a court order, no? We can't just go barging into the bank and saying we want to see her bank accounts!" said Tzilla excitedly.

Michael glanced at his watch. "It's nearly one o'clock. We've got a funeral to go to. After the funeral I'm going to Bethlehem, and Eli's coming with me, so you can get moving on it, Tzilla. After Bethlehem I have an appointment with the family—who knows how long that will take—and the rest will have to wait until tomorrow. There's a limit, after all. Eli, you can join Tzilla after Bethlehem. You can start questioning the people who were at the party. And, Tzilla, you'd better work out how many bank accounts we need to look at, any accounts Neidorf deposited checks in. After a few days they return the checks to the vaults of the banks on which they were drawn."

He concluded with suppressed fury: "We'll trace him in the end, though it may kill us first," and turned to Eli: "Do me a favor—take the receipt for the Zeligman file to Forensics. Maybe they'll be able to come up with something from the signature. I want us to leave for the funeral together. Tzilla, get hold of the photographers and the two extra men and see that they arrive separately; nobody knows them yet. I assume Shorer will send Raffi and Manny Ezra, but find out for sure."

When he was left alone in the room, he looked again at the list that lay under the desk lamp together with the five copies Tzilla had made of it. She had listed the names alphabetically, in her big handwriting. The first name was Dr. Giora Biham, which appeared neither on the list of Neidorf's patients nor on that of her supervisees. He apparently worked at Kfar Shaul Hospital, and Tzilla had ticked off his name; she had presumably made contact with him and set a time for his interrogation. It occurred to Michael that there would be no point in any of the Institute people trying to hide their professional contacts with Neidorf. The man in uniform who took Neidorf's file must have been someone from outside, someone who knew enough to have gone to the accountant in the first place. He said this to Eli, who came into the room and told him that he had left the receipt with Forensics to be examined by their handwriting expert.

Eli swore and said: "Where the hell is she? We have to get going."

Tzilla came back and reported that the others were already on their way; there was a photographer and Manny Ezra was coming too. "Thank God for small mercies, at least there'll be someone nice around."

Eli ignored this sally, which appeared to be directed against him, and the three of them left the office. When they passed the door of

Shorer's office, Michael looked in. Shorer, who was still sitting behind the mountain of papers on his desk, raised his head and asked what was new, and Michael told him in two sentences. Shorer sighed and said it would complicate things no end, with the banks it was a whole procedure, and he didn't know how they would be able to hide it from Levy, who, he didn't have to tell Michael, would be delighted. Michael said no, he didn't have to tell him, and he didn't intend hiding anything from anyone. "Do you feel like going to a funeral?" he asked.

Shorer shook his head vigorously: "Going to graveyards is bad luck. I never go unless I have to. When you've got anything more inviting to suggest, let me know." Michael shrugged his shoulders and looked back down the long winding corridor. He was standing on the threshold, between the doorpost and the half-closed door. Tzilla and Eli were waiting patiently at the top of the stairs. "What's up? Have you lost your confidence? Do you need a nursemaid, or what?" Shorer's voice was rough. In an instant the whole atmosphere changed. "A couple of fuck-ups and you collapse? What the hell's the matter with you? I stick my neck out for you, recommend you to the whole world, they all believe you can walk on water—you think I'm going to let you make me a liar? No more fuck-ups, you hear? One more thing goes wrong, and I'll make your life such a bloody misery you'll wish you'd never been born. And wipe that pathetic expression off your face, or I'll wipe it off for you. Pull yourself together!"

Michael shut the door and walked toward Tzilla and Eli. I know I asked for it, but he's acting like a sonofabitch anyway, he thought as he started the car and set off for Sanhedria. Every time he drove toward the funeral parlor in Sanhedria he wondered how long it would take him to cross all the red lights on Bar Ilan Street. And how long he would have to sit in his car watching all the dark coats, payis, and streimils on the ultra-Orthodox men, and the ubiquitous pregnant women, who took forever crossing the street. It would be ages before he could turn left to the crowded funeral parlor.

Tzilla sat next to him, Eli in the back seat. The sky was black, but it wasn't raining. They didn't exchange a word all the way. When they arrived, Michael parked the car, handed Tzilla the keys, and disappeared into the crowd of mourners.

Like instruments in a practiced trio, Tzilla and Eli went their separate ways, and the Renault with the police license plate remained parked among the Institute cars.

11

Michael Ohayon lit a cigarette, cupping the flame with his hand. He knew he shouldn't smoke there, but he couldn't help himself. He remained outside the hall at the head of the broad flight of stairs. Tzilla went in, and he stood on the corner of the top step, watching the people streaming into the hall. In spite of all the corpses he had seen, it was still hard for him to be in places like this. And the sight of the body being buried in the earth was even harder. At such moments he always thought enviously of the splendid Roman burial sarcophagi, of the other possible ways of parting from the dead. Only not this stretcher, this body wrapped in winding sheets.

Linder walked past him. A woman was leaning on his arm, and from the intimate, unselfconscious way in which she held on to him, Michael knew she must be his wife. Linder himself looked serious and absentminded; he glanced at Michael without actual acknowledgment, only the flicker of anxiety in his eyes betraying the fact that he had recognized him.

Dina Silver, wrapped in a fur coat and a black scarf, was mounting the steps with a young, bald man whose chin was covered with a thick beard. With a feeling of relief, he recognized the young photographer with the camera over her shoulder and the press tag on her coat collar as a plainclothes policewoman. She nodded to him discreetly and aimed her camera at the pair. Michael hoped she would get everybody, but he knew it was impossible.

On the bottom step stood the second photographer, fingering a cigarette lighter. There were genuine reporters there too, and press photographers aiming their cameras at the crowd ascending the stairs to the rounded stone hall.

Old Hildesheimer, supported by Rosenfeld, whose mouth looked naked without its cigar, climbed heavily from step to step, his shoulders stooped, his head bowed, a dark hat hiding his face. On Rosenfeld's other side was a woman Michael did not know. He imagined that most of the analysts would come with their families, or their spouses at least. Many people moved slowly and heavily up the broad flight of stairs. All wore heavy winter coats. Since the storm Saturday night, a penetrating cold had set in.

Many faces seemed familiar. Many of them were known to him from the Institute on Saturday, others he remembered from the university. The crème de la crème, thought Michael, the city's elite. What was generally referred to as a dignified funeral, but at the same time fraught with emotion.

The signs of sorrow and grief were evident on every face. Two weeping women mounted the stairs, and from the mourners clustered at the entrance to the hall, which was already packed with people, came sounds of sobbing.

There was something in the air that undermined the solidity of the crowd, who looked as if they came from the strongholds of bourgeois respectability. Eva Neidorf had not died of an illness, or in an accident, or of old age. And in addition to the usual signs of sorrow and grief, other emotions were evident on the faces of the mourners: there was fear in their eyes, and anger, sometimes even rage, on their faces.

Litzie Sternfeld, whose tears on Saturday he remembered vividly, mounted the stairs supported by two young men. She was not crying.

Her lips were grimly pursed. She looked like a person who had no illusions about what she was up against. Like a big black bird, she shifted her eyes from face to face as she advanced to the top of the stairs. She's looking for the alien passenger too, thought Michael. They all appear so respectable, the ultimate in good, law-abiding citizens, and if I didn't know better, this is the last place I would look for him. But they're looking at each other too, and they're afraid. All of them are afraid.

Gradually the stream of people ascending the stairs thinned, and the silence that now fell, interrupted only by sobs, told Michael that the ceremony had begun. Someone was delivering a eulogy; it was a man whose voice he did not recognize, and from where he stood the words were inaudible.

Then the cantor's voice rose, and finally there was silence; the ceremony was over. The body was borne by six men, among whom Michael recognized Gold and Rosenfeld. He looked at the bundle wrapped in winding sheets, and the sight of the body's contours sent shivers down his spine.

After the stretcher bearers, the family emerged from the hall. Michael saw Hillel, the son-in-law, supporting a young woman, apparently the daughter. Next to him was a young man whose resemblance to the dead woman was unmistakable. Hildesheimer supported the daughter on her other side. Now his face was clearly visible under the big hat covering his bald head. He passed very close to Michael, and Michael saw the tears rolling down his cheeks. People began following the family down the stairs and getting into their cars. Tzilla was behind Hildesheimer. After her came a long procession of people, many of them wiping their eyes, some leaning on others, some supporting their fellows. The sky was gray; it looked as if it was going to rain, and there was an icy wind blowing. The sound of cars starting came from the street. Dina Silver descended the stairs, leaning on the arm of the balding, bearded man. And then Michael saw him for the first time, the young man standing a few steps below him, on the other side, leaning on the balustrade and staring at Dina Silver and her escort. For a moment Michael thought that he was going to attack them.

He had a desperate, haunted look in his eyes. He doesn't belong to this crowd, thought Michael, sensing that he was different without knowing exactly why. Dina slowed down and turned her head, and her eyes met those of the young man, only for a second, and then she quickened her step again. The man at her side looked back curiously, stared for a moment, and then matched his step to hers. It was unclear whether she had noticed Michael, who did not take his eyes off the young man and hoped that one of the cameras had caught him. "The youth," Michael called him to himself, a word he did not normally use. As soon as he saw him he was flooded by a sense of impending catastrophe. There was a threat in that beauty, in the desperation reflected in those eyes.

Even a person insensitive to beauty would have noticed it. It was impossible not to notice the exquisite lines of the face framed in the raised hood of the duffel coat. It was impossible not to hold your breath at the sight of those burning blue slits with their despondent hungry look. The jutting cheekbones stamped his expression with a rarefied, spiritual quality. But there was sensuality in it too, especially in the full lips and the mop of golden curls. Michael's first association was with Tadzio in *Death in Venice*. After that he thought of Greek sculptures. The youth did not look more than twenty.

The policewoman, who had only now emerged from the hall, aimed her camera at him and pressed. There was a click, and she moved on past the youth, who appeared oblivious to her and her camera. Michael followed her down, and when he turned his head he saw that the youth was still standing there, in exactly the same posture as before.

On the bottom step he encountered Raffi Cohen, who looked at him with "What now?" on his face. Michael told him to follow the handsome young man in the duffel coat standing at the top of the stairs, to stick to him and not let him out of his sight. Raffi turned his palm up and wagged his hand in a gesture of mute inquiry, and Michael muttered: "I don't know yet myself; just stay with him and find out who he is." Raffi nodded, his face took on a thoughtful, concentrated expression, and Michael, who looked back again, saw him moving slowly up the steps toward the youth, his eyes on the ground. Although he was well aware of Raffi's skill and experience, he held his breath, like a hunter afraid his partner would make a noise and put the prey to flight. He considered the possibility of shadowing the youth himself but immediately dismissed it. I can't be everywhere at once, he told himself firmly, and walked over to the parking lot.

Where, he wondered as he got into the car and sat down in the passenger's seat, do they direct their suspicion? They must all assume that one of them might be involved in the murder. What do they do with their mistrust? How do they share their sorrow, drive in the same cars, without knowing who it is? Then he asked the same question aloud. Tzilla, who had taken her place in the convoy, was the first to answer. "Well," she said, choosing her words, "people have defense mechanisms. Everyone denies the possibility that the murderer is someone close to him. The people he loves and thinks he knows are above suspicion."

Eli kept quiet at first, and then he said that as far as he could see Neidorf's colleagues looked more depressed and sad than suspicious. "Maybe it takes time for it to dawn on them. A funeral isn't the place for suspicion." He sighed from the back seat. Behind hands cupping the flame of his match, Michael remarked that as far as *he* could see, the dominant emotion was anger. "They look sad and frightened, but mainly they look angry." And then there was silence until the winding road that led to the cemetery in Givat Shaul. It began to rain in a fine drizzle. Tzilla switched on the windshield wipers, which as soon as the glass was dry made a squeaking sound that gave Michael gooseflesh. Tzilla switched them off, and on again as raindrops covered the windshield once more, and complained of the poor visibility and the slippery road.

It was only when they were within half a mile of the cemetery, passing the tombstone factories, that Michael mentioned the youth, describing him in terms that made Tzilla wonder aloud how she could have failed to notice him.

Again there was a silence, and then Eli brought up the subject of the trip to Bethlehem. Why not bring the gardener in for questioning to the Russian Compound, he asked, and anyway, why did they both have to go?

Michael was afraid that he wouldn't manage with his Arabic. "You can't conduct an interrogation when you're busy trying to convert Moroccan into Jordanian Arabic; you have to be fluent and precise."

But Eli insisted. Why not let him go alone, then, freeing Michael for other things; it was a waste for both of them to go. Yes, Michael agreed, but he didn't like disappointing Gidoni; he was expecting him for coffee. Tzilla snorted contemptuously: "Well, really, what a reason!" But more than that neither of them dared to say. Although Michael did not keep an obvious distance between himself and his subordinates, they always knew just how far they could go.

Tzilla parked the car as close as possible to the stone wall separating the graves from the path.

The rain grew steadily heavier, and as they stood around the open grave it started coming down in floods. Michael could not distinguish between the raindrops and the tears. No one opened an umbrella, and Michael had the feeling that they were abandoning themselves willingly to the rain, that they had deliberately left their umbrellas behind in their cars. He looked around him and saw that the whole crowd of people was inside a big gray cloud. Despite the early hour, it was almost dark. All around them were graves, some fresh and some surmounted with slabs of stone. He thought of his mother, who was buried in the sands of Holon, outside Tel Aviv; he heard her low, warm voice. Hildesheimer was standing at a little distance from him, looking straight ahead of him with a stern, grim expression. Neidorf's son said Kaddish. There was absolute silence; not even a whimper was heard.

And then a terrible scream rent the air. Several seconds passed before he identified the word "Mommy." No one moved, and the only sound was that of the raindrops splashing steadily on the ground. Then people placed stones on the grave, and in the custom of Jerusalem Jews, the men formed themselves into two rows and the son walked between them. The women waited to one side. Some of them went up to Neidorf's daughter, Nava, who was standing at the graveside with her head bowed, supported by a woman Michael did not know. The men began trudging through the mud toward the cars. Nobody stopped to speak to anyone else; nobody uttered a word. Some of them touched Nava's arm; some glanced at Hildesheimer, but nobody touched him. Linder approached him and offered his arm, and the old man leaned on it as he made his way heavily toward one of the cars. Rosenfeld, Michael observed, who brought up the rear, sat down in the driver's seat, with the handsome man from the Training Committee sitting behind him.

Tzilla was waiting behind the wheel. Michael got into the car and looked at Eli's glum face. "So what do you suggest?" he asked after clearing his throat. "That we bring him here?" Eli nodded and shivered. There was a smell of wet wool in the car, and Michael opened the window in spite of the rain. Then he bent over the two-way radio and asked the control center to tell Gidoni to send the parcel to them. At the entrance to town, a voice on the radio said that Gidoni wanted to know if his people should deliver the parcel themselves. Yes, said Michael, he would prefer it. From the back seat came a sigh of relief. Tzilla smiled, and Michael shrugged his shoulders and lit a cigarette. The rain kept on coming down, and Eli began explaining in an apologetic tone that the interrogation could easily take hours. "Getting stuck in Bethlehem in this weather . . ." He didn't finish the sentence. Tzilla stopped the car next to their usual steak joint in the Mahaneh Yehuda market off Agrippas Street, and no one quarreled with her statement: "I'm always hungry after a funeral."

Just as Tzilla had predicted while sticking her fork into one piece of meat after another on the plate heaped with her mixed grill, when they arrived at the Russian Compound Ali Abu Mustafa was waiting in the detention room. Michael smoked nervously. The transition from the funeral to the restaurant, with Tzilla's energetic chatter, Eli's steady silence as he picked gloomily at his food, and the thought of the interrogation ahead of them, filled him with tension.

"Just imagine if we'd arrested a Jewish settler from around Bethlehem and chucked him into a detention cell in the Russian Compound," said Tzilla with a disapproving grunt as she maneuvered the car skillfully into a parking space. They relieved the policeman guarding the prisoner, who sat huddled in a corner of the room. Michael looked at the slack limbs, at the eyes, which contained the defeated expression of someone who knew that the game was lost in advance. Michael sat in the opposite corner, as Eli began to take down particulars. Ali tried to guess which of them was the senior officer, and his eyes darted from one to the other and settled finally on Eli, who asked him calmly why he had not come to work today. After a long silence, he repeated the question. Michael, who understood Arabic well but was always nervous about differences in accent and vocabulary, about missing nuances, kept his eyes fixed on the young gardener, who finally said that he was sick.

Eli inquired as to the nature of the sickness, and Ali pointed to his head and said that he had been feverish all night. After a slight hesitation, he asked if his absence from work was the reason for his arrest. There was no irony in the question, only the resignation of a man who had grown used to the fact that you could be arrested for anything. Eli explained that the arrest was not political but connected to the investigation of a murder.

Ali sat up, repeated the word "murder" as a question, in astonishment, in indignation, and in the end delivered himself of a long sentence that boiled down to the assertion that he didn't know what they were talking about. Eli drew little boxes on the sheet of paper that lay in front of him on the table.

The room in which they sat was on the second floor of the interrogations wing. The walls were a dirty yellow, and the only window overlooked the backyard. The table with its two chairs were gray, and the whole atmosphere, as Michael noted every time anew, was exceeding depressing. Eli waited, then said something about working on Saturdays, causing Ali to jump up from his chair and declare that he hadn't done anything wrong, that he worked on Saturdays for religious reasons, that the maintenance supervisor knew, that it was a private arrangement, which had been made for him because he was such a good, reliable worker.

Eli raised his eyes from the sheet of paper and the little boxes that were rapidly filling it and asked what religious reasons could possibly make a Muslim choose Sunday as his day off from work. Later he explained to Michael that the great majority of the population of Dehaisha were Muslims, so he hadn't taken much of a risk. Ali's face looked gray as he stammered that most of his friends worked on Saturdays, so that the social life of the refugee camp and its environs took place mainly on Sundays. The answer was persuasive, but Eli looked skeptical and suddenly asked how long his brother had been in jail. The prisoner trembled and tried to explain that there was no justification for his brother's administrative detention. He wasn't blaming the authorities, he said, only his brother; he was so young and foolish, he didn't know what he was saying, and because of this he had had been arrested on suspicion of rioting and incitement, whereas the truth was that he didn't even know how to throw a stone straight. Then he swore again that he hadn't done anything wrong.

In that case, said Eli as neutrally as if he were asking him to describe the landscape of the place where he had been born, why didn't he tell them about the pistol? If everything was so open and aboveboard and he hadn't done anything wrong, why hadn't he brought the pistol to the police? asked Eli with a frank, innocent air that made even Michael's blood run cold. He did not take his eyes off the young gardener, who was bathed in sweat despite the coldness of the room. Ali wiped his forehead with a trembling hand and asked, What pistol? Why, the one he had found in the hospital, said Eli, as if it was obvious to everyone what he was talking about; the one he had tried to hide and hand over to his friends in Dehaisha, of course.

Ali swore he had no intention of doing anything with the pistol; all he wanted was not to get in trouble. After this declaration, which was made in an impassioned voice, he sank back into his chair and looked at Eli as if he were the greatest magician in the tribe. Michael held his breath. He knew, like Eli, that if the gardener had wanted to use the gun, it would never have been found so quickly.

In the tone in which one asks a child why he didn't come to his mother with a problem that could have been so easily solved, Eli asked again why he hadn't brought the pistol to the police. Then Ali began to describe the events of Saturday morning, from the minute he saw "it" glittering in the bushes to the minute Tubol picked it up. His voice was a monotone, without any rising or falling inflections; it was clear to him—Michael sensed it—that he could no longer hide anything and there was no point in trying. When he was finished, Eli asked if he hadn't noticed the police cars outside the hospital grounds.

Yes, Ali replied, of course he'd noticed them; that was exactly why he had done what he did with Tubol. He thought— His voice broke. Eli did not press him. What he had thought was too obvious to need putting into words. Michael asked: "What did you think?" The prisoner looked at him fully for the first time, a wary, frightened look, and replied that he thought that if he went to give the pistol to the police he would be arrested on the spot. With an assumed innocence that made him feel disgusted with himself, Michael asked the reason for his apprehensions. Ali shrugged his shoulders and recalled his brother, who had been standing next to their house without doing anything after an army jeep driving through the camp had been stoned, and they had arrested him before he could even open his mouth. And even though he, Ali, like his brother, had done nothing to justify arrest, who would believe him?

Eli replied, with a dismissive wave of his hand, that they weren't talking about his brother now, and he had never heard of a prisoner yet who didn't claim he was innocent, but stones were thrown in Dehaisha nevertheless, and somebody must be throwing them. What interested him now was the precise time when he, Ali, had found the pistol, and a description of the same. He wrote down the gardener's answers, and in the end he asked if he had noticed anything—a vehicle, a person, anything he could recall—before finding the pistol.

Ali explained that he had been going from one rosebush to the next, working without looking up until the very moment when it had caught his eye, which was only a couple of minutes after he had reached the row next to the fence. Nevertheless, insisted Eli, perhaps he had heard or seen something unusual on that Saturday, even afterward—it didn't matter—and would he please make an effort to remember. The last words were said sharply, and at the same time the policeman stood up with a sudden movement that frightened the prisoner and made him raise his hands to his face. When Eli remained standing next to the table without coming any closer, he dropped his hands and swore that he hadn't seen anything. Only patrol cars and a lot of other cars, but all that was after he had found the pistol. Before that he wasn't anywhere near the fence. Eli looked at Michael inquiringly, and the latter raised his eyebrows with an expression that said as clearly as words: That's it, we're not going to get anything else out of him. But Eli made one last effort. Who had he seen in the hospital that morning, he asked.

Only the doctors who worked there on Saturdays, said Ali: that one with the mustache, and the lady doctor with the curly hair whose name he couldn't pronounce, and Tubol, and later the fat nurse. But he was afraid of her and he always tried to keep out of her way and she didn't see him. And that was all. He had seen the doctors when he arrived in the morning, and Tubol in the garden, right after finding the pistol, he replied to the question asked by Michael, who now stood up and called the policeman waiting outside and beckoned Eli to follow him out of the room.

They agreed that Ali's story was true. Eli asked how long they would keep him, and Michael shrugged his shoulders. "Let him sign a statement and promise to stay put, and he can go. I don't want to keep him for nothing, but I don't want him doing a vanishing act either."

Back in the room, Eli explained slowly to the prisoner, who apparently had some difficulty taking it in, that if he did what he was told, they would let him go for the time being. He signed the statement and promised to remain in Dehaisha, but he would not go back to work. Michael wanted to know why, and in the end Ali expressed the fear that if he returned to the hospital now, they would lynch him. At the moment, Eli reassured him, the only person who knew anything about Ali's part in what had happened was the maintenance supervisor, and as far as they were concerned, they would like him to go back to work and keep an eye out for anything unusual. Ali nodded mechanically, and Eli asked if he would return to work the next day. He would do whatever they asked him to. When would he be allowed to go home? Today, said Eli. And then, only then, the hatred flashed in the young

Arab's eyes as it dawned on him that he had been tricked, and although he was being released, he was trapped.

It was six in the evening by the time they had finished the paperwork and decided what Gil Kaplan would say to the press. (Michael tried as far as possible to avoid direct contact with journalists; his picture spread over the back page of the papers, as today again, embarrassed him profoundly.) The rain had stopped. He knew that he should leave for his meeting with the murdered woman's family, but he put it off to give himself time for a quiet cup of coffee. With Michael, coffee was always a good reason for postponing things.

But Tzilla refused to let him be. Frowning, she said that they should get busy on the application for a warrant to see Neidorf's accounts. Without permission from the district court, they would never get it, and then, as you very well know, the bank managers will say that we haven't got the right to see anyone's accounts." Michael sighed. "We'll have to make sure that the hearing is held *in camera,*" he said wearily. "We don't want the press to get hold of it." Tzilla registered a protest about the restrictions placed by due process and democracy on efficient police work. "You can't move an inch without permission from the courts," she said indignantly. "Don't knock it," said Michael sternly. "You want to live in a place like Argentina? It's a price we have to pay." And then he thought that if only he had placed a guard on Neidorf's house, the whole thing wouldn't have come up in the first place; or if only, at least, he had got to the accountants in time; or if only . . .

When Tzilla hurried from the room to ask for Shorer's assistance in speeding up the application to the district court, Michael was left alone with his rapidly cooling coffee, staring at the wall opposite him and at the smoke whorls rising from his cigarette. Even before he asked himself what was stopping him from getting up and driving to the German Colony, the telephone rang, the white one—an outside call.

When he heard the husky "Hello" on the other end of the line, he couldn't help smiling. Her timing, he thought, was always perfect. As if she knew he had just come back from a funeral. Funerals invariably induced in him a deep desire to take refuge in a woman's body. Maya said "Hello" again, and he sighed: "I thought we'd decided something." The sentence was said, as always, without the necessary conviction, and she, of course, heard his longing. For five years Michael had failed, in spite of repeated attempts, to break up with her. He had known from the beginning that there was no possibility of their ever living together. At their first meeting, when the tone of absolute frankness characteristic of their later relationship had been set, she had made it clear that she would never leave her husband. "As far as divorce goes, I'm a Catholic," was the way she put it. "And don't try to understand; that's just the way it is."

At first this declaration had produced nothing but happiness and relief in him, but the time came when, as she had predicted, the pain was fiercer than the joy. The time came when the brief meetings and the impossibility of spending a whole day and night together gave rise in him to a feeling of loss more intense than any he had ever known. Ultimately the separation was unavoidable, and Michael was able to bear it only when he threw himself into his work. But Maya, who had announced her intentions in advance, was ruthless in her attempts to get him back, and she never failed.

He had tried to leave her nine times. The last time had lasted the longest. He hadn't heard her voice for a whole month. "I missed you," the husky voice said now, with a simplicity that stabbed his heart. "What are we going to do?" asked Michael, as if he weren't the one who had announced that this time it was over, and for good. "It doesn't matter; the important thing is that you're alive and that you love me," said Maya joyfully, and he remembered her laughter and the light that shone from her eyes. "Okay," he said despairingly, "but what are we going to do with this love?" And Maya said: "Whatever we can."

He couldn't help smiling. The temptation was so overwhelming, and once more the separation seemed like a pointless attempt not to compromise.

"In the end I'll have no alternative but to leave the country," he said.

"Yes, to Cambridge. You'll get there one day, but in the meantime," said Maya impatiently. She still had the key to his flat, and she said that she would be able to come that evening.

For a moment he felt the old anger, the desire to tell her that he had other fish to fry, other women, another life, but the prospect of embracing her again, of hearing her laughter, her tears, her moans, was stronger than anything else. And he asked himself again what he was doing here, in this dreary room, in this lousy job, and why he didn't get up and drive to the university this very minute and see Porath, who had been a young lecturer when he was a student and was now head of the History Department.

Whenever Michael met one of his former teachers, especially Professor Shatz, who had supervised his M.A. thesis, he was always asked why he didn't come back and do his doctorate.

Eight years ago, just before the divorce, he had hated Nira more than ever because their marriage and then their divorce had prevented him from taking up the grant he had been offered and going to do his Ph.D. at Cambridge. Today he knew that he had been at a crossroads then. And that the road back, as opposed to what he had thought then, was not so simple.

In one of his conversations with Shatz, the professor had tried to bring home to him what dropping out of the academic rat race meant. Michael refused to take him seriously and clung to the belief that his chances of a brilliant academic future depended on his intellectual ability alone. He tried to persuade Shatz, a Hungarian, who was fond of him and saw him as his successor, that since he had been offered the grant once, there was no reason he shouldn't be offered it again, in a year or two, after he had "sorted things out."

Shatz had accused him angrily of being naive, of not understanding that new young scholars, no less gifted than he was, would take his place, and he would not have a second chance. Yuval was six years old then, and Michael explained that the child would not be able to cope with the separation from his father, who had taken care of him more than anyone else and to whom he was particularly attached. Shatz could not dismiss the problem lightly—he had children of his own—

but he tried to find practical solutions while Michael, who could not bring himself to tell anyone about Nira's vengeful refusal to allow the boy to spend even one month a year with him abroad, kept quiet. If she wasn't coming with him, she said, if she wasn't going to be part of his brilliant academic career, he wasn't going to go either. And if he went, he could say goodbye to their son.

Cambridge and the grant would have been possible only at the price of continuing his marriage or giving up his child. It was a price Michael couldn't pay. The marriage was absolutely impossible, and he knew that Nira realized this too, yet couldn't bear the thought of his going ahead without her. As for the child, from the very first night Michael had wakened when he cried, sterilized the bottles, changed his diapers, rocked him in his arms for hours on end—this at a time before women's liberation changed men's lives, when his fellow students were still being supported by their wives and taking care not to have any children. He could never give up the child. Youzek, of course, offered generous financial assistance. What wouldn't he have done to be able to call his son-in-law "Doctor"? If he was poor and a Moroccan, then at least let him be a professor, as Michael flung at Nira when she pressed him to accept her parents' help.

Today he thought he had behaved foolishly. He should have accepted her parents' assistance and made life easier for both of them. He needn't have fought with Nira over every new dress she bought with their money. But he had principles then, he thought bitterly, stupid principles that had interfered with his daily life. In any case, there had been no chance of saving the marriage; it was doomed from the word go. He felt no love or concern for Nira. The sight of her swelling belly in the first year of their marriage meant nothing to him but the price he had to pay for his sense of obligation and responsibility. Nobody knew how hateful his situation was to him. Even his mother did not understand how much her youngest son suffered when he married the spoiled only daughter of well-to-do Polish parents. She only guessed something after Yuval was born, for she knew the signs only too well: cold politeness, reserve, and rare outbursts of the kind she had not witnessed since he left home.

He rejected out of hand Nira's suggestions of counseling. At that stage he thought that he would be able to write his doctoral thesis while holding a full-time job in Israel. He turned down the offer of a teaching assistantship because the salary would not have been enough to pay for separate accommodations and the alimony that Nira ruthlessly demanded, and he took the job with the police. He was sent first to an investigators course and then to an officers course, and in the end he found himself in the Major Crimes Unit, solving murder cases, while the subject of his Ph.D. grew more and more remote.

In his present way of life, it was impossible to write anything, and when he was wakened in the middle of the night to go and look at a corpse, the subject of professional guilds during the Middle Ages seemed very dull and sterile. Observing misery and suffering, squalor and pain, at close quarters made him see the expression "Ivory Tower" in a new light. He knew that devoting himself to his thesis, getting back into the closed circle of academic life, would necessitate his leaving the police force. Often he felt that the longing to return to the university was a superficial one, that it was not in the History Department that he would find his real place; at other times, like now, he felt despairingly that his life in the force was meaningless, and then the guilds, the Middle Ages, the History Department, the library, seemed to hold the promise of salvation.

It was half past six when he drank his coffee, completely cold, to the dregs and pulled himself together, standing up slowly and heavily to go to the Neidorf home. The daughter could hardly be asked to come to the Russian Compound on the day of the funeral, especially since she was free of the least trace of suspicion—nobody had a better alibi—but the thought of returning to the elegant house in the German Colony, to the abstract paintings on the white walls, filled him with profound reluctance.

The door opened, and Tzilla, with the enthusiasm belonging only to those whose work absorbs them body and soul, announced that they would be able to apply for the court order the next day. Shorer had pulled every string possible, she said proudly, as if he had done it just for her, and now, while Michael went to Neidorf's place, she would get onto all the party guests she hadn't managed to contact yet. Manny was in the interrogation room, she said, with the first on the list, Rosenfeld. "What an ass," said Tzilla, "with that cigar of his." Michael wondered where she got her energy. He felt old and tired and wanted, above all, to sleep.

He left his office, huddled into his parka, waved wearily at Eli, who was on his way to question another of the party people, told him to give all the material to Tzilla at the end of the day, and asked him to organize a team meeting the next morning. He would take care of it, promised Eli, after the interrogation, and meanwhile Michael had better just tell Tzilla. "She's the coordinator, after all," he said, and smiled ironically. "She's the one I take my orders from, isn't she?"

Michael refrained from asking what he meant; he was sick and tired of Eli and Tzilla's games too. Everything was stupid and pointless; in the end they wouldn't find anyone. The end of the story would be that she had killed herself and fairies had wafted the pistol away. Who the hell cares anyway, he asked himself.

He was obliged to mobilize fresh energy to fend off the keen young reporter who was standing next to his car in the hope of obtaining an exclusive interview for a women's newspaper. She had despaired of getting him on the phone, she said imploringly; she had been standing there for hours; just a few words. Michael apologized politely and said he was in a hurry. He referred her to the spokesman, with the assurance that she would get all the information she wanted about the case from him. "But I'm not interested in the case from the police point of view. I wanted to write about you. The personal angle. A portrait in depth. You seem like an interesting man, and I'm sure the public would be fascinated by the psychology of a high-ranking detective." "Sorry," said Michael, and got into his car, giving her long, shapely legs an appraising look and asking himself how she could stand wearing such thin shoes and stockings in such freezing weather, and what it would be like to go to bed with her, with all that keenness and enthusiasm. "I'm not allowed to give interviews while I'm working on a case. You can try after it's all over, if you like," he said affably.

"When, in your estimation, will that be?" asked the young woman, and she pressed the button of the miniature tape recorder she was holding in her hand. Michael pointed to the ceiling of the car, started the engine, and said as he turned the wheel: "Ask Him, if you're on speaking terms with Him," and then, to avoid any possible misunderstanding, he thrust his arm out the window and waved his hand at the sky before driving off in the direction of the German Colony.

12

"Yes," said Nava Neidorf-Zehavi, and she rocked the infant on her shoulder, one hand supporting his head. Gently Hillel took the baby in his arms and left the room. Up to that moment, all his efforts to separate the mother from her child had failed.

"She's clinging to him for dear life. I don't think you'll be able to get any sense out of her today," he had said when he opened the door to Michael.

It was only when he asked if Eva Neidorf had met anyone abroad apart from the members of her family that Nava began to focus on the man opposite her. Although she had greeted him politely and expressed her wish to help the police "find whoever did it," she had shown no interest in the information Michael gave them. Her brother, Nimrod, did most of the talking. He reacted to the news that the house had been broken into with an outburst of anger. He had not been surprised to find his mother's consulting room in a mess because he assumed that the police had searched the house. In his mind, that accounted for the broken kitchen window too.

A superficial examination revealed that no articles of value or paintings had been stolen. As for her jewelry, said Hillel, they would have to see what had been left in the safety-deposit box in the bank.

Michael conscientiously wrote down every suggestion they made about motives for the break-in. After an hour of this, he finally told them about the missing patient list and address book. He said nothing about the lecture notes. Hillel leapt up from his chair, waved his arms about in excitement, and almost shouted: "Nava, did you hear that? Do you understand what he's saying? It was no coincidence that—" But Nava reacted with such horror that he broke off immediately. He went to sit down beside her and began stroking her arm. It was then that Michael asked whether Dr. Neidorf had met anyone outside the family circle. "During all the time that she stayed with you," he stressed, "even something that may seem completely trivial," and he looked into Nava's eyes as she said "Yes" and burst into tears for the first time.

The tears, which were quiet at first, gradually turned into a storm of childish sobs.

He waited patiently. Nobody spoke until she began to calm down, and then Hillel took up the story: "She returned via Paris; she had a stopover of twenty-four hours. I bought the ticket for her. Until then she didn't see anyone but us. She only came to be with Nava for the birth. She arrived two days before the baby was born, everything was a bit frantic, she helped us get his room ready, and then Nava's labor started and she was right there with us in the hospital the whole time." He stroked his wife's arm. "It took hours. Nava was at the hospital for a week. During that week, Eva and I were together the whole time. We visited her and got everything ready, baby clothes and all the rest. It's not like it is here, with everybody pitching in and helping; you have to do everything yourself. In the evenings, Eva sat and worked on the lecture she was supposed to give on the Saturday when . . ."

He stopped and looked at Nava apprehensively. She had stopped crying, her eyes red and full of rage. Suddenly she looked very like her younger brother, who was sitting at the other end of the pale sofa, the same sofa on which Michael had sat Saturday night. (Was it really only the day before yesterday? he asked himself.) They were both staring in front of them with angry scowls on their faces, and Nava Neidorf appeared to have finally understood: "What you're saying here is something I find difficult to believe. You're saying that"—she swallowed and took a deep breath—"that my mother's death was due to her work?"

"Because of the lecture?" continued Nimrod, with an expression of dawning comprehension. "You're saying that everything was because of that lecture?"

Michael told them about the missing copies of the lecture, about the search of the Institute and its environs, which had failed to turn up anything. Perhaps, he asked, she had left a copy in their house in Chicago?

They looked at each other. Nimrod sat holding his breath, looking tensely from Nava and Hillel to Michael and back. No. She hadn't left any copies behind. It was a big house, they explained, in the suburbs. Eva had a separate wing, with her own bathroom, "so that she could rest a bit," said Hillel. They hadn't even seen the lecture. If there were any drafts, the maid who came every day must have thrown them out.

"There's no chance," said Hillel. "You can't imagine how tidy Eva was."

Nimrod hung his head and moaned. Hillel looked at him and fell silent.

"But what about the flight to Paris that you mentioned?" said Michael. "What were you going to say?"

Hillel removed his spectacles and wiped his eyes. Then he said: "When Nava was in the hospital, the day before she came home, I found Eva in the kitchen at two o'clock in the morning. At first I thought she couldn't sleep for excitement, like me, at the thought of Nava coming home with the baby, but as soon as she began to talk, I realized that her nervousness and tension were related to the lecture. She kept saying that if only she could consult Hildesheimer, it would be a weight off her mind. I asked her why she didn't call or write, but she said that it wasn't something that could be discussed over the phone or in a letter, and she wouldn't have time before the lecture. I almost suggested that she go home early, but I thought she would be hurt after coming all that way to help us with the baby."

His voice grew thoughtful, as if he was going over things in his mind in the light of the new information. "I asked her if there was nobody else she could consult, and she opened her eyes wide and said, 'Of course; why didn't I think of it before?' and that's how the idea of returning via Paris came up. There's a certain analyst, a friend of hers, who lives in Paris. I don't remember her name, but I've got it written down, and the phone number too. Eva called her the minute it was a normal hour in Paris and made an appointment to see her. I don't understand French, or hardly, and I was astonished to hear how fluent Eva was in the language."

Nava began weeping silently again, the tears streaming down her cheeks. She wiped them away with the back of her hand, until Hillel noticed her sniffs and brought her a box of tissues from the kitchen.

Michael didn't know where to start. Hildesheimer had not mentioned any visit to Paris. Had he known and was he hiding it? But why on earth should he?

Was it possible that Eva hadn't told the old man? And what about the story that she had flown back to Israel with Hillel? He himself had questioned Hillel on the day of the murder, and it had been obvious that they had arrived on the same flight, the discussion in readiness for the directors' meeting, the first-class tickets.

Aloud he said only: "Didn't you fly back with her?"

Yes, of course he had; he'd said so to the chief inspector at the hospital, hadn't he, in the waiting room outside intensive care on Saturday?

"But how could you have?" asked Michael in confusion.

"What do you mean, how? On a flight from Paris, of course. I left for Paris the day after Eva," said Hillel.

"Why didn't you tell me this on Saturday?" asked Michael suspiciously.

"I thought you knew; I thought it was obvious; I didn't think it mattered. How do I know why? I didn't realize then that it was important, and mainly I thought you knew."

Rapidly Michael summed up the new information. Eva Neidorf had met a colleague in Paris, she had flown back to Israel with her son-in-law from Paris and not from New York, and she hadn't mentioned the meeting and the stopover in Paris to Hildesheimer.

He asked Hillel to tell him about the flight again. "Yesterday was supposed to be the annual meeting of the board of directors. It was an important meeting." Hillel stole a glance at his wife and brother-in-law, who were staring in front of them but obviously listening.

"I had to prepare her. She didn't have a clue. At home we never got around to it—the baby kept crying and she was busy with the lecture and we never had a chance—and we kept putting it off and saying that we would do it on the plane. I took an indirect flight to Israel with a stopover in Paris, and Eva boarded the plane in Paris. We arranged it all in advance; I made the bookings for both of us. So we flew back together from Paris, and all I know is that she met the analyst. I asked her about the meeting and her stay in Paris, and she said that it had been very important. She looked a little tense, but that's all I can tell you. I don't know what the lecture was about or what her problem with it was."

Michael looked inquiringly at Nava, who shook her head. She hadn't even known why her mother had flown to Paris. She thought it was just for fun. She had just given birth; she hadn't thought about it one way or the other, she said, and her eyes filled with tears again.

Yes, she knew the French analyst. She couldn't remember her name; it was hard to pronounce.

Nimrod remembered. "Catherine Louise Dubonnet," he said firmly, pronoucing every syllable separately. It was evidently a name that had left a profound impression on him.

Yes, Hillel and Nava agreed, that was the name. Nava, it transpired, had met her a number of years before, when she stayed with them during a congress at the Institute. "She seemed a thousand years old to me then, as old as the hills with her snow-white hair. I never spoke a word to her because I didn't know any French, or English either." She spoke between sobs, in a low voice. Nimrod, however, claimed that she wasn't much older than their mother. "They corresponded regularly after that," said Nimrod. "I know because of the stamps; I was still a kid then, and I collected stamps."

"When was this 'then'?" asked Michael, growing impatient.

Nimrod made a mental calculation, then said: "The first time I saw her was nine years ago. After that she stayed with us two more times, both during congresses. The last time was two years ago, and she still brought me stamps, even though I'd stopped collecting them by then. I was already in the army."

Hillel left the room. After a couple of minutes he came back, announced that the baby was sleeping, and handed Michael a note with a name and a Paris telephone number on it. Michael turned to Nava and asked her if the Frenchwoman and her mother were close to each other.

Nimrod answered first: "As close as she was with anyone. She called her Cathie. I don't believe she had any close women friends; my mother wasn't the kind for intimate chats over the phone. But I think she must have liked her, because she once told me that she respected her very much."

Nava gave her brother a forgiving look and explained that while their mother may have been reserved, she certainly had friends.

"Who? Go on, give me an example," Nimrod burst out, and quickly added: "Never mind; it doesn't matter."

Michael said he was afraid it did matter. Nava kept quiet, Nimrod withdrew into himself, and Hillel explained that it was difficult to know anything about Eva's social life, she was very reticent, but that she had described the Frenchwoman as "a friend I can confide in." He remembered the words precisely, because coming from her they had sounded strange.

Why hadn't she told Hildesheimer? Michael asked himself, and out loud he asked what her relations with the old man had been.

For the first time, all three smiled; even Nimrod raised his head and smiled. "Have you seen him?" he asked inquisitively. "Isn't he something?" The smile gave his face a naive, childish look.

Hillel said apologetically that he'd only met him a few times, but he seemed to be "a real personality or, more correctly, a monument," and he stopped smiling abruptly.

Nava said the relationship was warm and close. "He's the person closest to her—was, I mean," and her eyes filled with tears again. "I regard him as family," she said in a choked voice and wrapped herself more tightly in the big, shapeless dressing gown she was wearing.

She's not pretty, thought Michael, plain, if anything, and he remembered the scream at the open grave. He couldn't help wondering how she had felt next to her beautiful mother, how they got along together, how Eva Neidorf, with her highly developed aesthetic sense, had felt about the unimpressive appearance of her daughter, who wore her brown hair scraped back behind her ears, where any wayward lock was quickly and unthinkingly pushed back into place.

He asked about Neidorf's relations with the Institute people. All three, each in his own way, replied that everyone had admired her. "If you're looking for enemies, as you people say," said Hillel, "people who wished her harm, you won't find any. In all her life she never harmed a fly, and nobody would have wanted to harm her."

He himself realized the irony of his words, and quickly added: "Up to now, in any case, I never knew of anyone who wanted to harm her," and he straightened his spectacles.

Cautiously Michael asked if they would object to having their house in Chicago searched. "What for?" asked Hillel, and then: "Ah, the lecture notes? There isn't a chance, but as far as I'm concerned, go ahead."

Michael asked if anyone there had typed the lecture for her.

"No," said Hillel. "We've got a Hebrew typewriter, and she typed it herself, after writing it out in longhand." He gave Michael the address and asked if the house would "remain in one piece" afterward. Michael promised. Nava said nothing and picked at the tissue in her hand. Nimrod left the room and went to the kitchen.

There was a ring at the door, and Hillel said: "Who can that be? Nobody pays condolence visits on the day of the funeral."

Nimrod opened the heavy door and found Rosenfeld and Linder, who asked hesitantly if they could come in. He invited them in with a gesture and said to the people sitting in the room: "Rosencrantz and Guildenstern." Only Linder smiled. Nava glared at her brother and said: "Stop it, will you?" Rosenfeld stuck a cigar in his mouth and lit it. Michael said that they would finish their talk another time.

"Whenever you wish, we're at your disposal," said Nimrod sarcastically, and gave Linder a hostile stare.

Michael felt uncomfortable. He would have preferred to see Rosenfeld and Linder at the Russian Compound. On the other hand, he didn't want them to think that he was running away from them. Besides, he thought, he was sure to pick something up, obtain some additional information, if he stayed for as long as it took to smoke a cigarette. He lit one and stayed where he was, the same question nagging at his mind: Why hadn't Neidorf told Hildesheimer about her visit to Paris?

It was clear that the two analysts felt equally uncomfortable in the presence of the policeman. Linder sat down next to Nava and spoke to her in a whisper. Michael heard the words: "Sorry . . . feel guilty . . . " and wondered if he was talking about the pistol. Rosenfeld sat silent. After a while he opened his mouth and told Michael that he had just come from "your police station, from giving evidence. I thought you were in charge of the investigation," he said with a slightly offended air.

Michael tried to remember Rosenfeld's written statement after the meeting of the Training Committee. He wondered if Manny had asked him about Linder's sleeping tablets and couldn't call what Rosenfeld had done on Saturday morning and the night before, but he did recollect that he was apparently in the clear. Manny was supposed to have asked him about the party and about his relations with the dead woman. When he got back, he would find it all with Tzilla, in Manny's small, erratic handwriting, which no one but Tzilla could understand, and until she typed it out he would have no way of knowing what Rosenfeld had replied to his questions. Rosenfeld asked Hillel if there was anything he could do to help them, and Michael doused his cigarette in the big ashtray and said he had to be going.

To Hillel, who accompanied him to the gate, he whispered that he would be grateful for a report on what was said by the people who came to call. "Everything?" asked Hillel in astonishment. No, he didn't mean "everything," of course; just anything that sounded out of place, any strange or unusual behavior. "And any reference to the lecture, absolutely anything about it."

Hillel nodded and said: "It puts us in a very awkward position, having to spy on people and suspect them, and with Nava and Nimrod in the state they're in, I don't know. . . . " Michael cast a glance down Lloyd George Street, to where the police surveillance vehicle, a Peugeot van, was parked. Thank God they don't have to know about that, at least, thought Michael, or the bugging during the next seven days. "There really is a difficulty here," Hillel went on, looking mistrustfully at Michael in the light of the streetlamp, the same light by which Michael had forced the door of the house two nights before. Of this, too, Hillel was ignorant. A head shorter than Michael, he strained to look into his eyes as he mumbled that Nava wasn't so strong, and the very idea, the thought that anyone who came into the house might be ... But here he stopped talking, because a car drew up next to them and Dina Silver stepped out of it. Her face waxen in the lamplight, her hair shining with a blue gleam, she looked like a ghost as she shook Hillel's hand and said that she simply had to come, she felt she couldn't wait until tomorrow, and asked if she could come inside. Hillel said: "Yes, why not; there are some other people here already," and she nodded at Michael, who gave her a long look as she walked gracefully up the path leading from the gate to the front door.

Another day gone, thought Michael as he started his car and heard the radio signaling. Raffi was looking for him, he wanted to contact him urgently, the voice said, and Michael looked at his watch, wondered whether Maya was waiting for him, and said that he would be at home. Raffi could contact him there. When he turned the car around, he saw a long figure in a dark duffel coat come out of the shadows of the old Semadai movie house and stand next to the blue BMW from which Dina Silver had just emerged. Over the radio he now heard Raffi's voice: "Don't go yet; I'm right here. Just drive to the corner."

A dim figure descended from the Peugeot van on the corner, and Raffi got into Michael's car. "First give me a cigarette," he said, "and then tell me what's going on. He's been sticking to her like a leech. He was waiting next to her car outside the funeral parlor, and after the funeral he followed her on his Vespa to Rehavia and waited for her there until she came out."

"Where in Rehavia?" asked Michael, and received a detailed description of the clinic on Abrabanel Street he had visited the day before.

"After that he drove behind her like a pro, without lights, and followed her here," Raffi continued. "With looks like his, you'd expect to find him in the Hilton with some rich American tourist," he said, and stroked his hair.

Michael lit two cigarettes and handed one to Raffi. Then he asked the youth's name.

"The Vespa's registered to Elisha Naveh; I haven't checked yet if it's him. Balilty found out that the father's something in our embassy in London. We've got nothing on him, on the boy, just a couple of traffic offenses, and the Vespa's not stolen, no one's reported it missing. All I have to do now is verify that this lunatic is Elisha Naveh. What his story is with her I haven't a clue."

Michael asked if they'd spoken to each other.

"No; she doesn't know that he's still on her back," said Raffi, opening the window to shake out cigarette ash. "She saw him standing next to her car outside the funeral parlor, and she said something to him then. I didn't manage to hear what it was, but she looked grim. She's some piece, hey? I've got the particulars on her. You know who her husband is?" The last question was asked with a smile, and Michael nodded. He'd heard, yes, he knew who she was and who her husband was, and they could talk about it tomorrow morning, at the meeting. In the meantime, he should just stick to the boy.

"Ohayon," said Raffi plaintively. "I'm freezing and starving. Who's going to take over from me?"

"How many men are there in the Peugeot?" asked Michael.

"Come on, give me a break; you know there's only two of them.

The replacements are coming at eleven, and who knows how long she's going to be inside?"

"Who, in your opinion, can take over from you?" asked Michael wearily.

"Okay," sighed Raffi. "You needn't say any more. We'll fix it up between us. Ezra owes me one, I'll get onto him, and until he turns up, I won't budge from here. As long as something comes out of it, hey?"

Michael inquired dryly if he wanted a signed guarantee. No, he didn't want one. All he wanted was for Michael to leave him his cigarettes. "And if anything happens I can phone you at home, right?"

From the inside pocket of his parka Michael extracted the squashed pack of Noblesse, made of cheap Virginia tobacco, and laid the four remaining cigarettes one by one in Raffi's expectant hand. Raffi got out of the car, looked around him, and walked off in the direction of the Peugeot.

As Michael drove home it began to rain again, and the thought of Maya waiting for him excited him so that he went through a red light. It was half past nine when he parked outside the apartment. As he walked up to the front door, he could already hear the strains of Beethoven's fourth piano concerto coming from inside, and he couldn't understand how he had managed for a whole month without her.

13

"What exactly do you mean when you say he was uptight?"
Michael asked Manny, who had interrogated Colonel Yoav
Alon, military governor of the subdistrict of Edom, when
he came to give evidence as a participant in Linder's party. They were
in the middle of their morning conference, and although it had been
going on since seven-thirty, they were still nursing their coffee cups.

Intelligence Officer Balilty looked at his watch; Michael lit his
third cigarette. After an hour of intensive discussion, they were all leaning back in their chairs with a feeling that the essential points had all
been taken care of. Michael had delivered his bombshell about Catherine Louise Dubonnet and explained that Interpol were helping to
locate her. On holiday in Majorca, she had gone off on a sailing trip
and wouldn't be back to her hotel for two days.

Tzilla remarked that she thought psychiatrists only took vacations
in August. "Like in Woody Allen movies," she said, directing a viva-
cious look at Eli and receiving a scowl in return.

They had reviewed the events of the past couple of days and

agreed that Eli would handle the banks. A lot of time had been devoted to reviewing the funeral. They had all listened to Raffi's report on the youth he'd tailed. Balilty, who had gathered the information from the Foreign Office ("I've got connections in all kinds of places," he replied to Raffi's question), told them that Elisha Naveh was nineteen years old, had lost his mother at the age of ten, and was the only son of one Mordechai Naveh. "Officially he belongs to the Foreign Office, but he's actually from the Prime Minister's Office, presently attached to the embassy in London. The first secretary, if that means anything to you," said Balilty in a tone that deflected further inquiry. Naveh had been at the London embassy for five years, continued Balilty, glancing at his notes. The boy had returned to Israel when he was sixteen. He couldn't adjust to life in London and to the Jewish school he attended there, and his father had finally given in to his pleas. When he came home he lived for two years with his grandmother, who had died a few months ago. His army service had been deferred, "only for a year—you know what they're like," on the grounds of psychological unfitness.

Since his grandmother's death he had been living in a flat registered in his father's name. He was studying at the university—Balilty pulled a face—"something like Far Eastern Studies and Theater. The arty type, if you know what I mean."

Yes, he was in therapy, not with Neidorf but at a mental health clinic. There was a psychiatric evaluation in his file at the recruiting office, but he had not told the army psychiatrist that he was in therapy. Balilty had found his name among the patients listed at one of the mental health clinics in the northern suburbs, but he had not succeeded in discovering the name of the psychologist yet. The last word was emphasized.

Tzilla asked if there was anything in the army psychiatrist's opinion to suggest that he might be dangerous.

"Look," said Balilty, "the conditions under which I received the information didn't allow me to read the material myself. My sources reported on a 'maladjusted personality' and 'suicidal tendencies.' One phrase was repeated three times: 'Foreign Office children syndrome,' and there were all kinds of other things, but nothing to suggest that he was dangerous to others."

"But what's he actually done?" Eli asked Raffi. Raffi said that Elisha had followed Dina Silver home and sat on a stone outside her house until midnight and then gone home. Someone was living with him in the flat. Balilty was checking on the name he'd found on the mailbox, but he hadn't come up with anything yet.

"Don't worry, he will," said Tzilla. "It slays me how you manage to find things out so fast. I wouldn't like to fall into your hands, that's for sure. Tell me, do you know what he eats for breakfast yet?" Balilty, with a twinkle in his little eyes, was about to answer, but when he saw the expression on Shorer's face he thought better of it and kept quiet.

"Good," said Michael, still holding his coffee cup. "At nine I'm meeting the Silver woman. We'll see what she's got to say for herself."

"You haven't got much time," said Tzilla.

At the beginning of the meeting she had placed before everyone a list of known patients and supervisees, a reconstruction of Neidorf's work schedule (Tzilla had spoken to the maid), a list of Institute members, a list of guests at Linder's party, a photocopy of the signed note that Michael had brought back from the accountants' office, and the Identi-Kit drawing of the man who had taken Neidorf's file. The documents were inside manila folders, and everyone at the meeting received a folder from Tzilla, who reported, as she skipped with inexplicable gaiety from chair to chair, that Linder was in the clear, that his wife had handed in the dinner menu, the dinner guests' baby-sitter had confirmed the time they had come home, the upstairs neighbor had been awakened early on Saturday morning by the noise. "It's all there in the file, and anybody who wants to can listen to the tapes as well," she said as she finally took her place at the table and pushed a thin hand through her boyishly cut hair.

"Linder's in the clear," confirmed Shorer, snapping his last match and dropping the pieces into the tin ashtray. Michael asked him in a whisper if he would see to getting the court order for the banks. "Yes," said Shorer, "but I want Bahar there with me, so he can go straight to the bank before someone else gets there first this time too."

Michael looked at him apprehensively, and Shorer said: "I was only joking," and then Manny reported on his interrogations of Rosenfeld and Colonel Yoav Alon, military governor of Edom.

"Did you see how gorgeous he is?" Tzilla asked Manny, who ignored her and went on with his report. But she jumped right in again, with a bounciness that exasperated Michael: "They say he's the up-and-coming star, that he'll be the next chief of staff. And he looks so young, not more than thirty-five."

Manny gave her a withering look and asked if he could continue. Michael put his hand on her arm and said quietly: "Why don't you sit still and listen for a minute? Just drink your coffee and keep quiet, okay?" She kept quiet and Manny went on and said: "The subject seemed uptight." Michael asked what he meant, and he stared at the Identi-Kit picture of the man who had taken Neidorf's financial file.

"I don't know exactly what I mean," said Manny hesitantly. "You'd expect a colonel, a military governor in the territories, to be a bit more cooperative, you know, glad to help. But he kept looking at his watch, saying he was in a hurry; he looked tense and . . ." Suddenly there was silence in the room, an atmosphere of concentration and attention. For the first time since Michael had reported on his visit to the family and the discovery of Neidorf's stopover in Paris, there was tension in the air, the suppressed excitement that precedes the possible discovery of a fresh lead.

Everyone looked at Manny as Michael said: "Look at the drawing for a minute. Does it ring a bell?" Manny looked, and so did everyone else. Tzilla shook her head hesitantly, but all the others turned to look at Manny, who said: "I don't know. You didn't get much out of her, did you? Maybe without the dark glasses; there isn't even anything to go on with the eyes. I don't know, but let's say it isn't impossible."

"I don't suppose you happened to ask him what he was doing on Monday morning, when the file was lifted?" asked Balilty.

"Actually"—Inspector Manny Ezra wiped his forehead—"I did, and he said that he had come late to work because his car got stuck on the way to Bethlehem, next to Beit Jalla, and he had to wait an hour before someone came to get him. And for your information, I asked everyone the same question, including Rosenfeld. You think you're the only person around here who knows what he's doing?" And he put the manila folder down on the table, his hands trembling slightly with anger, and asked if anyone else wanted coffee.

Michael looked at him in astonishment and then at Balilty, who tucked his shirt into the belt above his paunch and looked around him in embarrassment. Shorer defused the atmosphere by asking if there was any connection between Colonel Alon and the victim. "No connection," said Manny, standing at the door, and Shorer said: "Just a minute; the coffee can wait. I want details."

"Sir," said Manny, and resumed his seat. "You can listen to the tape; there's no connection between them. He's a close friend of Linder's, he's known him for twenty years, he admitted to buying him the revolver, and he knows the girl too, the one they had the party for, Tammy Zvielli; she's a childhood friend of his, and that's what he was doing at the party. But he said he didn't know Neidorf."

"And what's his alibi for Friday and Saturday?" asked Shorer, and the tension in the room rose.

The hands of the clock stood at five to nine. Dina Silver was supposed to wait for him in the corridor outside his office, thought Michael as he stood up to open the window, which overlooked the backyard. He glanced at the bright blue sky—the glare hurt his eyes—without missing a word that Manny was saying.

On Friday night, said Manny, Colonel Alon had gone to bed early. "His wife was visiting her parents, in Haifa, with their two children. He was alone; he doesn't know who saw him. On Saturday morning he went for a walk around the French Hill; it was a nice day. He came home at around eleven, he didn't meet anyone, but that doesn't mean anything," he said defensively. "Since when do people go around organizing alibis?"

Shorer said nothing and looked at Michael, and Michael told them about the phone call Linder had made from the Institute.

"What time?" asked Shorer.

"Half past twelve."

"In other words," reflected Raffi aloud, "he knew then that she was dead. What does that tell us?"

"All kinds of things that it's too early to think about yet," said Michael. "Let's wait until we see the bank accounts. I've got a funny feeling, but still . . . We need the full list of patients and supervisees and the Frenchwoman's evidence."

Shorer was the first to understand. "You think he's the missing patient? Is that what you think?"

Michael replied that he didn't know; meanwhile it was just a hunch, and he wanted to see the bank accounts first. "Okay, so let's hear your hunch, then. You think there's a connection between him and Neidorf, don't you?" insisted Shorer. "We all know the way your mind works. Come on, nobody's going to sue you for libel."

Everyone looked at Michael, whose high cheekbones gave his smile a quality that had captured the hearts of many women but not of his teammates as they waited now for him to speak. Finally he said: "We all know that strange things happen in life. Even the coincidence of finding the gun in the hospital grounds sounds too good to be true. Which leads me to conclude that fact is stranger than fiction and that things may get even stranger before we're through." He looked at his watch and said that there was a lady waiting for him, from whom he was about to receive, among other things, the name of an additional patient.

The tension relaxed, as if the room had taken a deep breath and let out a sigh. Balility remarked: "Have you ever known him to keep a beautiful woman waiting?" They all smiled and began allocating the day's tasks among themselves. One after the other, they left the room. Tzilla, Manny, and Raffi went to question the party guests who had been invited to present themselves at the Russian Compound that day. "If we're lucky, we might get through ten today," Tzilla said with a sigh. "It's no joke: forty people."

Shorer and Eli left for court, where the hearing was scheduled at ten. Balility was about to leave too, when Michael touched his arm. They were standing in the doorway, and Michael, who had intended asking him to explain the meaning of Manny's defensiveness, found himself asking first if Balilty could gather intelligence information on Colonel Alon without anyone else knowing.

"Not even Shorer? No one at all?" asked Balilty.

"No one. Not Shorer, not Levy, no one from the military government—absolutely no one. Can you do it?"

Balilty stared at the toes of his shoes and tucked his escaping shirttails into his belt. Then he passed his hand over his head and said: "I don't know. I'll have to check. Give me a few hours to check out my contacts. I'll get back to you later today, okay?" Michael nodded, and Balilty was already on his way out when Michael caught up and asked: "What was that business with Manny all about?"

"Ah, that," said Balilty in embarrassment. "It's a long story. Nothing to do with the case. I'll tell you one day," and he headed briskly down the stairs leading out of the building.

The conference room was too close to Michael's office to allow him any time for reflection about his meeting with Dina Silver. She was standing in the corridor, looking pointedly at her watch and then at him. Michael ignored her silent comment on his lateness and thought that red and blue suited her better than her present black, which emphasized her pallor and made her lovely face look older. He opened the door of his room and lit himself a cigarette. With an expression of disgust, she rejected the one he offered her, and Michael opened the window, telling himself that this was the last concession he would make to her.

As soon as he had seen her in the corridor, he had put on his poker face and felt the hostility streaming through him. A cold beauty, every movement under control. I'd like to see you tremble, he thought, and the impulse he felt as he stood in the doorway and let her go in before him, the impulse to upset her self-control, her slow, emphatic speech, began to express itself in words.

He knew that she would have an explanation for her conversation with Hildesheimer on Sunday afternoon. He remembered Linder saying that she had been in analysis with the old man, and he was certain she would invoke this to account for the way she had accosted him in the street. By the time he sat down in the chair behind his desk, he had formulated his question about her relationship with the youth. "You've got no grounds," he heard a warning inner voice, "you've got no grounds at all, you don't know anything, you haven't found anything, you just think she might have a motive, but there's nothing to back it up, there was another candidate the Training Committee were going to vote on too, wait until you've spoken to him at least." The more he sensed the aggression in him seeking an outlet, the more slowly and politely he spoke.

Her flashing eyes, which were more green than gray, contained both anger and anxiety as he asked her about her movements on Friday night. In her low voice, with its precise enunciation, Dina Silver replied that she had gone to bed early. "How early?" asked Michael.

"After the variety show, before the movie," she replied, and he felt his tension begin to evaporate.

"So early? Do you always go to bed so early?" he asked in a tone of affected curiosity.

"No, actually I don't usually," and as she opened her mouth to say something more, he cut in: "And on the night before the vote on your presentation too?"

Here she smiled for the first time, but only with her lips—there wasn't the hint of a smile in her eyes—and said that actually she couldn't fall asleep. "But I wanted to be rested, for the lecture and the vote." Her hands fiddled with the high neck of her blouse. She sat there with her coat open, a long, soft fur coat, giving off a pampered air.

"I thought," said Chief Inspector Ohayon, and lit another cigarette, "that candidates didn't take part in the voting."

Fear flashed through her eyes as she explained that she had intended waiting outside the room, and then, if the vote went in her favor, they would call her in and she would know the same day.

"Well, and did you manage to fall asleep in the end? When?" said Michael, breathing in the cigarette smoke intently.

"Late, maybe after midnight," she said hesitantly.

"And what did you do until you fell asleep?" he asked with the same interested curiosity.

"What's that got to do with—" she began to say, but changed her mind and said that she had tried to read but couldn't concentrate.

"Read what?" asked Michael, noting signs of a loss of control and expecting an outburst of anger.

"Giora's presentation—the other candidate they were going to vote on. We're the first of our year, and—"

With a show of righteous surprise, Michael asked if she hadn't yet read her colleague's presentation.

"But they hadn't distributed them yet; only the members of the Training Committee had copies. He only gave it to me on Thursday; I hadn't shown mine to anyone except him either."

"Ah," said Michael. "And Saturday morning? What did you do on Saturday morning?"

"I was at the Institute, of course," she said quickly.

"From what time?" asked Michael. "Let's say eight o'clock—were you there then?"

Dina Silver grew even paler. Her face was gray. She had arrived at the Institute at ten. At eight she was only waking up.

She explained that she got up late because she hadn't slept well, but her face was hostile, and when he asked her if she was alone in the house, she burst out furiously: "What are you getting at? Of course I wasn't alone, I'm marr— My husband was at home with me."

"Have you got any children?" asked Michael.

Yes, she said, she had, a ten-year-old daughter. But she was sleeping over with a friend and only came home at lunchtime, she explained without having been asked. Michael studiously wrote down the friend's surname and telephone number.

"But what are you going to ask my daughter? Do you question children too?" she asked with open anxiety.

"Madam," said Michael coldly, "if necessary we question everybody. If necessary." And he added: "And does your husband know what time you went to bed and what time you got up?"

Dina Silver looked at him, and suddenly she smiled, the same humorless grimace as before, and said that she felt the situation was unreal. "I don't understand; am I suspected of . . .?" Michael waited and then asked her to finish the sentence. "Of murder—am I suspected of murder?" she asked in a tone of indignant incredulity.

"Who said anyone suspected you?" Michael inquired curiously. "Did I say so?"

No, she admitted, he hadn't said so, but the kind of questions he asked made her think that perhaps he imagined she might have God knows what reason for doing it.

How, Michael wondered, did she know what kind of questions they asked murder suspects? And observed with satisfaction the scrambled sentence structure, the slight loss of breath, the rapid spate of words, as she explained that television movies and thrillers were the source of her information. She was looking, Michael sensed, for the right way to get to him, just as he was looking for the right way to get to her. Now she appealed to him with a helpless expression and asked if that wasn't the way things really happened, like in books and television.

"I don't know," said Michael. "Do you read a lot of thrillers?"

No, only sometimes, when she couldn't fall asleep.

"And what do they do to you?" he asked.

"What do you mean?" she asked, placing her hands on her lap to keep them from trembling.

He meant, said Michael innocently, what made her interested in them, what attracted her to this kind of literature.

She wasn't a violent type, if that's what he meant, she said. He shrugged his shoulders, as if to say that he hadn't meant anything in particular.

Her interest was psychological, she said.

"Ah, psychological," he said, as if this explained everything. And what about her husband: did he know what time she went to bed and what time she got up?

She gave him a despairing look and asked if these were the kinds of questions they asked everybody.

Michael decided it was time to change his tune. Yes, he said, he asked everyone the same kinds of questions. Perhaps she would like coffee? She hesitated, looked at him, and then nodded. He brought her coffee and watched the trembling hand holding the mug. In a paternal tone, he explained that he was investigating a complicated murder case; it was his duty to ascertain all the facts.

He leaned over the desk, coming as close to her as he could, as if he were taking her into his confidence, placing some special trust in her. She relaxed, she thawed, and of her own free will, without his having to repeat the question, she explained that her husband had spent the night in his den in the basement. He was thinking about a court case, she said, he was a district judge, and whenever he had a trial on, like now, he would shut himself up in his den and go over the evidence by himself without talking about it to anyone. And so she hadn't seen him when she got up in the morning or when she left the house either.

"But I'm sure there won't be any problem about verifying your statement," said Michael in a friendly voice. "Did you walk to the Institute?"

No, she had gone by car.

The blue BMW she had got out of last night outside Neidorf's house? asked Michael familiarly.

Yes, that was her car.

"Then there certainly won't be any problem. There's always some-one who sees something." She could leave it to him, he continued, and looked into her eyes, where he read bewilderment at his changed tone, relief mingled with suspicion. "Just tell me exactly when you left the house. Five to ten?" He wrote something on the form in front of him and looked at her again with a air of satisfaction, as if she had been of the utmost assistance.

"There's something I'd like to ask you," he said, and leaned over the desk again, putting her on her guard. "What's the relationship between you and Elisha Naveh?" Michael sat up a little more erectly in his chair and waited for her reply. He saw the surprise in her eyes, and a new fear, of a kind that had not been there before.

When she recovered she asked calmly why he wanted to know. "What's his connection with all this?"

"None that we know of," said Michael matter-of-factly, "but since I saw the two of you talking next to your car, I thought . . ." Michael fell silent. He saw quite clearly the impulse to protest, to say that he couldn't have seen them, that he wasn't anywhere near, but also the calculation. Dina Silver looked at him and said: "And what about my professional ethics?"

"Ah," said Michael. "He's a patient of yours?"

No, that wasn't strictly accurate, she said, but he had been once. To Michael's questions about where and when, she replied that she had treated him from the age of sixteen to eighteen, at a mental health clinic in North Jerusalem.

"Two years, that's to say until a year ago," Chief Inspector Ohayon reflected aloud. "And you completed the treatment?"

It was a complicated story, she said, which had nothing to do with the case and was connected to the kind of relationship the patient had developed toward her. "Actually the treatment was terminated and not completed," she explained. "He couldn't be helped by me anymore, but you'd need a knowledge of professional terminology to understand."

"What terminology do you have in mind? What about the term 'transference'—would that be of any help here?" inquired Michael, and observed with enjoyment the expression of surprise and new respect that came into her eyes.

Yes, she admitted, it would certainly help. "Look," she said in a didactic tone, "I don't know, of course, how familiar you are with the field, but the boy began acting out. Do you know the term?"

No, he didn't. Could she explain?

"In other words"—a serious, self-satisfied expression began to spread over her face, and Michael made no attempt to interfere—"he began to pester me with telephone calls, with unexpected visits, with demands that I fulfill his erotic fantasies."

"Do you mean that he fell in love with you?"

"Putting it simply, yes. In professional terms, I would speak of a transference neurosis that found its expression in acting out rather than in verbalization during the therapy sessions."

"And when that happens the therapy is broken off? I thought that transference was one of the conditions for continuing it."

Again there was a flash of surprise, and she said: "On principle you're right, but in this case I had a countertransference, and . . ."

"What do you mean?" asked Michael impatiently. "Do you mean that he got on your nerves, or that you became emotionally involved with him?"

Yes, that was what she meant. He occupied her thoughts outside working hours to such an extent that she couldn't continue the therapy, and she didn't know what had become of him since. . . . The first time she had seen him since the termination of the therapy was next to her car at the funeral.

"In other words, you didn't see him for a whole year, and then suddenly he turned up at the funeral?" asked Michael, and he held his pen poised over the paper. "Are you sure? There was no contact between you?" Again the hostility in his voice, without his being able to control or account for it. He suppressed it and explained to her that whatever he wrote down had to be accurate.

"Yes, but why do you have to write anything?" asked Dina Silver, without concealing her annoyance. "I wouldn't like confidential medical information to be made public. It's unethical."

Michael asked if during the entire year the patient hadn't bothered her at all.

"No, only a few times on the phone," she said hesitantly.

"Where did he telephone to?" he asked, holding his pen.

"To the clinic. I only left there six months ago."

"And you hadn't heard from him since then?" asked Michael, who felt his tension mounting and sensed that something was preventing him from seeing the facts clearly.

No, she hadn't heard from him since leaving the clinic, and yesterday at the funeral was the first time she had seen him.

In that case, why, asked Michael, had the boy followed her yesterday from the funeral to Linder's consulting rooms, and from there to Neidorf's house, and after that to her home?

Her face turned ashen, and she said hoarsely: "Are you sure?"

He nodded and asked what he had said to her at the funeral.

"He said that he had to meet me, and I explained to him that I was only seeing patients privately now and so I wouldn't be able to see him. It's considered wrong and unethical for a therapist to receive patients privately after treating them in the framework of the public health services. I referred him back to the clinic," she said, but Michael sensed that she was thinking about something else, and he asked her if she was afraid of Elisha Naveh.

After a brief pause for thought, she said that she wasn't afraid—he had never been violent—but she didn't know how to interpret his behavior.

Michael asked if there was any possibility that he had been in contact with Neidorf. Dina Silver shook her head vehemently. "Impossible," she said. "She couldn't have accepted him for treatment, she didn't have the time, and he never met her anywhere else. I would have heard about it from him." Her face was still gray when Michael asked her in a fatherly tone if there was anything that was making her feel nervous. She replied that she had been in a very sensitive state ever since what had happened, everything made her feel anxious, but there was no rational basis for her anxiety. "It's part of the reaction to Dr. Neidorf's death. It will pass," she said, and she smiled with the corners of her mouth again. After a brief pause she remarked that she was worried about the boy, and for this reason she would like to suggest that Chief Inspector Ohayon refrain from questioning him until he "calmed down."

Michael said nothing, but his mind registered the fact that Dina Silver was afraid of contact between himself and the youth.

Again he asked her about her relations with Neidorf, and again she spoke of the debt she owed her, about all she had learned from her. There was no feeling behind the words, not even the kind of feeling that had been behind Linder's words. It was like a tape recording, as if she were repeating words she had learned by rote.

Was there any truth in what he had heard about the dead woman's coldness and remoteness? he inquired.

No, she had never sensed anything of the kind; the relations between them had been close and trusting. Neidorf had simply been a withdrawn, reserved woman, but not cold, said Dina Silver, and there was no hint of enthusiasm or any other manifestation of feeling in her voice.

And then he asked about the meeting with Hildesheimer, on Alfasi Street, outside his house, on Sunday afternoon. She looked at him in dismay, but she didn't ask him how he knew or make any clever, evasive remark, and after a moment she said that Hildesheimer had been her analyst.

Michael asked her how long it had taken, and she said that the analysis had been concluded a year and a half ago and had lasted for five years. She had met him in the street by chance, when she went out of the clinic she shared with Linder to buy a newspaper.

In that case, why had she spent such a long time walking up and down in the street outside his house? asked Michael. This time she did begin to ask him how he knew, but she cut herself short. The smile appeared on her lips again, like a grimace, and she explained that she had no desire to confess to him what a bad state she was in and so she had tried to hide the fact that she had waited for Hildesheimer outside his house. She wanted to ask him to see her for an hour there and then, she explained in embarrassment. There was no chance that he would have agreed over the phone, and she wanted to accompany him to his consulting room right away, but he had an appointment to see someone else, and he couldn't see her that day, or the next, because of the funeral. He would only be able to see her next week.

Michael glanced at his watch; it was already half past eleven. She was beginning to button her coat when he asked if she knew about Joe Linder's pistol.

"What do you mean, did I know?" she asked.

"Did you know that he had a pistol?" asked Michael. He had taken care not to publish the fact that Linder's pistol had been the murder weapon and wanted to know if Linder had told her himself.

Of course she knew, she said with a perceptible relaxation of her body. "Who didn't?" she asked, and smiled again, a grotesque smile, her eyes dull, her face gray. "Joe spoke about it ceaselessly." Michael noted the affection in the way she spoke and asked her about her relations with Linder and his family.

"It's a very complex relationship. There was intense competition when I received supervision from both him and Dr. Neidorf. Before that our relations were warm and simple. I don't know if you grasped how important it is to Joe to be sure that he's loved. He was very worried about my professional relationship with Dr. Neidorf."

Did she know where the pistol was kept in Linder's house?

Yes; somewhere in the bedroom. That's where he went to get it whenever he wanted to show it off, but she didn't know exactly where in the bedroom.

Of course she went into the bedroom on the night of the party, to get her coat.

No, there was nobody in the room. She had peeped at Daniel, who was sleeping in his parents' bed, and she was alone in the room. All the coats were piled on the sofa.

No, she had never used a pistol. In the army she had conducted psychological tests.

Yes—and she smiled again—she had learned to use a firearm in basic training, a Czech gun, and she had never succeeded in hitting the target once. She had no technical skills. Joe had once explained to her how his pistol worked and mentioned that it was always loaded, but she hadn't tried to shoot it, although he urged her to. Weapons frightened her.

The last words were said with a certain archness; the dimple in her chin came into play; she even fluttered her eyelashes. But Michael felt as if he had opened Pandora's box and shut it again without putting his finger on the essential facts.

Before parting from her in his doorway, he asked her in a neutral tone, as if in an afterthought, if she would be prepared to take a polygraph test. The wary look in her eyes betrayed a certain apprehension, but she only said that she would have to think about it. "There's no hurry, is there?" No; he shook his head; there was no hurry.

He had no way of knowing, he thought, if she was cautious by nature or if she was trying to gain time. In Michael's experience, most people who had nothing to hide had no objections to taking the polygraph test, but there were also some who hesitated and were afraid even if they had nothing to hide.

Finally, next to the door, he asked if she knew anything about Neidorf's lecture.

No, she didn't know anything about it; she had only heard what the subject was; but she did know that Hildesheimer always helped Dr. Neidorf to prepare her lectures, and she looked at him inquiringly.

Michael did not respond, only thanked her politely. His face betrayed nothing of the confusion and ambivalence he felt. Back at his desk, he rewound the tape and listened to what had been said in the room over the past three hours. Still listening, he picked up the phone. From his third-floor room, Balilty answered breathlessly: "I've just come in—I'd forgotten what working with you is like. I'll be there in two minutes," and he put the phone down.

The two minutes turned into fifteen, and Michael leaned back in his chair, stretched out his long legs, and listened over and over again to the last part of the conversation, where they had spoken about her relations with Neidorf, with the youth, with Linder and with Hildesheimer.

When Balilty came into the room, short of breath and holding a cup of coffee in his hand, Michael pushed a sheet of paper toward him and asked if he wanted to go over the questions with him. "Sure," said Balilty, "but first I've got an answer for you in the matter of the colonel." Here he paused to take a bow, and Michael obliged with the mandatory exclamations of admiration and surprise. If only Balilty had been a modest man, he thought, he would have been perfect. But the praise he demanded was not too high a price to pay for his cooperation. "You're incredible; there's nobody like you," said Michael, and the intelligence officer grinned from ear to ear, tucked his shirt into his belt, pulled down his sweater—it must have been knitted by his wife, thought Michael, dimly remembering a plump, comfortable woman, by all accounts a first-rate cook—and continued: "So we said you didn't care how I got hold of the information, right, as long as nobody knew? But it's going to take more than a few hours, I can tell you that. It's a complicated business, I'll need time, and when I say time I mean days, not hours." Michael whistled and asked cautiously how many days he thought he would need. "Two or three, maybe five. I can't explain why, but I told you in the beginning. And now you can show me your questions," and Balilty sat down and laid his big hands on the sheet of paper on the desk.

After reading rapidly through the questions Michael had jotted down, he raised his eyes and asked: "Who is she? The piece who was waiting here? The one you were talking about? That the boy followed? Raffi said she was married to 'The Gavel'—is that right?" Michael nodded, and Balilty took a cigarette from the squashed pack of Noblesse on the desk. "Screwing him will be a pleasure, believe me. Maybe she's fucking around? Trust me. You want details of her army service? Registration of firearms? Connections with the mixed-up F.O. kid? Is she seeing him? Come on! She's old enough to be his mother!"

Michael explained that Dina Silver had been Elisha Naveh's therapist and added that he vaguely remembered the judge's life being threatened in the past; he wanted to know if a pistol had been purchased and if anyone in the big house in the exclusive Yemin Moshe neighborhood had learned to use it.

"Why don't you just check with the computer?"

Michael explained that discretion was necessary here.

"It's a long time," said Balilty slowly, "since we've had a case involving so many important people. Judges, military governors, psychologists—you name it!"

"You can't say life isn't interesting," said Michael, and switched off the tape recorder. "Let's go and see how they're getting along downstairs." He picked up the pack of Noblesse, and they both left the room and went down to the interrogations wing.

Tzilla was busy questioning Hedva Tamari, the young doctor from the Margoa, and when she saw Michael through the window she left the interrogation room and wiped her forehead. The subject never stopped crying, she reported. "All I have to do is mention the victim's name and she bursts into tears. I've been with her for an hour, and I haven't found out anything we didn't know before, except that she's got a special arrangement with her senior on call, who stays at the hospital the whole day whenever she's on call. The things people are prepared to do for a pretty girl!" Michael was not deceived by Tzilla's volatility; he knew that she was a sharp-witted, efficient interrogator. He had listened to the tapes. Any childishness or sweetness in her voice was calculated to serve the ends of the interrogation. All her cute, girlish airs, he knew, were part of the atmosphere of intimacy she strove to create with her colleagues.

"The first interrogation today took longer, about two hours. That Dr. Daniel Voller from their Training Committee; remember him? The one with the gray hair. Nothing there either, except for a few spiteful remarks about Linder. They're both prepared to take a polygraph," she added without being asked.

Manny, in the next room, was questioning Tammy Zvielli, the young woman in whose honor the party had been given, a faded blonde with pink eyes. She too, said Manny, was willing to take a polygraph test.

Raffi had made no discoveries either. "One way or another, they're all covered. Not as if they'd planned it; just the normal things people do: they were with their families, they watched TV, they went to bed, got up late on Saturday. I've got nothing special on anyone."

Balilty went about his business, and Michael returned to his room to keep his appointment with Dr. Giora Biham, head of a department at the Kfar Shaul hospital. He turned out to be the bald, bearded fellow who had escorted Dina Silver to the funeral parlor.

Dr. Biham spoke in a thick Latin American accent, rolling words around his tongue as if he enjoyed the sound of them. On Friday night he had had friends to dinner, and on Saturday morning he had taken his children mushroom hunting in the Jerusalem forest. He had returned at nine-thirty, left the children (two boys and a girl, all under eight) with his wife, and driven to the Institute.

Dr. Neidorf was his teacher at the Institute, that is to say, she had taught his class, ten of them, for two years. He had not been in analysis with her, nor in supervision. He admired her greatly, he explained, but she didn't have any room. That is to say, he explained when he saw the puzzled expression on the chief inspector's face, she was unavailable; she had a waiting list two years long.

The way he was sitting, leaning back with his legs crossed, stuffing his ornate mother-of-pearl pipe, the gold lighter that he took out of his waistcoat pocket, the gray suit, the neatly trimmed little beard, told Michael all he needed to know about Dr. Biham's attitude toward himself. The pleasure he took in hearing his own voice left not a moment of silence. He had an answer to everything, even when he had nothing to say. Certainly he had been at the party, he adored parties, and he had been as drunk as a lord too—the life and soul of the party, no doubt. He liked Linder very much and had received supervision from him for two years. It was impossible to get a word of criticism regarding his colleagues at the Institute out of him.

At some point in the conversation, which despite all Michael's efforts to change the tone remained light and superficial, Michael asked Dr. Biham if he imagined that he, Chief Inspector Ohayon, was a secret member of the Training Committee; perhaps this was the reason he refused to say a bad word about any of its members?

Biham burst out laughing and asked if he could quote him. Then, without the least trace of tension, he explained frankly that until he had made his way to the top of the Institute heap, he had no intention of allowing himself to "feel negative feelings about anyone there."

In spite of the jokes and the relaxed, easy tone, Michael, who was beginning to wonder what had drawn the man to his profession, picked up a signal of profound sadness, expressed particularly in the subject's eyes, which were neither anxious nor tense, but tired and lifeless.

He didn't believe, he said firmly, that anyone at the Institute was connected to Dr. Neidorf's tragic death, he simply didn't believe it, never mind what evidence the chief inspector might produce. Yes, he knew how to use a gun; of course he had seen Linder's pistol. He didn't remember if he had gone into the bedroom—he must have been too drunk to remember; or perhaps his wife had taken the coats. He had no objections to a polygraph test; it might be a fascinating experience.

But for the sadness in his eyes, he might have been talking about some curiosity, thought Michael, and the sadness seemed deep and essential, unrelated to external events.

In reply to the question about how he had felt on the morning when they were supposed to approve his presentation, he said he had been very nervous. He had told himself that the worst thing that could happen was that they would demand corrections, and so he had prepared himself in advance for this eventuality. He had no doubt that they would approve his membership in the Institute. In the last analysis, he said, "once someone's reached their eighth year and been given permission to treat three patients, they'd have to do something really drastic not to be accepted; I can't even imagine what," and his eyebrows rose comically as he lit his pipe. He didn't take his eyes off Michael, who smiled in spite of himself.

Michael asked curiously what his reasons were for deciding to become a psychoanalyst.

Dr. Biham smiled mischievously, his eyes as sad as ever, and explained that he had heard how hard it was to be accepted and couldn't resist the temptation to try. "And it's interesting, you know, really interesting. And I'd already gone into psychiatry. I had all kinds of ideas for new methods and approaches in the running of psychiatric hospitals, which was why I went into psychiatry in the first place, but as far as the Institute is concerned, it was pure ambition. It took me a long time to persuade Hildesheimer, who was one of my interviewers, to take me seriously, but I had a successful record at work, and I had a good friend who had graduated from the Institute, and he recommended me too."

The man was ready to chatter away about any subject under the sun, and even when his face grew grave, when Michael brought up the murder, there was no sign of fear or tension in it. But this time, too, Chief Inspector Ohayon was left with an obscure sense of malaise as he accompanied the subject to the door. You can't believe that what you see is what there is, he said to himself. It never is. What you see is only the tip, less than a fifth of the iceberg. But maybe he really has no connection to the case, he thought as he glanced at his watch, rewound the tape, and told Tzilla—who opened the door without knocking and announced that it was three o'clock and time to take a break for lunch—that he had too much work to do. But all his attempts to put her off were in vain. "We'll only go to the corner; you know I hate eating alone, and Eli's not here, and he hasn't even phoned." With a sigh, Michael slipped on his parka and gave Tzilla his arm, and on their way out they picked up Manny too. "Nothing's going to run away," said Tzilla complacently. As Michael sipped the strong Turkish coffee that the old man from the café at the corner of Heleni Hamalka Street had cheerfully placed on the shaky little table, it suddenly occurred to him that what Dr. Biham had displayed more than anything else was a desire to please, to be liked, although with nothing like the desperation of Linder, who was already at the end of the road. Still, this thought did not help him to understand the sadness in the man's eyes. One of these days he would have to ask Hildesheimer about it.

In the two weeks since Michael had sent Balilty to gather information on Colonel Yoav Alon, the intelligence officer had gone to ground. At first Michael had taken no notice, but after five days, he began a frantic search. When he finally located him, late at night at home, Balilty refused to say anything. "I'm working on it, Ohayon. When I've got anything to say, you'll be the first to hear, believe me."

Michael believed him, but he was impatient. "What about the woman? Give me something on her at least." But Balilty warned him not to say anything else on the phone.

Things settled into a routine. The weather improved. The party guests and the patients were all questioned. The polygraph showed that they were all telling the truth. Dina Silver had not yet taken the test. She was suffering badly from sinusitis, she said, and asked for a postponement. No new facts came to light. Michael felt that it was time for them to step in and shake things up, "stage a drama to make something happen," as he said to Eli at one of their daily meetings.

Whenever Michael was working on a case, his colleagues claimed, he was "possessed by a dybbuk." Shorer referred to it during one of their talks during the interim period. "Is she your dybbuk now? I'm not saying you've always been wrong, but you tell me if you've always been right. She's got pneumonia; I talked to the family doctor, and even if she's not dangerously ill, you've got no grounds for harassing her. You've got nothing to go on except a hunch. Don't forget who her husband is."

Outside his office, at a late supper in the Mahaneh Yehuda market, Shorer admitted that if she hadn't been married to "The Gavel," he would probably have been less delicate. "But," he said, striking his fork on his plate with a bang, "it's your fault too. Bring me someone who saw her car on Saturday morning. Bring me something!"

Michael, who had lost his appetite in the last week, told him gloomily about his talks with the neighbors, the people playing tennis that morning on the court opposite the Institute, even the civil guard patrolling the street. "No one saw her leave. Dozens of people saw her arrive at the Institute at ten o'clock on the dot, but not early in the morning. But still, I've got a funny feeling."

"Feelings aren't enough," said Shorer, wiping beer foam off his lips. "Not that I discount their importance or relevance, but with all due respect to your intuition, we're talking about the wife of a district judge here; she's got pneumonia, and she's not running away from the country; and last but not least: I don't see her motive. You yourself said they told you at the mental health clinic that she was first-rate at the job, and Rosenfeld assured you that there was no doubt about the Training Committee's approving her case presentation. So what could her motive have been?"

Michael opened his mouth to say something, but instead he pushed some salad into it and nodded gloomily.

Nira had gone for her trip to Europe, and Yuval was staying with him. In the mornings the boy complained that he had heard his father grinding his teeth in his sleep. Michael withdrew into himself and sank into a depression that he himself did not fully understand.

With Yuval in the flat, he couldn't bring Maya there. In their rare meetings at Mav, their little corner café, she didn't complain, but she looked at him longingly. He couldn't answer her questions. All he wanted was to curl up in bed and be held without having to talk. Maya claimed that he fell into a depression every spring, that it was a recurrent pattern, but he thought that the case was to blame.

The questioning of the witnesses had not brought anything new to light. Their statements were interesting but unhelpful. Michael spoke again with Hildesheimer, and the old man said, sadly, "The Institute is sick," and he looked at Michael questioningly.

The pressure from the press didn't improve the situation. Police reporters complained bitterly about the lack of information. Every morning the police spokesman appeared at the conclusion of the team meeting and received, as he put it, his "daily briefing on how to say nothing in as many words as possible." "When are you going to give me a bit of meat to throw them?" he would ask Michael accusingly. His daily meeting with Ariyeh Levy, the Jerusalem commander, did nothing to improve Michael's mood.

Catherine Louise Dubonnet arrived, and she was the only ray of light during those two weeks. Michael himself went to meet her at the airport on Friday, four days after first hearing of her existence from the dead woman's family.

Waiting at Ben-Gurion and sniffing the scent of faraway places, he thought enviously that it was years since he had been abroad. Once again he imagined living quietly in Cambridge, plunging into the Middle Ages, taking trips to Italy.

He stood next to the passport officer and looked at the long line of people. Finally his patience snapped and he had Dr. Dubonnet's name called over the loudspeakers.

Three times he spoke to her. The first time was in the car, on the way from the airport. She had asked for a room in a hotel in spite of the warm invitation extended to her by the Neidorf family; she could not bear Eva's absence, she explained. They had booked her a room in a cheap hotel, but as soon as he saw her, Michael drove straight to the King David, where Tzilla, contacted by radio, had taken care of the details.

Catherine Lousie Dubonnet, Michael had learned from his Paris counterparts, was the most important analyst in the Paris Institute. Even Hildesheimer spoke about her with profound respect and admiration, in spite of his reservations on principle about "the French in general." Her passport told him that she was sixty years old. Her white hair was gathered in a thick bun on her neck, and her brown eyes, which shone with intelligence and warmth, were huge, like a baby's. Before he looked into her eyes she seemed to Michael like a sweet granny on her way to the kitchen. She wore a dark, shapeless dress, and over it a shabby coat; her face was innocent of makeup; and the irregular teeth exposed in her friendly smile gave her an air of neglect. Her flat brown shoes didn't match her dress. She contradicted all his stereotypes of Frenchwomen. Where's the famous chic everyone talks about? he thought when she shook his hand warmly at the airport, until he looked into her eyes and the question of chic became irrelevant.

Yes, Eva had spent the day with her, she told him in the car, in a Parisian accent that gave him much pleasure. After the first few minutes of awkwardness, his own French came back to life.

His first question was about the secrecy of the meeting. He wanted to understand, he explained as he maneuvered the police Ford onto the express way, why Eva Neidorf had not mentioned the stopover to Hildesheimer.

"Ah," said the Frenchwoman with a smile, "she had her coquettish side. She was angry with him and wanted to make him jealous by thanking me for my help at the beginning of her lecture."

This explanation did not fit his picture of Neidorf, and once they were on the highway, after lighting himself a cigarette, Michael said so. Without taking his eyes off the wheel, he sensed her probing look on his face.

She sighed deeply and said that most of his information about Eva came from people who knew only certain sides of her personality or took a very limited view of it. Not that Hildesheimer didn't know her, said Dubonnet, but there were a number of blind spots in his perception of her. Although he was certainly aware of the extent of her dependence on him and his help, he didn't really understand how important they were to her, or how intimately related to her *amour-propre*. She was insulted, the Frenchwoman explained in a tone that was at once amused and sad, by his very need to free her from her dependence on him. A feminine wound to which he was completely oblivious, she said, and added something about the limitations of the male sex in general.

And then she smiled again, a smile he saw only in profile, and she said that absurdly enough, she believed the old man would really have been jealous. "Perhaps not as jealous as Eva would have liked, but jealous enough. She intended telling him about it after the lecture," she said, and sighed. After that they talked about the special relationship between the two women. The geographical distance was what had permitted the closeness between them, she said. Eva experienced difficulties in sustaining intimacy on a continuous, day-to-day basis, and it suited her that they met only once or twice a year at the congresses of the International Psychoanalytic Society. "We were very fond of each other, and she could talk to me about her relations with Ernst, her patients, the Institute, everything, absolutely freely, I wasn't a party to anything."

Michael checked her in at the King David—if she was impressed by the grandeur of the lobby, she gave no sign of it. He accompanied her to her room and opened the curtains and pointed out to her the breathtaking view of the Old City walls. Her eyes turned sad, and she mumbled something about tragic beauty. When she asked him about the famous explosion during the British mandate, wanting with child-like curiosity to know which wing of the hotel had been damaged and how they had renovated it, he saw her eyes again and was completely captivated. It wasn't only the geographical distance that had made the friendship between them possible, he thought, but this woman's warmth and spontaneity, two qualities that had apparently been lacking in Eva Neidorf.

They met again that evening, in Maswadi, a little restaurant in the Arab part of the city, and there, among the assorted salads of the Oriental hors d'oeuvres, he asked her about the lecture. It was difficult, explained the Frenchwoman, who wore a dress very similar to the one she was wearing earlier, to convey it in the short amount of time available to them. The question bothering Eva was whether she should expose examples of unethical behavior by patients. There were cases of child abuse, for instance. Should the therapist respond therapeutically, or judge the patient openly and perhaps even report him to the police? And there were issues of professional discretion, such as the way therapists in so small a country should take more trouble to disguise the identity of patients in conversation with their colleagues. There was also a long discussion of when it would be wrong to demand payment for a session that did not take place.

Dubonnet explained the therapeutic relationship as one involving a long-term mutual commitment. Consequently, she stressed, if a patient failed to show up for a session he had to pay for it, apart from exceptions at the therapist's discretion, such as illness or childbirth. Eva was uncertain about giving examples, whether certain people might be embarrassed by them, whether they were appropriate to the subject of the lecture, whether therapists who took payment for appointments missed due to army reserve service, which she defined as *force majeure,* should be included in the discussion from the ethical point of view.

When she saw the disappointment on Michael's face, she interrupted the flow of her words. She compared his situation to that of patients disappointed after a few sessions because no dramatic breakthrough had yet occurred. "What exactly were you looking for?" she asked.

He told her that all the copies of the lecture had disappeared, together with the list of Neidorf's patients and supervisees and the file containing her financial records. She had heard about it from the family, she said, when she visited them that afternoon, "and the children are in a terrible state, especially Nimrod, because Nava gets it all out, and her relations with Eva were loving, whereas Nimrod's were very strained, and he's too reserved altogether." But that wasn't what he wanted to talk about, she apologized. Her clever brown eyes observed him as he explained that he had hoped to find out from her what had been in the lecture to account for its disappearance, or even for the murder itself. Her low forehead creased in a frown as she went over the details known to her. She had not kept a copy of the lecture, as she had no Hebrew, she said. And there was something that was disturbing Eva very much, but she refused to talk about it explicitly.

"Eva was shocked by the behavior of one of the candidates," she said reflectively. She hadn't mentioned the individual's name or sex, but Eva had been very interested in something that had happened in the Paris Institute: a very senior analyst had "conducted a passionate love affair with one of his patients." Dubonnet's face clouded over when she mentioned the incident, and for a moment the light in her eyes went out. Then she took a sip of wine and continued: "How did we know for certain, she asked me late that night, when I was already very tired, that the patient was telling the truth? I told her," said Dr. Dubonnet, "that I had demanded and received proof: eyewitnesses at restaurants, hotel registrations—a hateful, ugly business, but one has to make a thorough examination of the facts before expelling someone from the analytic society and disqualifying him from practicing his profession. But I'm not sure"—and here she looked intently into his eyes again—"that it was part of her lecture. I was exhausted after a hard day's work, with a hard day's work ahead of me. I was about to go on vacation—patients always react badly—it demands all one's energy, and I'm not so young anymore." She smiled and added with great sadness that it never occurred to her that it would be their last meeting. Her eyes filled with tears as she said that it was always like that; one always felt, she said as if to herself, that one had all the time in the world.

The conversation with Catherine Louise Dubonnet had pointed again to one of the patients or supervisees as the key to the affair, reflected Michael. Perhaps the lecture was the murder motive, but perhaps not. On the face of it, she hadn't presented anything new, but actually, he thought, she had confirmed that they were looking in the right direction. There were grounds for various motives here. It was clearer to him than ever that someone had been terrified lest Neidorf expose some information she possessed. Neidorf's interest in the case of the Paris analyst made him think of Dina Silver, but he had nothing to go on apart from his suspicions, and he silently cursed Balilty, from whom he had not heard for ten days.

The third meeting with Dr. Dubonnet took place on Sunday morning and was more formal. Catherine Louise made a sworn statement and promised faithfully that she would offer any assistance she could. Later that day she left the country.

Every morning at the team meeting, all eyes turned to Eli Bahar, who without a word would pass around the bank accounts he had finished going over the day before. It had taken two days just to write down the information disclosed in Neidorf's current account. Bahar had checked her bank deposits for the past two years and drawn up tables with the assistance of the police computer man, who helped him to establish a pattern. Some of the deposits were regular monthly checks, and some were in cash. "It could have been so simple," Eli lamented after they had all understood the results of the previous day's labors, which boiled down to a reconfirmation of the fact that all the patients and supervisees known to them had, indeed, paid Dr. Neidorf.

To Tzilla he complained of the monotony of the routine. For two weeks now he had been feeling like a bank clerk, he said. Every morning, when the bank opened, the manager took him down to the vault, where the checks drawn on customers' accounts were filed, and in the afternoon he met Michael and presented him with the fruits of his labors. The computer man, who had been co-opted to help, drew his attention to a regular cash deposit every week for the past year. After working on Neidorf's account for a week, Eli discovered that she had deposited a similar sum, this time in a check, drawn on a bank account that never appeared again.

Michael had learned, from both Hildesheimer and the accountants, that most patients and supervisees paid once a month. A few preferred to pay once a week, and there were rare cases, Hildesheimer had explained, where patients preferred to pay after every session.

After Eli Bahar discovered the check deposit exactly one week after a cash deposit in the same amount, he informed the team that he would be spending the morning in a suburban branch of the National Bank, where he had not yet been; the bitterness of his tone implied that this was a rare distinction indeed. Michael tried constructively to explain to Eli how important his work was, how much you could learn about people by looking at their bank accounts, but Eli looked unconvinced. He complained of the stuffiness of the vaults, the boredom and routine.

Tzilla predicted confidently that the check would turn out to belong to the missing patient and by the end of the morning they would know who he was.

Michael pointed to her and said to Eli: "Listen to what she says; I'm sure she's right. Now get going."

The appointment had been set up with the assistant manager, a thin, oily man who kept straightening the knitted skullcap that threatened to slip off his head. The manager was on reserve duty, explained the assistant, who with an air of urgent self-importance explained to one of the clerks—she reminded Eli of Zmira, at Zeligman and Zeligman—what the gentleman would be doing there this morning. After studying the account number that Eli handed him, he pulled a gray drawer out of a large filing cabinet in the basement of the bank. Eli's tired eyes lit up as he saw the name of the owner of the account.

A man of thirty, an inspector in the police force, does not jump for joy when he discovers that his work has produced results, thought Eli Bahar as he requested permission to make a phone call. They were still at the meeting, and Raffi lifted the receiver and passed it to Michael without saying a word. At first the others took no notice, until Tzilla tugged Manny's sleeve and drew his attention to the expression on Ohayon's face, which was attentive, tense, and excited. In the end he stood up and said: "Who says there's no God? Take a photo and get back here damned fast."

When he put the receiver down, pale with excitement, the atmosphere was expectant. Tzilla fell on Manny and planted a kiss on his cheek. Several seconds passed before Michael opened his mouth and said, in a hoarse voice, that their problems were only beginning.

"I don't know if you realize what this information means," he said. "You realize that we'll have to bring him in for questioning now as a suspect? Do you remember who he is?" Tzilla, naturally, was the one to jump to her feet and protest: "So what? Is he above the law?" And Michael was obliged to remind her that all they knew for certain was that the man had given a check to Neidorf, but the members of the special investigation team knew that he was as excited as they were.

At this point Balilty popped up out of nowhere, grinning complacently, and refusing to believe that Michael was actually anticipating someone else's arrival.

After Chief Inspector Ohayon had seen the clearly signed check with his own eyes and passed it to Tzilla as if he were handing over a fortune and asked her to see that the signature was compared with the scribble on the note from the accountants' office—only then, after he had heard her talking over the phone to Forensics and sent Eli, with a pat on the shoulder, to "take a little rest in the sun," did he turn to Balilty, whose smile had by now faded somewhat, though he still looked excited and refused to talk to Michael anywhere inside the building.

They sat at a corner table in Café Nava on Jaffa Street, and they spoke in whispers. Balilty kept raising his head to make sure that nobody was listening to them.

He had two things to say, said Balilty. Mrs. Silver was a terrible liar, that was the first thing; and the second thing, he said, lowering his voice even further, concerned Colonel Yoav Alon. "Where do you want me to begin?" he asked, wiping from his lips the deposit of cream from his coffee.

Michael said: "Start with the colonel," and lit a cigarette. He opened his eyes wide when he heard what Danny Balilty had to say. "How the hell do you get to know something like that? I don't understand—were you in bed with him, or what?"

For once, said Balilty, he would let Michael in on his investigative methods. Only this once, mind, and only because he had nearly killed himself to get the information. His little eyes twinkled as he spoke.

Balilty, a heavyset, balding, paunchy man in his middle thirties, sloppy in dress and coarse in manner, was a big hit with the ladies, as he had confided to Michael years before. Michael couldn't understand what they saw in him, but he knew that even though modesty had never been his strong point, the intelligence officer was telling the truth. He had no guilt about his double life, Balilty had explained on the same occasion. His wife was a good, warmhearted woman, with modest demands from life, whose interests centered around her home and children, and he loved her very much. Let there be no mistake about it, Balilty stressed, he considered his marriage a happy one. But he refused, on principle, to give up his extracurricular activities. Whenever he sensed that he was in danger of getting too involved, he broke it off—in a way that left them friends for life, he stressed.

He was in the middle of an affair now that was terrifying him, he said. She was an unmarried woman, something he had always avoided like the plague. "And that's not all; she's only twenty, sweet as pie, and the worst thing is," he said with winning honesty, "this time I've got myself involved. I'm in it up to my neck, and it's all because of you."

Michael raised his eyebrows, but the starry light in Balilty's eyes squelched any obligation to protest.

"She was the only source from whom I could obtain information without anyone knowing why, and that was all I had in mind. But I got caught. What can you do? There aren't any guarantees against it."

Michael could only light another cigarette, suppressing his curiosity. Balilty refused to come to the point. It took several long moments of background material before Michael understood that the intelligence officer had seduced the personal secretary of the military governor of Edom, Colonel Yoav Alon. "I wasn't the first. She's attracted to older men," he said with some embarrassment. "And the long and short of it is that before me, she had an affair with Alon."

Michael ordered two more cups of coffee, and while they waited for it to arrive, the threads began to come together in his mind. Balilty watched the waitress walk away before he said: "And she was the one who told me about Alon, that he couldn't get it up. It was awful, she said. She went into all the details; it was awful for her too. And now he only talks to her about work; you can cut the atmosphere with a knife, she says. She's very mature for her age, but still, she was very upset."

Michael stirred his coffee and asked when it had happened.

"She's been there for two years; she signed up for a stint with the standing army. She'll be demobilized in a month. It happened after the first six months. She's not pretty; I never imagined I'd get so serious about her. All I thought was that I'd go out with her a bit and get the dirt on Alon."

Michael wasn't interested in Balilty's love life. It cost him an effort to pretend to be sympathetic, even though he understood very well the desperate need to relive the encounter by talking about it. Everything was falling into place in Michael's mind and making sense. He told Balilty about the bank account, about the payment to Neidorf, and Balilty grew suddenly grave, all the enthusiasm of a man in love vanishing in an instant. "Yes," he said hesitantly, "even a colonel would go to a therapist if he couldn't get it up. And he wouldn't publicize it either; you don't get to be chief of staff if you need therapy. So that's it, eh?" Michael nodded. Neither of them felt happy or triumphant; there was only a sense of oppression and a grim awareness of the difficulties ahead.

"Everything fits," said Balilty. "He was at the party, he even bought the pistol, he was Neidorf's patient, and he's got motive, means, everything. What a story!"

But Michael, who had surprised himself by not feeling the familiar tension before the breakthrough, did not feel the familiar relief now. Instead he became aware of a spreading uneasiness, which left no room for any other emotions. "But I don't understand why he had to shoot her," he said. "She wasn't going to talk about his sexual problems or broadcast the fact that he was in therapy with her. The motive doesn't seem so clear."

Balilty shrugged his shoulders. "Who knows what else he told her. One thing's sure: he was in her hands, and if she felt like illustrating something by referring to his case—in the lecture, that is—he could have said goodbye to his career."

"What about Silver?" asked Michael. "Why is she lying?"

"Ask and I'll tell you. First of all, she met that guy, the diplomat's brat who looks like a gigolo, at least twice before the funeral—never mind how I know—at her home and at the Institute. And who says she doesn't know how to use a pistol? They've got one in the house; it's registered to the lord and master, but the lady herself has hunted in the Bois de Boulogne, and she's a first-rate shot. She's no more afraid of guns than I am of dames. That's why she's lying. Apart from which, she doesn't sleep with her husband, if you want to know. They've got separate bedrooms, and that whole marriage, if you ask me, looks like one big farce. It's a pity I couldn't get hold of Master Naveh's roommate; he's abroad. Everybody's abroad except us. I'll give you any odds you like that he would have had a lot more to tell us about glamour boy's meetings with his girlfriend, who's old enough to be his mother."

Michael paid for the coffee, and they went back to his office. Balilty said that the secretary, Orna, had talked a lot about the colonel's problems at work. "It seems he's a nice guy, too nice to do what he has to do." He smiled with a mixture of patronizing pride and pity. "Who knows, maybe he did something that Neidorf couldn't take; I don't have to tell you the kind of thing that goes on there."

When Balilty left at last, Michael considered his next steps.

He would have to tell Shorer to inform Alon's superior officer. They wouldn't be able to interrogate him here; they would have to take him somewhere isolated and protect him from any possible leaks, at least until they had proof, he thought wearily. His long legs carried him with unfamiliar heaviness to Shorer's room, where he found his chief bowed over a pile of files and documents, as usual.

Shorer raised his head and smiled. "Anything new?" he asked in the tone of one who did not expect an answer, and he tensed when he heard that there was, indeed, something new.

Shorer's face grew steadily graver, and the heap of broken matchsticks on his desk grew higher as Michael talked. He asked to see the check as soon as possible, listened to the story about the colonel's importance, inquired about his alibi for Saturday, and then he said: "It's about time. Two and a half weeks already, and this is our first decent lead. But we'll have to put Levy into the picture, I'm not sticking my neck out on this one without him. There *is* the possibility that he's not guilty, and you don't ruin a man's life just because he's impotent. We'll need a search warrant, if you want to check his shoes; we'll have to run a voice identification with that typist of Zeligman's. What a mess! What a country, I'm telling you. . . . Okay. Give it a few hours, and you can start tonight. And not here! You hear? And no leaks!" Michael nodded and agreed to wait until he got the green light.

It was six o'clock when Shorer informed Michael—who had not dared to leave the building, except to go down to the corner for a supply of Noblesse—that the suspect had been detained for questioning.

Shorer had taken care of everything, including the flat on Palmach Street that was used for special occasions such as the present one. Raffi, who had taken part in the arrest, told Michael later that evening about Yoav Alon's wife, who was in a state of shock. She had asked for time to get the children out of the house before they conducted the search. Raffi mentioned her tightly clamped lips, the fact that she hadn't insisted on knowing what it was about and only asked one question, which nobody had answered.

The arrest was made outside the entrance of the apartment on Bar Kochba Street, said Raffi, when he came home from work. His protests stopped when they told him that the arrest was being made with the consent of Central Command and that for the sake of discretion he had better come quietly.

Professor Brandtstetter, from the second floor, nodded at the young man he knew as the tenant of the Palmach Street flat. Although they met only rarely, in the stairwell, the professor always had a greeting for his pleasant young neighbor. The young man, who apparently worked for the Defense Ministry, paid his contributions to the maintenance committee on time, and ever since he had rented the apartment, the student parties that had kept the building awake had ceased. The professor watched him climb the stairs with a small group of men and a woman, on their way, he assured his wife, "to some secret defense meeting, no doubt. There was a very high-up officer with them," he said solemnly, and he warned her not to gossip to the neighbors. "We're talking about state security, don't forget," he reminded her sternly.

Mrs. Brandtstetter had no intention of gossiping to the neighbors, something she had never done in her life. But she did not protest at his warning, just as she did not protest about many other things her husband said. Mrs. Brandtstetter couldn't bear rows. Only at night, when she couldn't sleep and began wandering back and forth between the kitchen and the living room, trying to forget the sounds that had haunted her ever since she was twenty years old in Berlin, she would suddenly hear the noises from the upstairs flat, like a bad dream come true. Crying, screaming, stamping feet, sometimes men, sometimes women. Often she thought it was her imagination, but she knew that the figures she had seen in the stairwell were real. She knew very well, Mrs. Brandtstetter did, that the young man who paid his contributions to the upkeep of the building on time was a bad young man, who only looked like a Jew. Ever since he had come to live there, she had tried to go out as little as possible.

Through the peephole in the door that night, the minute her husband went out with the garbage, she had seen them filing up the stairs. There were two other young men besides the tenant himself, and a girl. And there was a man in army uniform, but Mrs. Brandtstetter knew the uniform was only a disguise. The only thing that confused her was the appearance of the "army officer," who crept up the stairs between the two young men, one in front of him and one behind, and didn't look in the least authoritative, as he was supposed to. Afterward she saw the tall one too, who sometimes came to visit the tenant who paid his dues on time. In the beginning she thought he might be a member of the family, because he never arrived with the rest of the gang. When she put the facts together, she realized that he always came after the sounds of furniture being moved had already been heard. Then he arrived, like the flood after the pestilence, she thought. He frightened her more than any of them, because of his handsome face. Once she had seen him face-to-face, when she came back from the grocery store and he opened the door of the building, holding it for her until she was inside with her shopping bag. But he couldn't pull the wool over her eyes with his gentlemanly manners, thought Mrs. Brandtstetter. And so far from winning her over, that handsome face, those penetrating eyes, that charming smile, only reinforced her in her belief that he was the really evil one.

If Mrs. Brandtstetter had seen Michael's eyes this night as he climbed the stairs to the third floor, before he tapped out the prearranged signal on the door, she might have changed her mind. His eyes were fixed on the step in front of him. He was thinking of the difficult days ahead, and more than anything else, he felt the weariness spreading through all his limbs.

There was something wrong about the file, he thought. Something very wrong. He tried, unsuccessfully, to imagine Colonel Yoav Alon in the flat that the General Security Services were kind enough to lend them for special occasions such as this. Three rooms, a bathroom, and a kitchen, functionally and economically furnished. In one room, the living room, there were two plain armchairs of the kibbutz fifties style and a black-and-white TV set, as well as a small table upon which reposed the "oxygen of the flat," as Tzilla put it—a black telephone.

The other two rooms held beds, two in each room, and a few chairs. There were army blankets in the built-in cupboard in the hall. There was always someone from the Investigations Division there, and members of the team took shifts when the interrogation lasted more than a day. And the interrogation always lasted more than a day, because it was only the secret interrogations that took place here, and they were always the most difficult and complicated.

Colonel Yoav Alon, military governor of the subdistrict of Edom, an officer who had risen with unprecedented rapidity to his present position and of whom great things were expected in the future, was sitting on a chair in the room that overlooked the backyard. He had not taken off his army parka. Opposite him sat Raffi, playing with a bunch of keys. Tzilla went back to the living room, where she and Manny were waiting for Eli Bahar to arrive with the results of the search of the suspect's house. When Michael entered the room, Raffi got up and went to stand next to the window, which was closed, and peer outside before he let down the blinds. Then he remained where he was, looking at Yoav Alon, who looked at Michael and asked, in a tone of great restraint, if he was the man who would inform him of the reason for his arrest. Chief Inspector Ohayon sat down and lit a cigarette. He whispered something to Raffi, who approached him and bent down to listen, then went out to the kitchen, where a clatter of glasses was heard. The chief inspector shut the door.

The pale man sitting opposite him huddled in his coat, who did not raise his voice when he asked again why he had been arrested, looked like a TV advertisement for the Israel Defense Forces. His blond hair was close-cropped, his eyes were clear, his full chapped lips hinted at desert winds and army jeeps. He appeared strong and well-built, although the parka made it difficult to distinguish the outlines of his body with any precision, and his skin underneath the pallor was bronzed. For the third time since Michael had entered the room, he asked why he had been arrested. This time he added that nobody had spoken a word to him. Apart from the fact that his C.O. was aware of the arrest, he knew nothing. This remark was made in a tone of suppressed rage.

Michael asked if he really didn't know the reason for his arrest.

He didn't have the faintest idea, said Alon, and the only reason he was still keeping a civil tongue in his head was his awareness of the need for cooperation between the different branches of the security forces. But his patience was wearing thin, he warned; he wanted to know what the hell was going on, and pronto.

Michael reminded him that the police were legally entitled to detain people for forty-eight hours without giving a reason for their arrest and concluded by saying: "And this being the case, I must ask you not to threaten us but to cooperate. You know very well why you're here."

Alon looked at him and said: "What the hell are you talking about? Just tell me what it's about, and I'll explain everything, and then you can apologize and take me home. Who are you anyway?" On the last question his voice rose furiously, and Michael looked at him calmly for a long time and said nothing. Then he recited the usual warning that anything he said might be used in evidence against him. The prisoner lost control. He mentioned Kafka, Soviet Russia, the Latin American dictatorships, and ended by yelling: "This is crazy, it's absurd—tell me at least who you are and why I'm here!"

At this point Raffi appeared, holding two steaming glasses that gave off a smell of Turkish coffee. He set one of them down at Michael's feet and the other at the feet of Colonel Alon, who looked at it and then at Michael and at Raffi's back as he left the room and shut the door behind him, and then he kicked the glass, which did not break but overturned and spilled its contents, leaving an oily black stain that spread between them on the floor. Michael did not stir or open his mouth. Sounding more desperate now, Alon said: "Look, you say that it's with the C.O.'s permission, but I haven't got any proof, and if you're lying I'll get you; I'll make you wish you'd never been born. What do you think, that I was born yesterday? Do you know who I am? You know how many interrogations I've conducted in my life? I know every trick in the book, believe me. I know that you have to identify yourself, and I demand to know what's going on!" The helpless rage covered everything, the color had returned to his cheeks, and Michael, who decided that it was time for the fear too, said calmly that he was waiting to hear from the prisoner himself why he thought that he had been arrested.

"Primitive, my friend, primitive. You won't hear a thing from me. There's no reason for my arrest, and I have no intention of speculating."

And then Manny came into the room. Colonel Yoav Alon gave him one look and paled, and this time you could see the fear plainly. Manny was the only one he knew, and with expert timing he had waited for this moment to produce himself like a rabbit from a conjurer's hat.

Michael asked if he recognized Manny.

"Yes," said Alon, in a new, humbler tone. "He's the officer who took my statement a couple of weeks ago, so I imagine that's what it's all about. But I already told him everything I knew. Why am I under arrest?"

Manny remained standing at the door while Michael revealed his name and rank and also what it was "all about." The investigation of the murder of Dr. Eva Neidorf, he explained, was the reason for the colonel's presence here. He should be grateful to them for keeping his arrest under wraps; even his wife had not been told anything, and she had been warned not to say anything about the search.

"What search?" yelled Alon. "What could you possibly find? And what about a warrant? You needn't take the trouble to reply; I know all your tricks. I'm telling you again, you know how many interrogations I've conducted myself?"

But for Alon's heavy breathing, there was a silence in the room. Then he said: "And don't give me that stuff about being 'grateful'! Who's stopping you from interrogating me publicly? I've got nothing to hide and nothing to add. You could have asked me to come to the Russian Compound, for all I care. You won't hear anything more from me here either. I didn't even know the Neidorf woman, except from stories."

"What stories?" asked Michael, who perceived that the fear was overcoming the anger. His face was pale again, his hands were trembling, the clear eyes had darkened.

"Just stories; what does it matter? They've got nothing to do with anything. You've got no reason to hold me here. I'm leaving!" And Colonel Alon stood up and took a determined stride toward the door, which was four steps away from his chair.

Michael did not move from his seat, Manny did not budge from the door. Alon reached the door and raised his hand to Manny, who with lightning speed bent his wrist and pushed his arm back down. No one uttered a word. Manny resumed his post at the door, Alon returned to the chair with the puddle of brown liquid at its base and the overturned glass next to it, and Michael lit a cigarette and asked if he suffered from claustrophobia. There was no response. If not, said Michael, why didn't he just sit quietly and cooperate?

"Cooperate? With pleasure. At home, in the Russian Compound, with an official request; not here. I've got nothing to say that I haven't already said! Are you deaf? I didn't know the woman! How many times do I have to tell you?"

"No?" asked Michael, and breathed out a column of smoke. "Are you prepared to submit to a polygraph test on that?"

"I'm prepared for anything, just so long as it's not here. I know this place. I understand that I'm here because you suspect me of something. First let me go, and then we can talk about the polygraph. Here you won't get a word out of me!"

Michael took a folded piece of paper out of his shirt pocket and handed it to the suspect, with the words: "That's a copy; don't bother to destroy it; we've got plenty of others."

The suspect examined the paper and threw it into the puddle of coffee. His lips trembled as he asked: "What's this? What's it got to do with anything? I don't understand. Just say what you want to say and get it over with."

"That's your handwriting, isn't it?" Michael asked quietly, and tapped his cigarette ash into the empty glass he was holding in his hand.

"Let's say it is my handwriting. Anyone could sign my name, but for argument's sake let's say it is. So what? What's the big deal? A note to a girl, so what?" His voice grew louder, and he stood up again. In a flash Manny was beside him, pushing him roughly back onto his chair. Michael asked if he would be more comfortable in handcuffs. Alon remained seated and did not reply. His shoulders were stooped, his eyes were fixed on the spilled coffee and the crumpled note, which was stained brown. Then he raised his head and gave Michael a look full of hostility and said: "If you put every man who writes a note to a girl under arrest, you'll have to arrest the whole country. And I'm still not saying that I wrote it."

"You don't have to say everything," said Michael simply. "Sometimes others say it for you." He took another sheet of paper out of his pocket, identical in appearance to the first, ran his eyes over it, and then read aloud: "'Orna, sweetheart, sorry about yesterday, I want to explain. Meet me at seven at the usual place? I'll be waiting for you. Yoav.'" Then he took another sheet of paper from his pocket—it, too, a photocopy, as he explained to the suspect, who read it and blushed— a page from the registration book of a Tel Aviv hotel. According to the hotel register, Colonel Yoav Alon had spent two days there in a double room, with his wife. "And your wife, has she ever heard of the hotel in question?" inquired Michael. "Would you like us to ask her?" Alon said nothing. "Perhaps you'd like to tell us what it was you were sorry about in the note you wrote to Orna Dan?"

Alon raised his head and looked at Michael with hatred. Then he said: "So what? I had an affair with a girl. What's it got to do with your investigation? Go on, tell my wife. Big deal. So the girl's a whore and she told you. Why did you want to know? What business is it of yours?"

"Ah," said Michael, and dropped his cigarette butt into the dregs of the coffee in his glass, "but it is. There's something that makes it our business. Shall I tell you what you were sorry about in the note? Do you want me to tell you? Or do you want to tell me?"

In a slow, halting voice, the suspect said: "I don't remember; it was a long time ago. I suppose I couldn't make it to a date I had with her, or something." Beads of sweat had begun collecting on his forehead, just under his cropped hair. He made no attempt to wipe them off.

"No, my friend, you remember very well. It's not the kind of thing one forgets. But I'll remind you if you like." Alon's face twisted in pain as Chief Inspector Ohayon said very quietly: "It's connected to the case because you couldn't make it with the girl. And don't tell me you don't remember."

Manny pounced on the uplifted hand, but there was no need. The hand dropped back with the slumping of the body, which for all its strength suddenly looked limp and lifeless. Michael nodded to Manny, who left the room.

"Supposing it's true," whispered Alon. "You think that's a reason to arrest somebody? What's the connection? Why don't you get off my back?" His voice was weak, and the last words sounded like a plea.

Michael shut his face against any trace of feeling as he said: "I can't get off your back if you don't cooperate, and you know it as well as I do. If you cooperate, I'll get off your back. You know that I know that you knew Neidorf, that you went to her with your problem for a whole year, Mondays and Thursdays, in the evening. You know that we know all about it already. We know that you didn't tell anyone that you were in therapy, not even your wife, and that when you said you were waiting for your son to finish his judo lesson you weren't waiting outside at all but racing to Dr. Neidorf's place instead, and that's why you always got home late. The boy couldn't understand why you always arrived to pick him up at eight, when the lesson finished at half past seven. You see, we know. If you like, we can even tell your wife about the pizza and falafel you would buy the kid on the way to account for your lateness. You know that I know that you lied when you gave evidence the first time. Why don't you just tell me the rest?" Michael stood up as he spoke and approached Alon, stood over him and looked into his eyes, which looked back completely blankly, even the fear gone. The man dropped his blond head and stared at the pool of coffee. In the next room the telephone rang. They both listened to the ring, which was cut off when a female voice said "Hello," and that was the last thing they heard.

With a final, weak bluster, Alon said: "You can't prove a thing; you're just talking."

"No?" said Michael. "You think I can't prove it? I've got witnesses, people who saw you going into the house. But I've also got this," and he pulled a third photocopy out of his pocket and handed it to the suspect, who stared at it for a long time. The signature on the check was very clear, and the handwriting was the same as the handwriting on the note to Orna Dan. On the top line, next to the printed words "Pay to the order of," Eva Neidorf had written her name in her own handwriting. "You gave her an incomplete check, but she was a woman of orderly habits, and she didn't pass the check on to her grocer, as you expected, but filled in the details and deposited it. We've got it all sewed up, and from now on you can cut the crap about 'proof.' They say you're a clever guy, you say you've had a lot of experience with conducting interrogations, and I think the time has come for you to confess and start cooperating."

Colonel Yoav Alon began to shake, and then he uttered a kind of whimper. Michael understood that the strange sound came from vocal cords unused since childhood, and once more he wondered why he didn't feel happy or triumphant. The weariness that had vanished when he began the interrogation now returned and demanded his attention. He sat still and lit a cigarette and thought about Yuval, about how proud he was of his father and how hard he tried, unsuccessfully, to hide his pride. He thought about Maya too. Would she have loved him now. In the second room, the members of the team heard the pause; the interrogation was being recorded from there. The door opened, Eli Bahar's head popped around it, nodded to Michael, and vanished again.

Yoav Alon didn't even raise his head when Michael began to speak. "We have proof that you broke into Neidorf's house too," he said. "Just reconstruct the murder; that's all I'm asking you to do."

As he had expected, the suspect came to life and said in a new voice: "But I didn't murder her. Why should I murder her? I swear to you"—here he stood up, and Michael made no attempt to stop him— "I tell you I didn't murder her. I had no motive." But Chief Inspector Ohayon didn't seem interested. And then Tzilla came in and suggested a break. They'd prepared some food.

Michael left the room and looked at what was waiting for him next to the telephone. Tzilla remained with the suspect, who, it turned out, did not touch either the sandwich or the fresh coffee she offered him.

Only Eli Bahar's wrathful look made Michael force himself to taste the hot meal they had produced from God knows where. The maternal vigilance his teammates, especially Eli and Tzilla, exhibited toward him amused Michael but also touched him. In the end he pushed the plate aside and concentrated on the coffee. The apartment was cold. Manny explained that the building's central heating wasn't working. In the living room, where they sat, an electric heater was burning.

Michael stretched out his legs and ignored the nausea the smell of the food had induced. With a tremendous effort, he listened to Manny talking about the search as he sat in the armchair opposite him. He hadn't stayed till the end, Eli interjected, but he was there when they found the shoe. The rubber sole had been examined and compared to the photo of the plaster cast. It was a perfect match. "It was him who broke in, took the documents, everything," said Eli with satisfaction. "All I'm waiting for now is for them to find the documents in his apartment, together with the file from the accountant. Have you got the strength to carry on?"

Michael glanced at his watch; it was half past ten. The date, he saw, was April 6, and suddenly he remembered that it had been parents' day at Yuval's school, that the boy had got his report card today—Michael had forgotten everything, even though Yuval had been with him that evening. He picked up the receiver and dialed his home number. The phone buzzed ten times in his ear before the receiver was picked up on the other end. Yuval's sleepy voice said that they would get their report cards on the sixteenth. "There's another ten days to go, and I'll remind you. Yes, I ate what you left me. I'm dead tired. When are you coming home? No, I've got a test tomorrow, Bible studies. I'm going back to sleep."

Though reassured about parents' day, Michael could not rid himself of guilt. Eli asked hesitantly if he wanted him to take over. "Not yet. Let's wait until he confesses to something. Whimpering doesn't amount to a confession." And he went back into the room. Alon requested permission to use the toilet. Manny accompanied him. The little bathroom window was barred; Manny waited outside the door and escorted him back to the room that overlooked the dark backyard.

The lights burned all night. The interrogation was over long before they thought it would be. By morning they had the whole story.

Michael kept going until five in the morning, when Colonel Alon signed a confession in the presence of the entire team. He left the reconstruction and the details to Eli Bahar, who had gone to sleep at two A.M. and was wakened at five.

When the suspect had returned from the bathroom and sat down opposite Michael, he asked for a cigarette. After Michael lit it for him, he coughed as he inhaled the smoke. He looked at the cigarette in his hand, remarked that he hadn't smoked for years, and fell silent. Then he burst out that not only had he not killed Neidorf but he would love to get his hands on whoever had done it.

In the terminology of the Institute, Michael knew, transference had taken place, but he himself would have called it love. Which is what Colonel Alon called it too, repeating emphatically that he loved her, worshiped her, would have trusted her with his life. And although

Michael could not see his eyes—the man was talking to the dry coffee stain on the floor—his voice expressed the right feelings, pain and grief. There was no fear anymore, in neither his voice nor his eyes, which looked straight at Michael for a moment and seemed hurt and wounded but not afraid.

Michael asked for the whole story, in detail.

It all began, said Colonel Alon to the circle of spilled coffee, with his present posting. Until then, until he had become a military governor, he never had any problems; not in his marriage either.

But when the problems began, they really hit him for a loop, he said bitterly; even the one and only time in his life when he tried to have a little fling, he had failed. At first, when he couldn't work up any interest in his wife, he thought he was simply sick of her. They had been dating since high school. And now he had lost all interest in having sex with her, he couldn't function, he didn't even have the energy to try. That was why he had started with Orna, who was so young and so special. "It took me six months to work up the courage to try, and afterward I was sorry I did, I didn't really want her either, and then I realized that it wasn't only sex, it was everything." Neidorf would explain that his feelings of apathy and futility were symptoms of depression.

Michael smoked in silence. From time to time Alon looked at him, to make sure that he was listening, and then he went back to staring at the floor.

Without making a sound, treading as delicately as a cat, Manny left the room, and Michael knew that from now on he would be sitting next to the tape recorder in the next room without missing a word. What was the cause of his depression, Michael was on the point of asking, but Alon anticipated him. His main task as military governor, said Alon, was issuing permits. "I don't know how familiar you are with the picture, but those guys need a permit to piss. You can't believe the kind of thing I have to deal with; nobody could believe it."

Although he thought he would be able to cope—for a time he had been seconded to the previous governor—although he had men under him from the different security branches to bear the brunt of the daily load of frustration, it began to get to him, to haunt him. He had never suspected that he would have so many difficulties in his new job. "I'm not exaggerating," he said to Michael, man to man. "You wouldn't have been able to stand it either, believe me. You don't look the type, you're not brutal enough, and it's got nothing to do with politics; I've never gotten into the political side of things. It's a simple question of humanity, of how far you're prepared to play God, and I've never been much good at that, but up to now I've never had to be."

At three in the morning, Manny brought them more coffee. Michael asked Alon if he wanted anything to eat. He didn't want anything to eat; all he wanted to do was talk. "It's like a flood," said Manny to Shorer, who dropped in at four o'clock in the morning. "You can't stop him. From the minute he started talking, he hasn't shut his mouth." Shorer didn't go into the room; he sat and listened in for a while and went on his way. Michael heard the knocking on the door, the footsteps, but he didn't move from his chair, where he sat listening intently to the man sitting opposite him and emptying his guts. The words streamed out of him, all kinds of things connected to the case and unconnected to the case, and Michael didn't stop him.

He spoke about his elderly parents, Holocaust survivors. About the fact that he was the eldest, the only son; his sister didn't matter so much, he explained, he was their "Kaddish," the one who would say the mourner's prayer when they died; and Michael pushed Nira and Youzek and Fela out of his mind, almost in so many words: "Move aside, get out of my way, you're distracting my attention." Alon spoke about the Hashomer Hatzair youth movement and the ideal of equality, about volunteering for tough combat units in the army as the highest value, about his distinction as a student, about his promotion in the army and the expectations that he would rise all the way to the top. Everything was all mixed up; there was no order in his words.

Afterward he spoke about his first day as military governor in the territories. He had signed a permit for an old peasant to grow olives on his ancestral land, and the peasant had looked at him in a way that made him feel like an arrogant fool. From day to day, said Alon, he had tried to make himself more insensitive, and he had succeeded, or so he

believed when he signed expulsion orders, when he forbade family uni-
fications, "all in accordance with policy, just doing my job. And with
the G.S.S. breathing down my neck all the time. I don't know what
your political opinions are, but it's completely irrelevant, believe me.
No one can be a liberal military governor; those are two mutually contradictory terms." Yoav Alon looked into Michael Ohayon's eyes: "You
don't understand the connection, but I can quote what Dr. Neidorf
said. She said that the things I failed to express spoke through my
body; those were her exact words. There were days, before I went to
her, when I even thought of putting an end to it all, life seemed so
futile. There was no point in anything. Food, sex, books, friends,
movies—nothing turned me on. You can't live like that, not for long
anyway, and then I went to a doctor about my sexual functioning and
he couldn't find anything wrong physically. I had to come to the obvious conclusion. I hope you're not recording this bit, but the fact is I
don't really care anymore; everything can go to hell."

After getting the background story off his chest, Alon got to the
details that interested Michael. He had been in therapy for a year,
twice a week, and he had been careful to pay in cash, because even
Osnat, his wife, didn't know anything about it. He couldn't explain
why he didn't tell her. Maybe he was afraid she would tell Joe; not
even he knew. He had chosen Dr. Neidorf because his old high school
friend Tammy Zvielli never stopped talking about her, and Joe sometimes mentioned her too. Although she had a two-year waiting list of
people wanting analysis, she was able to fit him in twice a week. He
didn't have to worry about meeting her socially, because she never
came to Joe's place. He had relied on her discretion, and rightly so.
Nobody in the world knew that he was in therapy with her, and if she
hadn't died the way she did, nobody would ever have known.

He had heard about her death from Joe at lunchtime on Saturday;
Joe had called to cancel a luncheon appointment and told him. Of
course, it hadn't occurred to Joe to warn him; he knew nothing about
the connection between them. At first he didn't know she'd been murdered—Joe only said that she was dead—and he was worried about the

discovery of the notes in her consulting room and his name being exposed. "In the army, they think you can't trust a man who goes to see a psychologist, certainly not in my position. And the funny thing is, they're right. They were simply mistaken in me; the truth is I'm really not suited to the job." After talking to Joe, he got into a panic and didn't know what to do. Joe had told him about her return to the country and her lecture, and he assumed that it would take some time to organize the family, so he waited for dark—it wasn't raining yet—and that same evening he broke into her house through the kitchen window and took the papers in her consulting room.

Michael raised his hand and asked him to stop for a moment. There were a couple of things he would like to get clear, he said gently.

Why did he have to break into the house when he had a key? he asked in tone of friendly concern, and he saw the incomprehension spreading over Yoav Alon's face. "What key? How could I have had a key? I don't know what you're talking about," and Michael dropped the question of the key and concentrated on the details of the break-in.

"No problem. I used an iron bar to bend the bars on the kitchen window and broke a pane of glass to unlock the window. It overlooks the back garden; nobody saw. And then I went to the consulting room. I searched all the drawers. I took the list of patients—it had written on it, in big letters: 'In case of emergency'—and also the timetable of patients' hours I found there," he said in embarrassment. "You have to believe me, I didn't read a thing. I burned it all, including her address book, where I found my number."

"And the lecture too," said Michael as if stating a fact.

"The lecture?" repeated Alon in bewilderment, and then he said: "Ah, the lecture she was supposed to give that morning? Why should I have taken that; what do I care about lectures? I never even saw any lecture there, but then I wasn't looking for it, was I?"

"So you didn't go through all her papers?" asked Michael, who knew that Alon was telling the truth but hoped against hope that he was mistaken.

"I didn't sit there for hours reading all that stuff, no. I just looked for anything that might expose me. The whole business didn't take more than half an hour. I wasn't in the mood for wasting time; someone could have arrived at the house at any minute."

Michael lit a cigarette and asked if he had worked with gloves.

"I don't know why you want to use the word 'work,' but yes, I did wear gloves while I was there, since I'm aware of the fact that breaking and entering isn't exactly legal. I assumed the police would check out her office."

"I thought you didn't know how she died. Why should you have thought of the police?" Michael did not take his eyes off Alon as he asked.

"No, I didn't know; Joe didn't say a word about how, and he only told me about the police and everything afterward. I can't give you any other explanation for the gloves; it was instinct; you'll have to believe me. Can I have another cigarette?" Michael gave him a cigarette and asked him to describe his movements in Neidorf's house in detail, which he did, again denying that he had seen the lecture.

"Okay, so you broke in and took the papers. What did you do with them?" asked Michael tensely.

"I got into my car and drove—you won't believe this—to the cemetery. I wanted—I don't know what I wanted, but I knew that I wouldn't go to the funeral. And I burned them all there."

"What time was it?" asked Michael.

"Maybe half past eight, maybe nine; no, later, because I was home by ten." Michael thought to himself that it had only started raining at around ten, on that Saturday when he was sitting with Hildesheimer. He remembered the shutter, the open window, the thunder and lightning, and decided that the storm had in fact begun sometime after nine.

"And afterward? What did you do after that?"

"After that I didn't do anything. The next day I talked to Joe when he got back from his session with you, and he told me about the murder, about his pistol, which I myself bought for him in '67 right after the war, when I was only eighteen years old. And then I got really nervous. The thought of a murder investigation . . . I've already told you that I know a bit about the way things work. I tried to think about where else my name might appear as a patient of Dr. Neidorf's." Alon fell silent and stared at Michael, who took care not to alter the expression on his face, which, or so he hoped, showed nothing but polite and steady interest, and not the knowledge that this was the critical moment: would Alon tell him about the accountant of his own free will? And if he didn't, did that mean that it was all a lie?

But he did. He told him about the receipts she was so scrupulous about giving him, although she knew he would never use them. She knew that being in therapy was a terrible secret as far as he was concerned, but nevertheless she would write out a receipt every time, and he would tear it up the minute he was alone again. He remembered Joe once telling him that he had changed his accountants and was using Zeligman and Zeligman, on Neidorf's recommendation. It was from Joe, who was always complaining about his financial affairs, that he had learned in the first place about how they passed on their receipt books and medical diaries to their accountants. He had called up the accountants' office and notified them that he was coming to get the dead woman's file in connection with police inquiries, and the girl who answered the phone said that the police had already been in touch and said they were coming for it that morning, at about nine. And so he had gone early, he was there at twenty past eight, and he signed a bit of paper and took the file. All the details fitted in with Zmira's story. There was no doubt that Alon had done what he said he had done. The question was, had he done anything else?

"What did you do after that?"

"I drove out of town in the direction of kibbutz Ramat Rachel. And over there, in a field where they haven't started building yet, I burned the file, that is, the papers inside it. The folder itself I took back to the office with me; it's exactly the same as the others. And my car really did get stuck; there was a fuel blockage. I wasn't thinking of an alibi; it just worked out like that. Not that it helped much, as you know."

"And afterward?" Michael persevered.

"There wasn't any afterward; there was nothing left. Afterward you brought me in for questioning and I was nervous, but I didn't do anything else. I thought it was over. Actually, I didn't think about it at all; I thought about Dr. Neidorf and wondered how I was going to manage without her. She went and died on me in the middle of the job, all the pus outside, and now it has to be cleaned up and there's no one to do it. Tell me, do you think that all this can be kept secret?"

"Kept secret from who?" asked Michael, and lit another cigarette. It was a quarter to five in the morning. His whole body was crying out for sleep.

"From everybody, I suppose. The army, the press, my wife, everybody."

Michael said that the arrest had been made with the consent of O.C. Central Command. They had told him only in general outlines what it was about, but he would demand an explanation, and Michael didn't know how they could avoid giving him one. And they would have to verify certain facts with his wife. And the higher ranks in the police force were aware of the basic facts, he said, and shrugged his shoulders, like Hildesheimer.

"In short," said Alon bitterly, "I'm finished."

"No, you're not finished," said Michael dryly. "You simply won't be able to continue your army career, and that's not because of the therapy either, but because of the way you broke the law—breaking and entering, concealing evidence, impersonating an officer of the law. We don't tend to take such things lightly. The truth is that you're not sure yourself that you're the right person for the job of chief of staff, or Commander Central Command either. I can only try to keep the papers from going to town on the story, not because I want to protect you but out of concern for the reputation of the army and the military government. But in the meantime, until the exact reconstruction of the crime and the polygraph test, you'll remain in custody. The forty-eight hours aren't over yet. After you've given us your full cooperation, and only then, we can talk about what we might be able to do for you."

Alon bowed his head and buried it in his hands, which were resting on his knees, and for a long time nothing was said. Michael suppressed a burst of pity and reminded himself of the two weeks he had spent with Eli Bahar at the banks, of his own frustration and depression. Then he filled with anger, which he suppressed too, looked at his watch again, and said that they would have to check out his alibi for the presumed time of the murder. "Inspector Eli Bahar will be with you for the next few hours. When you want to sleep, tell him. He hasn't got any plans for torturing you; not as long as you cooperate, at any rate," he said, and stood up. His legs were numb, his eyes burning. He walked out of the room, and Eli, who had been wakened by Tzilla, walked in.

"All that work with the banks and the accountants, and we're at a dead end again," said Tzilla bitterly when Michael sat down next to the phone in the living room before leaving the apartment.

"You sound sorry that he's not the murderer," said Michael, and he didn't smile.

"That's not what I meant, only that I can't understand why he went to such a lot of trouble and took such terrible risks, just to keep the fact that he was in therapy secret. Don't you think that's going too far?"

"I know it's going too far. But that's nothing new in our line of work. Do you think that killing someone for a hundred thousand dollars, for instance, isn't going too far? Or how about murdering a girl because you've made her pregnant and you don't want to admit paternity? You wanted to say something else. You wanted to say that we hoped he was our man, and we know even before the polygraph that he's telling the truth. And now we have to begin all over again."

On the second floor, Mrs. Brandtstetter peeped through the peephole and immediately recognized the tall man going down the stairs at half past five in the morning. She smiled in satisfaction at the thought that a man leaving a flat at half past five in the morning was no innocent uncle or cousin. No, it was proof that she was right, that he was the worst of them all. As long as he was there, upstairs in the flat, they had moved furniture around and answered the telephone. Now that he was leaving, perhaps she would be able to sleep.

They spent three days with Colonel Alon. They interrogated him again, with a polygraph, and it turned out that he hadn't been lying. They demanded to see the file folder he had taken from the accountants' office, a big plastic file that had held the receipt book and the medical diary. Zmira identified his voice, although she wasn't certain; and the footprint they found under the tree in Neidorf's big garden became an important piece of evidence against him.

He took them to the places where he had burned the documents, in the cemetery and on the hills outside Ramat Rachel, where he showed them the charred remains of the diary cover hidden under a rock. They gathered them together and put them into a big plastic bag.

They questioned Linder again; Alon's wife, Osnat; his secretary, Orna Dan; and his upstairs neighbor too, Mrs. Steiglitz, who assured them that you would have to get up very early in the morning to escape her vigilant eye. And in fact, she had seen him leaving the house on Saturday morning, on foot. More than that, to her regret, she was unable to tell them. The key to Neidorf's apartment was nowhere to be found. They searched his house, his car, his office, without coming up with anything new. During all these three days Michael took part in substantiating the evidence, but his heart wasn't in it. He knew the man was telling the truth and that just as Tzilla had said, they had reached a dead end again.

Shorer warned him that his hunch about Dina Silver was an obsession, that there was nothing to it. "You haven't got a leg to stand on. I don't know what you've got against her. Why don't you check her out with one of your friends at that Institute of theirs, with what's-his-name, for example, that old guy you're so crazy about."

In the end Michael had Elisha Naveh brought in for questioning. The youth had continued hanging around outside Dina Silver's clinic and then outside her house (she was still ill in bed), and he was looking more and more neglected, according to Raffi, who had been put on his tail.

He refused to cooperate, denied any connection with Dina Silver, and even when Michael reminded him of the fact that he had been in therapy with her at the mental health clinic he didn't blink an eye. There was no way of reaching him.

Michael told Hildesheimer afterward that throughout the interrogation he'd had the feeling that the youngster "wasn't there. He was in another world, hearing other voices, not mine. I even tried threatening him that we would get in touch with his father, that I would arrest him for drug possession, but he only looked at me with that blank, staring look, as if I didn't exist. It was only after I let him go, which I regret to this day, that I realized he was beyond fear, and when that happens, there's nothing you can do." But this conversation took place long after it was all over.

He let the boy go without having succeeded in getting anything out of him, and once more he was at a loss. Again Yuval complained about the grinding of teeth he heard at night.

In the end they got a warrant to tap the telephone at the Silver residence, in spite of the husband's position, and Michael hoped that his salvation would come from there. For two whole weeks he listened in, to nothing. He was forced to admit that she wasn't a chatterbox, not even when she was ill, and the fact that she was ill was irrefutable. The only people she spoke to on the phone were her patients, Joe Linder, and a few other analysts from the Institute.

It was only later that Michael remembered the phone call on the day that he was summoned to the Hadassah Hospital in Ein Kerem. Dina Silver said "Hello" several times, there was a silence on the other end of the line, and then a click. They traced the call, to a "public telephone on Zion Square," as they told Michael, and he didn't give it another thought until after he was summoned to Hadassah. But by then it was too late, as he told Hildesheimer afterward.

Since completing his residency in psychiatry, Shlomo Gold was on call at the hospital only twice a month. Six times a month he was on call at home, but it was only rarely that he was called out at inconvenient hours. He always made sure that Hadassah Ein Kerem was not the duty hospital on the nights when he was on call there; that way, he could expect relative quiet, as he explained to Rina, the head emergency nurse.

Tonight, he said to her on that Tuesday night at half past ten, when she began her shift, the duty hospital was Hadassah Mount Scopus, on the other side of town, so he expected to have time to write up the sessions with his analytic patients, as he hadn't managed to do during the week; tomorrow he had supervision with Rosenfeld. But he would be happy to chat awhile and put off the evil hour. Rina, a rather dumpy single woman in her early forties, looked at him seductively over the counter, her flat, broad face close to his, and asked archly if he really had to write tonight.

Gold blushed in confusion. He had never managed to emulate the lighthearted banter of some of his friends, who flirted with Rina without committing themselves and spent the long nights on call, as they reported the next morning, in passionate fun and games, on condition, of course, that the hospital wasn't the duty hospital that night.

His embarrassment amused Rina and caused her to press even closer. He stood with his back to the door and tried to arrest the blush that was spreading over his face. In the end he said: "I wish you'd stop it. You're embarrassing me," his pale eyes avoiding her amused ones. The situation was saved by the physician on call in respiratory intensive care, to whom Rina directed all her resources the moment he arrived and leaned on the counter next to Gold.

Unlike Gold, Dr. Galor was a young man with a light, open manner. He wasn't particularly handsome, but he radiated the kind of confidence Gold had never succeeded in acquiring. Galor smiled invitingly at Rina, crossed to the other side of the counter, put his arm around her shoulders, and began playing with the collar of her white zippered tunic. The zipper began to part under the busy fingers of Dr. Galor, who ignored the mild protests of its owner.

Gold, blushing even more deeply, was about to leave the emergency room when the stretcher bearers came in. Rina's face suddenly froze, and she said firmly: "We're not the duty hospital today." In the silence in the emergency room, which was almost completely empty, her voice sounded like a determined bark. Gold was sure she was going to throw them out, but then Yakov rushed in, and Rina's expression changed to one of interest and concern. "What is it, Yakov, is it someone you know?"

Yakov, a fourth-year medical student, who worked in emergency as a paramedic and aroused in Rina maternal feelings that no one before him had ever succeeded in eliciting, didn't say a word; he only nodded his head and pointed at the stretcher, from whose side an arm attached to an infusion protruded. The paramedics carrying the stretcher began gently to roll the patient onto the nearest empty bed, next to which Yakov was standing.

Rina looked at the young man on the bed and then at Yakov and said: "Isn't he the one who lives with you? The good-looking one? What happened to him?" Yakov wiped his face with his sleeve and said in a faltering voice: "He took all kinds of pills and drank something too. His pulse is very weak." He looked at Rina in despair and said: "Do something—why don't you do something! What are you all standing around for?"

And then what Gold always called the dervish dance began. Suddenly Galor was there, his hand on the pulse; suddenly Rina cried: "Respiratory senior on call—I need the senior too," and somebody said something about an active-carbon gastric lavage. Galor pronounced that there was no time for an X-ray, the emergency room began to fill up with people in white coats, the bed was wheeled toward the corridor, and Yakov was asked for details. Running after the bed, he replied that he had seen a bottle of brandy, he didn't know how much of it Elisha had drunk, and empty drug packets. According to his calculations, he said, Elisha had taken twenty antidepressants and ten barbiturates and washed them down with alcohol.

Galor looked worriedly at Yakov. "Stay here; you don't look good. I'll tell you when to come up, I promise," and he ran into the corridor after the speeding bed.

Yakov began to shudder violently, covered his face with his hands, sat down on the bed closest to the counter, and quavered: "He isn't going to make it. I found him too late. Oh, God, he isn't going to make it."

In a second Gold was beside him. His arms went around the medical student, who was everybody's favorite, who was always smiling, who worked three nights a week in the emergency room to support himself, who never complained, and whose face always wore an expression of admiration for the doctors, compassion for the patients, and childish veneration for the science of medicine in general.

Only a week before, Gold knew, he had returned from London, where his parents were in the diplomatic service. Yakov had been living on his own since their posting there. After completing his army service and being accepted into medical school, he had supported himself.

The only thing he didn't have to pay was rent, because he acted *in loco parentis* to his roommate, whose father was also posted to the London embassy.

Several months before, Gold had been talking to Yakov one night when he was on call, and the medical student had revealed his confusion about what to specialize in. He was considering psychiatry, Yakov had said very seriously, looking at Gold as if he were God. And then he had told him about his roommate. "A very gifted boy, who's messing up his life. You can't imagine what a waste," Yakov said sadly, and added that he was very attached to the youth. "He's like a younger brother to me, and I don't know what to do."

Behind the thick lenses of his glasses, his brown eyes peered out, anguished, intelligent, and trustful, and Gold found himself delivering a long lecture on psychiatric specialization. Without additional clinical training, said Gold, the qualified psychiatrist finds himself fit only to do drug therapy. If Yakov intended to specialize in the field seriously, he would have to get training in addition to that provided by the hospital. Finally, looking into those serious, trusting eyes, Gold smiled and said that by the time he graduated from medical school, Yakov would probably change his mind a dozen times. Then Yakov replied humbly that he might well change his mind, but what Gold had said interested him very much, and he really didn't know what to do about his roommate, who was also his charge. Gold suggested referring him for treatment to one of the city's mental health clinics. At that moment, Gold remembered, the student's face took on a bitter expression, and he asked him if he had heard of a Dr. Neidorf.

Gold smiled a knowing smile and said that he did indeed know her, personally.

"Well, Elisha's father knows her personally too—Elisha's the guy who lives with me—and he went to see her, and she referred him to the mental health clinic in Kiryat Hayovel, and since he's been going there he's in worse shape than ever, and I think that what happened there is a disaster."

But then Gold had been summoned to the ward, and the interrupted conversation slipped his mind. It must have been over a year ago, thought Gold, and until this moment he had forgotten all about it. He hadn't taken the trouble to find out what had been so terrible about the mental health clinic and what it was that was upsetting Yakov, who sat beside him now, staring blankly in front of him.

Rina took Yakov by the hand and led him to the back room, where the physicians on call and the emergency room staff ate their meals. She sat him down and put in his hand a cup of coffee containing a lot of sugar. Winking at Gold as if to say "Get to work," she walked out of the room.

Gold had to repeat his question about what exactly had happened several times, at first warmly and then insistently. At last Yakov spoke. He had gone to an early movie—he needed a break from studying—and when he left the house he thought Elisha was sleeping. When he came back, at ten o'clock, all the lights were on; he saw them from outside the house. He went inside and called out, but there was no answer, and he went into Elisha's room and found him lying on his back on top of his unmade bed. Next to him was an empty bottle of brandy, and the room stank of alcohol. "Elisha hated alcohol, you have to understand," said Yakov, and for the first time he looked at Gold, who nodded and asked him to go on. Yakov told him about the packets lying next to the bed, from which he had learned what Elisha had taken. "Those little health service packets—I don't know where he got them. One of them had 'Elatroll' written on it and the other one 'Pentobarbital,' and I don't know how many he took, but I do know that it would be hard to imagine a more destructive combination," he said, and burst into tears.

Gold said nothing and let him cry. The door opened, and Rina's head appeared. She looked inside soberly and shook her head. Gold signaled her to stay outside and shut the door, and she obeyed.

During the two hours that Gold sat with Yakov, he managed to talk to him about the feelings of guilt accompanying the shock of the discovery. Part of the guilt stemmed from the fact that he himself had once told Elisha "how you couldn't die," as he put it. They were watching a television movie, and the heroine tried to commit suicide by taking Valium. "And I had to be the genius who told him that to die of Valium you would have to swallow two hundred pills, or something, and that you don't die of sleeping pills unless you take vast quantities. He wanted to know how you could succeed in committing suicide, and I asked him if he had any plans in that direction, and he told me not to talk rubbish. Then, after the movie, I said something about Elatroll and the danger of combining it with alcohol and barbiturates." Gold murmured something soothing, but Yakov ignored him and continued passionately: "All that waste! I don't know if you managed to see how beautiful he is. Women are crazy about him. And he's clever and interesting too, and he's got a sense of humor and a lot of charm. People are drawn to him like flies to honey. Not even because of his looks, but because of the feeling he gives you that he needs you so much, and he gives that feeling to everyone. And we were very close, I've already told you, and I believed him, although to be on the safe side I hid the pistol they had in the house, because even before I went to London I felt there was something wrong, but I never thought he would be able to get hold of Elatroll, you can't get it without a prescription, I don't know who could have given it to him."

Yakov went on blaming himself, and alternately crying and shouting, and Gold was glad to see that the young man had recovered from his state of shock, which had been replaced by anger and rage. And then he explained to him, in the most positive tone possible, that there was no way of stopping someone who had decided to end his life. "If someone has really made up his mind, you can only postpone it; you can't prevent him from doing it. The act has to be seen as the consequence of illness, like any other mental illness, and it's not your responsibility or your fault; you couldn't have prevented it."

As Gold finished speaking, Rina stuck her head in at the door again and gave him a meaningful look. The boy's dead, thought Gold, and she wants me to tell him. But Yakov, too, had seen the look and understood its meaning, and he put his head in his arms on the table and burst into tears.

Later Galor came into the room, exhausted, and explained in an apologetic tone that they had tried everything they could without success. "He did a thorough job. Even if he had arrived earlier, I doubt if we would have been able to do anything." And he laid his hand on Yakov's arm. Yakov wiped his eyes and said: "Thanks; I know. I knew you wouldn't be able to save him," and he burst into tears again.

"We tried everything in the book on him, but he developed heart failure. Actually I was optimistic in the beginning, I thought we'd caught him in time, but it seems I was wrong," and Galor sighed and sat down in the chair next to Gold. "So young and such an idiot. You have to really want to die to do it that way."

Gold took the young man to the call physician's room in the Psychiatric Department and put him to bed after persuading him to take a Valium. He returned to the emergency room, where Galor was waiting for him; they would have to report it to the police, he said. Gold felt a chill, remembering the events of the Saturday morning two months earlier: the interrogation at the Russian Compound, the sense of helplessness he felt. But he knew there was no avoiding it. "Unnatural death; there are procedures; it has to be done," said Galor, and straightened his spectacles. "Go on, call the police. I want to be covered. He didn't die in your care, so don't look like that."

Why me? Why does it always have to be me? Gold asked himself bitterly when he saw Chief Inspector Michael Ohayon standing in the doorway of the emergency room. Gold had persuaded Rina to make the phone call and save him "all that hassle." And then the shift officer had arrived, the same redheaded guy who had escorted him to the Russian Compound that Saturday. Taking one look at the name of the deceased, he had exchanged a couple of words with Rina and asked for a phone. And then Ohayon arrived. "It's not true, it can't be possible," said Gold to himself as Ohayon and the redhead advanced toward the corner of the counter where he stood looking at them with a dread that grew with every step they took.

"So we meet again," said the redhead. "An unexpected pleasure, eh, Dr. Gold?" and he gave Gold a merry look.

Gold filled with rage and was about to protest at the man's facetious tone, but he stopped himself when he saw the tense, pale face of Chief Inspector Ohayon. Again, thought Gold in despair. Rina glared at the cigarette that Ohayon stuck in his mouth, and as she warned him not to light it, her eyes met his, and her face changed, taking on a slumberous look. Gold witnessed a new aspect of the head nurse's courtship behavior, no longer her usual automatic flirtatiousness but a seductiveness that derived from an attraction to a specific object, to this tall policeman with the dark, melancholy eyes—every common cow's dream come true, thought Gold viciously as Rina led Ohayon to the Respiratory Intensive Care unit in obedience to his request to see the body.

Again Gold found himself sitting opposite Michael Ohayon, this time on his own territory, where the chief inspector appeared quite at home, as if he had been sharing nights on call with him forever; but to his relief, he discovered that he was not at the center of the interrogation. It was Yakov that Ohayon was interested in, Yakov and what he knew about the dead boy.

When Ohayon had come back and asked Gold to take him to a room where they could talk, Gold reexperienced all he had felt on that Saturday at the Institute. It was only the chief inspector's expression, which was different from what it had been then, more strained, more exposed, that enabled him to collect himself and remember that things were different now.

The chief inspector's face had a hard, sharp look. And Gold saw something that reminded him of the expression on Yakov's face. A kind of guilt.

Ohayon asked impatiently: "What happened to the boy?"

He did not light his cigarette but set it on the corner of the table, and Gold saw the tooth marks on the filter tip.

Gold repeated everything Yakov had told him. The combination of pills and alcohol, the unstable personality.

He had written his thesis, Gold explained to Ohayon, on the lethal potential of psychotropic drugs. Actually, nobody in the entire hospital was a greater expert on the subject. Not that he said so in so many words; he simply confirmed what Ohayon had already heard from Galor when he went up to the ward. Pleasure flooded Gold as he explained to the chief inspector, who listened with grave concern, the dangers of taking Elatroll: the heart failure that was one of the side effects of taking an overdose, the danger of combining it with alcohol. Ohayon asked how the drug could be obtained.

"Ah," said Gold with a new and unfamiliar confidence. "All you have to do is go to any family doctor in a public health clinic and say that you're suffering from depression, and if he's worth anything, maybe not the first time but definitely the second, he'll prescribe Elatroll, in gradually increasing doses, and send you to the clinic pharmacy with a prescription for a monthly dosage. The thing is," explained Gold didactically, "that very few people who're not doctors know about the dangers of the drug; they don't know that an overdose endangers cardiac functioning. Most people"—and Gold blinked as he watched the trembling hand lighting the cigarette—"think that you die of an overdose of sleeping pills, or barbiturates, tranquilizers. They don't realize that you have to take huge amounts to die. But only specialists know that a combination of Elatroll in a sufficient amount— let's say two grams; in other words, twenty tablets of a hundred milligrams each, which is maybe a fortnight's dosage—a combination of that together with a few barbiturates, like he took, plus alcohol, gives you a very good chance of dying, especially if you're found only after two hours, let's say, by which time they can pump your stomach with active carbon, as they did to him, until kingdom come and it won't make any difference; the stuff will all have been absorbed into the bloodstream."

Michael asked him to go and wake up the medical student, Yakov, the roommate.

"Why do you need him now? He brought the empty packets with him, in his pocket. I took them when I put him to bed. I can tell you exactly what he took and where he got it," Gold said boldly. "The poor kid's exhausted; let him rest."

But Ohayon had recovered; his face had taken on the pantherlike expression with which Gold was familiar, and his voice was quiet but determined as he told the psychiatrist to wake Yakov immediately and not to tell anyone outside, or inside, the hospital what had happened.

Gold gave in and led Michael to the Psychiatric Department,

where without undue effort he woke Yakov. The young man sat up in bed, his eyes appearing naked without his glasses, for which his hand groped, and he looked at them miserably. His lips trembled when Gold explained, as tactfully as possible, who Michael Ohayon was. The chief inspector sat down on the bed, and with a gentleness Gold would never have believed possible, laid his hand on Yakov's arm and said: "I'm terribly sorry, but we need your help." Yakov collected himself, and while Gold went to get coffee for the three of them, he said despairingly that he didn't know how anybody could help anymore, it was too late to help, but he would do whatever they asked him to. His face twisted, and he seemed about to burst into tears, made vulnerable by his exhaustion and by the tranquilizer Gold had forced him to take, but he recovered himself and took a sip of the coffee Gold had brought from the urn in the corner.

Gold sat in the back of the room and listened to the conversation. Michael Ohayon did not ask him to leave, and altogether, thought Gold, the policeman looked as if something had snapped inside him.

It was four in the morning when Ohayon began the interrogation. At first he asked the predictable questions: the time when he found Elisha, the source of the drugs and alcohol, whether he had left a letter, a note, anything. Yakov said he hadn't looked; he was too busy trying to save his life. There was no note in a conspicuous place, he said.

Michael remarked that they were looking now, and Gold felt a shudder run down his spine as he imagined the police searching the young men's flat. Pictures of intrusion and disorder ran through his mind. When Michael asked about Neidorf, Gold suddenly comprehended the change in the chief inspector: he was still investigating the murder, almost two months after it had happened. Now Gold understood the significance of the dark circles under his eyes, and something, the faintest shadow of sympathy, of fellow feeling, began to steal into his heart, almost despite him.

And then Yakov was speaking about the mental health clinic. Elisha's father had consulted Neidorf nearly three years before. They were friends of the family. "Once they were neighbors or something, I don't remember exactly, but anyway Mordechai—Elisha's father—took him to see Dr. Neidorf, and she referred them to the clinic. Mordechai was extremely worried about Elisha—he wasn't an ordinary kid—and he went there for two years, twice a week, and then he stopped."

Yes, he said hesitantly, he knew why he had stopped going, but— he looked around him uneasily—it was a very delicate matter, and he wasn't sure that he should talk about it. Gold expected Ohayon to come down on Yakov like a ton of bricks, and he got ready to defend him. His hands were already clenched when, to his astonishment, he saw the chief inspector lean back against the wall in silence, his face relaxed, as if he had all the time in the world. Gold felt an urge to shake them both and scream. He stood up and went for more coffee.

In a different, slower tone, Ohayon asked what Elisha Naveh's state had been recently. He hadn't seen him much recently, said Yakov guiltily. He had come back from London only a week ago, and since then he had been cramming for exams. And Elisha would disappear for whole days; he didn't know exactly what he was up to, said Yakov despairingly. Now that he thought about it, he had looked odd and said strange, disconnected things whenever he bumped into him in the flat. But he had imagined his behavior was related to his love life, which was very complicated. And here he fell silent again.

Ohayon lit another cigarette and asked who Elisha had been involved with, and Yakov began gazing around uneasily again. Gold offered them coffee and looked at them in bewilderment. Yakov stared at the wall, and Michael focused on the coffee cup in his hand, then he asked, very quietly, if Yakov knew that Dr. Neidorf was dead.

The young man froze. In a trembling voice, he said: "When?" and Michael answered. And then Yakov asked: "How?" and received a brief summary of the facts. There was a long silence in the room. Yakov's breath was coming in rapid pants, and Gold, who could no longer endure the tension, went over by the window, where he could observe them both and try to comprehend what was going on. He couldn't understand the connection, and neither could Yakov, who asked in so many words.

In reply, Michael asked if he hadn't read the Israeli newspapers when he was in London. No, he hadn't, said Yakov, nor had his parents, or Elisha's father, but Elisha himself must have known, and he hadn't said a word about it. For the first two weeks, they had been on a trip to Scotland, he explained. Elisha's father had been somewhere in Europe; they had met only during the last few days. "But why didn't Elisha tell me?" he repeated, at first in bewilderment and then in anger.

Then Michael asked Yakov if he had ever met Dr. Neidorf.

Gold looked at the young man with curiosity and then in astonishment as he heard his reply. Yes, he had, he said; he had even gone to talk to her once.

Gold drowned the questions he was bursting to ask in his coffee cup and listened alertly as the chief inspector asked when the talk had taken place. "About three months ago. I don't remember the exact date, but it was about three months ago. Two weeks later she went abroad," said Yakov. He took off his spectacles, polished the lenses with the corner of the starched sheet, replaced them on his nose, and stared at Michael. Then he looked at the wall again.

"Why did you go to her, if I may ask?" inquired Ohayon, and Gold knew that this time he wouldn't let go.

"Because of Elisha," whispered the youngster despairingly, and he said he felt dizzy. Gold got him a glass of water and opened the window.

"What about Elisha? Why because of him?" asked Ohayon, and he lit a cigarette while Yakov gulped the water.

"Because of what happened at the clinic."

"What happened at the clinic? Do you mean the mental health clinic in Kiryat Hayovel?" asked Michael, and tapped his cigarette ash into the wastepaper basket, which he pulled toward him without taking his eyes off Yakov. Yakov nodded and said nothing.

Michael asked Gold politely to leave them alone. Yakov did not protest, but the look he gave the chief inspector emboldened Gold to ask if it was really necessary. Ohayon seemed hesitant, and then the young man asked if Gold could stay in the room. Gold looked at Ohayon, who shrugged his shoulders and said: "Whatever you like. I don't want to put you under any more pressure after what you've been through tonight." Gold sat down behind the dark Formica-topped desk near the window of the little room, which during the day was used for therapy sessions. Michael remained seated on the edge of the bed, next to the young man, who was leaning against the wall.

"What happened at the clinic?" he repeated quietly.

"Okay, it doesn't matter anymore, he's dead, and what I'm going to say to his father I don't know," said Yakov, and he looked despairingly at the chief inspector, who patiently repeated the question.

"What happened," said Yakov quickly, as if he wanted to get it off his chest, "is that that bitch fell in love with him."

Gold felt as if the room were spinning around him, and he gripped the edge of the desk. His throat was dry, and he felt somewhat as he had felt on the Saturday when he found Neidorf. He widened his eyes and heard Michael ask patiently: "Who fell in love with him?"

"His therapist, his psychologist, Dina Silver." Yakov looked at the wall opposite him, at a point just above Gold's shoulder. Gold was about to protest, when the words started pouring out of Yakov's mouth in a flood. In a monotonous, almost detached tone, the medical student from whom Gold had never heard anything but sense, and sometimes naïveté, said that at first he couldn't understand what was going on. Elisha, who always brought his girlfriends—who were usually older than he was and sometimes married—home without taking the trouble to find out what his, Yakov's plans were, had suddenly become careful, asking where he would be, when he would be out, "and I thought that he had something serious at last, you understand," and here he looked at Michael despairingly. "I thought that this kid, who had already laid the whole world—I think he must have lost his virginity in grade school, the girls ran after him so much—I thought that at last he had really fallen in love and that he was beginning to show some delicacy, because he wasn't particularly delicate when it came to sex, and that he didn't want to expose her, his new girl. He never talked about women, he never bragged, you know what I mean, and whatever I knew, I knew from what I saw for myself, from the telephone calls, the presents, the letters that came for him. But this time I didn't know anything, and I didn't dare to ask. The whole of last year there was some woman in the house, always when I wasn't there, when

I went to my aunt on the kibbutz or when I was at work in the emergency room. Then, about six months ago, I came home unexpectedly. I had a fever, and Rina sent me home in the middle of the night, and I thought he was out, otherwise I wouldn't have gone into his room, but I'd given him my aspirin the day before and I went in to get it. And they were in bed together, asleep. I switched on the light, and then I saw them. They didn't even wake up, and I took the aspirin and went out again. She was lying on her back, one leg was uncovered, and her face was fully visible in the light. I can't understand how she didn't wake up; he always slept like a corpse."

Yakov choked and breathed rapidly. Gold was stunned, but he still didn't understand the connection. He was stunned because, of all the things in the world, this was the worst that he could imagine. It was something that didn't even come up as a problem in the seminars. Even Linder didn't make jokes about it, thought Gold. The idea of having sexual intercourse with a patient was the greatest taboo in the whole profession—and Dina Silver, of all the women in the world! He thought of her cold beauty, of how he had never imagined her feeling any passion, of the way she flicked her hair off her forehead, of her ambition, of the fact that she was about to become a member of the Institute.

He heard Yakov's voice again, answering a question he had missed in his attempt to digest the shocking information.

"No, I didn't know who she was; I didn't make that connection at all. I thought she was beautiful, and she looked quite old; I thought, Another married woman. I saw the wedding ring on her finger; don't ask me how I took it all in. Anyway, I didn't intend making a fuss. He was over eighteen, and he had a way of shutting himself off when you said things he didn't like, and I went to bed and didn't say anything in the morning. But a few days later—you won't believe this—I was in the bank, waiting my turn, and I recognized her standing in front of me in line, and there was a new teller, and she was depositing checks, and he asked her who to credit them to, and she said the name, and I put two and two together and nearly fainted, because I knew his therapist's name and realized they were one and the same person. And then, when I went home, I asked him about his therapy, because he'd already told me that he'd stopped going, and that year was a catastrophe, with the army not taking him, and he wasn't sleeping and he wasn't eating and he looked like a shadow. So I asked him when he was going to go to therapy again, and he said he wasn't, he didn't need it. And in the meantime he was walking around as if he was stoned all the time, he wasn't attending lectures, he spent all day sitting next to the phone, and he started asking me questions about drugs and all kinds of crazy things. His father phoned me and wanted to know why he hadn't written and what was going on with him. There were days when he didn't seem to recognize his room or know where he was, and in the end, when I saw that he was going off the rails, I decided to go and talk to Dr. Neidorf about him, because she was the one who sent him to the clinic, so it was her responsibility, right?"

Gold wiped his brow and looked at Michael, who put his hand in his shirt pocket and touched what looked like a little square box. Suddenly Gold realized that it was a miniature tape recorder, like the one belonging to one of his friends, who was a reporter, but he immediately ordered himself to stop being so paranoid and began listening again.

"What happened at Dr. Neidorf's?" asked Michael, and the stream of words began again. Neidorf, said Yakov, when he called her and explained who he was, suggested that he bring Elisha, or get him to phone her, but he told her that it was impossible to communicate with him, "and I really did try to get him to go to her, but he laughed in my face and said he had never felt better in his life, and all kinds of stuff like that, and I could see that he was simply sick, really sick; you can't tell me that a healthy person can do nothing, but nothing, for months on end. Not read a book or go to a movie or see friends or work or study, just sit in a chair or disappear, and I was supposed to think that everything was all right. I even asked Dr. Gold once, but we didn't have the time for a serious conversation, and until I realized what was going on with his therapist, I thought that he still might go back to the clinic. Anyway, I finally persuaded Dr. Neidorf to see me. I didn't intend to go into all the details, I just wanted to describe the state he was in, but she maneuvered me into telling her about his therapist, and when I did tell her, she didn't believe me—that is, she believed me, but she asked me two hundred times if I was sure, and said that it was a very grave accusation, and all kinds of stuff like that. All I wanted was for her to take care of Elisha, but she kept asking me for all kinds of details, until at last I asked her if she wanted me to call her next time so she could see for herself. She said she didn't have time to treat Elisha herself, that she was going abroad in two weeks, but when she came back she would speak to him and refer him to someone reliable. When I came back I didn't have time to phone her. I hardly saw him; he wasn't home or he was lying on his bed and staring at the ceiling, and I didn't realize how urgent everything was. He hardly spoke to me. I tried to talk to him, I meant to phone Dr. Neidorf, but I never had the time." His voice died and turned into a deep sigh, and an expression of guilt and then one of helplessness came over his face.

Ohayon gave Gold an appraising look. Gold felt himself go pale, sensed the blood drain from his face. But he still didn't make the connection.

Michael asked him to step outside with him for a moment. Outside the room, in the long, neon-lit corridor of the seventh floor, Michael seated him on one of the orange plastic chairs lining the wall, gripped his arm, and in a chilling tone, unlike anything Gold had ever heard from him before, explained that everything he had just heard must be buried deep in his mind, and he mustn't say a single word about it to anyone. "You realize how important it is?" Gold didn't realize but nodded mechanically.

"I want you to understand: the entire solution of your analyst's murder depends on it. No one, not your wife or your mother or your best friend or anyone else. For the time being. And keep that boy here too; don't let him go home. Nothing must get out for one day, two days, no more. Not that he's dead, not the story about Silver, nothing. Understand?"

Gold wanted to protest, to ask questions, but the determination in the policeman's voice silenced him. Ohayon would notify the father, he said, he would take care of the hospital, they could keep the body for a couple of days, such things had been known to happen before.

Gold's job was, he stressed again, to hold his tongue and keep the boy from talking to anyone. "Give him a marathon, clean out his head; he's suffering from guilt and anger and bereavement and the whole works. You've got plenty to keep you busy; don't let him out of your sight, you hear?" Gold heard and promised. More than anything else, he felt frightened, frightened of Ohayon and frightened of what he had heard, but he had no one to share his fear with except Ohayon himself, and he found himself saying that the act of suicide had been committed against her, against Dina Silver. Gold was repeating words that Michael had heard from one of the members of the Training Committee on that Saturday: suicide was always a matter of revenge. Revenge, he corrected, and other things too.

Michael Ohayon asked only one question, a question that astonished Gold. Would they have suspended Dina Silver from the Institute for what she had done?

Gold looked at him in amazement. "What?" he said. "Suspended? That girl is finished professionally for the rest of her life! They wouldn't even take her in the Students' Counseling Service at Hebrew University, not even in some private quack sanatorium. It's the worst thing that anyone could do, and to an adolescent!" And only then did it begin to dawn on him.

He gave Ohayon a questioning look, and the latter nodded. "Yes, it's exactly what you think, and don't ask me for explanations now, because I can't give you any. Just do what I told you to, and don't take your eyes off the boy, or I'll have to take him into custody and maybe you too," he said threateningly, and the terrified Gold assured him that he wouldn't do anything except obey his instructions to the letter. But Ohayon did not look reassured, and finally he said: "Stay in the room and don't go out for anything—not to phone, not for anything. I'm sending someone to stand guard on the door."

It was eight o'clock in the morning, and the ward was already wide awake and the doctors' rounds were about to begin, when Chief Inspector Michael Ohayon left the hospital. He left Eli Bahar, whose breakfast he had interrupted, outside the door of the room on the seventh floor, after disconnecting the telephone with his own hands. He glanced apologetically at Gold, who made some remark about lack of trust. "My friend," said Ohayon, "this is a serious business. Too serious for games. We're dealing with a psychotic, and your young student is in danger of his life if somebody finds out what he knows."

Before disconnecting the phone, Ohayon made Gold call his wife with a cock-and-bull story about an emergency at the hospital; she was to cancel all his appointments for the next two days. An act of deception that left Gold with a feeling of uneasiness and anxiety hardly less oppressive than that which he had felt up to now, but also, he admitted to himself, with a certain feeling of importance.

At five to nine precisely, Michael drew up outside Hildesheimer's front door. He breathed in the fresh, crisp-morning air and waited on the other side of the road until he saw a man emerging from the entrance to the old building and knew, without knowing how, that he had just emerged from an hour with the old man.

In the brief time at his disposal from the moment he left the hospital to that of his arrival at Hildesheimer's, he had managed to send several messages over the two-way radio. He had dispatched Raffi to speak to Ali, the gardener from Dehaisha, who had returned to work at the Margoa Hospital as if nothing had ever happened. "What do you want me to do, for God's sake, hypnotize him?" said Raffi over the radio. "You think that if he saw a big new BMW he wouldn't have said so?" But he didn't wait for an answer, and put an end to the conversation with a hasty: "Okay, okay, I'm going now."

The redheaded policeman had left a message with Control: "If Ohayon wants me, tell him I've gone over the place and there's nothing; no letters. Tell him I'm in his office, waiting for the next step." Naftali quoted him word for word, and Michael said impatiently into the radio: "Tell him to go on waiting. Until he hears from me. And tell Tzilla to wait too; I've got work for her." Naftali refrained from commenting on Michael's impatient tone and merely said neutrally: "Message received, over. Are you leaving me a phone number?" But Michael did not reply.

The first patient of the morning having emerged, Michael approached the door. Hildesheimer opened to his loud knock and said in astonishment: "But, sir!"

There was no hint of intimacy in his voice, only a combination of anger and alarm, and Michael, without waiting for an invitation, pushed his way in and said, in his most pleading voice: "Professor Hildesheimer, I must talk to you immediately." Hildesheimer, who had recovered his composure, looked at him suspiciously. "But I have patients, all morning." The German accent was stronger than ever. And Michael said, in a more authoritative tone: "I'm afraid you'll have to cancel one of them at least, right now." Hildesheimer gave him a stern, questioning look, and then the doorbell rang behind them. The fair head of one of the candidates peeped around the half-open door. Michael remembered that Tzilla had questioned her, a skinny girl with short hair and a narrow, birdlike face. Hildesheimer looked helplessly at Michael, who did not budge from the door, and then, in a halting voice, the old man said he was sorry, but he would have to cancel the hour, because "something urgent" had come up, and he gave Michael an accusing look. The candidate's face paled, and she asked Hildesheimer if he felt all right. He felt fine, he replied; he was only very, very sorry that he couldn't let her know in advance, and they would have to meet next week. The girl accepted his apology with good grace, and it seemed to Michael that as long as the old man was alive and well, his clients would be willing to accept any explanation he cared to give them.

In a voice that was still angry, but less confused, the old man said it was fortunate for Michael that the woman was a supervisee, but the next one was a patient, and he, Hildesheimer, had no intention whatsoever of repeating the same performance. Michael Ohayon looked at his watch: five past nine. Only fifty-five minutes until the next appointment. He asked the old man to cancel it, and added that up to now, he hoped, he had not given Professor Hildesheimer any reason to doubt his discretion.

Without another word, Hildesheimer marched into his consulting room, where, after a quick glance at his diary, he dialed a number on the heavy, old-fashioned black telephone and to Michael's immense relief canceled the next session.

Then Michael, who had followed Hildesheimer uninvited into the consulting room, stood up and shut the door and, after a glance at the old man, drew the curtain on the inside of the door. Expectantly, the old man sat down on one of the armchairs, as Michael hurried to seat himself on the other. Despite the sun outside, the room was dark. The heavy curtains were drawn over the big window. There were traces of mud on the couch where the recent patient's feet had rested, and his head had left a dent in the pillow, which was covered with a white cloth. Suddenly Michael felt a great yearning to lie down on the couch and talk into the air of the room. The white cloth, ironed and spotless, despite the creases made by the patient's head, looked seductive and seemed to hold a promise of rest, a promise that he could safely abandon himself to other, reliable hands. He wanted the old man to sit behind him and to take sole responsibility for what was about to happen. It was not his longing for the couch, however, that he proceeded to impart to the analyst, who was sitting with his elbow on the arm of the chair, his chin resting on his fist, his face at once tired and expectant.

Michael knew that he had better justify his disruption quickly.

For an hour the old man listened without saying a word. Michael laid all the facts before him. He told him about Linder, about the pistol, about Colonel Alon, the missing patient, about the burglary, the accountants, the polygraph, the alibis, everything. One by one he described the events of the past weeks and, without any extraneous explanations, led him, as he himself had been led, to a dead end. Michael had no doubt that the old man was following every word, even though until the moment when Catherine Louise Dubonnet was mentioned he sat completely still. He had already heard about Dr. Dubonnet, he said, and the meeting in Paris too, he added in embarrassment.

It was already ten o'clock when Michael came to his conversation with Dubonnet. She had visited Hildesheimer before leaving the country and spent the whole of Saturday trying to console him for the tragedy. To Michael's surprise, his face did not light up at the mention of her name; he even looked discomfited. It was only afterward that Michael recalled Dubonnet's teasing remark about jealousy, and how even Hildesheimer was not immune to it.

At ten-fifteen he reached the suicide of the young man, after having described his appearance at the funeral, the way he followed Dina Silver, and Michael's interrogation of her, and then he asked Hildesheimer to cancel the next hour, a request the old man tried without success to fulfill. After dialing three times and getting no reply, he said with a sigh that if necessary he would send the next patient on his way, as he had done at nine o'clock.

From his shirt pocket Michael extracted the tiny tape recorder, and under the old man's astonished gaze he switched it on and set it to the highest volume. He preceded this operation only by saying that it was a recording of a conversation with the youth's roommate, and after that he let it run, while Hildesheimer listened.

At one minute past eleven there was a ring at the door, and Michael pressed a button and stopped the tape just before the story about the aspirin. When the analyst returned, Michael, without a word, switched the tape machine on again, and the old man sat and listened silently and impassively. His face did not change as he listened to the description of Dina Silver in bed with Elisha, or when Yakov spoke of recognizing her in the bank, or even when he mentioned Neidorf.

His expression reminded Michael of an ancient mask carved in stone he had once seen in Greece. "There is nothing new under the sun," was its message. "You will never penetrate me." And it did not change until the tape came to an end, at the moment when Michael asked Gold to step outside with him.

Then the old man bowed his head and covered his face with his hands. For a while he sat without moving, until Michael began to fear for him, and then the head lifted and the broken voice said: "She was my patient, you know, for five years. I never thought it was a good analysis." Again there was a long silence, after which he looked straight at Michael, who did not dare to move, and said: "I should have known. *Post factum,* I'm not surprised. It all fits, like the pieces of a jigsaw puzzle." Michael lit a cigarette, still not daring to say a word. The old man continued in a murmur: "Three supervisors . . . we should have known. . . ." And in the end he said: *"Ach!"* looked straight at Michael, shrugged his shoulders, and with an immense effort said: "One would have to feel completely omnipotent to think that we never make mistakes. No method in the world can prevent people from making mistakes."

Michael was wondering whether he had finished, when he heard the following exclamation: "Five years! Four times a week! And I thought she was making progress!" The old man seemed to be talking to himself, and then he looked straight into the dark eyes observing him once more and said: "I would have to be very narcissistic to think that it was all my own fault, but it's difficult not to nevertheless. We all have our blind spots. Sometimes the process makes you lose your sense of proportion." It was only then that Michael dared to say something. What he said caused the old man to look at him attentively and in the end to nod and say: "You're right. It may be ironic, but analysts know everything there is to know about their patients except their behavior as human beings outside the analytic hour. All we know is what we hear here, on the couch."

And once more he withdrew into his thoughts, until he said: "I don't even have to see that student for myself and hear the details all over again, although for the sake of closure I'll do it. But I don't really have to, because somewhere or other I've always known." And suddenly he fell silent, his face took on the stony, masklike look, and he sat staring in front of him, the only sound in the room the irritating ticking of the little clock that stood on the table between them. Its face was turned toward the analyst.

At one minute to twelve, Hildesheimer answered the last ring at the door for that morning, putting the supervisee off to the following week; then he canceled his two therapy sessions for the afternoon and turned to Michael with the request to "meet that student who spoke here on the machine."

They drove there in the police Renault without exchanging a word. The old man looked ahead at the road, and Michael smoked two cigarettes, until they arrived at the parking space next to the emergency entrance where he ignored the shouts of the guard and waved at the police license plate. The two of them then hurried to the elevator and rode up to the seventh floor.

In the corridor, opposite the elevator, they found Eli Bahar, sitting on an orange plastic chair, and in the room, which they entered without knocking, Gold was busy writing. Yakov was lying on the bed with his eyes half closed, but he woke fully when he heard the door opening. Gold leapt to his feet as soon as he saw Hildesheimer enter the room, and Michael almost smiled at the sight of his excitement. Tight-lipped, the old man asked Gold to leave him alone with the student, and Michael followed Gold out of the room.

They sat outside for about an hour in silence. Eli Bahar, too, said nothing. Michael smoked two more cigarettes and thanked Eli for the coffee he brought him. Gold refused coffee with a shake of his head.

When at last the old man emerged from the room, his face was gray, and Michael began to feel concerned about his physical state and suggested having something to drink in the cafeteria, a suggestion Hildesheimer dismissed impatiently. He nodded at Gold and began striding rapidly toward the elevator. The chief inspector had to quicken his step to keep up with him.

The moment they were inside the car, even before Michael had a chance to start the engine, Hildesheimer turned to look at him and said: "Good. What next?"

"Now," said the chief inspector hoarsely, "we have to prove it, which is the hardest part of all. We have motive, means, opportunity; her alibi can be broken, but we have to prove it."

"How will you do it?" asked the old man, tapping his fingers on his knee.

Michael had an idea, he said, but he preferred to wait until they got out of the car to explain it. "It's complicated, and it demands a lot from you." Hildesheimer did not react.

At half past one, they were sitting in the consulting room on Alfasi Street again, as if they had never left it.

Michael lit a cigarette and politely refused the halfhearted invitation to lunch offered by the old man when his wife's curly gray head popped around the door and asked him an angry question in German.

Hildesheimer listened attentively as Michael explained what was required of him. He repeated several times that conventional methods would get them nowhere, and emphasized twice, apologetically, that the situation in which the professor would find himself would oblige him to betray principles that were sacred to him. But the old man cut him short with the remark that it was also possible to see it in quite a different—in fact, opposite—light, as defending the very principles to which the chief inspector had referred. And so, at two o'clock in the afternoon, Professor Ernst Hildesheimer dialed Dina Silver's home number and asked her to come to his consulting room at four o'clock the same day.

At three o'clock precisely, Hildesheimer opened the door and let them in. The mobile lab team examined the house and checked the rooms, and Michael sat in the armchair in silence. The old man stood looking out the window. There was a knock at the door, and Shaul came in. He nodded at the wall and said: "Okay. It's all fixed. We'll have to position ourselves in the bedroom. There's a niche there, where the wall's thinner. We made a bit of a mess, but we'll clean it up afterward." And he looked at the old man inquiringly, although not apologetically enough to satisfy Michael, who had warned them several times to treat the analyst as respectfully as they knew how.

Michael added apologies of his own and promised that everything would be put back in its place, but Hildesheimer looked as if none of it concerned him. He was in another place, another time. He stood next to the open window and looked at the neglected garden, bathed in the sunshine of a spring afternoon, which did not penetrate the chilly room. A shiver ran down Michael's spine as he thought that two weeks before, the old man had turned eighty.

When the doorbell rang, at exactly four o'clock, Shaul, the forensics man, and Chief Inspector Ohayon were ready.

She was wearing the red dress, the dress in which he had first seen her. Her face was pale, and a lock of her hair, which had a blue-black sheen, was falling into her eyes. With a graceful movement, she tossed it back and asked with a smile if she should lie on the couch. The analyst pointed to the armchair. She sat down and crossed her legs sideways, like a model in a magazine. Her thick ankles made the pose slightly grotesque. Again Michael noticed the thick wrists, the short fingers, and the bitten nails, which paradoxically now gave her hands a strangely predatory look.

At first there was a silence. She began shifting about in the chair, and then she opened her mouth to say something but immediately closed it again. From his place of concealment, Michael could see Hildesheimer's face only in profile, but he heard him ask her how she was feeling, to which she replied: "Fine. Quite well again." Her voice was low and soft. Every syllable was clearly enunciated.

"You wanted to talk to me a while back," said the old man. "I understand you had a problem."

Again she tossed the hair off her forehead, crossed her legs, and finally she said: "Yes. I did then. It was just after Dr. Neidorf's death. But after that I was ill, and so I didn't call. I planned to get in touch with you when I was well again, but now it doesn't seem so urgent anymore. You wanted to see me. Is there anything new?"

"New?" the old man repeated.

"I thought that perhaps something had happened and . . ." She shifted in her chair.

Hildesheimer waited patiently. She did not dare ask him directly what he wanted, and her tension was evident only in her body, in the movement of her legs, which she uncrossed and crossed again. "I thought," she said in a firmer voice, "that it was in connection with my presentation; that you had discussed my presentation. That you had critical comments."

"Why do you think we had comments? Are you not satisfied with the way you wrote your presentation?"

She smiled, the smile with which Michael was already familiar, a grimace of the lips, and explained: "It's not a question of what I think or write. You have your own demands, which have nothing to do with my opinion."

The old man's hand rose into the air and fell back on the arm of the chair, and he said: "No. I wanted to see you in connection with your meeting with Dr. Neidorf."

"Which meeting?" asked Dina Silver, and clenched her hands.

"First of all, the meeting before she left the country, the one when the confrontation took place," said Hildesheimer as though he was referring to undeniable, self-evident facts with which they were both familiar.

"Confrontation?" repeated Dina Silver as if she did not know the meaning of the word.

Hildesheimer was silent.

"She told you about a confrontation?" she asked, and her hands slid over the fine wool of her dress.

Hildesheimer remained silent.

"What did she tell you?" she asked again, and still the old man said nothing. The question was repeated twice, and between the first time and the second she changed her position and shifted in the chair, and her hands began to tremble. Her voice rose as she reformulated the question: "You mean the meeting before her trip? She said that it was just between us and she wouldn't tell anyone."

Hildesheimer did not speak.

"All right, she criticized me, but it was a very specific, personal matter; it wasn't relevant."

Hildesheimer, Michael noticed, did not address her by her name even once. Without changing his position, he said in an icy tone: "What do you call a personal matter? Seducing a patient? Is that a personal matter in your eyes?"

Dina Silver went rigid, and then her expression changed, her eyes narrowed, and her face grew sly as she said: "Professor Hildesheimer, I think Dr. Neidorf had a countertransference problem. She was jealous of me, I think."

Hildesheimer was silent.

"I think," she continued when she saw that he was not going to reply, "that there was a certain rivalry between us, competition for your attention. I'm well aware of my own provocative role—we discussed it often enough—in manipulating her into a certain emotional situation. I gave her to understand that there was a special relationship between you and me, and I think that this was the background to her need to punish me, which came up so often in my analysis."

Michael was dying to see Hildesheimer's expression, but for the first time the old man turned his face aside and looked out the window. All Michael could see was his head, which was as bald as an egg, and the back of his neck emerging from the collar of his dark suit jacket. At last he turned his face from the window, looked directly at Dina Silver, and said: "Elisha Naveh died last night."

In an instant the sly expression disappeared. Her eyes widened, and her lips began to tremble.

Without giving her a chance to speak, he went on: "He died because of you. You could have prevented his death if you had performed your task faithfully and renounced immediate gratification."

Dina Silver bowed her head and burst into tears. With a mechanical movement, the old man took the box of tissues from the shelf and put it on the little table before saying: "You knew that Dr. Neidorf was familiar with the details of the case. The evidence she had is now in my possession. Together with a copy of the lecture. It's all written there; the third paragraph of the lecture deals exclusively with you."

"But I'm not mentioned there at all!" The words came out in a shriek. Then there was a silence, and her face went white.

Michael was afraid she would faint and all would be lost.

But then the blood rushed back into her face, and the old man said: "Don't try to look for a way out. The only person who saw that lecture besides Dr. Neidorf herself is the person who met her on Saturday morning before the lecture. The same person who phoned her early on Saturday morning and requested a meeting on a matter of life and death, a meeting that could not be postponed. I know your style, don't forget. And when Dr. Neidorf made it clear to you that there was no way back, that your transgression was unpardonable, you shot her.

"I only ask myself one thing: how come it didn't occur to you, when you shot her, when you took the key to her house, that before she opened the Institute door to let you in, Dr. Neidorf phoned me and told me that she was about to meet you? How is it that you didn't think of that, after thinking of everything else: the pistol you stole two weeks before you used it, the notes you hurried to steal from her house even before reading the lecture. How come you didn't think of something as simple as a phone call?"

"She phoned you first?" said Dina Silver in a strangled voice, and began rising to her feet.

Hildesheimer did not stir. He did not move a muscle as she said: "You haven't got any proof; no one knows but you and me. Maybe you've got proof about Elisha, I don't know, but nobody knows about the meeting with Neidorf; nobody saw me."

She was very close to him, to the old man who remained motion-less in his chair, when Michael came into the room and said: "You're wrong, Mrs. Silver. We have got proof, and plenty of it."

And then she fell on him, on Hildesheimer, and as if of their own accord, her hands encircled his throat. Michael Ohayon had to exert all his strength to pry the fingers with their bitten nails loose.

"And now," said Shaul after checking the tape and folding away the equipment, "we can get down to the real work." He was holding Dina Silver's fluffy blue coat in his hand as he spoke, and in a satisfied tone he announced that it was the item of clothing from which the thread had been detached. "I think," he added as he lifted the thread in its plastic envelope from his case and laid it on the coat, ignoring the racket around him as the Hildesheimers' bedroom was restored to its former state.

Hildesheimer himself was sitting in his armchair in his consulting room, his head thrown back in a gesture of unutterable weariness, his face gray.

Michael sat down opposite him, at an angle of forty-five degrees, and lit a cigarette. He didn't know why—perhaps because of the joylessness of the victory, or the depression that took hold of him at the sight of the old man's face, or the fatigue that relaxed his self-control—but of all the questions in the world, this was the one that escaped his lips: "Professor Hildesheimer, what did you mean when you said, in connection with Giora Biham, that Argentinians are different?"